RIDE THE GOLDEN TIGER

By the same author
OIL

RIDE
THE
GOLDEN
TIGER

BY JONATHAN BLACK

WILLIAM MORROW AND COMPANY, INC.
NEW YORK 1976

Library of Congress Cataloging in Publication Data

———————

    Ride the golden tiger.

    I. Title.
PZ4.V9453Ri [PS3572.042]   813'.5'4   75-30828
ISBN 0-688-03001-7

    Book design by Helen Roberts

For Roslyn Targ with Great Love
and Gratitude

"The days of the small prospector who went into a small operation and built it into a great mining concern are perhaps not over, but the more general line of development is now quite different. Commonly a successful prospector will sell his discovery to a mining finance house which undertakes evaluation and development. A small group of internationally renowned firms provide much of the capital for big mine projects. . . ."

—KENNETH WARREN, *Mineral Resources*

The London Gold Market handles over 85 percent of all the new gold coming onto the free market.

—BRIAN JOHNSON, *Politics of Money*

AUTHOR'S FREE TRANSLATION OF THE ABOVE:
Both the production and trading of gold are the shared monopolies of a very few, very powerful firms which are controlled by a handful of extremely wealthy individuals. The small-scale prospector or operator is completely at their mercy. If he bucks them, he does not survive—often in the strictest sense of the word.

Author's Note

On November 23, 1973, the free market price of gold stood at $90 per troy ounce. Then it began to rise sharply, passing the $100 mark within five days and continuing to go much higher. Many theories were advanced to explain the trend. All missed the true—and dismaying—reason for the phenomenon.

In actual fact, the world's gold markets were being ruthlessly manipulated. Men and institutions whose names are familiar to all were implementing a vast conspiracy to corner the world's available gold supply, to gain a monopoly over the precious metal. They did not care that their operations fed the fires of global inflation or that their success could—and probably would—create chaos with the already eroded monetary systems of the United States, Great Britain and Western Europe. Their concern was exclusively with their eventual profits, which they anticipated would be over $100 *billion*.

None of this became generally known, for the participants in the gold-corner cabal were enormously wealthy and powerful. They operated in the utmost secrecy and bought or coerced the silence of any who learned or guessed the nature and intent of their machinations.

By April, 1974, the gold market manipulators were on the verge of bringing off their gargantuan coup. The price of gold had more than doubled since the previous November. On April 3, it reached a dizzying peak of $197 per ounce on the Paris market, and various supposedly authoritative sources were freely predicting it would soon soar to $300, even $500, per ounce.

Abruptly—and apparently inexplicably—the upward spiral ceased and the trend reversed itself. By July 4, the price of gold had fallen back to $131 an ounce. This drop in price resulted in astronomical losses for the market manipulators, and they were forced to abandon their campaign to corner gold.

Only a very few insiders and government officials knew of the conspiracy and the mechanics of its implementation. The story never appeared in the news media, for even seasoned financial writers were at a loss to understand the real reasons that lay behind the sharp, steady rise—and then the sudden downward plunge—of free-market gold prices.

This book is, of course, a novel. It is fiction, the product of my imagination. But it has its original basis in hardcore—but necessarily, somewhat altered—fact. Needless to say, the characters, business firms, banks and other organizations I have created have no real counterparts. On the other hand, where appropriate, I have felt free to use the names of actual persons—ex-President Richard M. Nixon, French Presidents Charles de Gaulle and Georges Pompidou, for example, and of banking institutions whose names are household words around the globe. And, I would like to add, such incidents as Charles de Gaulle's carefully calculated plan to destroy the value of American and British currency are matters of historical fact.

Incidentally, I believe it is particularly important to note that some 85 percent of all the world's nonmonetary gold is traded on the London Gold Market. This market is formed by five member firms: Johnson, Matthey; Mocatta and Goldsmid; Samuel Montagu and Company; N. M. Rothschild and Sons; and Sharps, Pixley and Company. I have added a wholly fictitious sixth firm to their number. My purpose was to further the plot of the book but, at the same time, avoid causing any embarrassment to any of the real member firms, none of which were in any way parties to or involved in the scheme to corner gold.

—JONATHAN BLACK

Venice, Italy
1975

10

I
February 8-14, 1974

Prologue:

BOAC Flight 982 was on the final, Beirut-London leg of its trip from Calcutta. There were only forty-eight passengers in the tourist class section of the Boeing 747. Many had preempted entire four-seat center rows to stretch out and sleep. At seven P.M. the loudspeakers awakened them, announcing that the plane would be landing at London's Heathrow Airport shortly.

Flight attendants made their prescribed aisle patrols. Checking the aft compartment, Stewardess May Evans stopped at center seat row 55, the last in the cabin. A man lay across seats D through G, apparently still asleep. She tapped his shoulder.

"Sorry, sir, but we're about to land."

There was no response, and somehow the shoulder did not feel quite right to the touch. Stewardess Evans took a closer look.

The man was Asian. His eyes were open. He was dead.

May Evans used the nearest intercom to call the flight deck.

"We have a corpse in tourist," she told the captain. He would notify the control tower immediately. The authorities would cooperate. No one would come for the body until after the living passengers were offloaded. Immigration officers would obtain detailed information about those who disembarked—for possible future reference.

13

"Have the chief steward handle it for now," the captain instructed. "We'll be on the ground in five minutes."

The chief steward came aft and wedged himself into Seat 55-E to hold the corpse steady during landing. "Heart attack, I suppose," he muttered. A passport bound in red leather protruded from a pocket of the dead man's jacket. The chief steward took it out. The cover was gold-stamped with legends in Hindi, Tibetan and English: "Kingdom of Sakhana." A trilingual inside-page entry gave the anglicized version of the man's name as "Kalsi, Rafin." An Indian name.

During his twelve years with BOAC, the chief steward had seen only a half dozen or so Sakhanese passports. Citizens of the remote Himalayan kingdom seldom traveled abroad. As the steward replaced the passport, his hand brushed Rafin Kalsi's chest and encountered something hard and bulky. He opened the jacket and saw a shoulder-holstered automatic, a 7.65-millimeter Luger.

The steward cursed. When a passenger suffered a fatal heart attack or stroke aloft, it always meant extra work for crew members. They had to fill out endless forms and undergo hours of interrogation in order that the airline could be absolved of all liability. But when the deceased was a man with an Indian name who traveled on a Sakhanese passport and carried a gun—bloody hell, the complications were certain to be multiplied.

1

Matthew Robert Rutledge occupied Seat 2-A in the first-class section of the Boeing 747. Like all other passengers and as yet most of the cabin crew, he was unaware there had been a death aboard. Not that the knowledge in itself would have disturbed him greatly. He had seen men die and had himself come close to death more than a few times in his thirty-four years.

Matt Rutledge had the kind of handsome face that attracted women without creating resentful responses from men. It was a bit too irregular and roughly hewn to be called clean-cut in the conventional sense, and his jawline was strong. His complexion was weathered by exposure to sun and wind, and both his hair and eyebrows were coal black and thick. Clearly, he was a man who could control himself and his expressions, but now his features mirrored unease and apprehension. He was impatient, eager to have the plane land so that he could get on with what was the most crucial business negotiation of his career.

At last, wheels settled on runway and reverse-thrusting engines roared. A female voice rasped over the loudspeakers.

". . . apologize again for our late arrival . . ."

BOAC Flight 982 from Calcutta was due in London at 3:15 P.M. But "technical difficulties" had caused a four-hour layover at Khaldeh Airport in Beirut. It was now 7:28 P.M.

". . . and regret any inconvenience . . ."

Matt Rutledge scowled. He had had an appointment scheduled for five-thirty that afternoon in London. He had tried telephoning from Beirut to explain the delay, but Lebanese overseas circuits were clogged. In the end, he sent a telex. He could only hope it had gotten past platoons of aides and secretaries and to Sir David Auerbach personally. If so, he might still see Auerbach that evening. The meeting was urgent.

By proverbial time-is-money yardsticks, the dollar value of passing hours could be computed in six figures. To say nothing of other considerations that defied translation into terms of dollars or pounds sterling. Potential profits of a magnitude that few men could even comprehend were involved—as were the fate of a nation, its ruler and his subjects. And, Matt was aware, his success or failure could have wide-reaching, even global implications.

The Boeing's engines stopped. Matthew Rutledge

levered his six-foot-two frame out of the seat. A leggy blond stewardess who had fussed over him during the flight from Beirut brought his overcoat. She sensed him to be one of those rare males who was fine-tuned to women, and her look made it clear she would accept any invitation the attractive young American might offer. Any other time, gladly, Rutledge thought. He picked up his bulging Mark Cross briefcase and hurried toward the exit door.

Matt Rutledge was the first passenger from Flight 982 to reach the immigration counters. A pudgy immigration officer studied his much-stamped American passport and began asking the routine questions.

"The purpose of your visit, sir?"

"Business."

"And what might your line of business be, Mr. Rutledge?"

"Mining."

"I see. How long will you be staying in the U.K.?"

"About a week." Just long enough to get $20 million, Matt added silently. If things worked out, less than a week. If not—but he preferred to block any such possibility from his mind.

"Ah, you've been in Sakhana."

"Yes." Rutledge felt a prickle of misgiving.

The official squinted to read smudged visa-stamps in his passport. "You first arrived there in November, 1973. You made some trips back and forth to India and last exited Sakhana three days ago."

Rutledge's face was deeply tanned and this accentuated the sea-green color of his eyes, which now narrowed. The immigration officer was making statements rather than asking questions, and the statements seemed hardly relevant. Matt forced himself not to look down at the briefcase he had placed on the floor next to his feet.

"Sakhana must be a fascinating place," the portly official said. "Wedged up there between India and Tibet—sort of a Shangri-la, from all I've heard."

"Fascinating, yes. A Shangri-la—not quite."

"Mm. You said your business was mining. Nothing I've read about the country mentioned any mines there."

The immigration official's probing had brought him to a subject Matt very much wanted to avoid. "There aren't any—yet," he said coolly. "Could be iron deposits, though. We're still not sure." It was weak, but hopefully it would suffice.

Rutledge observed that other passengers from Flight 982 had arrived at the immigration counters. Their documents were being examined closely, too. His tension eased. He wasn't being singled out, after all.

"According to your landing card, you're staying at the Dorchester, Mr. Rutledge."

Matt said that was correct. The immigration officer made mysterious notations on the back of his landing card, stamped his passport and waved him through to the customs hall.

The conveyor belts had not yet begun spewing up luggage from Flight 982. Rutledge went to a pay telephone and called Sir David Auerbach's Belgrave Square townhouse. A servant answered. Matt gave his name and moments later heard Auerbach's voice. He spoke with an old-school-tie accent, but his tone was warm and cordial.

"I received your telex, Matthew, and kept the evening open. When could you drop around?"

"Would ten be too late?"

"Not at all. I'll expect you then."

Rutledge found his Mädler suitcases riding the luggage merry-go-round. A porter transferred the bags to a cart and reached for Matt's briefcase.

"Looks like it weighs a ton, guv."

"Thanks, but I'll carry it myself," Matt said. He followed the porter through a NOTHING TO DECLARE exitway. He felt safe. Any hidden sensors installed by Her Majesty's customs would be designed to detect ferrous metals. The contents of his briefcase were most definitely nonferrous.

It was February 8, 1974. Britain was crippled by fuel short-ages and energy crises, the result of Arab oil embargoes and domestic coal production slowdowns. Most industrial and business firms were operating on an emergency three-day-week basis. London was especially hard hit and had a bleak, near-wartime-blackout appearance. But none of these difficulties was evident at the opulent Dorchester Hotel whose lobby and corridors were as brightly lit as ever. Matthew Rutledge was given a luxurious two-room suite overlooking Hyde Park.

Matt bought a copy of the *Evening Standard* in the lobby and checked gold market quotations. The free market price had spiked to $145 an ounce that day, a record high. He grinned happily.

Rutledge unpacked, showered and changed clothes. By 9:30 P.M., he was outside, under the Dorchester marquee. The night was cold but clear and Belgrave Square was less than a mile away. His first impulse was to walk, but the awkward burden of his heavy briefcase made him take a taxi. The driver swung into Park Lane. With only trickles of gasoline available for private cars, there was virtually no traffic. The cab reached Grosvenor Place in minutes. Matt realized that he had miscalculated and would be very early for his appointment. Best not to seem *too* eager, he decided and told the driver to pull over to the curb. He got out and paid. The taxi drove off.

Matt was on the corner of Grosvenor Place and Hal-kin Street, two blocks from Belgrave Square. The elegant neighborhood was dark and silent. Drastic power cuts had left street lights barely glowing. Householders had drawn drapes shut to conserve what warmth was provided by greatly reduced heating-fuel supplies. There were neither pedestrians nor moving cars visible on Halkin Street, and Rutledge did not see the black Jaguar sedan that stopped some fifty yards away on Grosvenor Place. He started walking slowly along Halkin Street.

Halfway down the first block he sensed rather than heard someone coming up behind him—noiselessly and much too fast. Instincts that had served Matt well in the past caused him to act swiftly, reflexively. Side-stepping, he whirled around, his body braced. A man now barely five yards from him broke his swift stride and went into a knife fighter's crouch, arms held away from hips.

A fix-starved junkie using the brownout as a cover to rob, Matt thought. He snapped the briefcase up, holding it with both hands as a shield just as the man sprang forward, stabbing for his abdomen. A long double-edged blade punched through leather. Rutledge's assailant jerked the knife free and lunged again, slashing for his throat. Matt turned, swinging the briefcase by its handle. The knife ripped his overcoat at the shoulder and he felt a stab of pain as the blade sliced his flesh. But the briefcase slammed into the man's belly and sent him staggering back.

"*Sód ja Kyi!*" the man gasped, trying to regain wind and balance.

Now Matt saw that he had oriental features. Holy Christ, he thought. "*Sód ja Kyi*" meant "dog-to-be-killed" in the Tibetan-based dialect spoken in the Sakhanese highlands. This was a Sakhanese—and an assassin. The implications filled Matt with a surging fear. He forced himself back into immediate alertness and pretended to throw the briefcase. The man dodged. Matt dropped the briefcase and hurled himself forward.

As Rutledge and the Sakhanese crashed to the sidewalk together, Matt seized the hand holding the knife. He twisted it savagely until he heard an agonized groan and felt the wristbone snap. The knife fell. Matt snatched it up.

"*Kyod su yin*—whose man are you?" he demanded, holding the knifepoint to the man's jugular.

"*A-mai kyod-ta*—into your mother!" the Sakhanese snarled. He flung himself to one side, delivering a vicious kick to Matt's groin. Rutledge was momentarily paralyzed by pain. The Sakhanese rolled free, scrambled to his feet and fled in the direction of Grosvenor Place.

Matt waited for the worst of the pain to ebb and then stood up. He made no attempt to follow or to call for help. He could not afford to attract official attention to himself. He peered at the knife. It had an elaborately worked handle shaped like an attenuated letter "S"—undoubtedly of Sakhanese origin. He shook his head and tossed the knife into the gutter.

His shoulder was bleeding—not much, however, for miraculously the wound was superficial. He shoved a folded pocket handkerchief under his shirt to absorb the blood and, retrieving his briefcase, once more started toward Belgrave Square. Although still in pain, he walked much faster than he had before.

2

No flagstaffs jutted out from the white brick and stone facade above the double entrance doors to David Auerbach's townhouse. No brass plaques gleamed on the five-foot-high wall surrounding the property. Save for these omissions, the imposing residence might have been mistaken for one of the aristocratically staid foreign embassies located in Belgrave Square.

The house had belonged to successive heads of the English branch of the Auerbach family for well over a century. Its size, classic Georgian architecture and air of permanence befitted generations of men counted among Britain's most respected merchant bankers and ranked with the English Rothschilds. But then, there were other notable similarities between the Auerbach and Rothschild banking families. Both had long possessed enormous wealth, prestige and influence. Each had autonomous branches of different nationalities that nonetheless remained ever conscious of familial ties and Jewish heritage.

Sir David Auerbach (K.C.M.G. for public services) headed the London merchant banking firm founded in

1837 by his great-great-grandfather, Jacob Auerbach. At fifty-two, Sir David Auerbach exercised sole control over Jacob Auerbach and Company. His only brother had been killed in action during World War Two. His English uncles were dead. By some perverse trick of fate or genetics, their sons—David's first cousins—had neither talent nor taste for banking; David Auerbach was a widower with but one child, a daughter.

Phelan, the butler, took Matthew Rutledge's torn and dirt-stained overcoat and led him to the drawing room.

Museum-quality paintings—among them two Chardins, a priceless Cézanne and a Steen—were displayed on the drawing room walls. Fresh flowers filled superb T'ang and Ming vases. David Auerbach rose from an armchair. Slender, of medium height, he had a prominent forehead and his deepset brown eyes widened on seeing Matt's disheveled appearance and ripped jacket.

"Good God! What happened to you, Matthew?"

"Somebody tried to mug me." Rutledge gave a much expurgated version of the episode. The truth might have been self-defeating.

"We must call a doctor and the police," Auerbach urged.

"Neither, David. I don't want people asking questions. If you'd let me use a bathroom to clean up a little, I'll be okay."

"Of course."

Auerbach took Matt to a bathroom with a well-stocked medicine cabinet and stood by ready to help. Matt stripped off his jacket and shirt, exposing a lean, muscular torso as deeply tanned as his face. He pulled away the bloodsoaked handkerchief that was stuck to his shoulder. The wound was clean and shallow. He gritted his teeth, poured disinfectant into the cut and with David Auerbach's help plastered a large adhesive bandage over it.

"Do for now," Matt said, putting on his shirt and jacket.

The two men returned to the drawing room. Auerbach poured large whiskies from a cut glass decanter. They sat in chairs set at a complementary angle and drank. Then Rutledge reached for his briefcase. David Auerbach watched with keen interest.

Not yet thirty-five, Matthew R. Rutledge had amassed a $2 million fortune from gold mining ventures in various parts of the world. Three of these had been financed by Jacob Auerbach and Company. Rutledge had written David Auerbach in January, telling in general terms of his latest prospecting activities in Sakhana. Auerbach liked Rutledge personally and derived a vicarious sense of adventure from financing his ventures. Furthermore, Jacob Auerbach and Company was a member firm of the powerful London Gold Market and had profited handsomely from Rutledge's previous successes.

Matt had the briefcase open but straightened up without taking anything from it. Instead, he ran his fingers through a shock of thick, black hair and eyed Auerbach squarely.

"I might as well start with the punch line, David," he said. "I'm here to borrow twenty million dollars."

Auerbach's expression momentarily hardened. Jacob Auerbach and Company frequently made loans or arranged underwritings of much greater size, but the largest loan it had made to Rutledge in the past had been for only $3 million.

Matt lit an unfiltered Camel. "Stunned?" he asked.

"A bit nonplussed," the banker replied.

"This should ease the shock." Rutledge lifted a heavy object out of the briefcase and placed it on Auerbach's lap. About the size of a clenched fist, it was irregularly shaped with uneven jagged edges and gleamed brightly in the light from the table lamps. It was a lump of pure gold. "Two hundred and seventy-odd ounces," Matt said, grinning.

Auerbach stared at the nugget. More than seventeen

pounds of gold. Worth some $40,000 at the current free-market price. It was not, David knew, the largest on record. The Spaniards had taken 50- and 100-pound nuggets from the Carabaya fields on the Bolivian-Peruvian high plateau in the sixteenth century. In the 1850s, Australian fields had yielded enormous nuggets such as the 200-pound Holtermann and the 240-pound Welcome Stranger. But none the size of this one had been found anywhere in the world for decades.

"The placer deposits start at around nine thousand feet elevation," Rutledge was saying. "Unfortunately, I had only two men." He purposely avoided mentioning that he had gone into the Sakhanese Himalayas with six and what had happened to the others. "We took what we could carry in our back packs, period. I gave two other nuggets to the maharaja." Reaching into his case again, he produced some pieces of rock and handed them to Auerbach. "Ore samples from higher levels. They should assay twenty-five, even thirty, ounces to the ton."

Fantastic, the banker thought, blinking despite himself. Commercial producers were processing anywhere up to five tons of ore to obtain a single ounce of gold.

"You said twenty million dollars," he murmured.

Matt nodded. "Sakhana is still primitive. We'll have to build airstrips and roads just to get machinery and equipment into where—"

"Matthew, reliable sources inform me that there is unrest in Sakhana. If the Maharaja is deposed, your concessions will be worthless."

"Your sources are wrong. The Maharaja is in firm charge," Rutledge said with far more conviction than he felt.

"For how long? You've discovered what are probably the richest virgin goldfields left on earth. When their existence becomes generally known, any unrest in Sakhana will come to a furious boil. There will be a no-quarter struggle over who should control the gold."

"You forget the credit side of the ledger, David. The Maharaja has a constabulary that passes for an army. If you think it's a gamble, remember you'll be betting on the side that has the guns."

"I'll accept that as a major credit item. Any others?"

"In addition to interest, your bank will have a contract to buy given quantities of gold at three percent below market."

"An essential provision, considering the risks."

"What risks?" Matt snorted. "Free market gold hit a hundred forty-five dollars an ounce today. All signs are that it'll go higher yet."

Auerbach looked thoughtfully at Matt. "You know the facts as well as I, but let me remind you nonetheless." He went on to say that there were about 200 million troy ounces of "old" gold in the hands of investors and speculators and that the entire non-Communist world produced only some 40 million troy ounces of newly mined gold annually. Thus, with the production of "new" gold fairly constant year after year, the continuing scarcity of the metal was predictable.

"But," Auerbach added, "there are strange forces driving the price up—and the market is extremely sensitive. Say even thirty thousand troy ounces a ton of gold came out of a newly opened field. Thrown on the market, it could cause an appreciable price drop."

The banker cocked his head to one side.

"What do you estimate the Sakhana fields might produce when in full operation?" he asked. "A million ounces annually?"

"Two million, maybe more," Rutledge replied.

"Such quantities could drop the bottom right out of the market."

"Who cares?" Matt shrugged. "We'd make fortunes even at the official price." David appreciated the point Rutledge was making, for the official price of $42.22 an ounce, set by international agreement in 1973, was far below what gold brought on the open market.

"*If* you produced gold," Auerbach said. "There are determined pressures behind the upward price spiral. I have reason to suspect a syndicate is attempting to corner the market. In which case—"

Matt interrupted, "Now wait a minute, David. If a syndicate was trying to pull off a gold corner, you wouldn't 'suspect.' You'd know."

"Fallacious reasoning," Auerbach smiled. "Bankers are a secretive lot, especially among themselves. The massive buying orders coming into the London Market are from Continental and Middle Eastern banks acting as agents for clients whose identities they do not reveal. Whoever those clients may be, they have made immense investments. They would stop at nothing to prevent large amounts of new gold from being brought out of Sakhana and depressing—or breaking—the market."

Matt was aware of the dangers and risks Auerbach cited. Like every independent prospector, he had fought his share of schemers, scavengers, claim jumpers and cartels. But he was deeply troubled, for he feared that Auerbach was about to refuse the loan. The amount he needed was large, and money markets were tight. Auerbach knew him well, had dealt with him before—and he was the only banker Matt trusted implicitly. A no from David Auerbach would greatly diminish his chances of obtaining development capital anywhere; there was infinitely more than just gold and profits at stake.

Auerbach spoke again. "Actually, the venture rather appeals to me, Matthew. However, I'd like to give it—and the ramifications—more thought." He rose from his chair. Matt busied himself putting the nugget and ore samples back into his briefcase.

"Give me until tomorrow evening," the banker continued. "Come by for dinner at eight and we'll talk further."

Matthew Rutledge enjoyed the pleasant sensation of feeling that his fears might have been misplaced.

3

Charles J. Sturdevant, Sr., had founded an American industrial and financial dynasty that made the Sturdevant name a worldwide synonym for limitless wealth and power. He died in 1944 at the age of ninety-one, leaving behind four sons and eleven grandchildren. Charles Jordan Sturdevant III, the favorite grandson, inherited his grandfather's angular features, a large share of his huge fortune and a full measure of his fierce drives and ambitions.

Now forty-nine, Charles J. Sturdevant III was chairman and controlling stockholder of the Sturdevant National Bank of New York. Boasting $30 billion deposits, Sturdevant National topped David Rockefeller's Chase Manhattan Bank to rate as the third largest commercial bank in the United States.

Charles J. Sturdevant, Sr., had been coarse-grained— "a semieducated barbarian," according to his contemporaries. But money had transmuted third-generation Sturdevants into American patricians. Charles J., the grandson, was a product of Groton and Yale and belonged to such select clubs as the Union and Links. He was an influential member of organizations like the American Bankers Association and the Council on Foreign Affairs. He enjoyed renown as a philanthropist, patron of the arts and friend and adviser to presidents and foreign heads of state and was frequently invited or appointed to national and international policy-making bodies.

In February, 1974, Sturdevant was in Paris as the presidentially appointed American delegate to the World Economic Policy Conference. It provided reason for him to be in Paris openly while covertly conducting certain of his own business affairs that were awesome in implication, involving sums that ordinary individuals could not even comprehend and which demanded absolute secrecy.

The globe-hopping billionaire owned homes in three Western European capitals. In Paris, he used his mansion on the Avenue Foch as residence and personal business headquarters. On Saturday morning, February 9, Sturdevant ate the breakfast prepared and served by the large domestic staff and went into his study.

A lean and energetic man and, despite the sharpness of his features, not unhandsome, Sturdevant seated himself at a rosewood-topped Gilles Joubert desk to wait. A telephone call was due from London at nine. Two visitors were expected at ten. The Patek Philippe timepiece on the desktop read 8:53.

The telephone rang only a minute behind schedule. The conversation was astonishingly brief. "Yes on the first," the caller told Sturdevant. "No on the second." The billionaire hung up and glared angrily. He could not abide errors or the people who made them. Charles Sturdevant's visitors were ushered into the study, two men totally unlike save for the aura of wealth each carried.

Time Magazine had called one of the visitors, Emir Nasib al Rahman, "a Princeton-educated amalgam of Saudi Arabia's King Feisal and the late Aly Khan in their prime." Falcon-faced, suave and in his midthirties, Nasib al Rahman ruled the oil-rich Persian Gulf emirate of Hajar. The Hajari oil concessions were held by the American Ensign Oil Company—AMENOCO—which was controlled by Sturdevant dynasty interests. Sheikh Nasib received more than $3 billion annually in oil royalties from AMENOCO.

By sharp contrast, Michel Auerbach was loose-jowled, balding and near sixty. Michel headed the French branch of the Auerbach family and its bank, the Société Auerbach. A large financial institution by French standards, the Société Auerbach's balance-sheet total exceeded $5.5 billion. It had long collaborated closely with the Sturdevant National Bank and its European subsidiaries.

Sheikh Nasib, Michel Auerbach and Charles Sturdevant quickly got down to business. All spoke English, for despite education and extensive travel, Studevant's French was typically American, totally inadequate.

"You have heard from London, Charles?" Michel Auerbach asked.

Sturdevant glumly repeated what he had been told over the telephone. "We have to assume that Rutledge has spoken to your cousin, Michel," he concluded.

"Perhaps the situation can be corrected if another effort is made," Sheikh Nasib said, his full, expressive lips tightening.

"Out of the question," Sturdevant shook his head. "Too much chance it might be traced back to us."

Sheikh Nasib was wholly cosmopolitan and wore Savile Row suits, but he carried a *sibah*, a Moslem rosary. He toyed with it thoughtfully. "Rutledge cannot be allowed to return to Sakhana with the money he needs," he said.

Sturdevant and Michel Auerbach were in total agreement. Among them, they had already committed $3.5 billion in a scheme aimed at nothing less than cornering the world's gold market. They would be obligating much more in the near future, with their anticipated eventual profits above $100 billion. If Matthew Rutledge were to begin producing enormous quantities of "new" gold, market prices were certain to plummet and their plans would crumble, resulting in immense losses for all of them.

"We can still block Rutledge," Sturdevant said, turning to Michel Auerbach. "You must speak with your cousin, Michel."

Michel Auerbach frowned. "David is clever. If I intervene, he will comprehend everything immediately. We cannot allow that to happen."

"There are ways, though," Charles Sturdevant said. "Hint that your bank is acting for the Elysée Palace, that we've formed a syndicate to make some profits for ourselves by buying along with the French."

Michel's frown faded. "The idea is sound. David will believe history is repeating, that it is the same as it was with de Gaulle."

"It could hardly be the same," Sheikh Nasib interposed. "You will have to improvise some plausible variation on the theme."

Michel Auerbach nodded. The situation had changed greatly since 1965-1968 when French President Charles de Gaulle waged his monetary offensive to wreck the U.S. dollar and British pound sterling and make the French franc the West's predominant currency.

De Gaulle, too, had set out to corner gold. But in those years, nations and their central banks traded their gold reserves on the London Gold Market through the agency of a gold pool. France and French banks acquired vast amounts of the precious metal, increasing their holdings tenfold by early 1968, and their success was in sight. Only a final, all-out offensive was needed to achieve total victory. It came during four frenzied days in March of that year.

Some 85 percent of the world's gold is traded on the London Gold Market. Before March 11, 1968, the London Market's trading volume averaged about 5 tons daily. On March 11, the volume suddenly shot to 100 tons. The next day, it was 150 tons; the day after, 200. On Thursday, March 14, a phenomenal 400 tons were traded. The U. S. dollar and currencies linked to it plunged to record lows, causing chaos. American tourists abroad discovered to their dismay that they could not change their dollars into foreign money at any price.

Faced with monetary catastrophe, the U. S., Great Britain and six European countries took drastic steps. They decreed that none of their monetary gold reserves would be thenceforth traded on the market. All such reserves were officially valued at $35 an ounce—the long-standing U. S. price. Only privately held gold could come into the free market to find its price level according to the law of supply and demand. With this move, the French gold-corner scheme and monetary offensive collapsed.

Since then, there had been two increases in the official price of gold—to $38 in 1971 and then $42.22 in 1973, both serving to devalue the U. S. dollar. However, the free market in gold had been playing a progressively more important role in the international monetary systems and balances. Inflation, energy crisis and diminishing confidence in currencies made free gold a powerful factor. As its price rose, the buying power of U. S., British and other currencies lessened just that much more.

Yes, the three men agreed, it would be eminently plausible to suggest that the incumbent French President, Georges Pompidou, had decided to emulate his mentor, Charles de Gaulle—but with a somewhat different approach. David Auerbach—and others—would be very likely to believe that France had started the monetary wars anew, but was attacking through the free market in gold.

"I shall place a call to David now," Michel Auerbach said and went to the telephone on Charles Sturdevant's desk.

Matthew Rutledge had just finished dressing when the telephone in the sitting room of his Dorchester suite rang at 9:20 Saturday morning.

"Mr. Evan Moorhead of the Foreign Office and Police Inspector Thomas Kirkland to see you, sir," a desk clerk announced.

Foreign Office and police! It could only mean that someone had learned he had brought gold into the country without declaring it at customs. And that meant that news of his Sakhana find would soon become public property.

"All right," Matt said. "Ask them to come up."

Evan Moorhead and Inspector Thomas Kirkland apologized profusely for having disturbed Rutledge. Then Moorhead asked the first question.

"Mr. Rutledge, do you know a Rafin Kalsi?"

"Rafin Kalsi?" Matt thought a moment. "No. Who is he?"

"That is what we are hoping to discover," Moorhead said. "He was found dead aboard BOAC Flight nine eighty-two yesterday evening."

"Kalsi was murdered," Inspector Kirkland declared. "Preliminary postmortem examination indicates he was poisoned. We had hoped you knew him—or something about him."

"Why, for God's sake?"

"Kalsi had a Sakhanese passport. You were in Sakhana until a few days ago. Both of you boarded the same plane in Calcutta. These coincidences made us think you might be able to provide some information about the man. You see, very few Sakhanese come to England—"

"Very few of them travel anywhere outside their own country," Rutledge said. Though he said nothing about the Sakhanese who had tried to kill him the previous night, he wondered whether there was a connection between his own attempted murder and the death of Rafin Kalsi.

"Were there any other Sakhanese on the plane?" he asked.

Evan Moorhead said there weren't.

"Have you tried getting information on Kalsi from Sakhana?" Matt asked.

"We radioed Kangtek, the capital, last night," Inspector Kirkland replied. "So far, we've received no answer."

Moorhead and Kirkland stayed only a few minutes longer, for it was obvious that Matthew Rutledge could tell them nothing about Kalsi.

After they were gone, Rutledge sat moodily chain-smoking Camels, trying to ponder what he knew were imponderables. After half an hour, he gave it up. Only the $20 million loan from Jacob Auerbach and Company really mattered, he reflected. Once he had that, all puzzles would be solved and all problems would resolve themselves.

4

Vivian Auerbach had managed her father's household affairs for three years, since she was twenty-one and her mother died. Although spoiled and pampered, she loved her father and it pleased her to keep the domestic machinery functioning smoothly for him. Saturday morning the machinery faltered. She came downstairs to hear the parlormaid and her husband, the gardener, give their notice. They would be emigrating to Australia in March under the Assisted Passage Scheme.

"Australia's our chance, Miss Auerbach," the maid bubbled. "We'll be out of the rut, starting a new life."

Vivian's face had a beauty on two visible levels. At first glance, it was refined, superbly molded to classic contours—a face beautiful as ideal aristocratic faces are. Yet it expressed warmth and humor along with a sensuality and capacity for passion. Now she frowned, puzzled. The maid's words struck an unfamiliar responsive chord deep inside her. What could it be, she wondered. Envy? No, that was preposterous. She had everything she could possibly want—far more than most women could ever hope to possess. No, she told herself, whatever the feeling, envy had to be ruled out. Yet the encounter left her with a vague sense of depression.

Vivian breakfasted with her father, as she did every morning.

"Have anything on this evening?" David Auerbach asked when they had finished eating.

"Alan and I are going to a party." Alan was Alan Leopold, her fiancé. They were to be married in May.

"I've invited someone to dinner."

"Oh. All right, Daddy." If her father had invited a guest on such short notice, it was a business dinner, and he wanted her to stay home and act as his hostess. She was about to say something more, but Phelan interrupted to announce that Mr. Michel Auerbach was on the line from Paris.

David Auerbach was surprised. His second cousin Michel phoning on a weekend? Most unusual. "I'll take it in the library," he said.

Vivian sighed. The profusion of Auerbach relatives often made her feel claustrophobic, and she considered her French "Uncle" Michel a pompous, egocentric bore and worse. She went into the drawing room and phoned Alan Leopold.

"Bad news for tonight, darling," she told him. "Daddy's laid on a V.I.P. dinner. I have to stay and radiate charm and hospitality."

Alan was understanding and sympathetic. The very soul of consideration. As he always was about everything, Vivian reflected.

"We'll see each other Monday evening, then," he said.

Not tomorrow. It was the second Sunday of the month. When Alan *always* visited his paternal grandfather in Sussex. Families, Vivian thought, cradling the receiver.

Vivian Auerbach could have had any man she wanted, as five highly selective pre-Alan Leopold love affairs had demonstrated. But her choice of husband was limited by family canon and tradition. He had to be Jewish; in two centuries only five Auerbachs of all branches had married outside their faith. Then, because she was an only child and female, it was mandatory that her husband be a banker and from a banking family, for he would one day succeed Sir David Auerbach as head of Jacob Auerbach and Company.

Alan Leopold met all the criteria, and Vivian was content to marry him. *Content,* she mused, her large hazel eyes pensive. It was such a bland, pallid word—but, unfortunately, accurate. Their relationship fell short at some level. The sexual level? Perhaps. Alan's lovemaking did lack earthy spontaneity and imagination Yet, it wasn't just sex.

Vivian tugged absently at a strand of her long auburn hair. Whatever the flaw, Alan's reaction when she canceled their date for the evening was a symptom of it. He had made no objection or protest. He was acquiescent, compliant. But I have to forgive him for that, she thought. He's no less a Family Product than I am—damn it!

She joined her father in the library. Long-dead Auerbachs stared, glared or smiled from Watts, Millais and Augustus John portraits hung on the paneled walls. David Auerbach had finished speaking with Michel and sat at his library desk. He seemed downcast. Vivian sensed that he wanted to talk and curled her supple body into a leather armchair facing him.

"I take it Michel was peddling gloom," she said.

Auerbach took a deep breath. He frequently discussed business matters with his twenty-four-year-old daughter. While the man she was going to marry would eventually direct Jacob Auerbach and Company, she would inherit actual ownership of the bank. She needed to know about its operations and about banking in general.

"It has to do with our dinner guest," he said. "He's an American, Matthew Rutledge . . ."

The name meant nothing to Vivian, and she could not imagine what bearing Michel's call might have on any dinner invitation.

". . . who recently discovered gold in Sakhana. He came to me for a development capital loan. I was prepared to approve it. Michel learned that Rutledge was seeing me and asked that I refuse him."

"You're letting Michel change your decision?"

"Viv, when the head of one Auerbach branch makes a request of another—"

"It is always honored," Vivian broke in acidly. "Our most sacred family tradition." She seethed inwardly. "What grounds—or excuse—did Michel give for making the demand?"

"You know that I've suspected some sort of gold market manipulation for the last few months. It appears I was right. France is conducting another monetary offensive. Michel let that slip—"

"Nonsense! Michel never let anything 'slip' in his life You can be sure he had his own reasons for telling you."

"He did," her father admitted. "He and his bank are secretly acting as gold-buying agents for the French government. Michel is also part of a syndicate buying gold for its own account, investing very heavily on the assumption that the price will continue to soar. Word that Rutledge has made a fabulously rich find and obtained the capital to begin producing large quantities of newly mined gold could create havoc with the market price."

"Does Auerbach tradition force you to guarantee Michel's profits?"

Auerbach tugged at an earlobe. "There's more to it than that. French governments are notorious for retaliating against agent banks when their own plans go awry for whatever reason. Even the French Rothschilds learned that in 1968." He sighed unhappily. "Besides, Jacob Auerbach and Company has been handling the purchases of Michel and the Société Auerbach on the London Market."

"So you protect Michel."

"I'm protecting Jacob Auerbach and Company. As I said, there is a syndicate—"

"That's out to corner the gold market?"

"It might go that far, yes. Michel told me very little— but enough for me to realize it is an ambitious, even audacious, program."

"Program? It sounds more like a gigantic swindle to me."

"It's business, Viv. Harsh, perhaps, and on a vast scale, but still legal and legitimate business done in the open marketplace."

"For God's sake, are you afraid of this syndicate?" Vivian demanded.

"Not afraid. Prudent. The syndicate was formed by

Charles Jordan Sturdevant, according to Michel. I hardly need remind you what financial power and political influence he represents. It would be extremely foolish to antagonize Sturdevant and his financial empire."

Vivian had no further arguments. "Are we still having Mr. Rutledge over for dinner?" she asked.

"Of course. I have to tell him my decision."

It isn't your decision, Vivian thought bitterly. Michel made it for you. Being an Auerbach obviously meant that one gave every other Auerbach a blank promissory note good for a lifetime. It was all so archaic, unreasonable—and unfair. She found that all her sympathies were with Matthew Rutledge, a man she had never met but who—like herself—was a victim of a two-century-old Auerbach family code.

David Auerbach and his daughter received Matthew Rutledge in the drawing room. Phelan served martinis. Vivian studied Rutledge over the rim of her glass. She had expected him to be like so many of her father's business acquaintaines—a board-room type, middle-aged and stodgy. Instead, he was young, rough-hewn, handsome. He radiated a vital quality which, she guessed, was often and readily translated into exuberant sexual energy.

"Matthew and I first met ten years ago," Auerbach said for Vivian's benefit. "He had just obtained a mining claim in the Congo, in the part known as Zaire nowadays."

He likes Rutledge, Vivian thought. She looked at Matt, smiled and asked, "Did you open a mine and produce gold?"

"Produced it at the beginning," he said. "Not for long, though."

"Mind if I ask what happened?"

"I don't mind at all." Matt's grin was rueful. "I sold my holdings to a Swiss bank fronting for a dummy Lichtenstein corporation established by AMTORG—which in turn fronts for whatever the Russians want to hide. I had a hunch the Congo was ready to blow sky-high and got out from under. None too soon, I might add."

"Rebels and foreign mercenaries went on a rampage a month later," Auerbach interposed. "Matthew's intuition is remarkable."

It certainly isn't operating now, Vivian thought. He hasn't a clue to the letdown ahead of him.

The long, candlelit table could have accommodated two dozen guests. The china was Spode; the silver, Lamerie. Phelan and a footman moved silently, serving dinner courses and accompanying wines.

Matt Rutledge made his private assessment of Vivian Auerbach, who sat opposite him. High, delicate cheekbones and faintly almond-shaped eyes endowed her intelligent face with a vaguely Eurasian quality. Her figure was perfectly proportioned and there was sensuous grace to her movements. Forget it, he warned himself. She's David's daughter. Besides, she's wearing twelve carats of emerald-cut diamond solitaire on her engagement finger.

"It's so difficult to believe you're really a prospector," Vivian was saying. "In films, they're always dour, gnarled men."

"Matthew is a graduate mining engineer," her father said, a hint of reprimand in his tone.

"A prospector all the same," Matt said with a broad grin that displayed strong white teeth. "I've even done the burro-and-pick-and-shovel bit."

Vivian gazed at him from under her long lashes and made her own further appraisals. His sea-green eyes and jet black hair were a startling combination, but there was far more to him than physical attractiveness. Few women could ever ignore Matthew Rutledge, she mused. He was all male, independent and self-contained. Yet she sensed he was capable of far-ranging emotion, a man who would not be ashamed to be gentle and tender and not afraid to be hard and tough in the face of the heaviest odds. Without doubt, a relationship with him could quickly develop into total immersion. My God, she thought, looking away. My responses to him aren't cerebral—they're glandular!

There was coffee and superb seventy-five-year-old Otard cognac in the library after dinner. David Auerbach offered Matt Upmann panatelas. Rutledge refused and lit Vivian's Benson and Hedges and his own Camel.

Auerbach drew on his cigar slowly, a frown creasing furrows across his high forehead. He seemed reluctant to speak. Something was terribly wrong, Matt realized somberly and braced himself against the worst. It came soon enough.

"I slept on our last night's conversation, Matthew," Auerbach said at last. "This morning, I felt I should consult with two or three directors of the bank, and I spoke to them . . ."

David paused, looking very uncomfortable. He hates to lie to this man, Vivian thought.

". . . They reminded me of several internal situations in the bank that I'd failed to take into consideration last night. I'm afraid my decision has to be negative at the present time." Auerbach paused, smiled faintly. "In a few months, the picture will change, but I know you can't wait that long."

Rutledge emptied his *ballon,* tasting defeat rather than cognac.

"But there are other possibilities," Auerbach went on. "The Sakhana venture is most promising. Come to my office at ten Monday morning. I'll provide you with introductions to other banks likely to finance enterprises of that nature."

Matt had another brandy in hopes it would alleviate the sinking sensation. It failed to help. When he bid his host and hostess goodnight half an hour later, he was much too preoccupied to notice that Vivian Auerbach held his hand longer and pressed it harder than he might have expected.

Vivian Auerbach lay awake, her mind working, for a long time after she went to bed. The sense of depression that had come and gone all day returned and it was oppressive, suffocating. She had always mistrusted her "Uncle" Michel Auerbach. She felt he was making cynical use of Auerbach family tradition and loyalties—and of her father. She told herself it was this concern and not thoughts of Matthew Rutledge that prevented sleep.

5

Michel Auerbach and Sheikh Nasib al Rahman met again with Charles Sturdevant on Sunday morning in the study of Sturdevant's Avenue Foch house.

"What about Kalsi?" Sheikh Nasib asked.

"Brief items in the London papers," Sturdevant shrugged. " 'MAN FOUND DEAD ABOARD AIRLINER'—that sort of thing. According to the press, no one seems to know who he is or how he died."

"And the men who bungled?"

"They left England for Calcutta yesterday."

"Anything further to be done about Sakhana?" Michel Auerbach inquired.

Sheikh Nasib stared at him coolly. Pompous Jew, he thought. Nasib tolerated Michel Auerbach only because he was useful. Nasib was also aware that despite the wealth and power of Charles Sturdevant and Michel Auerbach, he himself held the whip hand. As Emir of Hajar, he could nationalize the Sturdevant-controlled AMENOCO oil holdings in his country with a stroke of the pen. By another stroke, he could withdraw Hajari deposits in Michel Auerbach's bank, and these deposits amounted to almost $750 million.

"If Rutledge returns to Sakhana empty-handed, that situation takes care of itself," Sheikh Nasib said. "Our job is to make certain that he does. He may go elsewhere for capital—and there's always the possibility he will get it. Since we were unable to eliminate Rutledge, we must eliminate the possibility."

"Simple," Michel declared. The Sturdevant National Bank and the Société Auerbach were international financial institutions of great stature and influence—to which other banks were obligated in one way or another. It was only necessary to pass a message through the tight fraternity of the banking world and loan applications by one Matthew R. Rutledge would be rejected out of hand. "You and I need merely drop the black balls tomorrow morning," Michel said to Sturdevant.

The American financier nodded. "And you might drop a few, too, Nasib."

The Emir of Hajar understood. He had billions of oil-royalty dollars deposited in banks around the world. An implied threat that he would withdraw his funds from any bank that granted Rutledge a loan was certain to be effective.

"I'll notify my finance minister to place the banks on notice immediately," Nasib assured the others.

"Another item," Sturdevant said. "We should thicken the smoke screen Michel laid for his cousin. We should commit several million dollars daily for heavy gold buying locally—on the Paris Market. That will drive prices up sharply here and convince David Auerbach that information leaks from French government sources have set off buying waves by French private speculators."

Nasib al Rahman inclined his head in agreement. "The ploy will make Michel's story completely believable." The sums that would be involved were negligible compared to the amounts they were pouring into buying on the London Gold Market.

"Will you see to it, Michel?" Sturdevant asked. "Naturally, the purchases should be spread out to make it appear there are great numbers of buyers."

"*Mais certainement.* Now what else is on our agenda?"

"Only a suggestion that you get in touch with your cousin again and find out if he's complied with your request."

It was a gray, dismal Sunday morning in London, and when Vivian Auerbach heard that her father had received another telephone call from Michel, her sense of depression returned anew.

"Why this time?" she asked.

"He wanted to know if I'd spoken to Rutledge," David Auerbach replied.

"You told him you had?"

"Yes."

"Daddy, be honest with me. Do you trust Michel?"

"Viv, he's my second cousin—an Auerbach."

"That's not an answer," Vivian said. "It's an evasion. So I'll ask another question. Does Matthew Rutledge have a chance of obtaining a loan from any other British bank?"

Her father averted his eyes. "I don't know, Viv," he murmured. "I really don't know."

Since Alan Leopold was making his mandatory monthly visit to his grandfather, Vivian spent the afternoon and evening with friends. They found her uncharacteristically distracted and withdrawn. Those who knew her best theorized that she and Alan might have had some sort of lovers' quarrel. There seemed to be no other explanation.

When Matthew Rutledge awoke, his first thought was that he did not want to move through the boredom of an English Sunday alone. He regretted not having asked the stewardess who had been so eager, for her name and number. He thought briefly of Vivian Auerbach—but, of course, she had to be counted out. Luckily, he knew many girls from his previous visits to London. After he showered, Matt slipped into his dressing gown and dug out his address book.

Vivian returned home at eleven that night. She bathed and went to bed. Again, she could not sleep. An attempt to read a book proved futile. She was unable to concentrate.

It was almost one o'clock in the morning when—without quite understanding why—she reached for the telephone on her bedside table.

The girl sharing Matt Rutledge's bed moaned softly, all her muscles contracting, her body arching up against his. Her fingernails dug deeply into his back. He did not feel their sharp bite, for he was caught up in the onrush of his own orgasm.

"I—I don't believe it," the girl gasped minutes later. "I've lost all count myself and you—"

"Never count in bed," Rutledge smiled, caressing her trim breasts. "That's like—now what the hell?"

He moved away from her and picked up the telephone that had rung once and was ringing a second time.

"Rutledge," he growled into the mouthpiece.

"Matthew—uh, Matt—it's Vivian here."

I'll be God-damned, Matt thought and said, "Good evening—or should I say good morning?"

"I'm terribly sorry to call you so late, but I was wondering if you were free for lunch tomorrow."

I have an appointment with her father at ten in the morning, and she wants to have lunch with me, Matt reflected. This makes no sense—unless she wants to sample every flavor before she gets the wedding band to go with her engagement ring. Which, remembering some of the looks she gave me last night, is entirely possible.

"I'm free for lunch," he said. "Any particular place you'd like to go?"

"Why not there, at the Dorchester?" The words came out in a tumble, as if Vivian had blurted them without realizing what she said. Evidently she had, for her voice was embarrassed and uneven when she hastily added, "It —it would be simpler to meet there, wouldn't it? Is twelve-thirty all right?"

"It's fine," Rutledge said. So what if she is David Auerbach's daughter, he thought. She's a grown woman and presumably knows her own mind.

"Will you meet me in the lobby?"

"Sure."

"Goodnight, Matt." The line went dead before he could say anything further. He replaced the receiver.

The girl in the bed spoke.

"I don't care who it was or what she wants," she said. "Just come back here with me." Her arms reached for him and her thighs parted.

6

Energy emergency decrees that placed steel mills and pastry shops alike on a three-day work week could not be applied to the City, London's financial center. Firms whose business was money did business as usual. This certainly included merchant banking firms like Jacob Auerbach and Company, whose headquarters were in a weathered stone building on Old Broad Street.

Matthew Rutledge was ushered into David Auerbach's office on the fifth—and top—floor a few minutes after ten o'clock on Monday morning. The office was a predictable setting for the head of a venerable merchant banking house—staid and decorous yet impressive, with magnificent old woods and rich leathers.

Auerbach sat behind a massive mahogany desk. He greeted Rutledge warmly and offered him a high-backed armchair drawn close to the desk. Depressing a lever on his intercom box, Auerbach instructed a secretary to begin placing calls to the officers of several London banks.

In less than an hour he arranged five appointments for Matt—two each on Tuesday and Wednesday, one on Thursday. Rutledge expressed his thanks.

"It's the least I can do under the circumstances," Auerbach said. Matt made as if to leave. "Wait a moment," the banker said. "Before you go, suppose we find out what gold is doing so far today." He reached for a telephone that was a direct line to the Jacob Auerbach and Company Gold Room. Both men were well aware of the power reflected in Sir David's Gold Room.

The official price of "monetary" gold—that is, gold held as reserves in national treasuries or central banks—is set by international agreement. To all intents and purposes, the free market price of the metal is set twice daily by the London Gold Market, through which the overwhelming majority of the world's nonmonetary gold is traded. There are secondary exchanges such as those in Zurich (which caters mainly to Continental nervous-money speculators), Paris (an almost exclusively domestic market), Frankfurt, Beirut and Hong Kong. But the London Market leads—and dominates.

Membership in the London Gold Market is severely restricted to six firms, most of them merchant banks. Insofar as their Gold Market activities are concerned, they are designated as "bullion brokers," but the term is misleading.

Member firms act as principals, issuing their own contracts. They may maintain their own gold inventories and buy and sell gold for their own accounts as well as for those of their clients. Each firm has its own "Gold Room" where the actual trading with customers is conducted.

The trading that takes place between the member firms themselves is limited to two brief sessions each weekday—at 10:30 A.M. and 3 P.M. At these times, a representative of each of the member firms goes to the N. M. Rothschild and Sons, Limited Building on Saint Swithin's Lane in New Court. They meet in the "Fixing

Room" on the ground floor, with the Rothschilds' representative acting as chairman. Since all gold trading is done in the utmost secrecy, extraordinary security precautions are taken during these meetings.

Each of the six men has a direct-line telephone to the gold trading room of his own firm. Each arrives knowing precisely what orders to purchase or sell gold have been received by his own firm since the previous session. The individual firms' cumulative orders are matched, balanced off against each other. A per-ounce price is then established. This is called the "fix." If buying orders exceed those to sell, the price will be somewhat higher than during the previous fix. If the balance is the other way around, a correspondingly lower price is fixed. These sessions usually last about thirty minutes.

Once the "fix" has been established, the men return to their own trading rooms. In their dealings between fixing sessions, the price of gold may fluctuate according to the "bids" and "asks" that each firm receives from its customers. The prices on secondary markets may also vary to some degree from the London Gold Market level, but the transactions on these lesser exchanges are inconsequential compared to London Market volume, where a $500-million trading day is by no means unknown.

On Friday, February 8, 1974, gold was bid up as high as $145 an ounce on the London Market. Late-hour sell orders from profit-takers softened the price to $141.50 by closing. On Monday morning the member firms set the 10:30 fix at $142 an ounce.

"We're already receiving bids at one hundred forty-four dollars," David Auerbach said after talking to the head of his bank's gold trading department. "Zurich quotes are the same at the moment. I anticipate another peak price to be reached before the day is over."

Auerbach did not mention that his Gold Room manager reported Paris Market quotations to be appreciably higher than London or Zurich—already at $148 an ounce. He preferred to steer clear of any discussion in which he might inadvertently reveal something of what he had learned from Michel about the French monetary offensive and the gold-buying syndicate that included Michel's bank.

David believed he knew the reason for the higher Paris price. Although the Market there was both small and domestic, it became volatile and responsive to all stimuli. He reasoned that word of the French government's campaign must be filtering down from the top levels. He could readily imagine a *sous* minister confiding to his mistress here, a clerk glimpsing a vital document there, and individual French speculators avidly following their government's lead.

"Will you be free for lunch later today?" Auerbach asked.

"Sorry, David," he said. "I already have a lunch appointment."

"We'll make it another day—best of luck on your meetings with the bankers."

Matt observed that Vivian Auerbach was following the current London high fashion trend, at once protecting endangered species from extinction and herself from heating-fuel shortages. Her coat was "fun" fur (but not that much less costly than the leopard it parodied). Beneath it she wore a white wool Cardin pants suit that accentuated both the reddish highlights of her auburn hair and the provocative curves of her body.

Once seated at their table in the Dorchester's Rose Room, Vivian asked for a dry martini and Matt ordered the same for himself. Vivian was obviously ill at ease. Then she stammered: "I—I shouldn't be here. . . . It's—well, I realize how much the Sakhana mines mean to you."

They're far from being mines yet, Matt thought, and what the hell does she care about Sakhana?

"Daddy couldn't tell you the truth . . ."

Rutledge's eyebrows rose in astonishment.

". . . that the French are cooking the gold and money markets—"

"My God, not a replay of the de Gaulle fiasco?"

"Something of the same sort, yes. Daddy's second cousin Michel phoned from Paris. He and his bank, the Société Auerbach, are working with the French and with your American tycoon, Charles Sturdevant."

I'll be a son of a bitch, Matt thought. A gold corner. Being engineered by the Société Auerbach and Charles J. Sturdevant III. Rutledge had encountered the Société Auerbach before, in the Congo and later in Venezuela. The French bank often served as a front for the Quai d'Orsay's schemers while raping freely for its own benefit in underdeveloped countries.

"We Auerbachs are all about family traditions and loyalties and Michel pulled out all stops, invoked the lot."

While she spoke, Rutledge was beginning to understand the many things that had inexplicably gone wrong. The incidents started the day he first arrived in Sakhana. Then there was the airborne murder of Rafin Kalsi and the attempt on his own life. The existence of a huge gold-corner conspiracy could be an explanation.

"You and my father have been friends for years. I felt you should know he was forced to do what he did."

Matt smiled gratefully, nodded and filed the information away for the moment. He concentrated on Vivian. Her slender hands rested on the edge of the table, right covering left, and she was nervously twisting the engagement ring on her finger. He recognized it as a giveaway, a woman's classic unconscious expression of emotional conflict over fidelity to one man and desire for another.

"Conscience bothering you?" he asked.

Vivian blinked. "I—I suppose so." She continued twisting the ring. "By Auerbach family codes, I had no right telling you anything."

"That isn't what I meant."

"I don't understand."

"Come off it, Vivian. We're adults—or reasonable facsimiles. Adolescent games have been out for a long time."

Their eyes met.

"I'm not hungry," she said. "Could we leave?"

Matt Rutledge closed the door of his suite behind them. Vivian flung her coat on a sitting room sofa and thrust herself against him, face upturned, mouth searching. Her kiss was ravenous, and then she abruptly pulled away from him.

"Was *that* an adolescent game?" she demanded.

Matt drew her back to him, right arm around her waist, left hand cradling the back of her head. He kissed her slowly, sensuously. Her response was volcanic, but he released her and his expression mirrored gentle amusement. Vivian misread it as patronizing and her hazel eyes narrowed with indignation.

"What was that?" she flared.

"Just a reminder that we're not in a hurry."

"I am. I don't want to wait."

He studied her for a moment. Her conscience again, he realized. Having gone this far, she didn't want to have time for second thoughts. He took her hand. "We're overdressed for the occasion," he said and led her to the bedroom. There, he reached for the buttons that fastened her pants suit jacket.

"I'll do it myself," she said. "I still don't want to wait."

Vivian undressed rapidly. Her body was lithe, flawless. Matt removed his own clothing. She turned to face him, her look eager and impatient, but it changed almost instantly.

"Your shoulder's bandaged."

"It's not important now," he said.

Vivian's eyes had shifted to his massively erect sex. "You're not circumcised."

"Does that turn you off?"

"Oh, no. It's only that I've never been to bed with a man who wasn't." Even the two Gentiles among her lovers had been circumcised. "But I want to. Now."

She lay down on the bed. He moved across the room and sat on the edge of the bed and began to kiss and caress her. His lips moved from her mouth to her shoulders and perfect breasts. Vivian strained against him, her hands seeming to savor the feel of his lean-muscled, sun-bronzed body. Then she grasped a handful of his black hair and raised his head.

"Inside me," she pleaded. "Inside me, please."

He positioned himself over her and felt her hand reach for his sex, hold and guide it. He lowered himself slowly, reveling in sensation as she raised her hips and her drenched sheath swallowed and gripped him, their bodies already moving in unison.

Vivian lay in Matt's arms. She was sated, drained. Matthew Rutledge had proved to be everything she had ever hoped for in a lover, infinitely more gratifying than any other man she had ever known. For some reason, her fiancé Alan Leopold was the last to enter her mind as she made the comparisons.

The drapes were drawn. Two soft lights burned in the room.

"What time is it?" Vivian murmured against Matt's bare chest.

"Little after six-thirty."

"What?" Vivian sat bolt upright. "That's impossible! We haven't—not for more than five hours!"

"We sure have—and they've been great hours."

"I have to leave. I'm supposed to be home and ready . . ."

Her voice trailed off. Alan Leopold would be calling for her at seven o'clock. He was always prompt. And she would have to change after she got home. But she could not tell Matthew any of this.

He kissed her cheek and swung out of bed. "I'll start

the shower running for you." He strode toward the bathroom door, paused and glanced over his shoulder. "Next time, we'll set an alarm or leave a call."

To her amazement, Vivian nodded. Until that moment, she had not even considered the possibility that there would be a next time.

7

Charles Jordan Sturdevant was in excellent spirits when he sat down at the breakfast table Tuesday morning. Two more days, and the World Economic Policy Conference to which he was a delegate would end. Sturdevant loathed the interminable meetings, but he had to attend them. They provided the pretext for his stay in Paris.

Sturdevant smiled to himself. He no longer needed the pretext. The master plan had been fully implemented and would move into its final stages as a practically automated operation. There was another ingredient in the mix that produced his sense of well-being. On Friday he would be on his way to the Persian Gulf emirate of Hajar as guest of its ruler, Sheikh Nasib al Rahman.

Sturdevant always looked forward to his visits to Hajar. The American Ensign Oil Company—controlled by Sturdevant interests—took millions of barrels of crude oil each month from its Hajari wells. The sight of AMENOCO wells ceaselessly pumping huge profits out of the Hajari sands never failed to fascinate and excite him.

Moreover, Sheikh Nasib entertained on a truly royal scale, providing the most lavish and exotic pleasures for his guests. These could be relished without fear of interference or scandal. The Emir's palace was a world of delights hermetically sealed off from the eyes and ears of media and public—a pleasure dome even Kublai Khan would have envied.

"Yes, more coffee," Sturdevant told the servant hovering at his side. Morning newspapers were piled neatly on the table. He selected the *International Herald Tribune,* turned to the Business and Finance pages, and his spirits rose even further. The Monday closing price of gold on the London Gold Market topped the previous high of $145 an ounce. On the Paris Market, the price had shot to $150. Our stratagem worked, Sturdevant reflected, not without pleasure. *My* stratagem, he corrected himself, remembering that it was his suggestion to buy heavily on the Paris Market.

"Beg your pardon, C. J."

It was John Nicholson, Charles Sturdevant's male secretary, who traveled with the financier everywhere—except to Hajar, of course. John Nicholson was forty, wispy-haired, efficient—a prototypal Great Man's Indispensable Aide.

Sturdevant acknowledged his presence without bothering to look up from his paper.

"Two calls for you. Mrs. Sturdevant from the States . . ."

It was a little after eight-thirty A.M. in Paris, six hours earlier in New York. If his wife, Lexa, had telephonitis at two-thirty in the morning, it meant she must have been drinking. Heavily.

"Tell her you just saw my car drive off," Sturdevant said. Lexa would have a few more drinks and go to sleep. He would talk to her that evening—if necessary. "Who else?"

"Mr. Michel Auerbach."

Michel calling before nine? "Bring me that phone."

An extension instrument stood on a Louis XV commode in a near corner of the dining room. John Nicholson brought it to the table, pressed a line-selector button and hurried off to deal with Lexa Sturdevant. The American banker picked up the hand set. "Hello, Michel."

"Are you alone, Charles?" Michel Auerbach sounded agitated.

Sturdevant dismissed the servant waiting on him. "I am now," he said. "What's the problem?"

"Only minutes ago I heard from a source inside the Elysée Palace. Pompidou is suffering from terminal cancer. He has only weeks. Perhaps only less than a month."

Sturdevant's face barely reflected a sudden sense of concern. If French President Georges Pompidou died, there would be national elections in France. Political opponents of his Gaullist party might discover that it was being made to appear that the French government was manipulating the gold markets. They would demand probes, perhaps make the matter a campaign issue. The consequences were unforeseeable and could be most dangerous for Sturdevant, the Emir Nasib al Rahman and most particularly Michel Auerbach.

"We must think ahead, prepare immediately for any eventuality," Michel was saying. "*Mon dieu*, the Société Auerbach cannot afford—"

"None of us can," Sturdevant said. "But let's not panic. We simply have to devise a new scenario. After I get to Hajar, Sheikh Nasib and I will talk the matter over. I'll be in touch with you from there—unless inspiration strikes me before I leave Paris."

Inspiration had already struck, Sturdevant reflected after concluding the conversation with Michel. It had been sparked by Michel's "*Mon dieu*, the Société Auerbach cannot afford—" Michel and his bank were not only the most vulnerable subassemblies of the operative apparatus but also the most expendable. The idea of using them as sacrificial goats suddenly had enormous appeal.

A Société Auerbach driven to the wall would be a most nutritious morsel for the Sturdevant National Bank's principal European subsidiary to absorb. Beyond that, the elimination of Michel from the master plan would add several billion dollars to the profits of Charles

Jordan Sturdevant III and His Royal Highness, Emir Nasib al Rahman.

Sturdevant rang for a servant. He wanted another plate of eggs, this time shirred.

Matthew Rutledge's first Tuesday appointment was with Edward Collings, a director of the Central Midlands Bank. He left his briefcase containing nugget and ore samples in the Dorchester safe, taking with him only the official documents verifying the exploration and development concessions the Maharaja of Sakhana had granted him.

Edward Collings listened politely to Matt's presentation.

"Most promising," Collings said when Rutledge had finished. "Naturally, you'd have to submit it to us in writing. After that, we here at Central Midlands will make preliminary studies before referring the matter to the full board. You should be able to expect an answer within ninety days or so."

Matt didn't have ninety days—not even thirty. But he understood. Collings wasn't giving him a direct no. He was delaying his response for so long a time that it amounted to the same thing.

At two-thirty P.M., Rutledge met with Sir Peter Vail of Lippert's Bank, Limited. Sir Peter was more forthright.

"Lippert's cannot possibly consider making a loan of the size you ask," Vail declared. Then, trying to be helpful, he added, "But you indicate that your personal net worth is around two million dollars and that you're willing to use your own money."

"I am. It's not enough, though."

"Why not form a company and sell shares? There's plenty of venture capital about, despite all the talk of a money crunch."

"It's something to think about," Matt said, but he

knew otherwise. Several months would be needed to organize a corporation and find investors with risk capital willing to put up a total of $20 million. Besides, there could be only two shareholders in the Sakhana enterprise —the Maharaja of Sakhana and Matthew R. Rutledge. They had to retain full control between them. That was why Matt was willing to pay high interest rates and had also offered to sell the lender part of the gold produced at preferential prices.

Rutledge returned to the Dorchester shortly after four P.M. There was a telephone message for him from Vivian. She asked him to ring her. And, Matt was informed, Police Inspector Thomas Kirkland was in the lobby, awaiting his return.

Kirkland? He's all I need, Rutledge thought. He found the inspector sitting in a lobby armchair reading a copy of *The Economist*. They went to Matt's suite. Rutledge offered a drink, and Kirkland accepted. Matt poured two large Black Labels at the tiny sitting room bar and gave one glass to Kirkland.

"I take it this is an official visit," Matt said.

The inspector grinned amiably. "We finally received a reply from Kangtek. The Sakhanese government verified that Rafin Kalsi was a citizen and a merchant. Otherwise, they know nothing about him. Rather unusual, wouldn't you say?"

"Not for Sakhana. It's a strange country—the Closed Kingdom, they call it. The Sakhanese are big on secrecy."

"Perhaps. But I do think this was unusual. There was an inquiry appended to the radiogram sent to us. His Majesty, Narayan Mahendra Karamchad, the King— or Maharaja—of Sakhana desires personal assurance that Mr. Matthew Robert Rutledge is safe, sound and in London."

Matt got to his feet and reached for Thomas Kirkland's empty glass. "I still can't help you with the Rafin

Kalsi puzzle, but I can pour us another drink and tell you a long story."

The account took almost an hour and two more refills. It omitted any reference to Matt's Friday night encounter with a would-be assassin, but was otherwise complete.

". . . so you can hang me for bringing gold into the country without declaring it at customs," Rutledge concluded.

"That's not my province," Kirkland smiled. "Incidentally, you might be relieved to know there's no suspicion that you were involved in Kalsi's murder. A stewardess remembers you clearly. You didn't leave your seat after takeoff from Beirut. All the same, I'd like to give you some friendly advice."

Rutledge waited for the inspector to continue.

Kirkland eyed Matt's big frame and strong, craggy face. "I don't doubt you can take care of yourself. Nonetheless, be a bit cautious."

"Any special reason?"

"Suppose Mr. Rafin Kalsi's killer might want to do the same for you." Kirkland drained his glass.

"That's pretty farfetched," Rutledge said, though in truth the same thought had occurred to him often.

"Perhaps. Old policemen have vivid imaginations."

"Another drink?" Matt asked.

"No, thank you. I'll be running along." The inspector stood up. "Oh, yes. I suggest you reassure His Majesty that you're in good health."

"Any chance of sending a radiogram through your channels? Commercial messages take a hell of a time getting to Sakhana."

"I suppose the regs can be stretched that far."

Matt took a sheet of Dorchester Hotel stationery from the writing desk. Using a ballpoint, he swiftly printed a message in clear, draftsman's letters and gave the paper to Kirkland.

"Some kind of code?" Inspector Kirkland asked.

"It's Hindi. Means *The doors have not yet been set into the frames.'* Hardly cryptic in view of what I've told you."

Kirkland departed. Matt placed a call to Vivian Auerbach.

"Are you free *all* tomorrow night, Matt?" she asked.

"I hadn't planned anything. Should I?"

"Please do. I'll be there at six." Vivian lowered her voice. "Everyone thinks I'll be staying overnight with a girl I went to school with."

Matt's pulse quickened, but he gave a good-natured laugh. "Your syntax is God-awful and you're ending your sentences with prepositions. I'll spend the night giving you grammar lessons."

"Bastard. I'll see you at six." The line went dead.

Rutledge cradled the receiver thoughtfully. Vivian offered generous compensation for the day's disappointments. He only regretted having to wait until the following evening to enjoy them.

8

Matt had appointments at two more banks on Wednesday. The meetings were unproductive, and he sensed there was something more than considered bankers' judgments behind the refusals he received. He had an excellent reputation as a successful gold prospector and producer, and the Sakhana find was without parallel in recent history. At the very least, the bankers should have shown sufficient interest to suggest sending representatives to Sakhana with Rutledge so that they could verify the existence of the fields. Instead, the men with whom he spoke rendered negative decisions which, it was apparent, had been made beforehand.

Puzzled and discouraged, Rutledge was not at his best when he met Vivian Auerbach in the Dorchester lobby at six o'clock. Either his interest in her had diminished, she thought, or, worse, he was taking her for granted.

When they entered his suite, Matt took Vivian's coat to hang in the entrance foyer closet. She went into the sitting room, flung her oversized Gucci handbag in a corner of the sofa and planted herself beside it.

"Well, here we are," Vivian said, her tone edged with ice. "You might offer me a drink."

"What would you like?" Matt asked, going to the miniature bar.

"A whiskey. A small one. With water." She spaced out the phrases and there was a pause before she added, "Please."

Matt frowned. For some reason, the gorgeous—and spoiled—Miss Vivian Auerbach had decided to be a pain in the ass. He poured a whiskey-water, brought it to her. "Antifreeze. May help you. Thaw out. I hope," he parodied her delivery.

Vivian's answering glare declared that her feelings had been unjustly wounded, that she was innocent of all wrongdoing—and that she was prepared to make a major issue of any trifle. It had always worked for Vivian, and she waited for the conciliatory protests, apologies and the culminating act of contrition.

"Sit right there," Matt said. "I'll be back in a couple of minutes." He left the suite before Vivian could speak. She fumed for ten minutes until he returned, carrying a large cardboard box from the lobby gift shop.

"Sorry," he said. "I forgot your birthday." He gave her the box and went to pour himself a drink. Vivian's first impulse was to say that her birthday wasn't until April and bait him into a quarrel, but curiosity proved stronger. She opened the box. It contained a white stuffed-toy panda. She recognized the medium as the message. Matt was telling her that she was being childish. She took the toy from the box and instead of being furious, wanted to laugh, at herself.

Rutledge stood directly in front of her, glass in hand. She put the panda doll aside, stood up and went to embrace him. As she did, Vivian accidentally knocked the glass from his hand. It fell, spilling liquor and ice cubes on the carpet, but she was in his arms and neither of them took notice of it.

"Undress me this time," she whispered against his lips. "Slowly."

It gets better and better, Vivian thought, her cheek against Matt's upper arm. They had made love for almost two hours. She had submerged herself in sheer pleasure, and she felt no sense of guilt, no conscience stirrings. She moved a hand down to his thighs and touched his sex. It became semierect instantly. It *can't* be, Vivian told herself, feeling his penis throb into full tumescence. Not after as many—

"Uh-uh." Matt took her wrist and eased her hand away. "It's quarter after eight. Dinner's at eight-thirty."

"You ordered it sent up?"

"Yep. Fish and chips, Yorkshire pudding, jam trifle—"

"Ugh!" Vivian grimaced. Then she kissed him. "What, no birthday cake?"

"Damn it, I forgot."

The overnight bag Vivian had ostentatiously packed at home for her mythical visit with a girlfriend had remained in her car. She could not bring it into the Dorchester. There was too great a possibility that she might meet someone who knew her and Alan Leopold. She now borrowed Matt's dressing gown. It was enormous on her slender, five-foot-six body. Rutledge put on shirt and slacks. When the room-service waiters knocked he went into the sitting room, closing the bedroom door behind him. Several minutes later the waiters left, and he opened the door and Vivian joined him.

An immaculately set portable table stood in front of the sofa on which the panda doll was propped in a sitting position. Vivian laughed. "The waiters probably think you have a teeny-bopper with you."

"Doubt it. Teeny-boppers carry hash pipes, not stuffed toys. Besides, nobody says *teeny-bopper* anymore."

"What are they called now?"

"Brats, I guess."

He had ordered caviar, chateaubriand, an assortment of side dishes and a magnum of Taittinger Blanc de Blancs '64. A candelabra was lit in the middle of the table.

"You forgot the cake but remembered the candles," Vivian chuckled.

Matt grinned at her. "Eat your caviar before it melts —brat."

When they had eaten Matt wheeled the service table out into the corridor and hung a DO NOT DISTURB sign on the doorknob. He took the champagne bucket and the two-thirds empty magnum of Taittinger into the bedroom. They undressed and returned to bed. Matt poured two glasses of champagne and gave one to Vivian.

"Salut."

Vivian drained her glass and turned it upside-down. A few drops of champagne fell on her breasts and flat stomach. "Empty," she said. "And you know, I'm a little smashed."

Rutledge took the glass from her and put it and his own on the nightstand. He turned back to Vivian and bent down, his tongue flicking at the drops of wine on her body. She held his arms and urged him to sit up. When he did, she kissed his mouth. Her lips were moist and chill from the cold champagne. Then she made him lie back and swung herself around in the bed. A moment later, her reddish-brown hair was cascading over Matt's thighs and her mouth was closing around his sex. Her lips were no longer cold.

The awareness that Matt was drawing her closer to him awakened Vivian and she realized it must be morning.

Matt's fingers conducted a gentle exploration.

"Useless, I'm afraid," Vivian murmured apologetically. "I'm never much good first thing in the morning."

"Honey, you don't know yourself. You're soaked."

"That's never happened before." Vivian was amazed. For once, she and her glands had awakened together. The discovery delighted her. She moaned with pleasure, moved her right leg up over his hips and locked him to her.

Rutledge had a ten o'clock appointment in the City. Vivian debated whether to take the lift down alone and leave the hotel by herself. There was a strong element of defiance in her decision. She would leave with Matt. If they encountered anyone she knew, it would happen and to hell with it!

Rutledge stopped at the desk to get his briefcase from the hotel vault. Today, he would take the nugget and ore samples with him. Vivian stood by, the white panda doll under her arm, gazing at his tall figure and wishing she could spend the entire day with him.

Matt had similar feelings when they parted outside the hotel. Then, hastily, he assured himself it was only what the psychiatrists called sensory fixation. Vivian was beautiful, and she was magnificent in bed.

"Any idea when you'll be through this afternoon?" she asked, holding his hand.

"I can phone later and let you know—will you be home?"

Vivian nodded. He kissed her on the cheek, and she hurried off to get her car. Matt told the uniformed doorman to signal a taxi from the waiting cab rank.

9

Brian MacIntyre, the chief loan officer of Claffley's Bank, was a grizzled and bluff Scotsman only a month away from compulsory retirement because of age. In his youth, MacIntyre had prospected for gold in Africa and had once worked as a mine foreman in Rhodesia. He sized up Matthew Rutledge immediately. He had known many men like Rutledge and regretted that they were a vanishing breed. For his part, Matt sensed a rapport with Mac-Intyre, and his hopes rose, but not for long.

"No bloody use my fiddling you around and talking balls," Brian MacIntyre said, glowering, but Matt recognized that the glower was not intended for him. "The powers that be in this countinghouse have already voted a unanimous nay. It's not my decision, Rutledge. Damn it, I'd probably let you have the whole store. The rumors are you stumbled across a bonanza."

MacIntyre had carefully chosen the word *bonanza*, which as Matt well knew is a term used in mining geology to denote a deposit of very rich ore, but usually one of limited extent.

"Bonanza doesn't begin to describe it," Matt said, opening his briefcase. He placed the nugget and ore samples on the bank officer's desk.

MacIntyre reached for the nugget and his eyes gleamed. "Jesus Christ and all twelve Apostles!" he exclaimed.

"Think that might make the powers that be reconsider?" Matt asked, lighting a Camel.

The bank officer shook his head. "Not likely." He was silent for a moment. "Oh, hell. In a few weeks I'll be out of here and tending my rose garden. I might as well be indiscreet." He reached for a battered briar pipe, lit it and continued.

"You've heard about little fleas having littler fleas. By something like the same token, powers have bigger powers. Some very big ones are biting those in charge here at Claffley's and elsewhere." He puffed at his pipe. "I'm afraid there've been blank walls built."

Matt's jawline tightened. Now the reactions he had gotten from bankers formed a plainly discernible pattern. Someone high in the freemasonry of banking had passed the word that he was to be blacklisted. He realized it should have been apparent. God knows it isn't the first time he had seen it done.

His father, Harold Rutledge, had owned a small but successful bank in Southern California's San Fernando Valley. Harold Rutledge had engendered the enmity of larger banking institutions by following a liberal policy in making loans and providing special services to small depositors. He took customers away from the large banks. They gave him two alternatives—change his policies or sell out to one of them. The elder Rutledge had refused to consider either course. He and his bank went on the banking mafia's blacklist and he was forced to close inside a year. Six months later, Harold Rutledge committed suicide.

"Mind telling me who's behind the boycott?" Matt asked.

"Damn it, man, I can't go all that far." Smoke billowed from MacIntyre's pipe. "On the other hand, there's nothing to prevent you from reeling off names. If you accidentally hit on the right combination, I'll probably react by showing surprise."

Rutledge remembered what Vivian Auerbach had told him. "I don't think I have to do much guessing," he said bitterly. "Société Auerbach and Sturdevant National."

MacIntyre took the pipe from his mouth and mimed a wide-jawed gape for a second. "Damn it, there I go. Can't keep a proper banker's frozen face anymore. Must be old age." He scowled. "Since you now know this much, I'll stick my neck out another inch. Any British or Continental bank you might approach for a loan the size of yours is beholden in one way or another to Sturdevant National or Société Auerbach."

"In other words, a total shutout."

"Afraid you'd find it so."

At last Matt knew exactly where he stood. But he was grateful to MacIntyre for telling him.

"Thanks, Mr. MacIntyre—"

"Don't thank me, Rutledge. Just find some means of beating the rotten bastards. I'll be cheering for you from my rose garden."

Matt called David Auerbach from a public pay telephone kiosk.

"Could you spare me a few minutes, David?"

"I believe so." Auerbach's tone was a shade hesitant. "When?"

"In the five minutes it'll take me to get to your office."

"Very well, Matthew. Come along."

Auerbach obviously felt embarrassed as he listened to Matt.

"You did me a great favor phoning people and making appointments for me on Monday. Did you know I was on the banking brotherhood's shitlist?"

"No, not then. I only learned of it Tuesday. I had hoped that all the banks to which I referred you weren't going along."

"They are, though. I'm blackballed."

"Matthew, if there was something I could do—"

"There isn't. I understand that. You're on the hook, too."

Auerbach's deep-set brown eyes seemed to sink deeper into his skull. "Have you any other plans?"

"God-damned right I have. I'm going to get the money I need. I don't care how—but I will."

* * *

Matt was deeply and gloomily meditative as he ate a solitary lunch at Wheeler's on Old Compton Street. Not even the superb chablis he had with his grilled Dover sole cheered him. He now comprehended the magnitude of the odds he faced.

The known and reasonably inferable elements combined to form a grim landscape. He had unwittingly made himself and his Sakhana venture a threat to the success of a global conspiracy mounted by men and institutions with overwhelming power. They could—and, if necessary, would—take whatever measures were needed to block or literally destroy him. As for the $20 million loan that was the key to his—and Sakhana's—future, he could not hope to obtain it anywhere in Britain or Europe. On the face of things, his situation was hopeless.

Rutledge grimly pondered all aspects of the situation, the scant few options open to him, drank a large cognac with his after-lunch coffee and returned to the Dorchester. He telephoned Vivian. She immediately expressed her eagerness to see him again.

"I've arranged things for tomorrow afternoon—"

"Sorry, Viv—"

"The day after, then?"

"Honey, I phoned to tell you I'm leaving for the States."

"Oh." Vivian's voice went flat. "When?"

"Today. I'll take the six P.M. Pan Am flight."

A silence, then: "You made up your mind very fast —or did you?"

"Less than an hour ago."

"Can't we see each other before you leave? I could be over there in fifteen minutes."

Matt hesitated, then said, "Better not. I've never been much for farewells."

"Will you be back in London soon?" she asked bleakly.

"I'm not sure. There's no telling what'll happen next. I can phone or cable you when I know anything."

Perhaps it was just as well that Matthew Rutledge was leaving, Vivian reflected. She and Alan Leopold would be married in a little more than three months. She remembered her thoughts when she first met Matt—and my God, was it really only last Saturday—a relationship with him could quickly develop into total immersion. She wasn't up that far—not yet, but his going now was none too soon for her to start working him out of her system.

Vivian experienced a momentary surge of relief. She could now write the Matthew Rutledge episode off as an exciting, short-lived affair. A fling, an adventure, nothing more.

"Please don't do either, Matt," she said. "No telephones, no cables." Once more, there was a silence as her sense of relief gave way to one of emptiness. Finally: "It was wonderful, Matt. Really. All the best luck—and happy landings." With that, she broke the connection.

Rutledge almost called her back. No, leave it as it is, he told himself, slowly replacing the hand set.

Rutledge knew that security officers made a physical search of all hand luggage carried aboard aircraft on flights from Heathrow to the United States. He consequently packed the Sakhanese nugget and ore samples in a suitcase that would travel in the plane's cargo hold. Hopefully, he could get past customs at Kennedy without having to open his bags.

Boarding the Pan Am 747, Rutledge settled into his first-class section seat and fastened his seat belt. A stewardess distributed copies of the London evening papers. Matt leafed through the *Standard* until he found the item he sought, a report of the day's trading on the London Gold Market. Gold had spiked to $148 per troy ounce at the 3 P.M. fixing, another record high, a 64 percent increase in barely more than two months. It had been only $90 an ounce on November 19, 1973, when Matt first arrived in Sakhana. He put the newspaper aside.

II

November 19, 1973-
February 8, 1974

1

Matthew Rutledge had wanted to be a mining engineer
from early childhood. By the age of fourteen, his ambi-
tion was focused on gold mining, and with reason. An
only child and perceptive, Matt saw his father lose everything when large financial institutions wrecked his small
bank. The boy came to realize that large banks and powerful bankers were ruthless—and more, that the value of
money was relative, subject to steady erosion by inflation.
Only gold was a constant, retaining its value throughout
history.

After his father's suicide, Matt Rutledge completed
his high school education in Southern California, then
worked his way through the Colorado School of Mines.
During his sophomore year, he read *The World's Gold
Supply,* and for the first time encountered a reference to
the Golden Mountains of Sakhana, a country he barely
even knew existed:

"The Kingdom of Sakhana is bounded on the south
by India and is walled off from Tibet in the north by
the Himalayas, which soar to heights of 25,000 feet and
more. The Sakhanese call the Himalayas the Cen-po Ri,
the 'High Mountains.'

"These mountains are for the most part uninhabited
and inaccessible, all the more so because Sakhana has no
rail or air transportation facilities and almost no roads.

The Ser-gi Ri—or 'Golden Mountains'—are reputed to lie somewhere in a particularly remote part of the Sakhanese Himalayas. Ancient manuscripts describe the Ser-gi Ri as abounding in placer deposits and with veins of gold so thick and pure that the metal may be cut from the rocks with a knife.

"According to Sakhanese historians, the goldfields were discovered in 1672, then 'lost' immediately afterward. Some Europeans and presumably many native Sakhanese have searched for the Ser-gi Ri over the ensuing centuries. None found gold. Most of those who went into the High Mountains perished there. Predictably, the Sakhanese have concocted superstitions about the Golden Mountains, saying they are cursed and the domain of evil spirits."

Matt Rutledge did further research and found other mentions of the "lost" Sakhanese goldfields. The stories caught his imagination. A legend that had endured for three centuries might indeed be true. Someday, he would go to Sakhana and search for the Golden Mountains. The idea remained a cherished fantasy for a decade.

Graduating from the Colorado School of Mines in 1962, Matt spent two years working for the Homestake Mining Company in South Dakota as a mining engineer. Upon his mother's death, he inherited a modest sum, all that remained of his father's estate. It was enough for him to go on his own as a shoestring independent prospector.

There is virtually no chance of discovering viable virgin goldfields in the United States. For the small-scale operator, the only possibility of success lies in foreign countries. Matt Rutledge went to the Congo. After several months, his innate prospector's instincts combined with sheer luck, and he found gold. British banks are far more willing to finance African gold mining ventures than those in America. Matt obtained some development capital from David Auerbach and his bank, Jacob Auerbach and Company. He exploited his find for a short time but prudently sold his holdings shortly before the Congo erupted in bloody revolt.

Rutledge shifted operations to Venezuela, where he made another strike and, after a brief period, again sold out to a giant mining combine that had the resources to develop the claim fully. By then, Matt was worth almost a million dollars. He decided to make New York City his home base and bought a comfortable condominium apartment there.

He next prospected in Canada, making a good find in Northern Quebec during the summer of 1972. Some months later, a large mining company bought his claim for a sum that raised his personal fortune to a little over $2 million. Matt now relaxed for a while, devoting himself to the enjoyment of various pleasures—mainly women. Then he grew restlessly eager to realize his fantasy of searching for Sakhana's fabled Ser-gi Ri.

Rutledge went to Calcutta, where he entered into correspondence with the Sakhanese government, requesting permission to enter the country and begin prospecting. It was a long, complicated process. Sakhana—the Closed Kingdom—was historically reluctant to allow foreigners across its borders.

The policy had been breached from 1922 until 1949, when Great Britain maintained military and civilian advisers and schoolteachers in Sakhana. But the postwar wave of nationalism that swept Asia ended British influence. The advisers and teachers were forced to leave. The Closed Kingdom sealed itself off from the outside world more completely than ever before. Sakhana maintained no ambassadors abroad, was not a member of the United Nations and did not tolerate the presence of foreign embassies in its capital city, Kangtek.

Matt drafted his letters with care, emphasizing that he was an individual having no connection with any government or large corporation. He provided documentation of his financial responsibility and suggested concession terms highly favorable to Sakhana. He finally received authorization to visit Kangtek and the promise of an audience with His Majesty Narayan Mahendra Karamchad, the Maharaja of Sakhana.

Rutledge bought a considerable quantity of basic prospecting equipment and gear, gambling that he would obtain the permission he sought. An experienced licensed pilot, he rented an STOL Porter Pilatus aircraft, had the equipment loaded aboard and flew to Darjeeling, near the border between India and Sikkim. He refueled there to have ample reserves for a return trip, for aviation fuel was not available in Sakhana. On the morning of November 19, 1973, he radioed his Estimated Time of Arrival to Sakhana's single radio station and took off for Kangtek, some four hundred miles northwest of Darjeeling.

The chronometer mounted on the instrument panel read 10:44 hours. The sky was clear, the sun bright. Matt Rutledge throttled back his plane's turboprop engine and swept over Kangtek at about fifteen hundred feet above ground level.

The Sakhanese capital had a population of less than seventy-five thousand, but appeared larger from the air. Its one- and two-story buildings were widely sprawled out. Then there was the great walled compound covering fifty acres in the center of the city. The structures inside it were huge and splendid, for it was the palace compound of the Maharaja. Looking down, Matt saw the upturned faces of the people in the narrow streets of Kangtek. An airplane was still a novel sight for the Sakhanese, some nine hundred thousand of whom lived thinly spread out over their country's landlocked, twenty-one-thousand-square-mile area.

Having memorized available Kangtek flight maps and charts—which had been made by the British before 1949 —Matt recognized prominent ground features. Sakhana's lone radio station—British-built during World War Two —lay to the west of the city, its hundred-foot antenna mast a latticed steel shaft thrusting into the sky. The country's single improved landing strip—constructed by the RAF during the war years—was five miles beyond Kangtek's eastern limits. Its sole, north-south runway was clearly visible.

Matt banked, skimmed low over the strip. There was no control tower, not even a windsock. Only a shabby concrete hut at the edge of the runway, which was surrounded by cultivated fields. Several men were grouped near the hut. Most wore what Matt recognized as outmoded British battledress. He made a 360-degree turn, landed and taxied the Pilatus over to the concrete hut, swung the plane broadside to the uniformed men and cut the engine. He opened the cabin door and climbed out, smiling. The smile faded instantly, and he froze where he stood. A dozen soldiers were pointing .303 Enfield rifles at him.

A sinewy, olive-skinned man of about forty stepped forward. He wore an obsolete British army officer's uniform complete with Sam Browne belt. Ornate shoulder-strap insignia seemed to indicate high rank.

"You are Matthew Rutledge?" he asked in excellent English. All Sakhanese spoke Hindi and a variant of the western Tibetan dialect. Many were also fluent in English, the result of earlier British influence.

Matt acknowledged that he was. The officer demanded his documents. Rutledge produced his passport and a letter signed by Tsering Dorje, Sakhana's Prime Minister, authorizing his entry into the country. The officer scrutinized the papers, then gave an order in Hindi. The soldiers lowered their rifles.

"I am Major General Dep Bahadur Singh, chief of the Sakhanese military forces," the officer announced. His name identified him as being of Pahari—Hill-Hindu —stock. He did not offer to shake Matt's hand or return his documents. "My men will unload your baggage. Come with me."

General Singh strode toward a 1950 Bentley sedan parked a few dozen yards away. A Leyland stake-bodied truck of similar vintage stood behind it. Rutledge's luggage and gear were unloaded from the Pilatus and put aboard the truck. Eight soldiers got on the truck. Four remained, apparently to guard the plane. Matt and the general got into the back seat of the Bentley. A soldier started the engine. The car eased forward. The truck followed, tailgating.

It was a thousand yards from the airstrip to a rutted dirt road. People on foot, carts drawn by horses or bullocks, and occasional bicyclists were going in both directions. Men wore loose-fitting tunics and baggy trousers. Women were dresssed in brightly colored sarilike garments. All gawked at the motor vehicles.

Although it was the third week in November, the temperature stood in the midseventies. Having read everything he could about Sakhana, Rutledge knew that the Closed Kingdom's climate was one of the meteorological wonders of the world.

Low hills along Sakhana's southern border formed a unique weather-front barrier. Immediately north of these hills was a great valley—long, broad and extremely fertile, containing two-thirds of the country's arable acreage. Kangtek was at the approximate geographical center of this valley, which enjoyed year-round near-tropical climate.

To the north were the Middle Hills and beyond them a plateau averaging four thousand feet altitude. There, the climate was far less stable and favorable, with hot summers and cold winters. North of the plateau were the Cen-po Ri—the High Mountains—where fall and winter weather went to savage extremes of cold.

Matt had been to other Asian countries in the past. The medley of odors filling the air was typical of the Orient. It was compounded of the smells of burning charcoal, dust, a faint trace of incense and above all the reek of excrement—animal and human—used as fertilizer in rice and grain fields and vegetable gardens.

Matt tried making conversation with Dep Bahadur Singh, but the general was uncommunicative. After twenty minutes of slow, bumpy driving, the sedan reached the outskirts of Kangtek. Rutledge noticed some rows of aging Western-style bungalows and correctly guessed they had been built originally as quarters for British advisers.

Then the car entered narrow, unpaved streets lined on both sides by purely Asian—and mainly ramshackle—buildings, shops and open-air stalls. Moments later, the thirty-foot-high walls of the palace compound loomed ahead. Car and truck drove through a gateway as sentries saluted.

Matt gaped at what he saw inside the walls. There were acres of lush, exotic vegetation. Chattering monkeys swung through trees. Birds with brilliant plumage flew about or perched on the branches of flowering bushes. The palace itself stood on a slight rise of ground, a huge and magnificent white marble structure. A pink marble pool larger than a football field stretched carpetlike in front of it. Palace and pool were reminiscent of the Taj Mahal, Matt observed to General Singh, whose response was quick and acid-toned.

"The palace dates from 1601," he declared. "Work on the Taj Mahal only began in 1632, and it is much smaller. The Indian Mogul Empire took its finer architectural inspirations from us."

The Sakhanese were chauvinists as well as xenophobes, Matt reflected. Strange. Slightly more than half the population was of Hill-Hindu origin. Most of the others were of Tibetan stock, descended from nomads who had negotiated the Himalayan barriers from the north many centuries before. But the two ethnic groups coexisted in harmony, sharing a deep disdain for all outsiders and a particular hatred of Indians, Tibetans and Chinese. The Sakhanese had evolved their own unique culture. Even their religion was unique, and though it did contain some elements of Hinduism, Jainism, Taoism

75

and Tibetan Lamaism, indigenous elaborations set it apart from all others.

All traces of the pernicious caste system found in Hinduism had been abolished many hundreds of years before. On the other hand, the Maharaja was not only the hereditary temporal ruler of Sakhana, but also venerated as an incarnation of Agni, the fire god.

The Bentley and truck drew up before an exquisite marble-walled villa. General Singh said this was the guesthouse where Matt was to stay. He accompanied Rutledge to the entrance doors. Two servants in colorful dress bowed deeply.

"The servants speak English," Singh said. "Ask for whatever you wish. I will return soon."

Matt remembered that his possessions were still on the truck. Singh anticipated his question. "Your things must first be examined by our customs inspectors. They will be brought to you later." He saluted and returned to the sedan.

Six soldiers dismounted from the truck and posted themselves around the villa. They faced in, toward the building, not away from it. It was clear to Matthew Rutledge that they had mounted guard over him. He was a prisoner in the guest villa.

2

Sakhana's ruler was a King, a "twenty-one-gun Maharaja" like the kings of Nepal and Bhutan, not a mere prince like the Chogyal of Sikkim, who rated only a fifteen-gun salute at official ceremonies.

Maharajah Narayan Mahendra Karamchad was the twenty-seventh of his line to sit on the Sakhanese throne. Intelligent, worldly, he had attended Oxford University in his youth. A realist, he recognized that his country and its people were trapped in a time warp. They were not ready to enter the twentieth century and needed a strong hand to govern them. After receiving the Twelve Rubies and Nine-Colored Scarf at his 1935 coronation, Narayan reigned as a benevolent despot. Whenever possible, he emphasized the benevolence but did not hesitate to exercise despotic power when he deemed it necessary.

When the British left Sakhana in 1949, Narayan's subjects rejoiced that their country would once again be the Closed Kingdom, free of foreign influence—and foreigners. But new threats arose to menace Sakhana's isolation and independence in the early 1970s. Huge Western multinational corporations on the order of—and including—ITT began eyeing Sakhana greedily. They believed the country possessed enormous untapped natural resources. Foremost among the great companies were those avidly eager to investigate the legend of Sakhana's Golden Mountains and, if they existed, to exploit the gold reserves.

The Maharaja rejected all their proposals. He feared an invasion by armies of Western technocrats. They were invariably accompanied by intelligence operatives, intriguers and cynical opportunists. They would quickly destroy the form and quality of Sakhanese life—and his own power.

The giant corporations persisted, employing methods that had always produced desired results for them in small countries. Agents on their payrolls were infiltrated into Sakhana to bribe and corrupt Sakhanese officials. Before long, the Maharaja began to sense tremors of discontent around him.

By 1973, Narayan Mahendra Karamchad was sixty-four and grimly aware that the most difficult period of his reign lay before him. While Sakhana was agriculturally self-sufficient, it was otherwise poor and primitive. Although the people would resist foreign military incursions, they were vulnerable to blandishments that promised them affluence through foreign investments in their country.

Narayan conceded that development of Sakhana's mineral resources would improve the Sakhanese economy —and rediscovery of the Golden Mountains could mean immense riches. But if the great multinational corporations were granted exploration and development concessions, they would eventually devour his people.

Faced with this dilemma, he seized on the letters Matthew Rutledge sent from Calcutta. Rutledge was an established and responsible gold mining entrepreneur with no ties to any multinational companies. It would be possible to deal with him as an individual, man to man— and easy to dispose of him if he failed to abide by agreements or tried meddling in Sakhana's internal affairs. Such was the reasoning that led Narayan to approve Rutledge's request for entry into Sakhana. He wished to evaluate the American personally.

Elections were unknown in Sakhana; the Maharaja appointed all government officials. After Narayan, the next most powerful man in the Closed Kingdom was his Prime Minister, Tsering Dorje. After Dorje came Major General Dep Bahadur Singh, who headed the Sakhanese armed forces. These forces consisted of a three thousand-man "army" called the Royal Constabulary and a few hundred frontier guards. There was also an elite Palace Guard unit, two hundred strong, but these troops were the Maharaja's personal bodyguard and not under Singh's command.

When General Singh left Matthew Rutledge at the guest villa, he went first to his own offices in the ministerial wing of the palace and supervised a meticulous search of Rutledge's effects. Then he reported to Prime Minister Tsering Dorje. The two men closeted themselves in Dorje's private audience chamber.

Plump, gimlet-eyed and in his midfifties, Tsering Dorje was of Tibetan stock, his skin a shade darker than Singh's, his facial features flatter and broader.

"*Kya karna hai*—what is to be done?" Singh said

moodily, speaking Hindi. "Rutledge brought no contraband with him." The general's expression grew cunning. "Of course, I can put something into his bags and say we found it there. We could then send him out of the country immediately and simply report to His Majesty we have done so and why we have done it."

Tsering Dorje shook his head. "We cannot go that far. We do not yet have the strength for a confrontation with the Maharaja."

Singh's mouth turned down at the corners. "Rutledge should not have been permitted to come here."

"It could not be prevented. Some fool gave his letters directly to our Living God, who insisted the American be granted entry. *Beshak.* We shall be rid of him soon."

"But His Majesty will ask to see Rutledge this afternoon."

"Doubtless," Dorje agreed. "And tonight, there will be a formal welcoming banquet—at which Rutledge will be made to appear the very worst kind of foreigner. He will become an object of contempt, leaving His Majesty no choice but to order his immediate expulsion."

"How is this to come about?"

The Prime Minister's reply was cryptic. "*Agniko spars karnese hath jalta hai*—the hand burns by touching the fire."

It was past four in the afternoon when Dep Bahadur Singh returned to the guest villa. His manner had changed. He was talkative and friendly. Soldiers came with him and brought Matt's baggage into the house.

"His Majesty commands me to bring you to him for a private audience," Singh said.

As they left the villa, Matt noted that the troops who had been stationed around the house were gone.

Matt estimated that the royal palace was larger than two Grand Central Stations. And, he guessed that he and Dep Bahadur Singh walked through a half mile of corridors before reaching the audience chamber in which the Maharaja was to receive him.

By contrast, the room itself was small and intimate, but splendidly furnished with couches upholstered in fine silks and woven fabrics. The Maharaja was attended by three aides. He dismissed them and General Singh after Singh presented Rutledge.

"Please sit there, facing me," the Maharaja said.

Matt's first impression of Narayan Mahendra Karamchad was highly favorable. Although in his midsixties, the Maharaja retained a firm, athletic physique and radiated vitality. Tall by Asian standards, he had saturnine features that reflected shrewdness and humor. His manner was gracious, yet Rutledge recognized there was an underlying strength in the man.

Narayan was hardly less satisfied with his initial appraisal of the tall, wide-shouldered American. Rutledge impressed him as being an independent and energetic individual, at once astute, enterprising and honest.

The Maharaja still spoke English with the accent he had acquired decades before at Oxford.

"So, Mr. Rutledge. You wish to search for the Ser-gi Ri. Countless others have tried in the past. All failed. Most never returned from the High Mountains." Narayan sighed. "Are you aware that huge areas of those mountains have never even been mapped?"

"I know, Your Majesty. I'll make aerial surveys."

"You sound confident. Perhaps you have not been told that the Royal Air Force tried making such surveys during World War Two. The efforts were abandoned. Several aircraft were lost. Those pilots who returned told of gale-force winds and such severe air turbulence that it was impossible for them to control their machines."

"My plane is a great improvement over the models that were available then. It's built for work under just such conditions." Matt paused. "Your Majesty, I would like to ask a blunt question."

"Please proceed."

"Do *you* believe the Golden Mountains actually exist?"

The reply came without hesitation. "I am certain of it. There are documents and other evidence that prove the Ser-gi Ri are real and not merely a legend."

Narayan smiled and indicated that the audience was over.

"We shall talk further in the days to come," he said. "Tonight, you will be my guest at a banquet." He made a resigned gesture with his hands. "One of those dismal affairs demanded by custom. My ministers and councillors must be allowed to see the visitor from abroad with their own eyes."

General Singh was waiting for Matt outside the Maharaja's audience chamber.

"I shall come for you at seven forty-five," Singh said. "The banquet will be formal, needless to say. White tie."

Matt had brought a wardrobe adequate for all occasions—including palace functions—as Dep Bahadur Singh was well aware. After all, he had personally inspected all of Rutledge's luggage.

3

The smallest palace banquet hall was being used. Its smallness was only relative, however. A fair-sized bungalow could have been erected inside the room. Once used to entertain British dignitaries, it was furnished in Western style.

Crystal chandeliers, a gift from Britain's George V, provided illumination—fitfully, for the palace compound's generating plant was old and temperamental. Refectory tables brought from England were arranged in a U-shape, the crossbar of the U arranged on a raised dais. The Maharaja sat in the center on the dais. He was flanked on the right by Matthew Rutledge, on the left by Prime Minister Tsering Dorje. Major General Singh was seated on Rutledge's right, and there were five other high-level officials at the dais table. Some thirty men of lesser rank were at the tables forming the arms of the U. All save Matt wore Sakhanese ceremonial dress —high-collared silk robes, the richness of their embroidery indicating the importance of the wearer's position.

The Sakhanese had few taboos about food or drink. Servants in baggy-trousered scarlet uniforms brought huge silver platters heaped with highly spiced sweetwater fish, game, fowl, pork, rice and a variety of vegetables. A strong rice wine was served throughout the numerous courses.

There were no speeches as there would have been in a Western country—and thank God for that, Rutledge mused. The main courses eaten, the tables were cleared and silver trays of sweetmeats appeared. Now there was to be entertainment.

The center of the U formed by the tables became a stage. A Sakhanese orchestra—string and percussion instruments and a single, flutelike reed—played music discordant to Matt's occidental ears. Then a troupe of doll-like and lovely young women with beautiful bare breasts performed several dances, all sinuous and graceful, some highly erotic.

The dances ended; the women filed from the room. Servants entered with rolls of thick, woven-fiber mats and laid them on the floor as carpeting. Two lithely muscled men, naked save for strip loincloths, appeared before the Maharaja's table. After bowing low, they went to diagonally opposed corners of the mat carpeting.

"Kai-Shee?" Matt asked.

The Maharaja was astonished. "You are familiar with Kai-Shee?"

"I've seen exhibitions in Cambodia and Hong Kong," Rutledge said. He did not think it necessary to add that he had taken lessons himself in that most difficult of all oriental personal combat arts. He listened politely while Narayan explained that Kai-Shee antedated judo, karate and kung-fu by centuries. Originally, it was practiced by slaves who—like Roman gladiators—fought to the death. While its forms had remained unchanged, the blows, holds and kicks designed to kill or permanently disable were eliminated in Kai-Shee sporting matches.

"The taller of the two contenders is named Danu," the Maharaja told Matt. "The other is Nirmal. They are Sakhana's leading Kai-Shee masters."

Danu and Nirmal faced each other at the center of the mat.

"*Kai!*" Danu called out.

"*Shee!*" Nirmal responded.

The match began.

Nirmal sprang at Danu in the arms-out Golden Butterfly attack. Danu whirled to one side and dropped in a squatting position. Nirmal overshot him, landed on the balls of his feet and spun around in the Blown Leaf maneuver. Danu's legs lashed out, struck Nirmal's chest and sent him sprawling to the mat. But Nirmal somersaulted, regained his feet and delivered a punishing Jade Lotus blow to Danu's head.

Rocked off balance, Danu fell, but as he did, his legs scissored those of Nirmal and brought him crashing down. Both men leaped up instantly. Danu performed the diversionary arabesque of the Thousand Poppies. Nirmal lunged in the low-diving tackle of the Great Serpent attack, which Danu spoiled with a downward hand chop and a sidewise kick.

Riposting, Nirmal caught Danu offguard with a whirling Reaper in the Field figure that sent Danu to the floor, where he lay immobilized as Nirmal's foot exerted excruciating pressure against his solar plexus.

Nirmal had won the first of the three *chen-ti*—or falls—that constitute a Kai-Shee match. The audience applauded and the combat began again. Danu won the second *chen-ti*. Nirmal won the third—and the match. The banquet guests applauded him enthusiastically.

Danu and Nirmal came forward and once again bowed low before the Maharaja. Then Danu turned toward Matthew Rutledge and addressed him in Hindi. Matt had learned some Hindi phrases while in Calcutta, but this exchange was beyond him. Narayan translated.

"It is a Sakhanese custom. The winner of an exhibition match challenges the guest of honor, who then offers him a sweetmeat, symbolically acknowledging the victor's superiority."

"Ah, but it was not always so," Prime Minister Tsering Dorje interjected. "Once, the challenges were in earnest."

"That is all long past," the Maharaja smiled.

Tsering Dorje stared at Matt Rutledge disdainfully. Matt suddenly became aware that everyone in the room was watching to see what he would do. And he knew that if he did not do something fast, he would lose one hell of a lot of face.

Matt realized too that if he refused the challenge, word would spread quickly that the American who wanted to seek the Golden Mountains was a coward. He rapidly weighed the pros and cons. Kai-Shee is a combat art at which small, wiry-lithe men excel. Matt was almost seven inches taller than Danu and outweighed him by perhaps sixty pounds. On the other hand, Rutledge knew himself to be in peak physical condition—and Danu had no inkling that he was familiar with Kai-Shee. Danu was sure to be contemptuously overconfident.

"With Your Majesty's permission, I accept the challenge," Matt said, easing back his chair.

Though he appeared to be pleased, the Maharaja was angry. He had been wrong about Rutledge. The man was just another blustering Westerner after all, a conceited fool. He would suffer a humiliating defeat and be a laughingstock. Afterward, he would have to be deported.

"Very well," Narayan said.

"Where may I undress?" Matt asked, standing up.

"You may do so here," Tsering Dorje replied.

Rutledge removed his shoes and socks, then stripped to the waist. He was about to take off his trousers, but glanced down at Danu clad only in the skin-tight loincloth. He slipped his dress trousers suspenders back up over his shoulders.

"The trousers will hamper your movements," the Maharaja warned. The fool was multiplying the odds against himself. He would be a lumbering, helpless victim.

"I prefer to wear them, Your Majesty."

Dep Bahadur Singh smiled. Now he understood what Tsering Dorje had meant when he said "the hand burns by touching the fire." Matthew Rutledge was about to be incinerated.

Matt faced Danu, towering over the Sakhanese Kai-Shee master. He could hear the derisive snickers of the guests. They expected Danu to beat him without effort.

"*Kai!*" Danu said, eyes gleaming.

"*Shee!*" Matt responded.

Danu stepped to his left, then forward, right hand chopping laterally. Matt recognized the elementary Bamboo Cutter blow but wanted to feed Danu's overconfidence and reacted slowly and clumsily. He took the hard chop on his left forearm. It was painful and he winced. The audience tittered.

Danu feinted with an Angered Buffalo head thrust aimed at the lower abdomen. Rutledge pretended heavy-footed confusion, retreating two steps. There was open laughter from the onlookers as Danu performed a slow pirouette to demonstrate that he was in complete command of the situation.

They faced each other again. Danu executed an arcing Silver Fountain leap. Matt once more feigned delayed reaction. The ironhard heel of Danu's left hand hacked into his neck where it joined the shoulder, striking a nerve center. The force of the blow sent Rutledge reeling sideways. He felt as though several thousand volts of electricity had jolted through his body.

Danu bored in, trying for a Jade Lotus blow to Matt's clavicle. Parrying with his right arm, Rutledge closed thumb and first two fingers of his left hand and drove a Flaming Lance thrust into his opponent's diaphragm. It was good. Danu staggered back, a look of astonishment on his smooth face.

"A lucky accident," Tsering Dorje commented at the table on the dais. "Danu will counterattack."

Danu did. Before Matt could evade, Danu drove the edges of both hands against Rutledge's skull just forward of the ears. These were the lethal Twin Blows of the Thunder God, never used in Kai-Shee matches that were only for sport.

Maharaja Narayan's eyes widened. The Twin Blows were forbidden. His first impulse was to stop the match, but he refrained. It would have been taken as a sign that he favored the foreigner.

Matt was dazed. Danu sprang at him in the Great Serpent. Rutledge went down as Danu's hurtling body slammed into his. The onlookers applauded. Danu locked and tightened a Hangman's Noose hold on Matt's neck. The hold was also prohibited, for it could easily break a man's neck.

Rutledge could no longer doubt that Danu was out to hurt him badly. He countered with the only possible defense, expanding his neck muscles and allowing the rest of his body to go completely limp.

"Danu must have lost his mind!" Narayan exclaimed.

"Majesty, he has only forgotten himself for a moment," Tsering Dorje soothed. "See, the foreigner is holding his own."

Matt had executed a version of the Geyser, arching his body and simultaneously snapping arms and legs outward. This move broke Danu's hold and Matt regained his feet.

Danu glared. He launched a vicious Devil-Hammer kick at Matt's groin. The audience gasped. The kick was used only in Kai-Shee battles to the death. But Rutledge's timing was perfect. As Danu's leg lashed upward, Matt dropped to his knees and bowed his head in the Praying Beggar posture. At the same instant, his hands shot up and seized Danu's foreleg. Matt levered Danu's leg on the fulcrum of his shoulder, executing a perfect Flaming Comet throw. Danu rocketed through the air, crashing to the floor three yards away.

Danu rose, shakily. He closed with Matt and once more attempted the Twin Blows. Matt sidestepped and responded in kind, battering Danu's head between the edges of his hands, using all his strength. Danu fell, his hands clawing for support. His fingers encountered the waistband of Matt's trousers and gripped it. As he fell, the claw clips of the suspenders gave way and the trousers were torn from Matt's body.

Rutledge kicked his feet free of the trousers and took a backward step, warily watching his opponent. But Danu lay where he had fallen, unable to rise.

At first the banquet guests did not believe what they had just seen. An occidental vanquishing an oriental Kai-Shee master! Then, led by the Maharaja, the audience broke into applause. The American had won fairly.

Narayan Karamchad's regard for Matthew Rutledge soared, but his mind was interpreting what had transpired. It was obvious that Danu had intended to humiliate—and seriously injure—Rutledge. Danu could not have done it on his own initiative. He had been ordered and probably well paid to do it. But by whom? Narayan knew the person responsible could have but one motive, to prevent Rutledge from remaining in Sakhana and prospecting there. It logically followed that the person must be in the pay of some Western corporation that wanted the mining concessions for itself.

Narayan turned to General Singh. "Arrest Danu," he ordered. "Interrogate him tonight. Use whatever means are necessary to learn who instigated him!"

Singh shot a glance at Tsering Dorje, whose face was impassive.

"Majesty—what if Danu refuses to talk?" Dorje inquired.

Narayan's voice was low, cold. "Danu violated the hospitality of my court. He attempted to do grave harm to an honored guest. These are acts against the Throne."

General Singh experienced a sense of deliverance. He could not silence Danu forever. "By Your Majesty's leave," he murmured, standing up and departing.

Clad now only in his jockey shorts, Matt faced the dais and inclined his head as a gesture of respect to the Maharaja.

Now, Narayan suddenly comprehended why Rutledge had insisted on wearing his trousers during the match. It had been an act of consideration for the feelings of the guests!

Sakhanese men—like many Orientals—believe that a man's virility is in proportion to the size of his sexual organs. However—again as with many Orientals—their genitals are usually notably smaller than those of Western males. Clad in the snug-fitting loincloths, Danu and Nirmal exhibited only comparatively small pelvic-area bulges. With Rutledge stripped down to his jockey shorts, his penis and testicles were huge by comparison. Rutledge had sought to save them loss of sexual pride.

Liveried servants lifted Danu from the floor. Matt retrieved his torn trousers and put them on. He had to hold them up with one hand as he made his way back to the dais. There he accepted the congratulations of the Maharaja, Tsering Dorje and the others—but he noticed that General Singh was not at the table.

The banquet was over. The Maharaja told Matt they would speak again together at eleven the following morning, and there was new respect for Rutledge in his tone and manner. He ordered two aides to accompany Matt back to the guest villa.

"I am certain you will have a pleasant night," Narayan said. Rutledge thought he detected a sly gleam in the monarch's eyes.

4

"A gift sent by His Majesty is in your bedroom, Rutledge *sahib-kamal*," the majordomo said when Matt returned to the guest villa. The significance of the honorific *"sahib-kamal"*— "one having excellence"—was not lost on Matt. Evidently, the palace grapevine had flashed word of his victory. He had gained much face.

He went upstairs, glad the bedroom had a large Western-style bed, for he was tired. He entered the bedroom. A single lamp burned on an ivory-inlaid table. Its forty-watt bulb gave only feeble light. There was a rustling sound. A girl stepped from a shadowed corner into the glow cast by the lamp. She was about twenty-one, Matt guessed, scarcely five feet tall. She wore a filmy white sari. Her heart-shaped face was a classic of Indo-Aryan beauty.

She was one of the dancers who had performed at the banquet—and the Maharaja's "gift." Matt racked his brain for an appropriate Hindi phrase. "*Salahm. Yah bahut ascharayaki bat hai*—[this is a great surprise for me]."

"My name is Sita." The girl's voice was musical. "I speak English." She smiled, her lips moist. "I saw you when we danced. Later, I heard how you defeated Danu. I asked to be the one His Majesty sent to you." She paused, her great dark eyes expectant. "A man who excels in the art of battle excels in the art of love."

Matt grinned. "An old Sakhanese proverb?"

"It is from the Ananga Ranga." Sita stepped close to him. Her long hair, a deeper black than his own, was lustrous and perfumed. Her sari was like fine gauze, translucent, and she wore nothing beneath it. The nipples of her exquisite breasts were rouged needlepoints.

Like most Asian dancers, Sita had also been trained in the esoteric erotic arts. When Matt kissed her, she thrust her tongue deep, broadening it like a leaf in the *pratata,* then made it quiver inside his mouth in the *kari* manner. Her supple, perfectly proportioned body pressed against his.

She eased herself away. "I will undress you," she murmured and drew him toward the bed.

Her hands titillated and tantalized. When she had removed Matt's clothing, Sita unfastened her sari and let it fall to the floor. She made Rutledge lie back. For the next several minutes she used her hands and lips to intensify his arousal.

He tried to draw her down beside him. "No," she said. "Tonight, you are weary." She positioned herself astride him, lowering her body to impale herself on the rigid shaft of his engorged sex. With her legs bent, Sita began a slow rotary movement of her hips and pelvis. Many more minutes passed as she gradually increased the tempo of this *bhramara* movement, but then her own desires took control. She was frenzied when Matt's muscles corded and he groaned loudly and their first orgasms exploded together.

The interrogation room was dungeonlike, with thick stone walls and a heavy iron door. Danu, trussed hand and foot, lay on the floor. Two men stood over him, General Singh and a deaf-mute Royal Constabulary corporal who held a heavy truncheon.

Singh nodded to the corporal. Mewling obediently, the man leaned over Danu and his arm swung. Danu screamed as the truncheon smashed into his face, breaking his nose and splintering his teeth. The deaf-mute continued battering him with the truncheon and Danu's shrieks rose. He totally misunderstood why he was being beaten. He thought it punishment for his failure to cripple the foreigner in the Kai-Shee match.

The corporal stopped wielding the truncheon. Danu tried to speak, to say he had done his best, to beg for mercy. But he could only swallow broken teeth as his torn mouth filled with blood. Singh nodded. The deaf-mute's arm flailed up and down again. His truncheon, coated with Danu's blood, cracked bone and pounded flesh into pulp. Danu lost consciousness.

Dep Bahadur Singh grunted approvingly. There was now ample evidence that Danu had undergone merciless torture in an effort to make him talk. No one could suggest that General Singh had been lax. He made a gesture.

The deaf-mute put the truncheon aside and drew a knife from a sheath on his belt. He squatted down beside Danu. One slash of the razor-edged blade cut away Danu's loincloth. A second amputated his genitals. The corporal leaned away to avoid being splattered by blood fountaining from the wound. The rest—demanded by Sakhanese law—was merely symbolic, for Danu was dead. The deaf-mute cut into Danu's belly. Intestines welled out. He drew out a long segment and looped it around Danu's neck.

Despite the lateness of the hour, Prime Minister Tsering Dorje was in his office. He sipped black tea laced lightly with ganja to ease his nervousness. At last, General Dep Bahadur Singh arrived. He was smiling.

"*Kaidi ki sakht saja hui*—the prisoner was severely punished," Singh said in Hindi. "Unfortunately, I was unable to learn who gave him the orders."

Dorje nodded with pretended solemnity. "A great pity. I shall express your loyal regrets along with my own when I make my report to our Living God."

Rutledge was ushered into the Maharaja's audience chamber in midafternoon. Narayan's look turned mischievous.

"Did my gift please you?" he asked.

"Very much, Your Majesty."

"She may remain with you until you tire of her." The monarch's expression grew serious. "Now, let us talk. The Kai-Shee match last night. I have reason to believe it was a trap set for you. I regret to say we do not know who set it."

"Has anyone asked Danu?"

"He was questioned. He remained silent to the end."

Sakhanese concepts of Law and Order went to Absolute Extremes, Matt thought grimly.

"I must assume Danu was instigated by someone who does not want you to search for the Ser-gi Ri," Narayan said.

"I would agree, Your Majesty," Matt said, lighting a Camel. "Gold breeds trouble. You told me that big companies have been after the concessions. So we're dealing with board room claim-jumpers. They stay safely hidden and operate through echelons of agents and intermediaries who do what's called the 'organic work.'"

"You speak as though you are aware of an actual conspiracy."

"Gold is an ongoing conspiracy. Half a dozen or so giant companies mine and refine almost all the gold produced in non-Communist countries. They enjoy what amounts to a shared monopoly of the Western world's output." Cigarette smoke drifted from Matt's nostrils. "Monopolies operate all the way along the line. Eighty-five percent of the free market gold is traded on the London Market, where six firms have a stranglehold on trading."

Narayan was listening with keen interest.

"Small independent operators are tolerated as long as they stay small," Matt continued. "If they start growing too big, they're bought—or knocked—out of business."

"Yet you want to search for the Ser-gi Ri. Why?"

"Gold fever," Matt replied, his sea-green eyes intense. "A man either has it or he doesn't. If those Golden Mountains exist, *I* want to find them."

"It would bring you great wealth if you did."

"That's a factor, of course. But prospectors are funny people—and I'm a prospector. The gamble and the gambling—"

"Are as exhilarating as the winnings themselves?"

"Yes, something like that, Your Majesty."

"Please come with me." Narayan led Matt into a room that contained an immense mahogany table, some teakwood chests and a few chairs. An old-fashioned metal strongbox the size of a four-drawer filing cabinet stood on the table. The Maharaja produced a key, unlocked the strongbox and lifted the lid.

"I told you yesterday there is evidence that the Ser-gi Ri exist," he said. "I had it all brought here from the treasury."

The strongbox contained twenty or more gold nuggets, the largest as big as an orange. Matt's blood pounded. Even the smallest was far larger than any he had seen during his mining career. Narayan took two leather-bound volumes from the strongbox and placed them on the table. He opened one of them.

"Documents written by the men who discovered the Ser-gi Ri in 1672," he said. "They were murdered by those who wanted their secret. Their documents survived, but the Ser-gi Ri were never found again. Countless attempts were made over the centuries, the most recent in 1963 by five brave officers from my Palace Guard. Like so many others, they never returned."

He pointed to the other volume. "There are even two sketch maps." He shook his head. "They reveal nothing."

The documents were in Sanskrit. Narayan sight-translated them for Matt. They were mainly narratives of the trek into the Cen-po Ri. Those describing the region where gold had been found were obviously deliberately misleading. As for the sketch maps, they offered no help. There were no compass references, no scale. The symbols drawn on them were arcane and bore no identification.

"A comparison with later maps might give us a clue," Matt suggested. Narayan brought a sheaf of maps from a teakwood chest. He unfolded one made by the British in 1948. It represented the entire 21,000-square-mile area of Sakhana. A great portion was virtually blank. Not even the RAF and Royal Engineers had been able to map a vast area of the Cen-po Ri. Matt Rutledge realized that if the Golden Mountains existed, they were somewhere in this uncharted region.

5

Sakhanese tradition required that bodies of executed criminals be exhibited publicly. Danu's mangled corpse was displayed on a wooden platform in the *bagica*—small park—opposite the palace compound's main gates. Placards proclaimed that he had been put to death for conspiring against the Maharaja.

Kangtek's residents flocked to view the grisly remains. Although the Kai-Shee master had been a great favorite, they did not question the justice of his punishment. No one placed red and yellow jasmine blossoms or lit sandalwood incense beside the body to speed Danu's soul on to its next incarnation. Some who visited the park even made the largely obsolete gesture of turning their backs on the corpse and dipping their knees as if to squat. This symbolized defecation on his memory—and his soul.

The public reaction was reported to Tsering Dorje and General Dep Bahadur Singh. The two men met in Dorje's office shortly after sundown. Their mood was glum.

"I expected public protests," Singh muttered.

Prime Minister Tsering Dorje's close-set eyes narrowed. "I've warned you. The monarchy remains strong. The people still revere their Living God. We must move with caution." He stroked his plump cheeks. "Narayan has begun to sense there is opposition and suspects it centers around the mining concessions. Fortunately, he does not connect us with any of it—yet."

Singh picked nervously at a tunic button embossed with the figure of a rampant three-headed dragon, the Sakhanese national emblem. "Narayan agreed to give the concessions to Rutledge today," he said. "The American must be disposed of quickly or you and I will lose valuable friends and much else."

"Nothing must happen to Rutledge for the present," Dorje countered. "Narayan would move heaven and earth to learn the truth—and we would share Danu's fate."

"But—"

"Wait. Rutledge will need men to accompany him on his expedition. We shall arrange to send some of ours, men we can trust. The High Mountains have claimed uncounted lives. Who will be surprised if they claim one more?"

"Our friends are impatient."

"What matter? They can accomplish nothing without us and must be content to move at our pace. Inform them of the latest developments and what we now plan."

Singh's long face grew longer. "Their agent, Ramesh Anwar, returned to Calcutta last week."

Ramesh Anwar was an Indian who owned and operated what was euphemistically called a "business liaison and public relations" agency in Calcutta. In fact, he and

95

his operatives performed industrial espionage and sabo-
tage for multinational companies based in the West—
and, when necessary, bribed and coerced Asian politicians
on their behalf. The huge corporations contracted with
Ramesh Anwar through intermediaries, avoiding any
direct contacts that might be traced and made public.

"Unfortunately, I cannot send Anwar a radio
message," General Singh continued. "Narayan would
learn of it. A letter is out of the question because it would
take days to reach him."

"Go to inspect one of our frontier posts on the
Indian border," Dorje suggested. "Once there, cross into
India and speak with Anwar by telephone."

Singh thought for a moment. The nearest frontier
post was at Chenagar, only 135 miles from Kangtek, but
the roads were abominations. Motor vehicles could travel
along them slowly and only in daylight. It would be an
overnight trip.

"I will leave at dawn tomorrow," he said. "By the
next afternoon, I'll be in Balapur, where there is a telephone central."

Matt dined privately with the Maharaja in Narayan's
palace apartments. Narayan said he would announce the
concession grant at a ministers' meeting he had called
for ten o'clock the following morning. He asked Matt to
attend.

Matt was jubilant when he returned to the guest
villa. The majordomo bowed him inside. Rutledge
stopped, stared around him. Masses of fresh flowers filled
the glazed ceramic vessels that stood in the entrance
foyer. To his left, an arched doorway led to the main
reception room. Lights burned inside and somehow the
room seemed brighter, warmer—and hadn't the furniture
been rearranged?

"Good evening. Would you like a drink?" It was
Sita. She wore a plain green sari. "There is Scotch

whiskey. It was brought from the palace by a servant of His Majesty."

Now Matt understood why the house seemed different. Narayan had doubtless sent Sita word that she was to stay—and she had promptly taken charge of the household. Just like coming home to the suburbs after a hard day at the office, Rutledge mused, and said, "Yes, I would like a drink."

Sita spoke to the majordomo in Hindi. He disappeared into the rear of the villa. "He will bring the whiskey to your bedroom," she said. Anyway, she's not calling it *our* bedroom yet, Matt thought with good-natured amusement. He kissed Sita, let her take his hand and lead him upstairs. They sat on a couch. The majordomo appeared with a silver tray on which there was a sealed bottle of Dimple Haig, a carafe of water and a single glass. He put the tray on a table and withdrew.

"Only one glass?" Matt asked.

"I do not drink whiskey."

Matt opened the bottle, poured himself a double. The whiskey went down well. "More?" Sita asked.

"No thanks. The one I had was the one I needed."

"Then I will bathe you."

The bathtub was huge, like those found in European luxury hotels built around the turn of the century. A charcoal-fired boiler downstairs provided hot water, which Sita perfumed with a piny scent from a crystal bottle. When Matt sank down into the water, she removed her sari and knelt naked beside the tub. The supple beauty of her body aroused Matt to a degree that was almost painful. His distended sex thrust above the level of the water.

Sita lathered his shoulders and arms with a scented soap, gently massaging his muscles. He wallowed in the sensations produced by her fingers. She varied the pressure and quality of their touch, sometimes stroking gently, at others pressing her fingernails against sensitive nerve centers.

She stopped, stood up. Matt climbed from the tub, his sex massively erect. Sita wrapped a drying sheet around him. He pulled it off and reached for her. She moved sinuously, easily avoiding him.

"You are slow—you have rusted in the water," she taunted, darting into the bedroom. Matt followed, and caught her. She spun around and flung herself into his arms.

Her response was no artificial display by a woman trained to give men pleasure. Sita wanted him as much as he wanted her. She kissed him with feverish spontaneity, the forms prescribed by oriental erotic manuals forgotten. Her right hand groped for his sex, seeking to guide it between her thighs.

Matt lifted her bodily, carrying her to the bed.

"I can wait no longer," she moaned. It was a plea.

"Neither can I, Sita." Matt covered her body with his own. Her arms were around him. He entered her. She thrust her hips upward, and her slender legs went around his waist, locking him into an embrace that achieved ultimate penetration.

The meeting in the Royal Council Chamber was brief. Maharaja Narayan Mahendra Karamchad stated that Matthew Rutledge was to have exclusive rights to prospect for gold in the Cen-po Ri. Rutledge would pay all expenses incident to his prospecting. The Sakhanese government would cooperate with him fully.

Narayan asked Tsering Dorje if he wished to make any comment.

"Only that I will insure obedience to Your Majesty's wishes," the Prime Minister responded, inclining his head.

Dorje was unflinching, Narayan reflected. He could be relied upon in all things.

Sita's heart-shaped face registered dismay when she found Matt packing a small overnight bag that evening.

"You are going back to America!" she exclaimed.

"Just to Darjeeling in the morning. I'll return in the afternoon—unless the weather closes down." He explained that he would make several shuttle flights to Darjeeling and ferry drums of aviation fuel to Kangtek. He needed to build a reserve stock for the survey flights he intended making over the Cen-po Ri.

"Let me go with you," Sita begged.

"How much do you weigh?"

"Weigh? Forty-eight *ser.*"

"If I take you, that's ninety-six pounds less spare fuel I can carry." He kissed her cheek. "The answer is no."

"Then we shall make much love tonight."

"Never has a non sequitur made more sense," Matt laughed.

One of the Maharaja's aging Bentleys drew up in front of the guest villa at eight in the morning. Matt was driven to the airstrip. Although Narayan had assigned Palace Guardsmen to round-the-clock sentry duty at the field, Matt took no chances. He checked the Pilatus to make certain no one had tampered with the plane. Satisfied it had not been touched, he took off.

Rutledge landed at Darjeeling less than an hour later. He made arrangements to have the plane's tanks filled and ordered more fuel in forty-two-gallon drums, the first batch of the drums to be loaded aboard the Pilatus as soon as possible. Then he went into Darjeeling, where he bought several bolts of fine silk as gifts for Sita.

Eighty-one miles to the east of Darjeeling, in the Indian border town of Balapur, Major General Dep Bahadur Singh was at the local telephone central. He placed a call to Ramesh Anwar in Calcutta. Two hours passed before the connection was made.

"We have had a setback," Singh told Anwar. "The concessions were given to Matthew Rutledge."

"You guaranteed that could not happen." Anwar's tone was gelid. "You were paid a very large sum for that guarantee."

"The problem is only temporary. All promises made to you will be kept."

"I can only inform my clients," Ramesh Anwar said. "They will relay your information to their principals, and they to theirs. When the top is reached, the process will be reversed. Further instructions will be passed down to me. Good-bye, General."

Dep Bahadur Singh found himself holding a dead telephone. He replaced the receiver thoughtfully. He did not know who Anwar's clients were, but he did know that those at "the top" were individuals with enormous wealth and power.

6

In 1933, a troy ounce of gold was worth $20.67. The following year President Franklin Roosevelt raised the price to $35 an ounce. The United States Government owned a great quantity of gold. The price set in Washington was adopted internationally and remained stable until 1968.

Then, sparked by Charles de Gaulle's monetary offensive, gold-buying waves sent the price to $44.36 an ounce. Some of the demand was met with stocks held by central banks. As their reserves dwindled, a monetary crisis developed. Disaster was averted by international agreement setting a two-tier gold-price system. Gold in national reserves would continue to be valued at $35 an ounce and used solely to settle international payments-accounts. Gold outside national reserves could find its own price level on a free market.

At first, it worked. During 1970, the free market quotation was often only a dollar or so above the official price. Stability ended in 1971, when President Nixon announced his "New Economic Policy." He called an end to the use of U. S. gold reserves in international payments settlements and abolished the already largely theoretical 25 percent gold cover on the American dollar.

Nixon devalued the dollar 8.5 percent by raising the official gold price to $38 an ounce. Less than fourteen months later, there was another dollar devaluation. The official price of gold was hiked to $42.22 per ounce. With that, gold began to soar on the free market.

Ostensibly, the Nixon Administration's "New Economic Policy" was the brainchild of Assistant Secretary of the Treasury Owen Raynor, widely hailed as a "monetary policy genius." Owen Raynor had come to the Treasury via the executive vice-presidency of the Sturdevant National Bank.

But Raynor secretly remained on the payroll of Charles Jordan Sturdevant III, board chairman of Sturdevant National. Owen Raynor received $250,000 annually in spotlessly laundered, untraceable funds from Sturdevant. The money was well spent and easily afforded by the man who paid it.

The Sturdevant family's holdings were by no means limited to the Sturdevant National Bank. They were to be found in every economic sector and included several huge multinational corporations. One was the American Ensign Oil Company—AMENOCO—a petroleum industry major. Another was Miramines, Incorporated, a sprawling conglomerate that owned and operated base and precious metals mines in many parts of the world.

It was Charles Sturdevant who actually prepackaged Richard Nixon's New Economic Policy and ordered Owen Raynor to present it to the floundering administration as his own. Both men knew that behind its embroideries, the policy would give the Sturdevant interests license for financial piracy on a staggering scale.

Charles Sturdevant and European subsidiaries of companies he controlled began massive gold buying early, far ahead of the speculative pack that quickly bid prices to record levels. Forewarned of international developments by Owen Raynor, Sturdevant sold at a July, 1973, peak, reaping over $1.5 billion in tax-free, windfall profits. His personal share of the booty exceeded $200 million. Strained through the sterilizing sieves of offshore corporations and Swiss banks, the money was added to his personal fortune. He promptly conceived an infinitely more ambitious scheme. He would gain a speculative monopoly over free-market gold. In short, he would corner the market.

"With you on the inside, it can't fail," he told Assistant Treasury Secretary Owen Raynor.

"I don't see how it can, C. J.," Raynor agreed.

Most reliable estimates place the total amount of gold available for free-market trading at 200 million ounces. Ownership of 125 million ounces would constitute an effective corner, Sturdevant calculated. When he began planning his master coup, free-market gold stood at the $90-per-ounce level. But he knew a sustained buying campaign would send the price spiraling upward. He believed the price he paid before he was through would average out at around $150 an ounce, which meant a commitment of almost $19 billion.

"The price will go to four hundred dollars an ounce, once you have your corner," Owen Raynor predicted.

This would represent a profit of over $30 billion when cornered gold supplies were fed into the superheated market. The profits could be greatly multiplied. Sharp rises in gold prices caused drops in the value of the dollar and other currencies. With gold high and money low, Sturdevant National and Sturdevant-controlled companies could pay off obligations at home and abroad in cheap money and buy valuable properties in expensive gold at a fraction of their true worth. Overall, the potential gain could be reckoned at $100 billion.

The scheme was virtually foolproof. The sole risk was that large quantities of "new" gold might reach the free market.

Quantities large enough to wreck Sturdevant's scheme could come from only two sources. First, from national treasuries or central banks. Owen Raynor provided insurance against this eventuality. He could—and would—block any sales of U. S. reserves and bring American pressure to stop such sales by other countries.

The second risk was the danger of a great new gold find. It was a remote possibility. There have been very few significant discoveries in recent years. Those made were by no means large enough to upset the market. However, Charles Sturdevant was determined to eliminate all risk. The only remaining area in the world reputed to have rich virgin goldfields was the Asian kingdom of Sakhana.

Sturdevant ordered executives of Miramines, Incorporated, to approach the Sakhanese government and obtain the exploration and development concessions in the country. Once he had them, his plan would be absolutely foolproof.

To Sturdevant's dismay, the ruler of Sakhana rebuffed all overtures made by Miramines. Sturdevant then ordered his subordinates to put the money-fueled apparatus of subversion into motion. Before long, agents made contact with the commander of the Sakhanese armed forces, Major General Dep Bahadur Singh, and the country's Prime Minister, Tsering Dorje. Each man was paid $100,000 and promised much more in the future. In return, they agreed to use their influence so Miramines would obtain the concessions.

Such strategies had never failed Sturdevant before. He felt the Sakhana problem was solved, and took the next step.

The gold-corner scheme would require commitment of $19 billion, but much buying would be done on margin. Still, at least $6 billion in fluid funds would be needed.

Like most financiers, Charles Sturdevant never used

his personal fortune in speculative ventures. He intended siphoning $2 billion from the Sturdevant National and from Sturdevant-controlled companies as low-interest loans to dummy corporations he established abroad. Four billion more was needed. He knew exactly where to go for the money.

Sheikh Nasib al Rahman ruled the Persian Gulf emirate of Hajar, where the American Ensign Oil Company produced millions of barrels of oil. Sheikh Nasib received $3 billion a year in oil royalties from AMENOCO, kept a lion's share of the money for himself. He had astronomical sums on deposit with Sturdevant National and other banks around the world. Yet, he was perpetually eager for more.

Michel Auerbach headed the French branch of an old and famous European banking family. His bank, the Société Auerbach, was one of the largest in France. Michel Auerbach had worked closely with Sturdevant in the past, and he also constantly sought new means for increasing his wealth and power.

In August, 1973, Sturdevant flew to Hajar in his private Boeing 727/100. When in the United States, the billionaire conformed to his patrician, Presbysterian image, a facade he could discard in Hajar. Like Sheikh Nasib, his drive to gain wealth and power was equaled in intensity only by his love for orgiastic sex. Sturdevant remained for a week. Sheikh Nasib provided platoons of women he had flown to Hajar from Beirut, Athens and Rome.

Between sexual bouts the men discussed business. The Emir Nasib al Rahman fell in with Sturdevant's scheme immediately and enthusiastically. He had only a single reservation.

"Michel Auerbach is a Jew," Nasib said. "How will he react to being associated with an Arab?"

Sturdevant's laugh was a snicker. "Michel's religion stops where his profits begin."

"As does mine," the falcon-faced Emir said, dangling his Muslim rosary beads from his fingers.

From Hajar, Charles Sturdevant went to Paris.

"Audacious—and irresistible," Michel Auerbach said when Sturdevant outlined his plans. "As you Americans say, count me in."

Meeting in New York a week later, the three men agreed their buying campaign would be conducted in utmost secrecy through dummy corporations, with buying orders channeled through numerous banks and brokers. The syndicate was now formed. The operation to corner the gold market got underway.

During the first week in November, Charles Sturdevant was informed that a Matthew Rutledge had appeared in Calcutta. A successful independent prospector, Rutledge was seeking permission to enter Sakhana and search for gold. The bribed Sakhanese officials had assured Sturdevant's agents that Rutledge would not succeed. The billionaire took it for granted that the issue was closed.

But on November 25, the executive who supervised the "Sakhana Project" came to New York from Frankfurt. He brought a report that had been relayed to him from Calcutta.

"Rutledge was given the concessions. However, General Singh guarantees—"

"To hell with the guarantees," Sturdevant flared. "Get this man Rutledge out of the way!"

"The action may have to be organic."

"That's your headache. Just be sure I'm never told any of the details."

7

By November 25, Matt Rutledge had built a sufficient stock of aviation fuel in Kangtek and stopped his daily shuttlings back and forth to Darjeeling. He began preparations for an aerial survey of the High Mountains.

Matt obtained exact copies of the ancient sketch

maps from the Maharaja and collected every other map of Sakhana he could find. He pored over them with Sita for days. The results were discouraging. There was only one very slender hope.

Rutledge scanned the seventeenth-century sketch maps for the thousandth time. "These squiggles are identical on both of them," he told Sita. "Let's suppose they're intended to represent the base contours of three mountains. They're clustered close together. Maybe this line indicates a stream or river running between them. The base of the mountain in the middle—if that's what this is—seems shaped like a lopsided letter Y."

They studied the British maps with a magnifying glass. There was no cluster of mountains even vaguely resembling those Matt theorized the sketch maps showed, in any parts of Sakhana that the British had succeeded in mapping. The Golden Mountains could not lie anywhere but in the unknown—and according to Sakhanese superstition, forbidden—portions of the Cen-po Ri.

"Nothing left except to start surveying this area," Matt said, passing his hand over the great blank space on the British map. He grimaced. "At least eight thousand square miles to cover."

"When will you start?" Sita asked.

"Probably by the end of the week."

"I will go with you."

At first, Matt did not take her seriously. "You want to go into the forbidden zone—where the evil spirits dwell?"

"Those are myths. I have never believed them."

"Even so, it's impossible. Last thing I need is a passenger—"

"Two sets of eyes can see more than one, even from an airplane. I know that, even though I have never been in one." Sita smiled triumphantly. "And I would not be a passenger. I would be your crew. I taught myself to use your camera during the days when you were away in Darjeeling."

Matt stared at her. Aerial photographs enable geologists and prospectors not only to map but also to recognize the patterns of rock formations and analyze terrain features and structures. He had brought a modified Fairchild K-22 aerial camera with him. It was stored in the bedroom.

"I'll show you," Sita said.

They went up to the bedroom. She lifted the heavy K-22 handily and demonstrated that she had, indeed, familiarized herself with its workings.

"Well, I'll be God-damned!" was all Matt could say. He would have to take Sita now. Having her to operate the camera would make the task of aerial survey much easier, for alone he could only take photographs when his hands were not needed on the plane's controls.

November 30 dawned clear, a perfect day for flying. The flight was in the nature of a test—and Sita passed it with superlative marks. She showed no fear. After fifteen or twenty minutes during which she exclaimed with delight at the sights below, she settled into the copilot's seat like a veteran air traveler.

For the first few days, Matt made preliminary reconnaissances over the Great Valley and the Middle Hills. He wanted to familiarize himself with the topography, locate sites that could be used for emergency landings and observe other features, all of which he marked on his maps.

On December 4, the weather closed down. Matt and Sita remained in Kangtek, in the guest villa. That day, the price of gold went to $105.50 an ounce on the London Market—a rise of $15 an ounce in the barely more than two weeks since Matt had arrived in Sakhana.

Major General Dep Bahadur Singh had issued Ramesh Anwar a permanent entry permit into Sakhana two months before. On the morning of December 4, Anwar presented himself at the palace compound gates and sent word of his presence to Singh, who had him brought to his private office immediately.

Sleek, slender and wearing a well-tailored Western-style suit, Ramesh Anwar's manner was coldly hostile.

"I have received my instructions," he declared. "You have one week in which to rid us all of Matthew Rutledge."

Singh and Tsering Dorje had considered every aspect of the situation and decided they held the upper hand.

"Do not give me commands!" General Singh barked.

"No?" Anwar sneered. "What if I inform the Maharaja—"

"You would lose your head at the same moment that mine is lopped off. And your precious clients would lose all chance of obtaining the concessions."

Ramesh Anwar was taken aback. What Singh said was true enough, but he had not believed that the Sakhanese general and Prime Minister would have the courage to take a firm stand.

General Singh's tone eased. "Our warranties are good—as long as the Prime Minister and I are alive and holding influential positions in the government. Tell that to your clients—and let us have no more idle and foolish threats!"

"My clients represent people of great—"

"Power," Singh agreed, finishing the sentence for him. "However, they can exercise it only where they have already established themselves."

"General, time is pressing!"

"My dear Anwar, time has its own rhythm here in the Closed Kingdom. And when Matthew Rutledge is in the High Mountains, for him the hands of the clock will stop forever."

The skies cleared on December 5. Rutledge felt ready to explore the southern fringes of the Cen-po Ri. He found the terrain to be the most rugged and forbidding he had ever seen.

Even the lower tiers of the High Mountains were tangled chains of jagged peaks slashed by narrow, twisting gorges or boulder-strewn moonscape valleys. High winds whipped the peaks. Savage air currents and down-drafts made it difficult for Matt to keep the broad-winged Pilatus on an even keel.

He was grateful for Sita. Whenever he pointed out a terrain feature he wanted photographed, the girl operated the bulky Fairchild K-22 with remarkable efficiency. She was very disappointed when he told her the films she took could not be developed and printed in Sakhana. He would have to take them to Darjeeling when the survey flights were completed.

The weather held. During the next four days, Matt made deeper sweeps over the Cen-po Ri, penetrating far into the forbidden zone. Flying conditions became progressively more difficult and dangerous as the mountains rose higher and higher. But by Decmber 9, Rutledge's maps no longer had such large blank expanses on them. He was gradually filling them in, marking the location of mountains, rivers and other terrain features, recording altitudes and compass bearings.

On the morning of December 10, Matt set a course to the northeast, toward an area of the High Mountains about two-thirds of the way between the Middle Hills and the Tibetan border. The peaks stepped up. He had to fly at above 16,000 feet to clear many of them. Matt and Sita had to use the oxygen masks with which the Pilatus was equipped. Outside the plane, air temperatures were 20 and 30 degrees below zero. They would be even lower, Matt knew.

Shortly after 10:30 A.M., they were cruising over a zigzag chain of serrated mountains and a particularly savage downdraft caught the plane, flinging it over on its right wing. Matt had to fight the controls to bring the ship back to level flight.

"Matthew!" Sita had eased the oxygen mask from her face. She pounded his shoulder with her fist. "Turn around—to where the wind tipped us over. I saw three mountains!"

Matt put the Pilatus into a wide turn, circling back over the ragged spine of the mountain range. Luckily, the air currents were not as bad as before. Moments later, Sita pointed down. Rutledge banked to the right, peering past Sita at the ground below. At first, he saw nothing— then his heart started to pound. By God, it could be! There was a tight cluster of three mountains. A deep gorge with a river at its bottom wound between them. The mountain in the middle had a base vaguely resembling a distorted Y.

Sita was working the K-22. They were past the mountains. Rutledge made a 180-degree turn and brought the Pilatus back over them again. He held the control column with his knees and grabbed for his maps. Checking his instruments, he made a number of notes. He repeated the 180-degree turn, made it wide and lined up on the mountains. He pulled off his oxygen mask.

"Hang on, we're going to take a closer look," he shouted to Sita. He put the plane into a dive. The altimeter began to unwind—14,000, 13,000, 11,500, 10,000 . . .

Sita had the K-22 pointed straight ahead and was photographing through the cabin windscreen. The Pilatus was down to 9,500 feet and flying through a narrow gorge. Rock walls sheered high on each side. The air turbulence was brutal, threatening to fling the plane against the cliffs.

"Matthew!" There was terror in Sita's voice, but Matt's reflexes were already operating. The gorge made a ninety-degree turn and the face of a mountain loomed ahead. He hauled back the stick and rammed the throttle forward. The Pilatus responded instantly, going into a near-vertical climb, the powerful turboprop engine pulling it up. Even so, it was close. The plane's underbelly missed scraping the mountaintop by fifty feet—or less.

Rutledge made additional—but more cautious—passes over the three mountains. Then he turned on a straightline course for Kangtek.

Matt and Sita were in Darjeeling the next day, early. He bribed the officer commanding the Indian Photo Reconnaissance Squadron based at the Darjeeling airfield. The squadron's photo lab processed the negatives and made greatly enlarged prints. The pictures were clear, crisply focused.

Sita was delighted to see the results of her work.

"Are they good, Matthew?"

"They're terrific!" he said, hugging her tightly.

Matt took his filled-in maps and the photos to Narayan.

"I'm willing to gamble," Rutledge said. "I'll get to these mountains overland—"

"You cannot land your airplane near them?" Narayan asked.

"Not within thirty-five or so airline miles—which means twice that distance or more on foot. The terrain's impossible." He explained he would select a flat area situated as near as possible to the peaks and establish a base camp there. "The big question is where I can find men who'll go into the forbidden zone with me."

"How many will you need?"

"Six should do."

"There are men in the Palace Guards and Royal Constabulary who have rid themselves of old superstitions. I will ask for volunteers."

"They'll be highly paid."

"Please—not too highly!" the Maharaja protested in mock alarm. "I would rather not have the outside world's inflation imported into Sakhana!"

* * *

General Singh was ebullient when he reported to Tsering Dorje.

"Rutledge will be leaving soon," he announced. "Narayan has asked me to find volunteers who will accompany him. He already has two from his Palace Guard, but I said I would provide the four others who are needed."

"Do you have them?"

"Certainly. Four stalwarts of the Constabulary whose devotion is beyond question."

"How can you be so certain?" Dorje asked.

Dep Bahadur Singh looked smug. "At one time or another, all have committed crimes punishable by death. I hold the evidence against them in my files—as they are very aware."

"What of the two men from Narayan's personal bodyguard?"

"They will be eliminated, along with Rutledge."

Matt selected the site he considered best suited for a base camp. It was thirty-seven airline miles from the three mountains he believed might be the legendary Ser-gi Ri. He tried a landing. The ground proved not much rougher than the landing strip at Kangtek. It was fortunate that the Pilatus was especially designed for STOL operations, for the flat space was scarcely eight hundred yards long.

Rutledge met the men who would go with him in General Singh's office. Capt. Pemal Nyamgal, Sergeant Lapka, Privates Ang and Kalu were from the Royal Constabulary. There were also two Palace Guard privates, named Kancha and Baki. Captain Nyamgal was a lean, taciturn officer. Sergeant Lapka was burlier, with the hard, immobile face of the typical career noncommissioned officer.

All six men were of Tibetan stock and had experience in mountain duty. Captain Nyamgal spoke fluent English. Sergeant Lapka's command of the language was almost as good. The others had at least some knowledge of English, Matt noted gratefully. He would have no problems communicating with the men.

"Would you care to brief the detachment on your plans?" General Singh asked.

Matt told them all the supplies and equipment needed would be stockpiled at the Kangtek airport within a very few days. He would then fly some supplies and two men to the base camp site and make shuttle flights to bring the remainder of the gear and the rest of the party. He would also fly in three pack mules.

The men had no questions. When Matt left, General Singh dismissed the four privates. He remained closeted with Captain Nyamgal and Sergeant Lapka.

Everything was ready at Kangtek by the evening of December 18. Matt would make the first flight to the base camp site the following morning.

That night, when he and Sita went to bed, Matt switched on his Braun T-1000 and listened to a BBC financial roundup. It was dismal. Problems caused by the Arab oil boycott were worsening. World stock markets were slumping badly. There were widespread industrial shutdowns with unemployment mounting.

Matt paid scant attention. He was waiting for gold price quotations. Sita stroked his chest and stomach, then moved to his inner thighs, eager for the mutual pleasure his already engorged penis would soon provide.

". . . today's afternoon fix on the London Gold Market was one hundred and nine dollars per ounce," the BBC newscaster said. Matt switched off the set and turned to Sita.

"They must be going out of their minds in the Gold Rooms," he said. Then he groaned with pleasure. Sita was bending low over him, his sex between her lips, her tongue flicking.

His right hand went to her breast, cupping it. His left touched the back of her head, stroking her soft hair.

Then both his hands clenched reflexively, and his back arched.

Sita had begun *karatikka,* the indrawn, trilling hum that in some mysterious way causes the nerves in the meatus to respond as though resonating. Matt was no longer aware of anything but pure and total sensual delight.

8

The London Gold Market is the world's most exclusive club. Membership is limited to six firms:

Johnson, Matthey
Mocatta and Goldsmid, Limited
Samuel Montagu and Company, Limited
N. M. Rothschild and Sons
Sharps, Pixley and Company, Limited
Jacob Auerbach and Company.

Trading among the member firms takes place during two ritual "fixing sessions" each weekday: at 10:30 A.M. and 3 P.M. At these hours, a representative from each firm appears at the headquarters of N. M. Rothschild and Sons on Saint Swithin's Lane in the heart of the London financial district. The men gather in the elegantly appointed "Fixing Room" on the ground floor of the ugly, penitentiary-modern-style building.

A fixing session is a matching up—or balancing off—of the buy and sell orders the firms have received from clients all over the globe. Each representative knows precisely what orders have been given his firm since the last previous fixing session. He remains in direct-line telephone communication with his company's gold trading offices—the Gold Room—in the event there are last-minute surges of orders that require him to reevaluate his firm's trading position.

Whenever this is necessary, the representative concerned raises a miniature Union Jack on the tiny flag-staff on his desk. Trading is "flagged"—suspended—while he makes his computations.

When buy orders held by member firms exceed those to sell, a price higher than that at the last fixing session is set. If it is the other way around the fix will be lower. Prices are always quoted in American dollars. The fix established, the men return to their respective firms' trading offices.

There was an air of subdued tension in the Fixing Room at N. M. Rothschild and Sons during the 3 P.M. fixing session on December 18, 1973. The morning fix had been $106.75 an ounce. Since then, member firms had received a heavy volume of buy orders. Each of the representatives at the fixing held the telephone tying him to his firm's Gold Room.

"Gentlemen, we are at one hundred and eight," the N. M. Rothschild man chairing the session murmured. "Shall we fix?"

"Sorry, I flag." The Mocatta and Goldsmid representative raised his tiny Union Jack and scrawled calculations on a pad.

"Flag here, too," the Sharps, Pixley and Company man said.

Trading was suspended. The firms reassessed their buy-sell balances. The results were heavily on the buy side. The afternoon fix was set at $109 an ounce.

In the Gold Rooms of the London Market's member firms, the scenes were anything but subdued. Traders and clerks shouted into telephones in a Babel of tongues —and to each other in English.

"Messmer Handlebank in Hamburg buying ten thousand ounces—"

"Open buy-order for five thousand ounces from Cipriani and Taglia in Milan—"

"Boekema in Amsterdam buying—"
It was going to be another record day.

Numerous banks and other institutions in various cities around the world also have their Gold Rooms, for they actively engage in gold trading on behalf of their clients.

Be they in great Frankfurt or Zurich banks or in third-string banks in Beirut or Hong Kong, all Gold Rooms have much in common. They are all but hermetically sealed off from other offices to insure maximum secrecy. Inside the trading rooms, the atmosphere is always tense, the activity always hectic—and very often frenzied. Telephones ring and telexes clack constantly, telegrams and cablegrams arrive in endless streams.

Gold Rooms are necessarily staffed by men fluent in half a dozen or more languages, yet capable of remaining silent in all of them. Their minds must work with computerlike speed and efficiency, making complex international currency conversions within split seconds.

Banks outside the charmed circle of London Gold Market membership have only limited stocks of gold of their own. When they cannot offset their clients' buy and sell orders against each other, they usually turn to the London Market, flashing orders to one of its member firms. Most often, these orders are telexed:

SELLING 100 KILOGRAMS PAREN 3,527 OUNCES PAREN PLS ACK

The reply arrives within moments.

OKAY YOUR 100 KILO SELL ACKNOWLEDGED

Jacob Auerbach and Company was a venerable merchant bank and a member of the London Gold Market since it was formally established as such in 1919. It belonged to the British branch of the famed Auerbach banking family. Sir David Auerbach, its head, was a second cousin of Michel Auerbach, whose Société Auerbach ranked high on the list of great French banks.

Kevin Sundbury managed Jacob Auerbach and Company's gold trading operations. On December 18, he made his late afternoon report to Sir David Auerbach.

"Our day's trading volume is a bit over a hundred million dollars," he said.

Sir David was silent for a moment. He had a reasonable idea of his bank's share of an average day's gold trading. The London Market volume for the day must be over $750 million, and the buying trend had been going on for weeks now.

"Any pattern to the buy orders, Kevin?" he asked.

"Same as it has been recently. Very large numbers of individual orders, mainly from the Continent and Middle East."

"There should be a profit-taking flurry soon," Sir David said.

"That's my feeling, too," Kevin Sundbury agreed.

Michel Auerbach, Knight Commander of the Legion of Honor and Sir David Auerbach's second cousin, had flown from Paris to New York. He met with Charles Jordan Sturdevant III in the seventy-three-floor Sturdevant National Bank Tower on lower Broadway. They lunched together in the board chairman's private penthouse dining room. After the main course—blanquette de veau—was served, Sturdevant dismissed the butler and footman.

"I spoke with Nasib on the telephone yesterday," Sturdevant said, cutting into his veal. "He agrees we should do some selling to divert attention."

"*Bien.* When do we begin?"

"Tomorrow. We sell just enough to make it look as though ordinary speculators are taking their profits."

"*D'accord.*" Michel Auerbach had not yet touched his food. "I came here because there is something troubling me, Charles."

"What?"

"Sakhana. Our campaign still has months to go. If this prospector—what is his name?"

117

"Rutledge."

"If Rutledge makes a major discovery, it will have a very negative effect on the market. We will have serious trouble."

"Stop being troubled, Michel," Sturdevant said. "I've passed along orders that payments for neutralizing Rutledge are to be trebled. That should ease your mind."

Like Sturdevant, Michel Auerbach had unshakable faith in the buying power of money.

"It does," he said, and reached for his knife and fork. "The veal looks superb."

9

Matt Rutledge calculated it would take a total of eight flights to ferry all his men, pack mules and materiel from Kangtek to the base camp. Allowing for loading and unloading time, he could easily make three round trip flights daily. He allotted three days for the shuttling task, but intermittent rain and heavy cloud cover wrecked his schedule. The job stretched out, well into the week before Christmas.

Matt fumed when he had to stay in Kangtek waiting for the weather to clear. Sita did all she could to divert and amuse him. It was difficult for her. She knew that when he made his final flight to the camp, weeks, even months, might pass before she saw him again, for he would then start into the High Mountains.

At the end of the December 21 trading day, the London Gold Market closed down for the long Christmas holiday. Matt listened to the BBC newscast. Gold closed at $106.75. The price had been sagging for a few days. The dip was ascribed to year-end profit-taking by speculators. Matt agreed that this must be the explanation.

December 23 dawned clear, and Matt could at last fly the final load to the base camp. It consisted of some additional food supplies and odds and ends. He had already shuttled men and mules to the site, along with the bulk of the supplies and equipment.

Sita went with Matt to the airstrip. She tried to maintain a cheerful exterior, but the facade crumbled. As Matt was about to climb aboard the Pilatus, she clung to him and wept openly. She was no longer able to hide from the premonitory fears that had been gnawing at her.

"Easy," Matt soothed her clumsily, almost absently, for he was eager to be in the air and on his way. "I'll be back before you get used to the idea I'm gone."

"Matthew." Sita was sobbing. She wanted to say that she loved him, but somehow managed to bite back the words. She knew that while Matt's feelings for her went beyond simple affection and sexual desire, he did not love her and never would. "I—I will burn incense for you."

"Not sandalwood, I hope." He grinned, desperately trying to lighten her mood. In Sakhana, sandalwood was burned only for the dead. "Wouldn't want to think you're writing me off. . . ."

Oh, Christ, I've said all the wrong things, he realized. Sita was staring up at him in terror, her body trembling.

"No!" she cried out. "No, Matthew!" She continued to shudder. For the past several nights, she had had recurring dreams—that she smelled the scent of sandalwood incense. Each time, she had awakened with a start, terrified, but had not told Matt.

After some moments, Sita succeeded in regaining her composure. The urge to tell Matt she loved him was greater than before, yet she again controlled it. She reached inside her sari, took something from it and pressed it into Matt's hand.

He looked. Like all Sakhanese, Sita owned a pair of small Yin and Yang idols, household gods symbolizing the male and female principle. They were considered precious, for their presence together was said to bring the owner good fortune and happiness.

Sita had given him the green jade idol symbolizing the female principle. He knew how much the Yin and Yang idols meant to her and tried to return it.

"I might lose—"

"You must take it." Sita was adamant. "Then it will be as though I am with you."

He put the idol into a pocket. Sita kissed him again, long and deeply, then broke from his arms and ran toward the Bentley that had brought them to the strip. Matt climbed into the pilot's seat, fastened the safety belt and switched on the ignition.

British missionaries had found it impossible to proselytize the Sakhanese. There were virtually no Christians in the Closed Kingdom. Christmas meant nothing to the Sakhanese, and Matt ignored it, too. By Christmas Eve everything at the base camp was ready for the party's departure on its overland trek.

Matt's plane and a reserve of supplies were to be left behind. The Pilatus was guyed down to prevent damage by wind. The supplies were stacked and covered with tarpaulins. There was no need to leave a guard. The base camp was deep inside the forbidden zone. None of the hill tribesmen living to the south and west on the fringes of the zone would dare venture into the area.

At dawn on Christmas Day, Matt and the six Sakhanese soldiers gathered around the campfire. Rutledge spread a map and several aerial photographs and held a final briefing.

"The photographs will help us. Many ground details don't show up on them, but others do," Matt said. "We'll head in the direction of that ridge about three miles to our right, but we'll have to make a wide sweep around it." He pointed to a photograph. "The reverse slope is a sheer drop. We couldn't get down it. The distance around the ridge is only eight or nine miles, but the terrain is broken, rugged. We probably can't make it until late this afternoon."

An hour later, the three mules were loaded and the party set off. Captain Nyamgal, carrying a Webley revolver and a canteen on his belt, led the way. His men were burdened with regulation military packs and Enfield rifles. The Maharaja had presented Matt with a splendid cut-down sporting model 1903 Springfield rifle mounting a telescopic sight. It was an ideal weapon with which to bag game for the pot while on the trail. Matt carried it slung over his shoulder.

Rutledge went with Captain Nyamgal at the head of the short column. Next were the mules, roped into a string and led by Kancha and Baki, the Palace Guardsmen. Sergeant Lapka and privates Ang and Kalu brought up the rear.

Matt's field thermometer read 22 degrees Fahrenheit, but he was warm in his parka, fur-lined cap and heavy boots. The boots had grooved soles, giving his feet a firm grip on the snow covering the rocky, fissured ground. Men and mules had to pick their way carefully.

Two hours out, they came to a wide, deep ravine that had not been visible on the aerial photographs. It could not be crossed unless the mules were let down by rope sling. Matt scanned the area through his binoculars.

"Ravine narrows—looks like it might even end—a couple of miles to the left," he told Nyamgal.

It was the first of what would be countless detours dictated by the terrain. At dusk, the party was two miles short of the spot Matt had designated as the first night's campsite. Two soldiers pitched Matt's tent, a lightweight nylon model popular with Alpinists, and spread his sleeping bag inside it. The Sakhanese had regulation shelter-halves with which they erected three tents. Captain Nyamgal and Sergeant Lapka would share one, Ang and Kalu the second. The third was for Kancha and Baki. Kancha acted as cook. He prepared preserved pork and canned vegetables for Matt, Nyamgal and Lapka. The four privates ate *dal bhat*—rice and lentils.

That night, the temperature plummeted to 7 degrees and gale-force winds whipped down from the north, bringing heavy snow. The storm continued the following day. It was impossible to resume the march. Matt spent the day inside his tent. He cursed the fact that he did not have a radio. Any set capable of overcoming the atmospherics and other barriers to transmission and reception in the High Mountains would have been too heavy and cumbersome to carry. Until the party returned to the base camp and Matt could use the radio in the Pilatus, there would be no communication with the outside world or even with Kangtek.

On the morning of the twenty-seventh, the wind stopped. The temperature rose to 20 degrees. Matt and Captain Nyamgal reconnoitered ahead. They found a route that enabled the party to cover seven miles before nightfall, but again on a course that veered away from the mountains Matt was seeking.

Matt Rutledge covered only seven miles in a day. In New York, Charles Jordan Sturdevant III had spanned thousands of miles in minutes. By telephone. Because of time-zone differences—eight hours to Hajar, six to Paris and five to London—he placed an international conference call at 4 A.M. It went through quickly. Michel Auerbach and Sheikh Nasib al Rahman were on the line more than an hour before members of the London Gold Market would meet to establish the morning fix.

Sturdevant had news to report and a suggestion to make.

"I received word from Calcutta late yesterday," he announced. "Rutledge has gone into the Himalayas." Unsaid but implicit, it would be a one-way journey. "Since we made our point by selling before the Christmas holidays, and because the London Market reopens today, I think we should start buying again."

His partners in the gold-corner scheme concurred. Within the next hour, an especially heavy volume of buy orders poured into the Gold Rooms of London Market member firms. This was reflected in the 10:30 A.M. fix, which was set at $111.75 an ounce—a full $5 above the December 21 closing.

Matt Rutledge and his men found the trail increasingly difficult and dangerous as they moved deeper into the Cen-po Ri forbidden zone. They were constantly aware of the menace of rockslides and avalanches. The valleys frequently echoed with the crash and roar of rock and snow masses plunging down mountainsides, both nearby and far away.

In the late morning of December 31, the party reached the crest of a mountain and began descending the reverse slope. Matt remembered that in countries using the Gregorian calendar—unlike Sakhana, which used a lunar calendar—it was New Year's Eve.

He thought of Sita, pulled off his right glove and thrust his hand deep into a parka pocket. Between his fingers he rubbed the idol she had given him. Damned if I don't miss her, he thought.

After the midday meal, the column resumed 'ts descent toward the valley. Matt, trudging beside Nyamgal, suddenly glimpsed a dark brown blur flashing among some trees about three hundred yards to his right.

"Boar!" he exclaimed, unslinging the Springfield. He worked the bolt to jack a round in the chamber and threw the rifle to his shoulder, leaning into the scope. The blur appeared again, between two trees. Matt had the crosshairs on it. The rifle cracked and bucked against his shoulder, the report echoing in the mountain silence. The blur froze into a shape and dropped.

"Fresh pork tonight," Matt chuckled. "Send a couple of men to dress the carcass, will you?"

Captain Nyamgal nodded. Sergeant Lapka had come running up to Nyamgal. The two men exchanged glances. Rutledge's reflexes and markmanship had suddenly become factors they would have to bear in mind.

123

10

They crossed a boulder-studded valley the next day and camped for the night at the foot of a great hill mass. Matt decided the slope would have to be climbed. It was the sole alternative to yet another sweeping detour.

Seen in the morning light, the mountainside was forbidding. Its face was scarred by serrated cliffs, the open wounds caused by countless rock slides. The ascent would be an ordeal. The single promising route was along a tentacle that hooked down toward the southwest. But the ridge line of the tentacle sprouted high, irregularly shaped rock formations. These knobs would prevent movement along the ridge line itself. The ascent would have to be made below the crest, along the side.

"What do you think?" Matt asked Captain Nyamgal.

"We should start climbing."

Rutledge had last-minute reservations. The knobs looked menacing; the rock appeared to be rotten. The fourth in line was the worst of all. It had a great bulge at its top that formed an overhang along the route they would follow.

"I think it is safe enough," Nyamgal shrugged.

The party started up the tentacle. After the midday meal stop, the column was five hundred yards short of being even with the fourth knob. Matt gave it a close look through his binoculars.

"If that overhang lets loose, we're finished," he said to Nyamgal.

"I will send men to inspect it." He snapped orders to Sergeant Lapka and Kalu in Tibetan. They set off, upslope. Matt and the others remained where they were, watching. Lapka and Kalu reached the base of the knob and started to clamber up the side of the snow-splotched crag. Matt had his binoculars trained on them. Kalu was ahead, Lapka a short distance behind.

"Nyamgal!" Matt yelled. "It's giving way!"

The overhang was crumbling. No doubt the two men had disturbed a precariously balanced boulder or broken off a shard of rotten granite to start the slide.

The knob was disintegrating. Tons of rock were cascading down. In moments, the debris would gather into waves and surge down the slope.

Matt snapped his head around. Captain Nyamgal was already running toward high ground to the right. Ang was sprinting after the captain. Kancha and Baki were still with the mules.

Rutledge ran to the two men, grabbing the lead rope. "Move!" he bellowed, starting for the rise of ground.

Rock, snow and uprooted trees were surging down the slope, gathering speed and mass. The noise was deafening. Matt, the mules and the two Palace Guardsmen made it to the rise only seconds before the rock slide reached the place where they had been standing.

Rocks flew into the air as the rolling mass thundered down the slope. They crashed down, smashing into fragments like exploding shells. A rock splinter sliced into Matt's right hand. A fist-sized stone struck Kancha in the back, sent him sprawling.

The noise level dropped. The avalanche had passed. It was moving downslope. Rutledge looked up to where the knob had been. There was only a jagged stump of it left, like a tooth that had been broken off by a hammer blow.

"Captain," he called to Nyamgal, hiding the contempt he felt for the officer because he had been the first to run. "We have to look for your men."

They started up, stumbling over the debris left by the slide. They had not gone far when they heard Sergeant Lapka's voice calling to them. They found Lapka cowering at the base of what had been the knob. His uniform was torn, and he was bruised and lacerated but alive and not seriously injured. By some miracle, the tons of crumbling rock had missed him. The miracle had not extended to Kalu.

Matt and Nyamgal discovered a human foreleg lying under the jagged boulder that had severed it. Some distance away, they came across two splintered rib bones that still had shreds of flesh clinging to them. Caught in the grinding boil of the rock slide, Kalu had been torn apart—pulped.

"We might as well camp," Matt said, weary and sickened. "There's nothing left up there that can fall on us."

Captain Nyamgal ordered Ang to burn the sandalwood incense that would speed Kalu's soul on to its next incarnation.

Kancha and Baki came up to Matt Rutledge.

"You save us, Rutledge *sahib-kamal*," Kancha said. "Our lives yours now."

Sergeant Lapka lay in the tent he shared with Captain Nyamgal. His cuts and bruises were painful, but his mind was on other matters. "Kalu is gone," he said. "Kancha and Baki now worship the foreigner as a god. We should remove one or the other—perhaps even both."

Nyamgal had some earthenware jugs of *rakshi*, the potent Sakhanese rice liquor in his pack. He held a jug in his hand and drank from it.

"We need Kancha and Baki to do work on the march," he growled. "We take action only after we reach the mountains the foreigner seeks. Understand?"

He took another drink, corked the jug and soon was snoring.

Each passing day taught Matt Rutledge another reason why the Sakhanese viewed the forbidden zone of the High Mountains with superstitious dread. Climate and terrain conspired against intruders with such ferocity that even the most rational of men might be tempted to believe it the work of supernatural forces.

Matt could no longer estimate how many miles the party had traveled overland. The march was a succession of circuitous routes dictated by the topography. Sudden and violent storms caused delays or forced the group to turn back from streams flash-flooding into torrents.

At the same time, Rutledge had seen ample evidence of Sakhana's immense wealth in natural resources. In many places where erosion had stripped away superficial deposits, the exposed rock showed iron, nickel and copper sulfides. But there were no signs of gold—and on the night of January 9, 1974, the party was still more than fifteen airline miles from the three mountains that were Matt's goal.

A deep-cleft saddle provided a pass over the next mountain. Reaching the crest, Matt saw that a narrow rock ledge angling down a sheer cliff face offered the only descent route for the first thousand yards. Nyamgal and his men indicated they believed it negotiable and were willing to proceed.

Nyamgal led, with Matt next and the rest of the column in single file behind them. Sergeant Lapka followed Matt. Then came Kancha leading the mules. Baki marched behind the animals. Ang was last in line.

The ledge was perhaps three feet wide, its uneven surface coated with snow. To the left, the cliff dropped away perpendicularly for several hundred feet. Two-thirds of the way along the ledge, the track narrowed abruptly. It was barely two feet wide.

The column edged forward. A few minutes later, the mules balked, setting their hooves and braying loudly. Kancha tugged at the lead rope. Baki prodded the rump of the last animal. It was to no avail. Captain Nyamgal stopped and turned around, as did Matt and Sergeant Lapka. The mules refused to budge.

Baki moved forward gingerly and joined Kancha.

Both men pulled at the lead rope. Their efforts were futile. Sergeant Lapka cursed and retraced his steps along the ledge. He snatched the lead rope from Kancha and Baki. Still cursing, he used the rope as a whip, lashing at the first mule's head and face. The end of the rope caught the animal in the eye, and it moved backward. Matt called out a protest. Lapka ignored him, struck at the mule again—harder. The animal panicked, tried to turn.

"You crazy bastard!" Rutledge shouted, going toward Lapka.

It was too late. The mule's hooves lost their purchase. Braying in terror, its legs flailing, the mule tore the lead rope from Lapka's grasp and rocketed over the side of the ledge. The rope linking it to the second animal snapped taut. Kancha and Baki reacted. They clung grimly to the second mule's harness to prevent it from being dragged over the side. Matt knew they could not hold long—a minute or two at most.

Lapka seemed paralyzed. Ang was somewhere up-trail. Matt whipped out his hunting knife and pushed past Lapka. There was only one chance of averting total disaster. He gripped the knife tightly and cut through the taut rope. The first mule plunged down into the chasm, but now there was no pull on the second animal. One gone, but two saved, Matt thought.

"What was that mule carrying?" he asked Kancha.

"Food, *sahib-kamal.*"

"*All* our food?"

"Not all." Kancha patted the second mule. "Some here."

"Anything else?"

Kancha averted his eyes. "Long box, *sahib-kamal.*"

Matt would have gladly shot the blundering Sergeant Lapka where he stood. The "long box" contained the prospecting tools, surveyor's instruments and a Hasselblad camera he had brought along for use in the field. Their loss was a catastrophe.

128

"All right, Captain," he muttered, his green eyes blazing with anger. "Let's try to get going."

It was, Matt reflected, anticlimactic.

On the morning of January 12, he and the soldiers reached the narrow mouth of a twisting defile. Immediately ahead, there was a valley. At its far edge, there were three mountains—in a cluster, almost as though they had been nested together.

These were the mountains Rutledge was after. The one in the middle had to be the mountain with the base shaped like a crooked letter Y. Were they truly the Ser-gi Ri, Matt wondered, unconsciously slipping his hand into his parka pocket and stroking the jade idol Sita had given him.

After all that had gone before, it seemed too simple and easy. For years, Matt had fantasized about rediscovering the Golden Mountains. For more than two weeks, he had been slogging through the High Mountains. Now he turned a corner, and there they were—directly in front of him.

His pulse was pounding.

"Rutledge *sahib*." It was Nyamgal.

"Yes, Captain." Matt did not turn his eyes from the three mountains.

"Have we reached our destination?"

"We still have to cross the valley. I'm going ahead."

Matt struck off at a fast pace. He reached the banks of the river winding between the mountains. There was a wide gravel strip along the bank. Matt slowed, stopped, bent his head and stared at the ground. He moved forward again very slowly. Then he stopped again, knelt down, his hands clawing at the gravel. He snatched up something and stared at it. He gave a triumphant shout that echoed and reechoed between the walls of the gorge through which the river flowed.

The object he held was a gold nugget the size of a grape.

129

11

In its native state, gold may be 99.9 percent pure, but 85 to 95 percent purity is more common, the gold being alloyed with silver, copper or other metals.

Widely dispersed through the earth's crust, gold generally occurs in very small quantities. It may, however, sometimes form rich veins or lodes in rock. Over the aeons, the rock may have been eroded by weather and water. Such action forms gravel, which washes down into river or stream beds.

This is how alluvial—placer—deposits of gold were formed. Nuggets or smaller particles of gold remained dispersed in the gravel or sand. Sometimes, the streams and rivers dried up, changed their courses or cut deeper channels, leaving the gold-bearing gravel exposed as surface deposits. In other instances, the rivers and streams continued to flow and quantities of gold remained in their beds. In yet others, thick blankets of sand and gravel covered over the surface deposits.

History's greatest gold finds and "rushes" began with the discovery of surface deposits. Men literally stumbled across gold that lay atop the ground or only a few inches below its surface. Surface deposits were exploited immediately. Deeper searches were made into the gravel in hopes there was more gold at lower levels. Prospectors scoured the surrounding countryside seeking the rock formations and mountains containing the veins or lodes from which the placer gold had originated.

There have been many spectacular placer finds. Early Spanish explorers took nuggets weighing fifty pounds and more from Central and South American placer deposits. California and Klondike placer fields yielded nuggets of large size. The biggest known nuggets came from the Australian goldfields in the 1850s. These included such "boulders" as the 1,117-ounce "Sierra Sands," the even heavier "Lady Hotham" and the giant 200-pound "Welcome Stranger."

But the rich placer deposits were found and played out long ago. For decades, two-thirds or more of the world's new gold has come from South Africa. There, the metal is found in ore bodies far below ground surface. South African goldfields are worked at depths of 12,000 feet and more. The ore contains only minute quantities of gold. Five and even more tons of ore must be mined and processed to recover a single ounce of the metal.

In South Africa, such mining is economically feasible because the blacks who labor in the mines receive bare subsistence wages. Their work—in cramped galleries where the temperature may stay at 135 degrees—is extremely dangerous. Hundreds of these men die in mine accidents each year.

But then, when measured in terms of gold, human life has always been cheap.

Matt Rutledge had found a bench placer deposit, a terrace of gold-bearing gravel just above the riverbed and running parallel to it. Matt scrabbled in the gravel, raking it with his fingers. Gold flakes were visible and, after several minutes, he found another nugget, this one somewhat smaller than the first.

When Nyamgal and the men caught up with him, Rutledge exuberantly showed them the nuggets. The captain did not appear greatly impressed.

"Our supplies are low," he grumbled. "We cannot remain long."

"Three days—maybe four," Matt said. He outlined the work ahead. They would sift and wash gravel from the bench deposit and riverbed to recover gold that would be proof of the find. Rutledge added he would reconnoiter upstream and look for signs that might indicate gold veins in the mountains higher up. "I'll also map the immediate area," he concluded, his tone bitter. The loss

131

of his "long box" and its contents would prevent him from doing much more than a sloppy job of mapping.

Captain Nyamgal and Sergeant Lapka wandered off, ostensibly to relieve themselves.

"Let me kill Rutledge tonight," Lapka urged, patting the trenchknife that hung from his belt. "I can slit his throat while he sleeps. After that, it is nothing to shoot Kancha and Baki."

"No. We wait until the last day."

"Why? Because of the gold? You, Ang and I can dig in the earth without the others. We will find some to take to General Singh to show we discovered the Ser-gi Ri— and more that you and I can hide for ourselves on the march back to Kangtek."

"You do not see beyond the end of your nose, Lapka. Rutledge will make maps and write notes of things we know nothing about. General Singh will reward us if we bring him this information, and punish us if we do not."

Lapka had nothing further to say.

The Sakhanese who first discovered the Ser-gi Ri in 1672 had not exaggerated. By noon of the following day, Matt Rutledge knew that he had found what were truly Golden Mountains. The placer deposits were fabulously—incredibly—rich.

Matt told the men to take the party's shovels, and he improvised some raking implements for them. He had them work over a section of the bench with these tools. Within hours, they had collected more than a dozen nuggets, including one that weighed over five pounds.

Rutledge's prospecting dish had not been lost. He took it to the riverbed and pan-washed sand there. The results were spectacular. Large numbers of big, plump gold flakes remained in the riffles of the pan each time he washed a quantity of sand. More nuggets turned up in the afternoon. Working near the riverbank, Matt unearthed a giant. Eighteen pounds.

It's real, Matt told himself over and over. I've hit—

hit what's probably the world's biggest gold jackpot. His elation was boundless, wild, that of the prospector long infected with gold fever who discovers an El Dorado surpassing anything he had ever imagined.

The fever raged that night. Matt lay in his sleeping bag, unable to sleep, waiting only for dawn, when work would resume. Realization of the magnitude of his strike had an aphrodisiacal effect. Matt developed an erection that was almost painful.

He smoked several cigarettes. His sexual excitement refused to subside. At last, he conceded his desperate need for some form of release and masturbated. Ejaculation eased his inner tension. He wiped himself off with a handkerchief, certain he would not be able to sleep.

It was just before he dropped off that Matt realized his masturbatory fantasies had all focused on Sita and not on any of the other women he knew and had bedded. Hell, it figures, he told himself drowsily. Sita was the last woman I made love with before starting into the mountains, and she'll be the first after I get back to Kangtek. Then he slept.

At sunup, Matt set off with Kancha, Baki and one pack mule. They went upstream, following the riverbank through the gorge. After they had gone two miles or so, Matt saw what appeared to be a relatively easy route up the mountainside. They climbed to the 10,500-foot level, 1,500 feet above the river. Leaving Kancha and Baki, Rutledge went off to explore.

He was stunned—staggered, he admitted to himself —by what he found. Much rock had been exposed by erosion on the mountainside. In several places, the rock was heavy with gold. The Ser-gi Ri legends had not lied when they told of thick veins. His gold fever returned, raging, as he broke off chunks of rock with the hand ax he had brought with him for that purpose. Here was ore richer than even the finds worked by the Spaniards in the Carabaya fields on the Bolivian-Peruvian high plateau.

Matt thrust the ore samples into the musette bag he

carried slung across his chest. It soon bulged, weighing him down. In midafternoon, he paused, took a long drink of water from his canteen and reached into his parka pockets, searching for a pack of cigarettes. As he fumbled, he became aware that the jade idol Sita had given him was gone. He turned out all his pockets.

"I was afraid I'd lose it—and I have," he muttered aloud. What the hell, he reflected. I'll buy her another—a hundred others if she wants—as soon as I reach Kang-tek.

Matt was away from the camp on the gravel terrace less than thirty-six hours. Nyamgal, Lapka and Ang had continued work while he and the two other soldiers were gone. The nuggets they had found were added to those recovered previously and piled on a square of canvas. Over 150 pounds of gold in all, Matt estimated, his mouth going very dry when he thought of how many *tons* of gold were waiting to be taken from the Ser-gi Ri.

"I'll finish my mapping tomorrow, and we can leave the day after," he informed Nyamgal.

Supper was meager, rice and lentils. After eating, Matt went to his tent. He wanted to add certain details to his notes while they were still fresh in his mind. Nyamgal and Lapka stayed by the fire.

"Ang has the *rakshi* and *charas*," Nyamgal murmured to the noncom, his eyes gleaming. "He'll cook his brew tonight."

Charas was the potent hashish of Sakhana. Boiled in water, *charas* produces a tasteless, amber-colored liquid. When added to the rice liquor, it acts as an extremely powerful sedative. A swallow of *rakshi* laced with *charas* "broth" was sufficient to knock a healthy man out for anywhere from twelve to eighteen hours.

Kancha stirred in his sleep. He thought he heard the clank of cooking pots. Puzzled, he came fully awake. He heard the sound again and cursed to himself. A mule must have gotten loose. Peeling away his blankets, Kancha put on his boots. He did not bother to wake Baki, who shared the tent with him, and went outside.

Kancha stood, listening intently. He caught the sound of human feet hurrying across the ground, away from the cookstove. The sound faded, stopped. A match flared about fifty yards away. It went out, and the bluish flame of a portable Coleman stove became faintly visible.

Baffled, Kancha made his way silently toward the dim glow. The moon was full, the sky clear. He could see where he went easily. A figure was hunched over the Coleman stove. Instinct made Kancha drop to his knees, crawl closer and lie flat behind a small fold in the ground. He raised his head cautiously, peered and recognized the figure. It was Ang. He had taken a copper kettle and was putting it on top of the small stove. The kettle seemed to have water in it.

Kancha continued to watch as Ang unwrapped an unmistakable triangular parcel. In Sakhana, only *charas* was wrapped this way. Ang took handfuls of dried leaves from the open package and dropped them into the kettle. There was an earthenware *rakshi* jug beside the stove. Kancha comprehended what Ang was doing. He crawled rapidly, went to his tent and awakened Baki.

"Ang is boiling enough *charas* to drug a hundred men," he whispered excitedly. "We should report it to the captain."

"And beg for punishment?" Baki snorted. "Nyamgal hates us. Ang is one of his men. What Ang does is none of our affair."

Kancha reluctantly agreed that Baki was probably right and began pulling off his boots.

Funny people, the Sakhanese, Matt reflected the next afternoon. It was their last day. In the morning, they would start out of the mountains. Under similar circumstances, Western soldiers would be inclined to be boisterous. The Sakhanese simply went about their tasks as they always did.

But Nyamgal proved unusually cheerful and expansive at supper. He laughed and joked with Matt and Lapka. When everyone had eaten, he produced a jug of *rakshi* and turned to Matt.

"A toast to our safe journey back?" he asked, uncorking the jug. "It is an ancient Sakhanese custom."

"It's an ancient custom almost everywhere," Rutledge grinned. "I'll be glad to drink to it with you."

Kancha and Baki exchanged quick looks. Now they understood. Kancha was on the verge of warning Rutledge, but it was too late. Matt had the jug and was taking a swig from it. He returned the jug to Nyamgal, who lifted it to his lips, then passed it to Lapka. Lapka appeared to take a drink, and so did Ang, to whom he handed the *rakshi* next.

Ang gave the jug to Baki. Clever, Baki thought. It was less than two-thirds full. No one would suspect that the three members of the Royal Constabulary had only pretended to drink. But he feared that Nyamgal and Lapka might realize the contents had not diminished when the jug was given back to them. He raised the jug, tonguing the neck and making a show of swallowing. As he lowered the jug, he let it fall. It struck the ground and some of the liquor spilled out. Baki mumbled apologies, retrieved the jug and passed it to Kancha, who also only pantomimed swallowing.

Nyamgal, Lapka and Ang got to their feet. "We will leave you now, Rutledge *sahib*," Nyamgal said. "We have many preparations to make for tomorrow." The three men got up and walked away.

Matt stood. He yawned and his legs were heavy. Making for his tent, he staggered a little. Funny, he thought, he had barely had any of the *rakshi*, but the stuff had really hit him.

Left alone, Kancha and Baki spoke in urgent whispers.

"Nyamgal and his men want the gold," Kancha said. "They think they have drugged us. They'll try to kill us when we are asleep."

"Come," Baki nodded. "They may be watching." He and Kancha went stumbling and weaving to their tent and crawled inside it and gathered up their rifles and ammunition belts.

"Loosen the back of the tent," Kancha said.

Ang was with Nyamgal and Lapka. The night was clear, the still large moon bright.

"They should be asleep by now," Sergeant Lapka muttered, fingering his long-bladed knife.

"The deep sleep will begin in ten minutes," Ang said.

Kancha and Baki slipped from the back of their tent and crept to the one occupied by Matt Rutledge. They tried to awaken the American. It was useless.

"We must drag him from the tent and then carry him," Kancha said. Although Rutledge was a big man and his limp body a heavy and clumsy burden, the two Palace Guardsmen were strong. They dragged him from the tent. The mules were tethered in a small bowl-like depression of ground twenty yards away. The approach to the depression from Rutledge's tent was not visible to Nyamgal and his companions. Rutledge had passed out wearing all his clothing, even his parka. Good, Kancha thought. Now he would not freeze outside. He and Baki carried Matt to where the mules were tethered and laid him on the ground. They flattened themselves on the ground near the lip of the depression.

"If we shoot first against Nyamgal, it is mutiny," Baki warned. "We shall be executed in Kangtek."

"Not if Rutledge *sahib* lives."

Baki mulled that over and nodded. Rutledge could go straight to the Maharaja and tell him the true story. In any event, Rutledge had saved his life and Kancha's. They had to protect his.

Kancha and Baki heard movement and snapped alert, peering into the camp. They were able to discern three

137

dark shapes approaching Matt's tent. One ducked low and entered.

Seconds passed. Rutledge's tent shook violently. The figure that had gone inside now burst from it.

"He is not there!" Sergeant Lapka said. "The foreigner is gone!"

Nyamgal kept his head.

"The tent used by Kancha and Baki," he rasped. He and the other two hurried to it.

Lapka and Ang ripped the shelter halves apart. There was no one inside.

Nyamgal had to vent his rage on someone. Ang was the logical choice. He whirled, struck Ang across the face with his revolver barrel.

"Fool! You said they would be asleep!"

"They could not remain wake," Ang groaned. "I swear—"

"Wait," Lapka interposed. "Being drugged, they could have wandered off and collapsed somewhere."

"Then we search for them!" Nyamgal snapped.

Kancha and Baki could see the three men fan out and begin their search. Kancha nudged Baki to keep watch. He went to the mules. Using his trenchknife, Baki cut one mule's tether rope and gave the animal a sharp knife-prod in the haunch. The mule started running toward the river. Kancha dived down beside Baki again.

"Now we will learn surely what they intend," he said.

Nyamgal, Lapka and Ang could feel their own tension. When they heard the sound of rapid movement, each whirled in the direction from which it came and opened fire. Nyamgal triggered his Webley, Lapka and Ang fired their rifles. Amplified in the narrow gorge, the shots sounded like heavy artillery fire. A bullet struck the running animal. It brayed in agony and dropped.

Nyamgal cursed. It was only a mule. The animal was still alive. Nyamgal finished him with a shot.

"Look," Sergeant Lapka said. "The rope was cut. At least one of them must be conscious and with the other mule."

"We go after them."

Kancha recognized the foremost figure. It was Sergeant Lapka. He held him in his sights. Ang was off to one side and to the rear of the noncom. Baki trained his weapon on Ang.

"Halt!" Kancha called out when Lapka was less than thirty yards from his rifle muzzle.

Lapka's reply was a shot fired blindly. Kancha pulled his trigger. Sergeant Lapka shrieked as the .30-caliber bullet plowed into his chest. He fell, blood gushing from his wound.

Ang would have run, but Captain Nyamgal had sprinted forward and was beside him. "Lie down!" Nyamgal ordered. They both threw themselves on the ground.

"Open fire!" Nyamgal shouted and began shooting with his revolver. Ang obeyed, emptying his rifle, reloading it with a fresh clip and firing again.

Bullets cracked over the heads of Kancha and Baki, spanged against rocks and whined off in ricochet. They did not return the fire. They waited until they could take careful aim.

Suddenly, their hearts sank. The single remaining mule brayed and fell, its body thrashing wildly. A bullet had struck the animal. That meant they would have no mules for the trek back over the mountains.

"Baki—"

"Quiet—look!"

Nyamgal and Ang had risen to their feet and were coming forward, firing as they came. Baki fired at Nyamgal, missed and fired again. The captain was slammed down on his back by the slug that punched into his belly.

Ang had seen enough. He flung his rifle aside.

"I only obeyed orders!" he pleaded, raising his hands high above his head. "I meant none of you harm!"

There was a silence. Then Kancha was sure he could not miss. He shot Ang squarely in the middle of the forehead.

Kancha and Baki scrambled to their feet and hurried forward.

Lapka and Ang were dead. Captain Nyamgal was alive, but suffering as only men who have been gut-shot can feel pain.

"It is good that he is not yet dead," Kancha said.

He took his knife from its scabbard again. The blade was razor-sharp, the point honed. Kancha leaned over Nyamgal, raising the captain's left eyelid with a thumb. He inserted the point of the knife between eyeball and eye socket. He began to cut, and Captain Nyamgal's shrieks grew louder and louder.

12

It was past noon when Matt Rutledge regained a painful, partial degree of consciousness. His eyes refused to focus. Everything was a purplish-gray blur. The God-damnedest hangover of my life, he thought. Only he could not remember how he got it.

"Drink tea," a voice urged. "Be better." An arm went around Matt's shoulder, raising him. A hand held a metal mug to his lips. Matt drank. The tea was scalding hot and very strong. His stomach churned for a moment, then settled. Slowly he began to recall what had happened. He had been sitting beside the fire after supper. He had joined Nyamgal and the men in a drink of *rakshi*. And now? The purple haze parted a little. It was daylight. He was in his tent.

Matt turned his head. The effort caused agonizing

throbbings inside his skull, but he recognized Kancha and Baki squatting beside him. "Call Captain Nyamgal," Matt groaned.

"No good, captain dead," Kancha said. "Sergeant, Ang dead, too."

"How the hell could that be? Help me up."

Kancha and Baki held Matt's arms as he stumbled out of the tent. The icy air helped revive Rutledge, but he was instantly sorry it had. Three frozen corpses lay on their backs in a row. Matt took several steps, stared down at the bodies. He saw that they must be Nyamgal, Lapka and Ang by their blood-soaked uniforms. Their faces were covered with blood—and the eye sockets of all three men were empty, gore-encrusted wounds.

Kancha spoke, relating what had occurred. The *rakshi* had been drugged. He and Baki knew this and did not drink. Nyamgal and his two men wanted to take the gold for themselves.

"We shoot like in battle," Baki interjected.

"Their eyes," Matt said numbly. "What about their eyes?"

"Here." Kancha brought out an oilskin pouch. He opened it wide. There were six ghastly lumps inside. "I take to His Majesty," Kancha declared proudly. He explained that three men had wanted to steal what belonged to the Maharaja. Their eyes had been cut out to prevent them from finding their way to the Golden Mountains in some future incarnation.

"We make *gama* on bodies," Kancha said. Matt had seen small lumps of human feces on the corpses. Kancha and Baki had defecated on them—and thus, symbolically, on their souls. The remains would not be buried, Baki said. They would be left for carrion birds and insects to devour.

Matt refrained from comment. He wanted to start the return journey but realized he was still weak and shaky and it was already early afternoon.

"We'll leave at sunrise tomorrow," he said.

Kancha made a helpless gesture. "Mules dead." He told how the animals had been killed.

Matt felt very sick again, and not from a *charas* hangover. Loss of the pack mules was a serious blow. It would be a long trek over the mountains. Whatever he and the two men took with them, they would have to carry it all on their own backs.

He turned away from the frozen bodies and began making a mental list of absolute essentials. Food. Bedrolls and blankets. The tents would have to be left behind. Weapons. Lengths of rope. One ax, one shovel. His maps and notes. A selection of the largest nuggets and some ore sample as proof of the find.

The supplies and gear to be taken were divided into three loads. Kancha and Baki would each carry about seventy pounds, Matt almost eighty.

The following morning, Rutledge was more optimistic. After all, they did know the most direct routes back to the base camp. There would be no long circling through the mountains. And, on reflection, loss of the two mules was not an unmitigated disaster. He and the two men could move faster than if they were leading the animals, coaxing and maneuvering them over rough spots and across streams.

They set out on the morning of January 17. Eight days later, they reached the base camp. By then, they were haggard, half-starved and close to total exhaustion.

The tarpaulin-covered supplies and the Porter Pilatus were intact. Kancha and Baki cut the tarps loose and dragged out cases of canned food. Matt climbed into the plane to start the engine. He made several tries, his heart sinking until at last the engine caught. He let it idle fast enough to generate electricity and avoid draining the batteries and switched on the radio, calling the Kangtek station.

As usual, the operators there were maddeningly slow in responding. Matt repeated his call for fifteen minutes before he got through and dictated a message to the Maharaja.

"We found what we went after. I told my men"— he carefully avoided saying how many—"that they can eat. After that, we'll secure the supplies here and take off. We should be landing at the Kangtek strip in about an hour and a half."

Prime Minister Tsering Dorje and Major General Dep Bahadur Singh were supremely confident that Captain Nyamgal would carry out his orders. Once Matthew Rutledge had reached his destination, he would be killed, whether there was gold there or not. Since Nyamgal could not fly an airplane and would have to come out of the mountains entirely on foot, it might be another two weeks before he arrived in Kangtek.

Neither Dorje nor Singh were thinking of Matt Rutledge at 10:45 A.M. on Friday, January 25. They were going about their normal official tasks when aides of the Maharaja summoned them to His Majesty's audience chamber. They found Narayan exultant, his aristocratically saturnine features screwed into an immense smile.

"Rutledge located the Ser-gi Ri," Narayan announced. "He will be landing in little more than an hour."

Dorje and Singh battled to maintain composure. Dorje gained his voice first. "Wonderful news, Majesty."

"You both are to be at the airfield to meet him— with a guard of honor," the Maharaja said. "Rutledge and the men with him are to be brought directly to me."

"As you command, Majesty." Tsering Dorje hid his hands in the folds of his robe. They were trembling. With frustrated rage.

Filthy, their clothing in rags, Matt, Kancha and Baki were a sorry sight as they alighted from the Pilatus. The honor guard presented arms.

Prime Minister Dorje and General Singh were effusive in their greetings. They had come to the field in a ceremonial seven-passenger Bentley limousine gaudily painted with the royal colors, scarlet and saffron-yellow. Matt insisted that Kancha and Baki also ride in the car, and he would not allow any of Singh's aides to take the heavy rucksack he was carrying.

The limousine started. General Singh stared at the backs of Kancha and Baki, who were perched ramrod straight on the limousine's jumpseats. "The other men in your party," Singh said. "Did you leave them at the base camp, Mr. Rutledge?"

"No. We left them in the mountains, General. I'll give His Majesty a full report."

Singh opened his mouth to speak. A glare from Tsering Dorje silenced him.

Matt and the two Palace Guardsmen were ushered into the Maharaja's small audience chamber. Narayan told Dorje and Singh they could leave, then asked his visitors to seat themselves.

"Rutledge, my friend!" Narayan exclaimed. "You look—"

"Pretty bad, I imagine, Your Majesty—and I'm sure we smell much worse." Matt opened his rucksack, up-ending it on the floor. Nuggets and ore samples tumbled out. Matt lifted the two largest nuggets from the floor and gave them to Narayan, who stared at them in wide-eyed delight. After a few seconds, his face grew serious. He put the nuggets aside.

"Six men went with you into the mountains. Where are the other four?"

Matt related what had happened. He, too, believed that Nyamgal, Lapka and Ang merely intended stealing the gold taken from the placer deposit and suspected no broader implications.

"Kancha and Baki were very brave," Matt concluded.

Narayan spoke to the Guardsmen in Tibetan, asking for their versions. When each had spoken, the Maharaja thanked them and said they would receive promotions.

Kancha took the oilskin pouch from a pocket. Bowing low, he presented it to Narayan. "Their eyes, Your Majesty."

Narayan opened the pouch. The stench of decomposed human tissue came from it. Narayan nodded gravely, closed the pouch and placed it on a table. He dismissed Kancha and Baki and turned to Matt.

"The gold of the Ser-gi Ri will work miracles!" he said.

Damn it, he hasn't a clue as to what it will take to get those fields into production, Matt thought and said, "We'll have to build airstrips and roads, buy and bring in heavy equipment and machinery. It'll take months and millions of dollars before there can be any miracles." He stopped. He was very tired. "May we speak further tomorrow morning?" he asked. "I'd like a bath, some sleep—"

"And to be with Sita?"

"Yes, that, too."

"Go, of course. We can meet again tomorrow, Matthew." It was the first time Narayan had ever called Rutledge by his given name. It was a token of confidence, gratitude and genuine friendship.

13

Sita was overjoyed at Matt's safe return. Her fears and premonitions had been unfounded. She insisted on undressing and bathing him, after which she made him go to bed, and she brought him food and drink. Matt quickly realized he was not as tired as he believed.

"Come to bed," he urged.

"In a few minutes." Sita went downstairs and told the servants to leave the villa and not return until morning. She wanted to be alone with Matt, to have him entirely to herself.

Returning to the bedroom, she undressed and sat on

the edge of the bed, her nipples already erect. Matt tried to embrace her.

"No, let me do this." Sita bent over him, her lips and tongue moving over his chest, then lower. When they reached his tumescent sex, they were avid.

"Not one way," Matt protested, holding her shoulders.

Sita raised her head and looked at him. "You are wrong." Her voice was husky. "When I taste what you have for me, I will explode, too."

They lay in each other's arms.

"Matthew, you have forgotten something," Sita murmured.

"Forgotten?" He was half-asleep. "What?"

"You forgot to put me back beside you."

Matt was thoroughly baffled.

"My *Yin* idol. It should be there on the chest next to Yang."

Matt could not bring himself to tell Sita the truth, that he had carelessly lost the jade figurine. "I left it in a special place in the Ser-gi Ri," he said and felt her body go taut against his.

Two things happened simultaneously inside Sita's head. She sensed that Matt lied—he had never lied to her before—and a feeling of foreboding swept over her. I'm being silly and superstitious, the girl thought. Feeling the hard press of Matt's erect sex against her thigh, Sita turned to face him; her lips parted and covered his.

In midmorning, Matt went to the Maharaja's palace apartments. Narayan was fascinated by every word Rutledge told him about the Ser-gi Ri. He asked questions endlessly, even during the lavish luncheon that was served.

It was understandable, Matt realized as he answered the barrage of queries. After so many centuries Sakhana might finally become a rich nation without sacrifice of its independence or of its ruler's sovereignty and power. No wonder Narayan was ecstatic and insatiably curious.

Their discussion continued after lunch, but Matt took the initiatives.

"Labor will be a major problem," he cautioned. "Most Sakhanese won't set foot inside the forbidden zone."

"When they hear that men went into the zone and came out alive, their fears will fade," Narayan said. His smile was worldly, knowing. "Especially when our people learn they will receive good pay for their work. Money can even exorcise evil spirits."

"That's bound to take a while. In the meantime, we'll probably have to import laborers and certainly the skilled men to supervise building and to run the machines. Their wages will be astronomical by Sakhanese standards."

The dialogue had come full circle, back to the question of money for financing development of the goldfields. Matt lit a cigarette and inhaled deeply.

"I said at the beginning that I'd commit all my own capital—two million dollars. But that's only a fraction of what will be needed."

Narayan repeated what he had told Matt on other occasions. The Sakhanese treasury was virtually empty. His own personal fortune was small.

"It's up to me to find the development capital," Matt said. "I don't think it'll be an insuperable problem. I've dealt with Jacob Auerbach and Company, the English banking firm, for many years. The man who heads it is my friend, and a project with the potentials of the Ser-gi Ri will have strong appeal for him."

"When will you go to England, Matthew?"

"Soon as the concession grants and our other agreements have been drawn up formally and signed."

"All the papers must be prepared in three languages —English, Hindi and Tibetan—and numerous copies must be made," Narayan said. "Our scribes work at their own pace, nothing or no one can hurry them, not even I. The task will doubtless take them a week."

"I hate to wait that long, but if there's no way around it, I'll just have to do so."

Tsering Dorje and General Singh strolled in the palace gardens.

"Another failure," Dorje muttered acidly. He paused in his steps to pluck a red jasmine blossom. "Our only consolation is that your men remained silent. Otherwise you and I would already be under arrest." He put the flower to his nostrils and sniffed its sweet, heavy fragrance.

A monkey scampered into their path, grimaced and jibbered at them and scuttled off into some bushes.

"What can I tell Ramesh Anwar?" Singh asked. "There is no excuse that will satisfy him or his superiors."

"Tell him nothing—yet," Dorje said, tossing the jasmine blossom aside. "We no longer have any choice. Rutledge must be removed here, in Kangtek. Only then should there be any report to Anwar."

Singh was thoughtful. "Rutledge and the dancing girl often leave the palace compound and go into the city by foot—or into the countryside in one of our Living God's automobiles. An expert marksman—"

"Do you have one in mind?"

"Yes, and I will speak with him today."

Royal Constabulary Lt. Gopal Rangaswami was another junior officer General Singh held on a tight leash. Singh held a secret dossier on Rangaswami. Its contents could cause the lieutenant to be executed a dozen times over. In the evening, the general and the lieutenant conferred for half an hour. When they were finished, Rangaswami understood his instructions perfectly.

Thusday was the last day in January, and this fact reminded Matt Rutledge that as yet he had done nothing about buying Sita a new pair of Yin and Yang figurines.

Sita eagerly accepted his suggestion that they go shopping. It was a lovely day, and they walked.

Once outside the palace compound gates, they became the center of attraction, as they always did when they went into the city. People in the narrow streets gawked at them openly, for they had all heard of the foreigner and his exploits. Many people called Matt "the giant who stepped over the High Mountains." Indeed, walking with Sita or compared to the average Sakhanese, Rutledge did seem to be a giant. Men talked of his strength and bravery. Women marveled that while Matt's hair was almost the same shade of black as their own, his eyes were a green such as they had never seen before. A few of the most curious—of both sexes—trailed after Matt and Sita, curious to see what the foreign giant would do.

The streets became more densely packed with people as they approached the great square that was the Kangtek marketplace. The jade carvers' shops were located at the corner of the square.

Matt and Sita threaded a path through the crowds. They held hands, and this simple act brought a few looks of mild disapproval. Normally, only small children of opposite sexes held hands in public.

The marketplace was thronged. Merchants offered wares of all kinds. There were vegetables, meats, fruits. In another section, bolts of cloth were displayed. In yet another, bicycles and large tricycles, which were used as pedicabs or to transport cargo.

Rutledge and Sita were passing the shops that sold copper and brass vessels. The jade carvers were next, but Sita stopped. She had glimpsed an ornamental brass vase that appealed to her.

"Please, Matthew. I want to look." She pulled him by the hand toward a minuscule shop. Almost all its wares were displayed outdoors under a tattered plaited-bamboo awning. A roly-poly merchant standing near the merchandise gave them a huge smile.

Sita bent down, examining the vase that had caught her eye. She pouted thoughtfully. "The one over there is finer," she said, reaching. "Yes, it is prettier—see?"

Sita straightened up abruptly, holding the vase out to Matt. In that same instant, a pistol cracked loudly. The bullet that had been aimed squarely for Matt's heart punched into the back of her head. Her eyes opened wide in a look of dismay. Blood gushed from her mouth and nostrils, and she began to fall. Matt sprang forward and caught her, but even as he did, he knew she was dead.

Matt's next impulse was to lower Sita down to the ground and go after whoever had fired the shot. He saw it would be useless. A mob of shouting people were already milling around, pressing in around him. The assassin would have no trouble losing himself. He was probably far away by then.

The Maharaja sent for Matt after members of the Royal Constabulary on police duty in the marketplace brought Sita's body back to the palace compound.

"You were the killer's real target, Matthew," Narayan said.

Matt nodded blankly. He was surprised at the sense of loss he felt.

"Matthew," Narayan said, "there are no clues to the identity of the killer, not even a description of his appearance. However, I have posted a large reward. I have also issued a royal decree. Anyone who saw the assassin and fails to report will be punished by me in both my temporal and religious roles."

Narayan's tone changed.

"You probably do not wish to stay alone in the guest villa. A suite has been prepared for you here, in the palace."

"There are other guest villas in the compound, Your Majesty."

"Yes, but none as safe for you as the palace itself." Narayan sighed. "I cannot afford to lose you, Matthew."

He spread his hands. "It is for this reason that I have already given orders to have all your things brought here."

Tsering Dorje's rage was molten.

"Impossible!" he rasped to General Singh. "Rutledge is a man—he is not immortal! Are your men so stupid—"

"Tsering, Lieutenant Rangaswami was aiming at Rutledge. If the woman had not put herself between his pistol muzzle and Rutledge at the very last fraction of an instant—"

"Why did he not fire again?"

"He would have been seen, perhaps even taken prisoner by the people in the marketplace."

"Excuses—is that all your men give you?"

"The next time, Rangaswami will—"

"Will do what?" Dorje sneered. "Shoot down the entire Palace Guard? Or have you not heard yet? An hour ago, Narayan gave orders that until Rutledge leaves Sakhana, he is to live in the palace. Two Palace Guardsmen —over whom neither you nor I have any authority—are to be at Rutledge's side constantly as his bodyguards."

General Singh had not heard of these developments before, and he cursed—long and volubly.

Do-Ce (literally "to become"), the Sakhanese religion, calls for burial within twenty-four hours after death. Services were to be held for Sita on Friday afternoon in the Docist temple on the palace grounds.

Accompanied by his bodyguards, Matt went to the Kangtek marketplace again. He selected the finest pair of Yin and Yang figurines he could find in the shops of the jade carvers. He arranged that the idols were to be buried with Sita.

Matt attended the Docist services. He placed great masses of red and yellow jasmine blossoms and burned sandalwood incense beside her coffin.

14

At the beginning of February, 1974, the Western world's chief concerns were with the Arab oil boycott, fuel shortages and the energy crisis. But stories of daily developments on the world's free gold markets were shouldering their way onto front pages and up among top items being reported on radio and TV newscasts. The price of gold was rising steadily, a phenomenon that promised to have repercussions on national economies and monetary systems.

There was an old but good Grundig radio in the palace apartments the Maharaja had allotted to Matt Rutledge. On the night of February 4, Matt tuned in the BBC. Gold had climbed to $132.25 an ounce on the London Gold Market.

". . . barely more than two months ago, the price was ninety dollars an ounce," the announcer said. "Few expected it to go much higher. Certainly few—if any— thought it would increase by almost fifty percent between then and now. London Gold Market sources attribute the rise to sustained buying by individuals and companies that have lost faith in national currencies and more conventional forms of investment . . ."

Matt switched off the set. He was not interested in theories about causes. To his mind, the one important fact was that gold was continuing to go still higher.

A federal law passed in 1934 prohibited American citizens and companies from buying gold bullion for investment or speculation. The law remained in full effect for four decades, but by the early 1970s it was being easily and frequently evaded. Wealthy Americans bought and sold gold bullion through foreign intermediaries. U. S.

corporations with overseas subsidiaries or affiliates made use of them as fronts to deal in gold.

Charles Jordan Sturdevant III had learned how to circumvent U. S. gold-ownership laws. When Sturdevant devised his scheme to corner the free market in gold, he knew that absolute secrecy was imperative. He could not afford to attract the slightest attention to himself. The actual day-to-day manipulation of the market would have to be conducted from abroad.

Sturdevant and the Hajari Emir, Sheikh Nasib al Rahman, agreed that their third partner in the gold-corner conspiracy was the ideal choice to perform this task. Michel's Société Auerbach had its headquarters in Paris. France and French banks possessed a long tradition of speculating in gold. Michel had a one-third interest in the scheme and so could be relied on to do his very best.

Charles Sturdevant and Sheikh Nasib were content to maintain low profiles, while Michel guided the actual buying and selling. But it was still necessary for the three men to meet periodically and secretly discuss the next steps in their campaign among themselves.

For Charles J. Sturdevant III, secrecy had become a fetish. When Sheikh Nasib suggested a meeting in Paris during the first weeks of February, Sturdevant agreed on the condition that he could find a cover for being in Paris.

The billionaire financier-industrialist turned to Washington. He enjoyed extremely close ties with the administration. Many of his cronies and former employees held key positions in Executive Branch agencies and bureaus. The most notable among them was Assistant Treasury Secretary Owen Raynor.

Thus it was no problem for Sturdevant to have himself appointed last-minute delegate to the World Economic Policy Conference being held in Paris. He knew he could attend a few of the boring meetings and spend the rest of his time conferring with Michel Auerbach and Sheikh Nasib.

Sturdevant arrived in Paris several days before the conference was scheduled to begin—but then, so did many other delegates. He often saw Michel and Sheikh Nasib in his Avenue Foch mansion. On February 2, the three men met there in the late afternoon.

"I want to ask you something, Charles," Michel said. "Have you heard further from Sakhana?"

"Nothing more than what I told you—Rutledge is in the Himalayas. He won't be coming back."

Prime Minister Tsering Dorje pinched his lower lip between his fingers and tugged at it.

"The scribes are almost finished with the concession documents," he informed General Singh. "Rutledge will be leaving Sakhana soon. You must finally gather up the courage to tell Ramesh Anwar the truth."

"He will be furious," Singh muttered unhappily.

"When his rage passes, he will see that we are co-operating fully." Dorje paused, spoke again. "Anwar or his clients will be able to intercept Rutledge once he is beyond our borders."

The Maharaja made an informal ceremony of the meeting in his Council Chamber on the morning of February 5. He and Matt Rutledge signed the numerous copies of the concession grants, royalty agreements and other documents that had been—at last—prepared by court scribes and checked over by Maharaja's ministers.

After the signing ceremony, Narayan announced the creation of a royal commission to explore means for recruiting a labor force that would work in the forbidden zone. He appointed another panel with considerable executive power to insure that Rutledge received whatever help he would need from Sakhanese government agencies when he returned to the Closed Kingdom.

There were bows and handshakes. Then Narayan and Rutledge went to the Maharaja's small audience chamber.

"Now it's my job to round up investment capital," Matt said.

"When will you leave, Matthew?"

"Day after tomorrow. I'll fly my rented plane back to Darjeeling, go on from there to Calcutta and then on to London."

Narayan sent for Maj. Rafin Kalsi, an officer in his Palace Guard. Kalsi was bound to the Maharaja by the fearsome blood oath Sakhanese tradition demanded from all members of the Palace Guard. Major Kalsi had but recently returned to Kangtek after spending several months overseeing municipal affairs in Changyo, a town on Sakhana's western frontier where there had been unrest. Matthew Rutledge had never met Kalsi, but the Maharaja arranged for Kalsi to get a good look at Rutledge.

"Leave for Darjeeling by car today," Narayan instructed Maj. Rafin Kalsi. "Wait at the airport for Rutledge. Follow him everywhere, but do not let him be aware of it. He would resent my assigning a guard to him. Your mission is to protect his life as if it were my own."

Narayan added that a passport, the names of certain persons in Calcutta and London and a large sum in Indian rupees and British pounds sterling would be provided.

Tsering Dorje was surprisingly calm and unruffled.

"Rutledge departs day after tomorrow," he informed Dep Bahadur Singh. He studied his plump hands. "I have also been told to issue a passport immediately to Maj. Rafin Kalsi. Our Living God is sending Kalsi to watch over Rutledge. You must go to Balapur and telephone Ramesh Anwar."

"Will Kalsi travel under his own name?" Singh asked.

"Yes, but identified as a merchant, not as a Palace Guardsman. Anwar's people will have no problem singling him out."

General Singh appeared a bit puzzled. "You are in remarkably good spirits, Tsering," he remarked.

"It is because I have been thinking and now recognize the opportunity Narayan and Rutledge have given us." He adjusted the folds of his official robes. "Have your agents go out and talk of the death and violence that followed Rutledge into Sakhana. Danu, your four men, the dancing girl—invent some others if you wish."

Dorje fussed again with his robes.

"The people should be told that the foreigner has a mysterious hold over our Living God and even that Rutledge and Narayan intend to keep all the gold of the Ser-gi Ri for themselves."

"That will stir much discontent."

"Indeed. Our cadres are small, but with an angered populace, we can accomplish what we have spoken of often in the past—lift Narayan off his throne. We replace him with his young son—and you and I act as regents."

"Our friends who want the mining concessions will give us much aid," General Singh nodded. "And when we are the regents—"

"They will pay us the royalties," Dorje said, finishing the sentence for him.

Ramesh Anwar recognized the urgency of the situation described by Maj. Gen. Dep Bahadur Singh. Anwar immediately passed the message to his clients. They were the next links in a complex and covert chain. The information was flashed upward.

On the evening of February 6, the intermediary who served as the next to final link on the chain flew from Frankfurt to Paris. He met privately with Charles Sturdevant and repeated what General Singh had told Ramesh Anwar.

"God-damned bunglers!" Sturdevant barked. He forced himself to relax slightly. "What do you recommend?"

"The same as Anwar does. He has the bodyguard eliminated first, by his own men."

"What about Rutledge?"

"There are several Sakhanese who were exiled by the

present Maharaja living in London. He proposes using two of them against Rutledge after he reaches London. That way, even if they are caught, it will seem to be a purely Sakhanese affair."

"Get back to this Anwar in Calcutta," Sturdevant directed. "Tell him he has a completely free hand."

On February 8, 1974, Matthew Rutledge boarded BOAC Flight 982 at the Calcutta airport. He traveled first class and carried a heavy Mark Cross briefcase into the cabin with him. He paid no attention to the other passengers, whether they were in first or tourist.

Rafin Kalsi purchased a tourist-class ticket on BOAC Flight 982. This would enable him to travel aboard the same plane as Matt Rutledge but minimize the chance that Rutledge might see his face and remember it.

Unlike Rutledge, Rafin Kalsi scanned the faces of all the passengers as they went through the boarding gates. The handful traveling first class was made up of British and European businessmen.

Tourist offered a more varied lot. Indians of both sexes, one couple traveling with small children. A few British and Americans, probably low-season-fare tourists on their way home after a fifteen-day package tour of India. Six Iranians and a Lebanese—Flight 982 touched down in Teheran and Beirut. An old woman with Slavic features. A young hippie who could be of any nationality.

Kalsi felt that if one of the passengers was aboard as a hunter, he would not make any move against Rutledge while the plane was in flight. The two stopover points and London itself were the most likely places for an assassination attempt. He kept Rutledge under surveillance at Teheran and later at Beirut's Khaldeh Airport, where the plane was held on the ground for some hours "due to technical difficulties."

When the Boeing took off from Khaldeh, Maj. Rafin

Kalsi relaxed. Nothing would happen before the aircraft landed at London's Heathrow Airport.

About an hour before Flight 982 would arrive in London, Kalsi got up to stretch his legs. He walked to the aftermost compartment of the tourist section. There he paused and looked without much interest at the magazines displayed in racks mounted on the bulkhead.

A man—an Indian—came aft, obviously very much in need of the toilets situated beyond the magazine racks. Kalsi sidestepped into the last center seat-row to clear the aisle and allow him to pass.

The man drew abreast of Kalsi and appeared to lose his balance. Kalsi held out an arm to support him. The man lunged. A hypodermic needle stabbed through Maj. Rafin Kalsi's jacket and shirt and then deep into his arm. His right hand reached for the Luger automatic he carried in a shoulder holster. The movement was abruptly arrested. The hand stopped as if suddenly locked in midair by paralysis. The swift-acting poison that had been injected into his body had already killed him.

The killer guided Kalsi's body to make it fall across the seats. He rearranged the corpse in a sleeping position. Then he returned to his own seat.

Kalsi's body remained sprawled across the seat-row until the Boeing 747 was about to make its final approach to Heathrow. Making her mandatory prelanding passenger check, Stewardess May Evans thought he was sleeping. She shook his shoulder to wake him so that he could sit up and fasten his seat belt. When she realized he was dead, May Evans thought it was an IFCA—Inflight Cardiac Arrest—case and notified the pilot over the intercom.

III

February 14-July 5, 1974

1

As all who have visited the Middle East are aware, Arab oil sheikhs have a passion for what can be best described as Eyesore Eclectic architecture. Since His Highness, Sheikh Nasib al Rahman, Emir of Hajar, had attended Princeton University, it might have been expected that his tastes would be somewhat more refined. They were not. Sheikh Nasib sought *sharaf*—honor—in the eyes of his fellow Arab rulers and built accordingly.

Nasib's residence complex was located ten miles west of Izra, the Hajari capital. Sprawled over a two-square-mile area, it was a garish hybrid of San Simeon and Disneyland executed in reinforced concrete, stainless steel and tinted heat-resistant glass. The buildings were Arabian Nightmare Camelots of varying sizes with Moorish arches and free-form Byzantine elaborations. Final absurd touches were provided by stylized minarets that substituted for crenellated towers.

The Emir had officially designated the complex as "Al Qsar"—which may be rendered as THE Palace, suggesting it was unique, the world's one *true* palace. The grounds were surrounded by a thick concrete wall similar to those around maximum-security penitentiaries. Armored cars maintained incessant patrols outside the walls. Inside, a resident 750-man garrison—the elite Al Qsar Battalion—was equipped with the latest in antiaircraft weapons, automatic cannon, machine guns and M-16 rifles.

Al Qsar had been constructed at a cost estimated to be $200 million. The sum was a trifle considering that Sheikh Nasib received $3 billion annually in royalties from the American Ensign Oil Company, which held the oil concessions on the Persian Gulf island emirate of Hajar. It did not include the cost of the weaponry in the hands of the Al Qsar Battalion and other Hajari army units. The armaments were paid for by American taxpayers. They were given to Nasib under a Military Assistance Pact engineered in Washington by Charles Sturdevant, who controlled AMENOCO.

Sheikh Nasib maintained that impregnable walls, troops and weapons were needed to protect Al Qsar—and his person—from possible Israeli commando raids. Western observers knew the claim to be preposterous. They were aware that Nasib feared the day when his 280,000 subjects, most of whom lived in mud huts or in the festering slums of Izra, would demand a share of Nasib's oil wealth. In any event, anyone seeking entrance to the grounds of Al Qsar was required to undergo body search and obtain clearance at three successive checkpoints.

Of course, there were exceptions to the rule, Charles Jordan Sturdevant III being among them. On Thursday, February 14, 1974—the same day Matt Rutledge left London for New York—Sturdevant's private Boeing 727/100 landed him at Izra Airport. Sheikh Nasib had sent a platoon of his highest ranking councillors and a fleet of gleaming Mercedes Benz limousines to meet his guest. The convoy traveled at eighty miles an hour along the six-lane divided highway that led from Izra Airport to nowhere save Al Qsar. The limousines slowed—but did not stop—at the checkpoints.

While Sheikh Nasib al Rahman's tastes in architecture remained unalloyed Arab, his manner had the chameleon-like quality of the true cosmopolite. When alone with American friends, Nasib was entirely American.

"Glad to see you, C.J.," Nasib grinned, giving Sturdevant a hearty handshake.

The Emir received Sturdevant in what might have been the cocktail lounge of a luxurious Miami Beach hotel. Although no alcoholic beverages were permitted in Hajar, the prohibition did not extend to the Residency. The huge bar was fully stocked.

Nasib seldom if ever got drunk, but he did enjoy convivial drinking—among less innocuous pastimes. Once, when he was a freshman at Princeton, Nasib al Rahman and some classmates went to a Philadelphia nightclub, where he drank several Chivas Regals. A member of the group asked Nasib how he reconciled drinking Scotch with the teetotaling tenets of his Moslem religion.

The question amused Nasib. The quick reply he made delighted his companions.

"The Koran forbids drinking the fermented juice of grapes," he declared solemnly. "Since when has Scotch whiskey been made from grapes?"

Nasib's answer failed to explain why he also relished vintage wines and champagnes and very old cognacs, but his classmates did not press the issue. Nasib was paying the nightclub check and all the costs the party would incur at an exclusive bordello later that night.

The Emir liked entertaining American guests in his Al Qsar replica of an American cocktail lounge. It helped put them at their ease. Even when they were men like Charles J. Sturdevant, who felt more at home in settings reminiscent of the Union Club rather than the Fontainebleau Hotel.

Authenticity of the cocktail-lounge atmosphere was heightened by immaculately white-jacketed bartenders and waiters. At the same time, it was totally destroyed by the presence of six granite-faced uniformed bodyguards. Oddly enough, Sheikh Nasib's apparently paranoid fears were operative only in his own land. When abroad—which was often—he traveled with a conventional retinue of servants and aides. He attended top-level diplomatic and social functions (to which he was ever being invited) alone and unarmed. Outside Hajar, Nasib had justifiably earned the "Playboy Emir" image that inspired the media to liken him to the late Aly Khan.

Nasib was thirty-six, Sturdevant almost fifty. The Emir handily managed to create an impression that differences in age as well as those of nationality, religion and the status of hereditary ruler versus that of commoner did not exist. But then, Nasib al Rahman possessed a large measure of charm, which he used whenever he considered it to be of advantage.

"I'm having absinthe over ice," he said to Sturdevant. "Might as well start stoking the fires for this evening. And what would please you?"

"The same, thanks." Sturdevant said. While appreciating the asphrodisiacal effects of the wormwood contained in absinthe, Sturdevant loathed the liqueur's bitter anise flavor. But, as a frequent visitor to Al Qsar, he recognized the promise in the Emir's slangy euphemism, "stoking the fires for this evening." Far from any place where he would have to maintain his Presbyterian patrician image, Sturdevant could anticipate immersing himself in sexual excess that evening and for some days ahead.

The drinks were served in seconds. "If there's any business we have to discuss, let's get it out of the way, C. J.," Nasib said, sipping absinthe.

Charles Sturdevant toyed with his Waterford crystal glass, bracing his taste buds against the first shock of the liqueur's bitterness. "There's very little you don't already know, Nasib. Rutledge was completely shut out in London. Every English bank he approached turned him down. I received full reports before leaving Paris."

"Something puzzles me," Nasib murmured. "If Rutledge could be so easily prevented from obtaining a capital loan, why did you ever order what you call 'organic action' against him in the first place?"

The American billionaire swallowed a bit of the absinthe, grimacing as it went down. "Several reasons. One, it was the means our contacts in Sakhana said they preferred. Two, by asking other bankers to blacklist him, we naturally had to risk their asking questions—of each other, if no one else—and perhaps discovering the nature of our operations. Three—"

"Never mind. I can guess." The Emir sipped his drink. "A question. Has Rutledge gone back to Sakhana?"

"I don't know. Does it make any difference now?"

"Maybe not, but in any case, Michel Auerbach should be told to keep track of Rutledge."

"Oh, yes, Michel." Sturdevant managed a fair-sized swallow of his absinthe. "I've some new thoughts on the subject of Michel Auerbach. He telephoned me hysterically to say Premier Georges Pompidou is suffering from terminal cancer—"

"My ambassador in Paris sent me a report on that today. Evidently, it's true. But what has it to do with us?"

"Michel was panicking. He claimed Pompidou's death would bring political upheavals in France and could result in investigations of our gold buying."

"What did you tell him?"

"That you and I would talk the matter over while I was here." Sturdevant stared into his glass. "You know, the thought struck me that Michel and his Société Auerbach could prove extraneous to our needs—yours and mine."

"Are you suggesting that we get rid of him?"

"Yes and no. First let's use him and his bank as decoys to draw any fire that may erupt—and then let them take the consequences."

"With the profits to be divided evenly between us, rather than among three—and Sturdevant National absorbing whatever is left of the Société Auerbach?"

"Those would be the inevitable results," Sturdevant said, adding, "One more item, Nasib. Michel's second cousin, David Auerbach, the London merchant banker. I'm not sure how much Michel has told him."

"Another Jewish flea," the Emir replied. "If he creates any problems, I will simply have his bank—Jacob

Auerbach and Company, isn't it?—placed immediately on the Arab blacklist. The bank will lose all business it does with Arab countries and all Western firms with North African and Middle Eastern interests will have to boycott it, too. Such wounds could be mortal, C. J."

"That seems to tuck in all the loose ends. I haven't any other business to talk about."

"Are you ready for another absinthe?"

"Can't say I'm ever really ready for the stuff—I think it tastes terrible. I will have one more, though." Sturdevant's eyes gleamed. "I want to build a large fire."

"You'll need to. The evening should be memorable."

It was 5:30 P.M. in Hajar, 2:30 P.M. in England. An hour later, the London Gold Market set its afternoon fix. Gold stood at a record high of $148 an ounce.

At eight P.M., Hajari time, Sheikh Nasib al Rahman and Charles Sturdevant dined together, but by no means privately. They had a dozen women with them—all young, highly attractive and even more highly talented. They had been flown from Rome to Hajar for the occasion. Nasib was fluent in Italian—as he was in several languages besides English and Arabic—but for Sturdevant's benefit he had specified that all must speak and understand English.

At the dinner table, Charles Sturdevant was flanked by a svelte brunette on his right, a voluptuous redhead on his left. Throughout the meal, they took turns fondling his genitals under the table and whispering to him the clinically explicit erotic words he loved to hear.

Afterward, Nasib took "his" six women to his apartments. Three armed bodyguards trooped behind them. They would remain with Nasib throughout the entire night, remaining awake and watching the women to insure that none sought to kill or injure their Emir. Whatever sexual acts the guards observed would not excite them; all three were eunuchs.

The other half dozen women accompanied Charles Sturdevant to the palatial third-floor suite the Emir assigned to him whenever he stayed at Al Qsar. The bedroom of the suite had mirror-sheathed walls and ceiling, an enormous round bed and a double-size couch permanently tipped at an angle so it could be more easily seen from the bed.

Sturdevant told the women to remove their clothing. He undressed himself. He could not bear to have a woman take off his clothes for him. Frenzied, his face flushed and his long but rather thin penis distended, Sturdevant flung himself on the bed, lying on his back. Now he could once again realize his secret sexual fantasies.

"You two—use the couch and go down on each other and make plenty of sound when you lap cunt."

Saying what he had been taught in childhood were "forbidden" words excited Sturdevant even further.

"You"—motioning to the brunette who had sat on his right at the dinner table—"get up here so I can lick your snatch and see them at the same time." He spoke to the red-haired girl. "Suck my cock—but don't swallow." He told the other two women to lie on either side of him. He thrust fingers of one hand into the vagina of the first, used his other hand to knead the breasts of the second.

He reached his first orgasm quickly. He sat up, pushing the brunette aside, and seized the red-haired girl by the back of her head. He crushed his lips against hers and greedily drank his own semen from her mouth.

2

Sir David Auerbach sat in the drawing room of his Belgrave Square townhouse, reading. His daughter, Vivian, was out for the evening with her fiancé. He did not expect her to return until long after he had gone to bed for the night. When Vivian came into the room a few minutes past ten, Sir David's features registered surprise.

"Home so soon—and where's Alan? Didn't you ask him in for a drink?"

"No, I didn't." Vivian Auerbach smoothed back her long auburn hair and lowered herself into a wing chair facing her father. "I asked him to drop me off early because I had a headache." An excuse which Alan Leopold, being his polite and unflappable self, accepted without question, she added to herself.

David Auerbach took off his reading glasses and looked more carefully at his daughter. Yes, there were circles under her large hazel eyes and her delicate face did appear troubled and drawn.

"Sure you haven't picked up a flu bug?" Sir David's high forehead wrinkled in concern. "There's one going around. Couldn't be otherwise with the heat turned down everywhere."

"No, I'm not infested with any viruses." Vivian took a Benson and Hedges from her handbag and lit it.

"Oh. Had a lovers' spat with Alan?"

"Not that, either." Alan was eternally even-tempered and forbearing, Vivian thought dismally. And I'm supposed to marry him in May. It'll be the monochromatic marriage of the century. Aloud, she asked, "Did you know that Matthew Rutledge left for the States today?"

Sir David blinked. "Why, yes. He dropped by to see me this morning." He took an Upmann panatela from the humidor on the table beside his chair and reached for his cigar cutter. "How did you find out he was going?"

"He telephoned me—to say good-bye."

"That's a bit unusual. Polite of him, though. You are the mistress of the house, and we did have him over for dinner."

"Yes, we fed the condemned man a hearty meal."

Auerbach frowned, put his cigar aside without lighting it. "What the devil are you driving at, Viv?"

"Only the facts as we both know them. You were ready to authorize his loan. Then that hypocritical bastard, Michel, played the Auerbach Family Tradition March and you made an about-face and saluted dutifully. Thanks to you, Michel, and Charles Sturdevant, Matthew Rutledge was turned down by every bank he applied to."

Auerbach's deep-set eyes narrowed almost imperceptibly. A vague suspicion had begun to form in his mind.

"Viv."

An only child, Vivian had always been close to her father, all the more so since her mother's death three years before. She could practically read his mind and, sensing the direction of his thoughts, prepared herself for what was to follow.

"Yes?" She stubbed out her cigarette in a silver ashtray.

"You saw Matthew alone while he was in London?"

"Three times."

"And neither you nor he saw fit to mention it to me?"

"Why should we?"

"Did you tell Alan?"

"No. If I had, Alan would have simply smiled that bland amiable smile of his and said, 'He must be a nice chap if he's one of your father's friends.' That, I guarantee you, would be the sum total of Alan Leopold's reaction."

Auerbach picked up his cigar again and stared at it for a long, silent moment. "Was there anything between you and Matthew?"

Vivian lit another Benson and Hedges. "I went to bed with him, if that's what you mean." Her tone was neither churlish nor defiant.

The corners of Sir David's mouth tightened. "You're engaged to be married to Alan Leopold."

"Please don't play the heavy mid-Victorian father, Daddy. After all, I *am* over twenty-four years old."

Auerbach finally lit his panatela. This gave him the moments he needed to organize his thoughts.

"Unfair shot, Viv. I'm aware you had a few affairs before you met Alan, and I assume the two of you have slept together occasionally." Sir David drew slowly on his cigar. "I'm hardly a prude. I assure you people did those things long before there was any era of sexual permissiveness or whatever you may choose to call it. But formal engagement to a man you love implies—"

"Suppose I *don't* love Alan?" My God, Vivian thought, there it is. Now that I've said it, I know it's true. I like Alan. Period. I don't love him, and I'm not in love with him.

"You can't be serious!"

"Daddy, I hate to tell you, but to my own dismay, I am."

Auerbach stood up, began to pace the floor. "You imagine yourself in love with Matthew Rutledge, is that it?"

"I'm not sure. I think so." No, damn it, I know so. "Yes." Vivian realized the effect this would have on her father. Although far from being devout—or even practicing—Jews, the Auerbachs were proud of their Jewish heritage. In centuries, only a handful of Auerbachs had ever married outside their faith. By admitting her love for Rutledge, she was implying a desire to break her engagement to Alan Leopold and marry a Christian.

David Auerbach's love for his daughter was limitless. But he had a deep and abiding sense of responsibility for her future—and for the future of the English Auerbach line. Steeped in Auerbach family tradition, he saw her carrying it on as Mrs. Alan Leopold.

"Impossible!" he blurted, hurling his panatela into the fireplace. "I like Matthew. In fact I admire him. But he is a man without roots—a prospector on one continent today, another tomorrow." He gestured helplessly. "Viv, Matthew Rutledge has no family background, and he's—"

"A Gentile, is that it?"

"Yes, that too. We Auerbachs—"

"Are obligated to maintain our pure Jewish blood-lines?" Vivian broke in with a harsh, cynical laugh.

"Vivian, I am not a religious bigot!"

"Of course not. You're like the American racist who boasts that he has nothing against Negroes—but he wouldn't want his sister to marry one. Only in your case, it's Gentiles and your daughter."

Auerbach stopped his pacing and stared at her.

"Has—has Rutledge asked you to marry him?"

"No. And if he had at any time before tonight, I would have laughed at him and refused. Now, I'm not so sure."

"Viv, you're overwrought."

"Very much so," the girl agreed. "All my protective maternal instincts have been aroused."

"What in God's name are you talking about?"

"The most ancient and honorable of all Jewish traits. The compulsion to side with the underdog." She shook her head sadly. "You, Michel, the world-famous Mr. Sturdevant and your billions and your banker friends all ranged against one man. It's sickening—and I'm on his side, not yours."

Vivian stood up and started for the door.

"Where are you going?" her father demanded.

"Right now, to bed," Vivian replied. "Tomorrow, I'll be going to New York. Matt needs all the help and support he can get. No matter how little it is that I can give him, it will be more than he has now."

"You can't go chasing after Rutledge. I refuse to permit it."

"There's no way you can stop me, Daddy. I'm of age—a free agent. Thanks to all the dead and gone Auerbach grandparents, aunts and uncles who remembered me in their wills, I have my own money." Vivian tipped her head to one side and her tone and manner softened. "I love you—and very much," she said to her father. "But this is something I have to do. I know it now, even if I didn't before."

3

Mark Rutledge's Pan Am flight from London landed on time at Kennedy. He was in luck with customs. A bored inspector merely glanced at his declaration and did not ask Rutledge to open his suitcases. The eighteen-pound nugget and the ore samples went through undetected.

Matt took a taxi to the high-rise condominium building on East Eighty-first Street between Park and Lexington in which he owned a six-room apartment. He had cabled ahead, saying he would arrive sometime Thursday evening, to Luis Hernandez, his general factotum who lived in the apartment and who looked after it during Matt's absences.

"God damn, but you're a pain in the ass," Hernandez greeted Rutledge. "No word from you since November. I was starting to think you fell down a mountain."

The relationship between employer and employee was close and unusual. With good reason. A Hispano-American and a veteran miner, Hernandez had worked for Matt in the Congo and Venezuela. While in Venezuela, an adit—a mine gallery—in which Luis was working collapsed. A slab of ceiling rock fell on his right leg, crushing it and trapping him. The leg had to be amputated in order to free him and save his life. Since there was no doctor anywhere within a hundred miles, Rutledge risked his own life to go into the adit and perform the amputation.

Luis was flown to a hospital in Ciudad Bolivar. After two months, he was fitted with an artificial limb. He could no longer work as a miner. Matt kept Hernandez on as a timekeeper. Completely devoted to Matt for having saved his life, Luis gratefully accepted the general factotum's job that Rutledge offered him when the Venezuelan claim was sold. That had been more than five years before. Luis proved himself unswervingly loyal and reliable, indispensable to Rutledge, and they had long since addressed each other by their first names.

"Booze or grub or both?" Luis asked.

"Just booze, Luis. Bring a bottle of cognac and two glasses into the study."

Matt removed his jacket and necktie and went to the study. He sat down behind his desk, planting his feet on its top. Hernandez brought a bottle of Gaston Briand le Paradis, poured two large shots.

"Glad you're in one chunk," Luis toasted.

"Me, too—believe me."

They drank.

"All your personal mail's in that tray." Hernandez pointed to a stack of unopened letters. "I took care of the bills and the business correspondence. Want to see the file?"

"Not now." Matt poured himself a refill and another for Luis.

"Phone messages are here—how about them?"

"Leave 'em for now. I want to turn in, get an early start tomorrow."

Hernandez was forty-three, nine years older than Rutledge, but he had a good-natured gargoyle face that belied his age. He screwed it into an inquisitive look.

"Time for the big question. How'd you make out, Matt?"

"You'll see the good news when you open my suitcases. I found a field with more gold than your Conquistador ancestors ever took out of Potosi."

"You're bullshitting me," Hernandez said, then saw the expression on Matt's face. "No, I guess you're not." His eyes shone with an old-time miner's gleam. "So you really hit a jackpot."

"I said that was the good news. The bad news is that it'll take twenty million dollars to develop the fields . . ."

Luis whistled, downed his cognac.

". . . and my friendly neighborhood banker and all his buddies refuse to put up a fucking nickel."

Hernandez scowled. "Think you'll get the dough here?"

"I'm going to bust my ass trying."

Matt was personally acquainted with several high-level bank officers in New York City. He telephoned three on Friday morning and obtained appointments with two for that afternoon. Their responses were replays of those he had received in London.

". . . you've been out of the country, Matt. you can't imagine what the energy crisis and the Watergate stink have done to business. Everything's at a complete standstill."

". . . the money markets are tighter than hell. People are scared shitless. Look at what's been happening on Wall Street."

There were large grains of truth in what he was told, but Rutledge sensed he was again being given evasive excuses. It was quite obvious that Charles Jordan Sturdevant and Michel Auerbach had dropped their black balls in New York, just as they had in London.

His spirits low, Matt felt the need to divert his mind for an evening. He telephoned an attractive fashion model he had dated, took her to dinner at La Grenouille and then, to her amazement, back to her apartment, where he said good night at the door. Neither she nor the dinner had served to distract him, and he was in no mood for sex.

It was almost midnight when Rutledge returned to his own apartment. He found Luis Hernandez in the living room watching television, his artificial leg elevated horizontally and propped up on a cocktail table. Luis took the leg off the table and turned off the TV.

"A girl with a high-society accent's been calling you

every half hour or so since about nine-thirty," Luis said.

"Did she leave her name?" Matt asked without much interest.

"Yeah. Miss Vivian Auerbach—"

"I'll be God-damned. From London?"

"From the Regency. Says she just got into town and wants you to call her no matter when you—"

Hernandez stopped in midsentence. Matt had brushed past him and was picking up the living room phone.

"Got the number of the hotel?"

"Wrote it down. Plaza nine four-one-hundred."

Rutledge was already dialing.

When a hotel operator answered, he asked for Miss Auerbach. A moment later, he heard her voice.

"Hello, Matt."

"Good guess, honey."

"No guess. It had to be you. You're the only person who knows I'm here. When can we see each other?"

Rutledge was momentarily speechless and perplexed. First by the fact that Vivian was in New York, then by the urgency of her tone. Only the day before, in London, she had made it clear that their brief affair was over. She had been insistent that he not even telephone or cable her.

"Uh—tomorrow's Saturday, Viv. I've got the whole day clear. Anytime—"

"Not tomorrow, Matt. Tonight."

Rutledge's right eyebrow rose. "Viv, are you all right?"

"I'm not sure—no, I didn't mean that. Yes, I'm fine. How soon can you be here?"

The Regency Hotel was only twenty blocks from Matt's apartment. "I can be in the lobby inside fifteen minutes. I'll call you on the house phone."

"Don't. I'm in suite nine-eleven. Please come straight up." She broke the connection.

175

Matt replaced the receiver, his expression one of complete bafflement.

"Trouble?" Luis asked.

"I don't know," Rutledge replied, putting on the overcoat he had taken off only minutes earlier.

Vivian had not allowed herself to reflect on the possible consequences of her sudden-impulse decision while flying across the Atlantic. The emotions that had motivated it were still strongly operative, and they sufficed as full justification.

After checking in at the Regency, she immediately telephoned Matt Rutledge at his apartment. A man she assumed to be a servant answered and said yes, Mr. Rutledge was in New York, but no, he wasn't in and there was no telling when he would return.

It was a letdown. Somehow, in a remote corner of her mind, Vivian had expected that Matt would be there, as eager to hear her voice as she was to hear his. She tried to shake off the initial sense of disappointment by keeping busy. She unpacked, hung up her clothes, telephoned again. Mr. Rutledge had not come back.

Another letdown.

Vivian bathed, changed into a casual pants suit, tried once more, with the same results. She left a message. Matt was to call her—at whatever hour. She thought of ordering a drink and dinner from room service, then discarded the idea because she felt herself becoming tense. A drink—or even several drinks—would not help, and she really couldn't face food.

The reaction began to set in, a realization of the implications of what she had done. She had opened a wide breach between her father and herself—one that could be permanent, and this thought was both painful and terrifying. And she had destroyed her engagement— and her future—with Alan Leopold, not even showing him the minimal consideration of telling him what was wrong to his face. She had not even bothered calling Alan to say she was leaving for New York.

Vivian stared at the huge diamond solitaire Alan had given her as an engagement ring. It's done and over with, and I'm not really sorry about that, she thought. She felt no pangs of remorse or sadness—none at all, she realized—when she took the ring off her finger and dropped it into her jewel case.

She called Matt's number yet another time.

"I'll give him your message the minute he comes in," the manservant assured her.

My God, Vivian thought, her depression deepening and new fears and uncertainties attacking her. She had told her father she was going to New York because she wanted to give Matt Rutledge help and support. And she did. Sincerely, desperately, with all her heart. But what could she really do? He needed a huge amount of capital —twenty million dollars to be exact. Banks that refused to lend Matthew Rutledge the money certainly would not change their decisions because of anything she said or did.

Her own fortune? Matt was welcome to that—every last pence of it, as conscience money for the actions of her father and Michel Auerbach, if for no other reason. She had over 300,000 pounds—about $700,000. A large sum—as a private fortune. Almost nothing compared to what Matt required.

What *am* I doing here, Vivian asked herself, and a numb, chilling fear settled over her. I made a terrible mistake. I'll go back to London tomorrow. I have to. It's the only way I can hope to pick up the pieces and try and fit them together again.

It was then that her telephone rang and she snatched up the receiver and joyously exclaimed, "Hello, Matt!"

She heard his voice, and miraculously her fears and doubts vanished.

* * *

177

Rutledge tapped on the door of Suite 911, and it was opened almost immediately by Vivian. The mutual desire that was so strong in London flared instantly. It was almost a tangible, crackling force. Matt stepped inside, took Vivian in his arms. There was a starved ferocity in their kiss. It left Vivian breathless.

She reluctantly eased herself out of his arms. Her hands were trembling when she took his coat and hung it in a closet. This gave her time to recover. She closed the closet door and turned toward Matt.

"Bewildered?" she asked, her voice still uneven.

Rutledge was on the verge of saying that he was most pleasantly surprised, but remembered that he had said very much the same to Sita months before, when he found her in his bedroom in the guest villa. Remembering Sita caused a brief but sharp pang of grief. He let it fade.

"Bewildered?" he echoed, and forced himself to smile. "That's close, Viv. I'd have to search through a thesaurus to find a word that's closer." He stepped toward her.

"Please, let's sit and talk," she said.

"Sure, honey." He eased himself down into a sofa.

Vivian seated herself in an armchair opposite. She began to talk, nervously at first, then more evenly and with growing confidence. She described the scene with her father and made a successful attempt to explain the reasons for her sudden decision without revealing her deeper feelings.

"They have you outnumbered, Matt—my Uncle Michel, Charles Sturdevant—and Daddy, even though he's an unwilling ally."

"Outnumbered and outgunned," Rutledge agreed.

"I've learned quite a bit about what they're up to," Vivian went on. "I thought that if I was here and perhaps went with you to the bankers, told them what I knew, well—you might have a better chance."

Jesus, Matt thought. She's bucking her father and

the whole Auerbach clan for me. He noticed her left hand. She was no longer wearing her engagement ring. Vivian had said nothing about having broken off with her fiancé.

"Viv, I'm grateful." He was—and more. "But coming with me, telling the bankers what you've learned can't accomplish much. If anything, it would make them even more certain I'm a lousy risk."

"Why?"

"Bankers' mentalities. As of now, they're only extending what you might call a sort of professional courtesy, saying no to me because Sturdevant or Michel Auerbach asked them to. There's still a chance that one —or some—of them can be talked around to saying yes. If they find out what's really going on, I won't even be able to get past their front doors. They wouldn't dare defy all the power the combine represents."

"There must be something I can do."

"Maybe, but I can't think of anything at the moment."

Vivian took a Benson and Hedges. Matt stood up and lit it for her with his Cartier lighter, then lit a Camel for himself and sat down again.

"Are you saying that you want me to go back home, Matt?"

"No."

"What if I stay? Will we see each other?"

"God, yes."

"And you'll let me try and help you—even if it's only with moral support?"

"I need plenty of that, Viv."

Vivian crushed her cigarette into an ashtray, stood up. Their eyes met.

"All the banks are closed until Monday morning," she said, her voice husky. "We have the whole weekend to ourselves."

She led him into the bedroom.

4

Sheikh Nasib al Rahman and a haggard, bleary-eyed Charles Sturdevant shared the Emir's sauna at Al Qsar late Saturday morning. Nasib was talkative.

"Believe it or not, I gave thought to the Sakhana affair last night," he said. "Perhaps it's because I am an Emir, but my weltanschauung appears to be broader than yours, C. J. It strikes me you've missed an excellent bet."

Sturdevant's grunt could be taken to indicate he wished to hear more.

"You have that lap dog, Raynor, in Washington."

"So?"

"Why not use him and your other marionettes? Have the American government bring pressure on the Maharaja. If it's done with a sufficiently heavy hand, your Miramines Company can move right in. You won't have to worry about Rutledge or what other banks will do. Make the administration do the work."

Sturdevant wiped his perspiring face.

"Miramines made its first approach through diplomatic channels," he said. "And got nowhere."

"Ah, you were using the gentlemanly approach then. I'm recommending a more effective technique. An economic squeeze. Perhaps even a threat to the Maharaja that the President will support any Communist Chinese —or, for that matter, Indian—territorial claims on Sakhana."

Nasib might have an excellent idea, Sturdevant conceded grudgingly.

"I'll put through a call to Raynor at his house." He made a mental time-zone calculation. "I'll make sure to wake him up. He takes orders best when he's half-asleep and unable to think very clearly."

Alan Leopold had telephoned Vivian Auerbach repeatedly on Friday. Each time, Phelan—the Auerbach butler —informed him that "Miss Auerbach is unable to come to the telephone" and refused to give any further information.

Leopold went to the Auerbach residence on Saturday morning. Tall, sandy-haired and not quite thirty, Alan was not given to displaying emotion. But, after he had spoken with David Auerbach for a few minutes, his handsome features registered a deeply concerned dismay.

"But—but it's just not possible!" he stammered. "I brought Vivian home Thursday night because she didn't feel quite right. A headache, she said. She mentioned nothing—not a word—about going to New York!"

Sir David Auerbach could not bring himself to look Leopold in the eye—or tell him the truth.

"Alan, I'm afraid Vivian is spoiled and willful. It's my fault, I suppose. She obviously had a sudden impulse —who knows why? Probably she doesn't even know why herself."

"Did she tell you how long she'd be gone?"

"Not really," Auerbach said, with great effort, making his tone casual and placating. "I'm sure she'll be back in a few days—a week at most, I'd imagine. Vivian is trying to prove some point known only to herself. Once the novelty of having asserted her independence wears off, she'll take the first available plane to London."

"And you don't even know where she's staying in New York?"

Sir David's eyes appeared to recede even further into their deep sockets. "She always used the Plaza on her previous trips there," he said. "I telephoned the hotel. She's not registered." Auerbach took a deep breath and shook his head. "No, Alan, I don't know."

"Perhaps if I went—"

"I advise against it strongly. The more you or I try to make her return, the more obstinate she'll be."

Alan Leopold stared down at the tips of his riding boots. He always went riding on Saturday mornings.

"Strangest thing I've ever heard," he muttered.

"There's absolutely no reason for Viv going off like that, is there?"

"No," David Auerbach said, hiding his intense distaste for his lies and evasions. "There is no reason."

When Owen Raynor came to Washington to be Assistant Secretary of the Treasury, he automatically purchased the obligatory Georgetown mansion. He and his wife, Adele, occupied separate bedrooms, as had been their custom for the last five years of their twelve-year marriage. They slept in the same bed only on those occasions when there was a third person—male or female—to share it with them.

On Friday night, the Raynors had attended a Canadian Embassy dinner party. Both had drunk a bit too much. They returned very late and retired to their own bedrooms.

Owen Raynor was sleeping deeply when the telephone beside his bed began to ring. Finally, his conscious mind was prodded into some semblance of wakefulness. Raynor switched on the bedside lamp. The clock on the nightstand read 5:10. He was still mumbling curses when he picked up the telephone.

"Mr. Owen Raynor, please. This is the overseas operator. We have a call for him from Mr. Charles Sturdevant in Hajar."

Sturdevant. That helped rouse Owen Raynor into a state of more than semiconsciousness.

"Yes. I'm Owen Raynor. Put Mr. Sturdevant through."

"One moment, please."

There were clicking and scratching sounds. Then: "Owen?"

"Yes, C. J."

"Are you functioning?"

"Yes, C. J." Raynor was scrabbling in the nightstand drawer for memo pad and ballpoint.

"What dealings does the Treasury Department have with Sakhana?"

Sakhana. Raynor fuzzily raked over his memory.

"None I'm aware of."

"Find out for sure. Today."

"C. J., it's Saturday."

"I don't give a damn if it's Christmas. Get some of your people cracking. Tell them it's an emergency."

"Right, C. J."

"And don't stop there. We own plenty of key people in State and Defense. Have them dig up every scrap of information on U.S. relations with Sakhana—especially as regards loans, aid programs and any other projects. I expect you to have a complete rundown by five tonight— your time. Call me then here, in Hajar. At the Emir's palace. The number is Izra one. Got that?"

"Yes."

"Thanks, Owen. I'll be waiting for your call."

The line went dead. Owen Raynor hung up his telephone and groaned. He set the bedside clock for seven A.M. and went back to sleep.

When the alarm went off, Raynor forced himself to get out of bed, shower, shave and dress. Then he started to work, phoning his own aides and giving them orders and placing calls to officials of the State and Defense Departments.

He had all the information that was available long before five P.M. It was little enough.

His blond wife of thirty-two looked in on him at around three in the afternoon. Her balding, portly husband had always been a nervous type whose face tended to become puffy when he was under strain.

"You look like hell," Adele Raynor observed. She saw that he had a stack of scrawled notes in front of him. "What's going on, Owen?"

He told her about Sturdevant's phone call.

"And?" Adele demanded, suddenly wary and concerned. Her husband owed his position and affluence to

183

Charles Sturdevant; the billionaire was entirely capable of taking away both if piqued.

Adele Raynor was very much an authority on Sturdevant, his nature and methods. She had been one of his confidential secretaries and secret mistresses before her marriage to Owen Raynor—which Sturdevant had arranged. It had long been the financier's custom to pension off paramours of whom he had tired by having them marry the men he secretly subsidized and maneuvered into key government posts. The ploy gave him foolproof two-way holds on husbands and wives. The most highly publicized of these matrimonial arrangements had been made between one of Adele's successors—the statuesque, pseudo-intellectual Alice McGregor—and Jeffrey Tillinger, Sturdevant's fair-haired boy in the State Department. There had been several others.

"I've been on the phone all day asking questions," Raynor told his wife morosely. "The answers aren't what C. J. wants to hear." Assistant Treasury Secretary Owen Raynor was thinking of the $250,000 a year that Sturdevant paid into his numbered Swiss bank account. He was terrified of losing the huge stipend.

"Christ, twist things around so they'll sound good," Adele said. "You know how to do it and still cover your ass."

"I can't," Raynor muttered. "Not on this. I have to give it all to him straight."

Raynor used official U. S. Government telephone facilities to call Charles Sturdevant in Hajar.

"The information I've gathered is discouraging, C. J.," he began. "Sakhana has received no loans, grants or aid of any kind from the U. S. Government. We've never managed to achieve a toehold. Every offer made over the years has been rejected by the Maharaja. He's even refused to allow trade missions and junketing congressmen into the country."

Charles Sturdevant made a sound that might have

been an impatient and annoyed growl. "Have you talked to Colby?" he demanded.

"Of course. He says that with all the operations he's run in Asia he was never able to put so much as a single C.I.A. agent into Sakhana."

"What about the Defense Department?"

"A blank there, too, C. J. Defense has practically nothing. Its whole Sakhana file consists of some long obsolete British intelligence reports and the usual spy-satellite photographs." Owen Raynor paused, cleared his throat. "I'm told that the whiz-kid McNamara once wanted to reequip the Sakhanese army with American weapons, but his military advisory team wasn't even allowed to cross the border. It all looks pretty hopeless."

"Nothing is ever hopeless," Sturdevant snapped. "There's always a rabbit somewhere in the hat. This time it's Jeffrey Tillinger, our illustrious Secretary of State. I want you to see him personally, Owen. Tell the conceited asshole that you're acting for me and that I damned well expect him to move fast. He's to contact reliable top-level people in New Delhi and Peking. He's to find out what they're willing to stir up over Sakhana if Washington keeps hands off—and maybe even gives them a diplomatic assist."

Owen Raynor swallowed, then wet his lips. "Til-linger will probably have to clear that with the Oval Office, C. J.," he said.

"*You* clear it for him," Charles Sturdevant ordered. "Work it through Stans or one of Bluejaw's Kraut watch-dogs. Lay it on the line. They don't get another cent from me or from anyone associated with Sturdevant interests if they give Tillinger any static on this." Sturdevant paused, chuckling. "And if Tillinger gives any sign of balking, make it clear that I'll call that half-million-dollar loan I made him two years ago."

Owen Raynor laughed to himself. He enjoyed being appointed Sturdevant's official string-puller on projects of such magnitude. He derived an enormous vicarious sense of power from feeling that he was the billionaire's secret associate in enterprises that made marionettes of government leaders and shaped the destinies of nations.

"With that much ammunition, I won't have any problems, C. J.," he assured Sturdevant.

"I know damned well you won't, Owen. Give me daily progress reports by phone—at five P.M. your time—for the next three days. After that, I'll be flying back to the States via a quick stopover in Paris. Arrange to have plenty of free time after I arrive. I'll want you in New York for a week or so."

"Right. Care to give me any hint as to why?"

"Gladly. There are a lot of screws we're going to turn together."

5

For a number of reasons, His Majesty Narayan Mahendra Karamchad, Maharaja of Sakhana, had been deeply troubled for several days.

First there had been the radiogram from British authorities in London, announcing Rafin Kalsi's murder. Fortunately, the British did not suspect that Kalsi was a major in Narayan's Palace Guard. They accepted the cover that he was merely a merchant traveling abroad on some commercial business. But this in no way lessened the impact of the knowledge that the man Narayan had sent to protect Matthew Rutledge was dead. And, the Maharaja realized, Rafin Kalsi had undoubtedly been killed at the behest of the same people who wanted to murder Matthew Rutledge.

Another radiogram from London—this one sent by Matthew Rutledge—had assured Narayan that Rutledge was safe. However, it also indicated that the American had not been able to obtain the loan he sought in London. A second radiogram from Rutledge, received in Sakhana on Friday, revealed that he was flying to New York, where he hoped to have better luck in finding the necessary capital.

Concerns over Matt Rutledge and the progress he was making had been overshadowed by developments inside Sakhana. Rutledge had barely departed from Kangtek when the Maharaja was made aware of new waves of unrest in his country. There were reports from outlying areas suggesting that subversive elements were at work.

Despite their veneration for Narayan, who was not only the Maharaja but, to the Sakhanese, a Living God, disloyal whispers and surly complaints were beginning to spread. In Kangtek, the capital, there were those who claimed that the foreign gold-prospector, Rutledge, had gained some mysterious hold over the Maharaja.

"It has all happened much too fast to be spontaneous," Narayan worriedly told his Prime Minister, Tsering Dorje, on the night of Sunday, February 17. "There must be agents, an organized effort—"

"Majesty!" Dorje interrupted deferentially. "The reports we have received are of isolated incidents." His tone sought to soothe and reassure. "We must remember that our people have deep superstitious fears, and word that there is gold in Sakhana will naturally excite their fears and cause them to talk wildly." Dorje smiled confidently. "The rumors will run their course soon—within weeks, at most." He paused, then added somberly, "If they do not, Your Majesty need only call on General Singh to silence the rumormongers."

Narayan's saturnine features grew grim. "No," he said—and it was clear that he was giving a royal command. "There will be no blood baths."

"But, Majesty, if we permit malcontents to flourish, it will become increasingly difficult—and eventually impossible—to govern." Tsering Dorje was being his most persuasive. If he could only prevail on the Maharaja to order out the troops, the coup d'etat that he and General Dep Bahadur Singh planned could be brought off swiftly and easily.

"You are being shortsighted for the first time since you have been my Prime Minister," Narayan said reprovingly. "We must take no action against our people who appear to be malcontents, as you describe them. They are not speaking from their own hearts and minds. They are being stirred up by agitators, by *agents provocateurs*. These individuals—and those who employ them—are the ones you and General Singh must seek out. It is my command that you pursue investigations to identify them. Now leave my presence!"

Alone in his small audience chamber, Narayan allowed his mind to travel far beyond the borders of his Closed Kingdom. Rutledge was in the United States. It was early morning there, the Maharaja mused—early Sunday morning. He wondered if on the Western world's day of rest there could be anything at all transpiring that might affect the future of his country or his throne.

Secretary of State Jeffrey Tillinger stared owlishly at Assistant Treasury Secretary Owen Raynor.

"The instructions are from C. J. himself?" he asked.

"Given to me personally—for delivery to you," Owen Raynor nodded.

"And you've—ah—cleared it?" Tillinger inquired, shifting uneasily in his chair.

"All you have to do is call either Hans or Fritz," Raynor said, nodding toward the telephone on a table in a corner of Tillinger's Chevy Chase mansion living room. "I got through to both of them last night after talking to C. J. They said you can play it by ear." Raynor smiled maliciously. "Which means play it the way your ear hears C. J.'s orders, wouldn't you say?"

Jeffrey Tillinger had the beginnings of a double chin. The fatty roll quivered slightly.

"I presume C. J. realizes the possible ramifications," he said. "We've got enough trouble in Asia as it is. If we encourage the Indians and Chinese to lay territorial claims to Sakhana, it's impossible to predict what kind of mess we'll start."

"Make it simple for yourself," Owen Raynor shrugged. "Don't approach both. Pick one or the other. We fucked up with India over the Bangladesh business. Flash the green light to New Delhi, and Uncle Sam will gain mileage with the Indians. Or give the nod to Peking. Hint that it's Washington's way of showing it wants to play more and bigger Ping-Pong matches."

Jeffrey Tillinger glowered. "You're not that much of a fool, Owen. If I encourage New Delhi, Peking will hear about it—and be enraged. If I offer the plum to the Chinese, the Indians will find out, and the administration will be in deeper shit than ever with them."

Owen Raynor studied his immaculately manicured fingernails and when he spoke, his voice was a purr.

"Problems like that are the administration's headache, Jeff. No matter what happens, the President will have to carry the can."

"Theoretically. But what about my reputation and record? If there's a blowup, the media will start asking questions—the Senate and House will appoint committees and start—"

"Look, Jeff. C. J. told me not to bring this up unless it was absolutely necessary, but there's one damned big question you've got to ask yourself. Who 'loans' you a half million dollars at a clip—the administration or Charles Jordan Sturdevant?"

Jeffrey Tillinger's clean-shaven pudgy face paled, evidence that he had asked himself the question and answered it.

"I'll talk to the Indian ambassador tomorrow," he said, his voice barely above a whisper.

Matt Rutledge and Vivian Auerbach skipped Sunday morning breakfast and settled for a bloody mary brunch served in the sitting room of Vivian's suite at the Regency.

"Anybody ever tell you there're two things you

should never do?" Matt smiled, raising his glass to Vivian in a toast.

"I've been told not to do a great many things," she smiled back at him. "What are your special prohibitions for me?"

"One, you really shouldn't ever wear clothes. Two, you should never get out of bed—when you're in bed with me, that is."

"The flattery isn't going to get you anywhere this morning—"

"It's twelve-thirty."

"As far as I'm concerned, it's still morning—and I'm not taking off my robe and I'm not going back to bed," Vivian laughed. "Not until I've finished my brunch. I'm starved." She took a sip of her bloody mary. "And it's the being in bed with you that got me that way."

"Which way? Stubborn?"

"No. Starved." Her hazel eyes were amused, but when she looked directly at Matt they glowed with an intensity that far transcended physical desire.

Rutledge had ordered an enormous brunch. They both ate with the ravenous appetites of lovers who had slept little, experienced great pleasure and felt very close and very much at home with each other.

Matt poured coffee from a silver pot.

"Oh, by the way, honey, I'll help you pack this afternoon," he said, grinning.

"Pack?" Vivian exclaimed and stared at him in dismay. "I'm not leaving, Matt, not for—"

"Yes, you are. Today. This afternoon. You're checking out of here—"

"Matt—what's gotten into you? I'm not going back to London—"

"Who said anything about going back to London? I only said you were going to pack and check out of here —so you can stay with me at my apartment."

Vivian was silent for a moment. Then she said, "That sounds like the sanest suggestion I've ever heard. The answer is yes."

190

"You're not drinking your coffee."

"I don't want it. I want to start packing."

6

I knew it would be like this, Vivian Auerbach told herself happily when she first entered Matt Rutledge's apartment. The apartment was entirely like Matt, a reiteration of him and of his nature and personality. It did not pretend. It *was*.

She was struck by the absence of the usual self-conscious attempts to make a bachelor residence reflect superstud masculinity. There were no playboy-pad embellishments designed to precondition visiting females to the inevitability of seduction.

Vivian could not help but compare Matt's apartment with the London flat of her ex-fiancé, Alan Leopold. Although proper and low-key, Alan's flat was replete with hunting prints, athletic trophies, gun racks and proudly displayed examples of the taxidermist's art. To Vivian, the sum of such efforts had always seemed a forced effort to prove exaggerated maleness and to dispel lurking fears of sexual inadequacy.

Matt Rutledge obviously needed no such stage properties to strengthen his male ego. His apartment was furnished in excellent taste that reflected both a well-developed esthetic sense and a love of comfort. Instead of hunting prints, there were better-than-fair paintings, mainly modern, but with a trio of excellent Dürer engravings. Athletic trophies, weapons and stuffed heads and bodies of birds and animals slaughtered in hunts or on safaris were conspicuous by their absence. But there were books—shelves and shelves of them, Vivian noted— and good sculptures and carvings that Rutledge had collected in Africa, South America and elsewhere on his travels.

"You have a lovely place," she told Matt. It's just

another proof that you're one of those rare—God, how rare!—men who have no insecurities about your masculinity, she added to herself. And you're able—and accustomed—to treat women as individuals and human beings.

Vivian was no less favorably impressed by Luis Hernandez, Matt's manservant, who was clearly more than that. Rutledge had told her about Luis. Meeting him now and seeing him with Matt, Vivian realized that the men were close friends, who had shared countless experiences and trusted each other implicitly. The extent of their mutual confidence and respect was evident in the manner with which Luis greeted Vivian and treated her.

Hernandez instantly recognized that Vivian Auerbach had already become a part of his employer's life. How large and important a part, he could not yet estimate, but it was obvious this was no casual affair. Luis approved of Vivian without reservation. The slender auburn-haired girl with the great hazel eyes was certainly a beauty—but far mare than this, Hernandez sensed that she was genuinely in love with Rutledge.

"Whenever you want anything, just tell me, Miss Auerbach," Luis told Vivian. "As far as I'm concerned, it'll be the same as if it was Matt—I mean Mr. Rutledge—talking."

"Lay off the Mr. Rutledge, Luis," Matt corrected him with a grin. "Or I'll start calling you Señor Hernandez."

Luis took Vivian's suitcases to the master bedroom. Somehow, this too seemed entirely natural to Vivian.

"Luis has a maid come in three times a week—Mondays, Wednesdays and Fridays," Matt said. "She'll be in tomorrow morning. We can have her come full-time if you want."

"No need on my account," Vivian said. "I know you probably won't believe it, but I'm not totally helpless around a house." She moved closer to him. He took her in his arms and kissed her. She stepped away, smiling. "I can even cook—and I'm good, even if I say it myself."

Well, I'll be damned, Matt thought. The possibility that Vivian Auerbach, daughter of Sir David Auerbach and heiress to one of England's great banking fortunes, could even boil water for herself had never occurred to him.

They were in the living room and he went to the bar and poured two Chivas Regals and water. He handed her one glass, raised his own.

"I'm glad you're here with me, Viv," he said simply, drank and then slanted his eyebrow at a quizzical angle. "Tell me something?"

"Mmm," Vivian nodded.

"How—and why—in the name of God did you ever learn to cook?"

"It's among the nicer Auerbach family traditions. We even have a collection of recipes that Auerbach women have passed on from one generation to the next. Both kinds of recipes."

"*Both* kinds? I'm afraid you've lost me, honey."

Vivian gave an exaggerated sigh. "Serves me right for getting involved with a goy. The two kinds are kosher and nonkosher. You'll have to try my gefilte fish someday. Or maybe you'd rather have blintzes?"

"Huh?"

"Blintzes. Crepes with a Jewish accent. Then, there're *kreplach*." Vivian's eyes twinkled with amusement as she teased Matt. "Or *kasha varnishkes*—"

"Hey, have a heart. I don't know what you're talking about, but all of a sudden, I'm hungry." Rutledge glanced at his watch. "No wonder. It's almost eight. We haven't eaten anything since brunch." He turned away from Vivian. "Luis!" he called out. "Is there anything you can do about making us all some dinner?"

Hernandez limped into the living room. "The refrigerator and freezer are both loaded, Matt," he beamed.

He looked at Vivian. "Is there anything special you'd like, Miss Auerbach? We've got just about everything—"

"No blintzes, I'll bet," Rutledge interrupted, giving Vivian a wink.

Hernandez was unruffled. "Matt, I can make the greatest blintzes you or Miss Auerbach ever tasted."

"Luis." Matt drained his glass and gave Hernandez a long, dubious stare. "What the hell do you know about blintzes?"

"Everything. When I was a kid, I worked in a kosher restaurant in Chicago. I was a busboy, but Mr. Weiberman, who owned the place, wanted me to work up to be a cook. So, I learned—"

"Never mind, Luis." Matt shook his head dolefully and poured himself another—and generous—Chivas Regal. Hernandez ignored him and spoke to Vivian.

"How would you like them, Miss Auerbach? With cheese? Or caviar, maybe? We have some great beluga—"

"Make some of each," Matt groaned. "And broil three thick steaks while you're at it."

Matt Rutledge's bed was large, with neither headboard nor footboard. It was an honest bed, Vivian decided, looking at it—one intended to provide its occupant, or occupants, with roomy comfort, whether it was being used for sleep or for lovemaking. The fireplace in the bedroom was honest, too. It was not there for effect but because Matt liked to turn off the central heating and read in bed or sleep with an open fire going.

Luis had built a fire. It was burning well, the logs crackling, when Vivian and Matt went into the bedroom for the night. Vivian noticed two features of the room for the first time. The bedspread had been drawn back. The bed was covered by a huge patchwork quilt.

"A Rutledge family heirloom," Matt told her. "According to what my folks told me, it was made by my great-grandmother." He nodded toward the fireplace. "In a funny sort of way it goes with that painting."

The second thing she had missed when looking around the bedroom earlier was a Miro, vital and vibrant with its bright primary colors. Yes, she agreed silently, the abstract painting and the patchwork quilt did "go" together. That is, they did in the free-form individuality of Matt Rutledge's apartment and bedroom.

"You really do trust your own tastes, don't you, Matt?" she murmured.

"I suppose so," he replied, then laughed. "I develop tastes, too—like for blintzes. Tell me something. Are yours as good as the ones Luis made?"

"Let me make them for you someday. You can decide."

They undressed. Vivian went into the bathroom. When she came out, she saw that Matt had taken the quilt from the bed and spread it on the floor in front of the fireplace.

"Be back in a minute," he said, kissing her mouth and then her bare shoulder. He vanished into the bathroom. He returned in a few moments to find that Vivian had removed the pillows from the bed and placed them on the quilt and had turned off the light. She lay on the quilt, her head propped up by a pillow, gazing into the fire. Matt lowered himself down beside her. He took her in his arms, turning her toward him. Their lips met. His rigid sex was a heavy and massive pressure against the juncture of her thighs.

"Do you do this often?" Vivian murmured against his lips.

"You mean make love in front of the fire?"

"Yes."

"I have, sometimes. Not often." His hand stroked her back. "Never before on great-grandmother's heirloom, though." His sea-green eyes gleamed like emeralds in the firelight.

"Is that the truth?" Vivian's body strained against his. Her right leg slid over his upper thighs, tightened.

"Yes." His mouth moved to her breasts.

Vivian moaned ecstatically. The play of light and shadow caused by the flames from the burning logs excited her more than she believed possible. Her body writhed and pulsed, her muscles seeming to flex and strain of their own accord. Her hands grasp at Matt's black hair and forced his head and lips harder against her breasts. She was already on the razor-thin edge of orgasm, and he sensed it, shifting his position ever so slightly so that the distended head of his sex pressed against her swollen clitoris. He contracted his thigh and buttock muscles, exerting more pressure against the mound of eager flesh, and held her more closely to him as the spasms of orgasm went through her body.

"Matt—oh, my God!" she gasped and then there was a renewed frenzy to her movements as she flung her legs open and one of her hands reached for his sex and her sheath enveloped it. I'm with him in his bedroom for the first time, and it's as though it was the first time ever, she thought, and I've lost myself in him.

They made love several times. Matt occasionally eased himself away from Vivian to add more logs to the fire, but she experienced a special joy because he returned to her very quickly each time and held her, and his kisses and caresses did not diminish in their intensity.

At four A.M.—perhaps later—the telephone in the bedroom rang. Matt was holding Vivian in his arms, and he did not stir, although he was wide awake.

"Matt," Vivian said on the third ring. "Shouldn't you answer?"

"Nope. Luis has an extension in his room. If he hears it, he'll take a message."

Another ring.

"Suppose he doesn't?"

"Who cares? It's probably a wrong number."

The ringing stopped.

"See?" Rutledge murmured. "There wasn't any

reason for me to leave you." He stroked her arms. "I should have switched the damned thing off anyway."

Moments passed. There was a tapping on the bedroom door.

"Oh, hell," Matt muttered, propping himself up on one elbow. "What's the big crisis, Luis?"

"Call for you from London, Matt. Man won't give his name, but he says it's important."

"Okay. I'll pick up." Matt kissed Vivian and stood up. He went to the bed, lifted the phone on the nightstand.

"Rutledge," he growled.

"Matthew—I'm terribly sorry to bother you." Matt recognized Sir David Auerbach's voice, and for a moment he was unnerved. "I had to talk to you—as a last resort."

"Yes?" It was all Rutledge could manage to say.

"It's—well, it's about Vivian, Matthew. She—that is, she left London. Said she was going to New York. To help you." Sir David Auerbach's voice was tight, hoarse. Matt could readily imagine what the call was costing Sir David in terms of his pride. "I've tried the Plaza, where she usually stays. Vivian's not there, and I've heard nothing further from her. I wondered—Matthew, do you know where she is?"

"Uh—I'm sorry, but I can't hear you very clearly," Rutledge lied in order to gain time. "Let me go into my living room and try another extension phone."

He cupped his hand tightly over the mouthpiece.

"Viv," he said softly. "It's your father. He wants to know if you've been in touch with me. What should I tell him?"

Vivian's reply surprised him.

"I don't want you to tell him anything." She had already gotten up and was coming toward the bed. "I'll talk to him myself."

"Honey, are you sure—"

"I'm absolutely certain." She took the telephone

from his hand and held it to her ear. "Hello, Daddy," she said into the mouthpiece. She was silent for a moment, listening. "Yes, I'm fine."

She listened again, and when she spoke, her tone was firm yet gentle and loving.

"I am sorry for upsetting and even disappointing you, Daddy—but I'm not sorry for anything else. I'm doing what I want to do—what I want to do more than anything else in the world."

She was silent once more and Matt guessed that Sir David was protesting and pleading with her.

"I told you in London, Daddy," Vivian said. "I'm a grown woman." A pause. "Yes, I am with Matt in his apartment." Her voice was strongly determined, self-assured and even defiant. "I'm staying with him. For as long as he wants me!"

Vivian listened once again. Matt could tell that whatever Sir David was saying to his daughter, he was only antagonizing her and increasing her determination. The firelight playing on Vivian's lovely face revealed that her features were hardening as she heard her father out.

"No, I don't give a single bloody hell what all the Auerbachs in the world say or think!" she said at last. "You're my father and I love you and I wouldn't hurt you for anything. But the Auerbach family and all its damned totems make me sick. For all I care, every last one of our precious relatives can have cardiac arrests or apoplectic strokes." She paused, took a deep breath, but even so when she spoke again, her voice was shaky.

"We'd best say good night now, Daddy. We'll talk later—when we're both calmer."

Vivian hung up.

"Matt, take me in your arms and hold me—please," she whispered, and he knew she was fighting back tears.

He did as she asked. Now, for the very first time, he realized fully what Vivian Auerbach was sacrificing to be with him. She had broken her engagement to Alan

Leopold. She had rejected her family and all its hallowed rules and traditions. By Auerbach standards, she was a traitor to her family and her heritage. She had even defied her father—perhaps alienated herself from him permanently.

He held her very tightly, finally comprehending how deeply she loved him—and, at the same time, becoming aware that he was in love with her, too.

7

The world's hundred or so most powerful bankers form a freemasonry that abides by its own arcane codes and is a law unto itself. True, major banks compete among themselves, often fiercely. But there is a line at which competition ceases, a line set by the men who really control the great banks, and it is scrupulously observed.

When a leading banker undertakes a personal project or financial venture, it is sacrosanct. No other member of the banking industry's freemasonry will encroach unless and until the particular banker abandons his project or—for some reason—clearly and finally fumbles his play.

The message that a given venture is off limits is discreetly flashed along the uppermost levels of the banking world's Old Boy network. It can be—and frequently is—accomplished as simply as that.

Thus, Morrison, chairman of U. S. and Southeastern Fidelity, will encounter Auchincloss, who controls American Guaranty and Trust, and Clarke, chairman of Transnational, at the Union Club.

"Delighted to run into you today," Morrison says over a martini. "Been meaning to tell you. I'm after Barton Industries—doing it through the bank, of course, but it's actually my own private enterprise."

Auchincloss and Clarke nod. They have gotten the

message, and it will spread swiftly through the Brotherhood. Morrison is out to take control of Barton Industries, a hundred-million-dollar corporation—by one means or another. Since it's his private venture, no other bank will attempt to outbid or outmaneuver him. Nor will any bank come to the aid of Barton Industries if Morrison's strategy involves a financial squeeze and the Barton management seeks help to ease the pressure and avoid being caught in the trap.

Listed in the order of their assets, the four largest commercial banks in the United States were the Bank of America, the First National City of New York, the Sturdevant National and the Chase Manhattan. Within the nation's financial community, the Sturdevant National was known—and often feared and hated—as being by far the most aggressive and ruthless of the Big Four.

But then, the Sturdevant National had much justification for its arrogance of power. It was the international banking apparatus for the vast, global financial and industrial empire owned or controlled by America's famed Sturdevant dynasty. The extent of the dynasty's wealth defied estimate. Not even Senate or House investigating committees could ferret out more than the wispiest shreds of information. A single Sturdevant Foundation (and there were several such foundations) had assets of more than $12 billion. The actual worth of individual members of the Sturdevant family was impenetrably camouflaged by battalions of accountants—themselves millionaires from the fees they received for their adroitness at hiding their clients' assets.

Sturdevant wealth made Sturdevant power pervasive. The merest whisper of a Sturdevant was a bellowed command that made great and famous stock brokerage houses jump to obey and could make or break Market trends and even whole markets—to say nothing of AAAA Dun and Bradstreet-rated corporations. This was hardly all.

The Sturdevant dynasty owned entire stables of politicians, legislators and members of the judiciary at local and national levels at home and abroad.

In Washington, crucial administration posts were filled by individuals who had been "recommended" for the positions by Charles J. Sturdevant III, de facto head of the Sturdevant dynasty. His "recommendations" carried the force of instructions—if not actually orders—with the Executive Branch. On Capitol Hill, legislation drafted to benefit Sturdevant interests and enterprises was time and time again dutifully passed by senators and congressmen who knew the power—and enjoyed the largesse—of C. J. Sturdevant.

Under such circumstances, it was a foregone conclusion that Matthew Rutledge would receive only more rebuffs and refusals beginning on Monday morning. During the first days of the week, Rutledge stubbornly refused to admit to himself that his situation was impossible. But the unwritten law that drew the banking fraternity's line had been invoked in New York and from there throughout the entire United States.

Charles Jordan Sturdevant III had demarcated Sakhana—an Asian kingdom about which bankers knew little and cared less—as his private preserve. The banking mafia was aware that Sakhana had been designated a "Sturdevant area of interest." This established the ground rules. If funds were to be made available to anyone for whatever purpose in Sakhana, they would have to come from Charles Sturdevant or the Sturdevant National Bank. No other bank, banker or financier with sufficient resources to provide $20 million would dream of transgressing.

By Thursday, February 21—a day when the price of gold reached $151.50 an ounce on the London Market—Matthew Rutledge was forced to admit that the shutout was indeed total.

"It's useless," he told Vivian and Luis when he returned home that evening. "Now I can't even get past third assistant vice-presidents."

"You sure you've tried everybody who might be willing to finance you, Matt?" Luis Hernandez asked.

"Everybody. I even went off the beaten path to men like Hightower and to Colson of LeMaine Brothers —people who're usually willing to take a risk for a higher interest rate." Matt downed the triple-strength Chivas Regal and water Luis had made for him and went to the living room bar to pour himself a refill.

Vivian, completely at home in checked pants and a shirt with rolled up sleeves, set the drink Luis had served her on a cocktail table. Her long auburn hair was brushed back and held by a gold barrette. The effect was to make her appear far younger than her twenty-four years, but her expression was serious and deeply thoughtful.

"Matt, you still have one person you should try— must try," she declared.

Rutledge, his glass filled, turned and looked at her. "Who? God?"

"He probably thinks he is—and so do a great many other people," Vivian said. "I'm talking about Charles Sturdevant."

Matt gaped at her. "Sturdevant? You must be kidding!"

"I'm not. Oh, I don't think for a moment that he'll help you get the loan, Matt. But I do feel that if you met the man personally, you could size him up, perhaps even learn more about his plans and intentions than you know now."

Luis Hernandez sat in a chair at one end of the living room. He leaned forward.

"Sure. If you can get to see the big wheel, he might make you an offer—"

"Last thing I want is an offer from Sturdevant!" Matt snorted.

"No one suggests you should take it if he does," Vivian said. "But anything he says, any information or even impression you can gain will help you evaluate the situation and possibly find some weak spot or loophole."

"You may have a point." Rutledge took a large swallow of Scotch. "I want to think the idea over, though." The suggestion did have its merits, he reflected. If he made approaches to Sturdevant and asked for a meeting, the billionaire would assume it was an attempt to surrender and salvage something from a hopeless predicament. That could make even the great C. J. Sturdevant overconfident and careless. On the other hand, such a move had to be given much thought. There were too many potential boobytraps and always a chance that Matt might make a slip of the tongue and give away information valuable to the banker-industrialist.

Rutledge said little for the next hour or so as he pondered the idea. He had not yet reached a decision when he switched on the TV for the seven o'clock news on Channel 2. He watched absently as Walter Cronkite and various correspondents reported the latest dismal developments in the Watergate scandals, the energy crisis and the Patricia Hearst kidnaping case.

Then Cronkite read an item datelined New Delhi and Matt snapped alert in astonishment.

"The Indian government has revived ancient territorial claims on the kingdom of Sakhana, a small mountainous country that borders on its northern frontiers—"

"Jesus Christ!" Rutledge groaned. "Now, of all times!"

"There has been no immediate reaction from Sakhana, which is linked to the outside world by only a single radio station located in its capital city of Kangtek . . ."

This is just too damned pat, too much of a coincidence, Matt thought. It must be that the Indians have heard about the gold—or it could even be part of a bigger pattern. His suspicions were verifield a moment later as Cronkite continued.

". . . However, in Washington, Secretary of State Jeffrey Tillinger commented on the development, which could possibly grow into a new Asian crisis. Secretary Tillinger announced that the United States was adopting a hands-off policy. 'This is a matter entirely between the two countries concerned,' he stated."

The next news item dealt with the opening of a three-day conference of Latin American and Caribbean foreign ministers. Matt levered his tall body out of the chair in which he was sitting and angrily switched off the television set.

"The dirty sons of bitches!" he bellowed.

Vivian and Luis looked at him questioningly.

"Tillinger and Sturdevant engineered it—there's no other explanation." Matt had begun to pace the floor. "I can smell it—and it stinks!"

"You ain't getting a bit paranoid, are you, Matt?" Luis asked.

"Paranoid?" Rutledge stopped pacing and laughed acidly. "Hell, you can add it all up on the fingers of one hand. Sturdevant wants the Sakhanese concessions. Jeffrey Tillinger was on his payroll for years. He was the head of Sturdevant's Foreign Policy Study Foundation— went directly from there to the State Department. He may be a glamour boy to the public, but he's still nothing but a pimp for Charles Sturdevant!"

"Could be," Hernandez conceded, "but it doesn't seem—"

"Look. I can only guess what the mechanics of the deal were. Sturdevant has large holdings—and plenty of pull—in India. Chances are he pulled strings in New Delhi, maybe paid off politicians in the Congress party— they come cheap enough, Christ only knows. He got them to revive the old border disputes. Then he laid down the law to Tillinger: No diplomatic interference by Uncle

Sam, period. And that puts Sakhana and the Maharaja right behind the eight ball."

"Matt, aren't you exaggerating?" Vivian asked quietly. Her expression seemed to indicate that she, like Luis Hernandez, believed Rutledge might be slightly paranoid after all. "Asian countries are forever at each other's throats. We British learned that a long time ago." She smiled. "We tried to sort out their squabbles. We called it the White Man's Burden—and only had our noses bloodied for our efforts. Now you Americans are determined to make the same mistakes—"

"Honey, this is no Rudyard Kipling or J. Arthur Rank-type hassle. It's being carefully staged—and stage-managed—in dead earnest. Believe me, I feel it—right at what we Americans call the gut level. The objective is to make things so hot for the Maharaja that he'll have to abdicate—and if he refuses, to shoot him off his throne."

"It might not be all that easy," Vivian countered. "From everything I've heard, the Sakhanese have managed to remain independent for what—a thousand years or more?—and they hate the Indians—"

"Viv. The Indians have a huge modern army and air force, and they're cocky as hell ever since they whipped the Pakistanis. The Sakhanese have an army of maybe three, four thousand men with no heavy weapons, no armor, no aircraft. If India moves against Sakhana, it'll be a massacre."

Matt walked across the living room to a huge sheet-glass window that faced out on Eighty-first Street seventeen floors below. He stared through the window silently for several seconds and made his decisions.

"Now I have to see Sturdevant, whether I like it or not," he said, turning away from the window. "Anything I can find out from him—even if it's only what I gather from his manner and attitude—will be valuable."

Luis Hernandez was at the bar, pouring fresh drinks.

"Then what, Matt?" he asked over his shoulder.

"I go back to Sakhana."

Luis handed around the drinks. Vivian held hers and stared at it.

"What good will it do if you don't have the capital you need?" she asked, not looking at Rutledge.

"A tenth of a loaf is better than none," Matt grinned, and drank. "I'm worth two million bucks. That won't finance more than a shoestring operation compared to what's needed to make the Sakhanese fields fully productive. But it's a starter. Somehow or other, I'll figure a way to bring some gold out of those mountains."

" 'Some gold?' " Vivian echoed. "What do you expect to accomplish by that?"

"A good question." Matt eased himself down on the arm of the sofa on which she sat. He slowly swirled the whiskey and water remaining in his glass. "Could be I won't accomplish a damned thing—except go broke. But there's an outside gambler's chance I can do a lot."

Luis Hernandez was watching Matt closely. Rutledge *was* a gambler—a big-stake gambler with no shortage of guts or balls—Hernandez mused. If anyone could beat what seemed overwhelming odds, it was Rutledge, and Luis was already silently cheering Matt on.

"There are all kinds of possibilities," Rutledge continued, still swirling his glass. "Let's suppose I'm able to get even a million dollars' worth to Kangtek in a hurry. That would be enough to prove to the whole world that Sakhana had huge gold reserves, and it'd strengthen the Maharaja's position—"

"And make the Indian government just that much more eager to take over the country," Vivian interposed.

"More eager—but less able," Matt said. "No other country in Asia would want the Indians to have the gold, and every diplomatic ploy would be used to keep them from laying their hands on it—or on Sakhana. Every other Asian—and for that matter, European—government would rather have an immensely rich independent little Sakhana than see India grab off the plum."

"Sounds reasonable," Luis Hernandez grunted.

"It is," Rutledge said. "It's also reasonable to figure that if Sakhana suddenly has a million dollars' worth of gold to sell on the market, Charles Sturdevant et al will have to throw in the towel or have it taken away from them."

Vivian now took a sip of her drink. "That last point escapes me," she said.

"Simple, Miss Auerbach," Hernandez spoke up. "If Matt actually manages to haul a big batch of gold out of those mountains, all the bankers and big money-men are going to decide that Sturdevant's lost more rounds than he's won. They'll all want a piece of the action—and the profits. They'll line up, begging Matt and the Maharaja to borrow dough from 'em. Right, Matt?"

"It couldn't be otherwise."

Vivian reached for Matt's free hand and held it.

"You have more than two million dollars," she said, her eyes shining and tender.

He stared at her, uncomprehending.

"You see, I have something over three hundred thousand pounds. No—please don't interrupt me. It's all in my own right. Neither my father nor anyone else can tell me what to do with the money—"

"Viv, you can't—"

"Stop it!" Her hand tightened on his. "You've been going from one bank to another looking for a development capital loan." She laughed throatily. "I'm not a banker's daughter for nothing. I'm always on the lookout for a promising investment."

She glanced at Luis, gave him a conspiratorial wink. Hernandez flashed a huge smile, nodded and raised his glass to her.

That night, Matt's lovemaking ran the gamut from the infinitely tender to the near-violent and back to the tender. Vivian responded totally to every nuance, and it was almost dawn when, happily exhausted, they fell asleep in each other's arms.

8

Charles Sturdevant returned from Hajar—via a brief Paris stopover—on Wednesday. On the following morning—as was his usual daily custom when in New York— he went to his board chairman's offices in the Sturdevant National Bank Tower on lower Broadway. Assistant Treasury Secretary Owen Raynor reported to him there. Raynor detailed the progress Secretary of State Jeffrey Tillinger had made with the Indian ambassador.

"India will maintain diplomatic pressure on Sakhana," he assured Sturdevant.

The billionaire nodded approvingly. "Now fill me in on the broader picture."

Raynor recited national and international economic facts and figures and much highly classified information. There was no possibility that the United States—or any other—government was contemplating any moves that could interfere with Sturdevant's campaign to corner the gold market.

Sturdevant arranged an intercontinental conference call with Sheikh Nasib al Rahman and Michel Auerbach, his partners in the scheme, and urged further increases in their gold buying. Nasib and Michel concurred. The appropriate orders were issued.

On Friday morning, Sturdevant and Raynor resumed their conference. Owen Raynor produced a telex and sounded a cautionary note. The morning fix on the London Gold Market was $158.50 an ounce, up from $151.50 overnight.

"Aren't you pushing things a little too fast, C. J.?"

Raynor asked. "If the price keeps rising so rapidly—"

"No problem," Sturdevant said. "Considering the quantities we've already bought, our cost average will be reasonable even if the price goes to two hundred dollars before we're through. Once we have the one hundred twenty-five million ounces we're after, we can hold on and keep the gold off the market for weeks, even months, until it hits four hundred dollars or more an ounce."

Raynor gave no sign of the sudden resentment that began welling within him. True Charles Sturdevant paid him $250,000 a year. But he, Owen Raynor, was doing more than any other single person to insure that Sturdevant would make tens of *billions*. And Sturdevant had never made the faintest suggestion of allowing Raynor any share in the profits. Raynor thought a hint might not be out of order.

"I've been meaning to ask you, C. J.," he said. "Would you have any objection if I did some quiet buying myself?"

Charles Sturdevant's angular features formed into an affable smile. "Hell, Owen, I took it for granted you've been going along, buying on your own from the start. I'm sorry to hear you haven't—and no, I have no objection. Go right ahead. You won't have any difficulties doing it secretly through your Swiss bank."

"Thanks, C. J.," Owen Raynor said. The answer spelled it out. Raynor would have to use his own money. Charles Sturdevant was not going to set aside any purchases for his account or make him any interest-free loans for buying gold.

The billionaire pretended to glance at a letter that lay on his huge, gleaming desktop. "Nothing like building more security for the future," he said and glanced up. "Oh, I meant to ask you. How is Adele?"

Having sensed signs of discontent in Raynor, Charles Sturdevant employed the ultimate castration weapon which he knew inevitably slammed Raynor back into his place. Adele Raynor had been Sturdevant's mistress before her marriage to Owen. Indeed, Raynor—then a Sturdevant National vice-president—had only married her on a suggestion that was tantamount to an order from Sturdevant. By taking her off the financier's hands, he assured his future.

The reminder had its desired effect. Owen Raynor shriveled inwardly from the renewed awareness that Charles Sturdevant could destroy him completely, at any time.

"Adele is fine," he said, struggling to keep his voice even. "She asked that I give you her best when I saw you."

Sturdevant shifted position in his chair. "We have several other items on the agenda, Owen. Let's start with the problems Sturdevant National has been having on that Bolivian loan. You and Tillinger were supposed to get the administration cracking."

Ordinary mortals could not hope to reach Charles Jordan Sturdevant III by telephone. All callers were screened by relays of secretaries. Even senior vice-presidents of the Sturdevant National had to wait—often for hours, sometimes for days—before the board chairman called them back.

Matthew Rutledge had a hunch that he would get through to Charles Sturdevant with remarkable speed. The banker could be assumed to harbor a megalomaniacal desire to gloat over a defeated opponent's plight.

Matt telephoned the Sturdevant National Bank at ten A.M. on Friday. He patiently talked his way up the ladder of successively higher-echelon secretaries, freely throwing out names that would impress them.

"Mr. Sturdevant and I have many mutual friends. There are the Auerbachs in England and France—and, of course, David of the Chase."

Eventually, Matt reached some kind of secretarial summit. The voice was flawless Katherine Gibbs via

Goucher and courteously authoritative, and asked for Matt's telephone number.

"Your message will be given to Mr. Sturdevant, Mr. Rutledge. Someone will telephone you soon and tell you if Mr. Sturdevant will be able to speak with you."

The call came less than twenty minutes later—from a man who identified himself as John Nicholson, Charles Sturdevant's administrative assistant.

"I've been instructed to inquire if you can be at Mr. Sturdevant's office at eleven-thirty, Mr. Rutledge."

"I'll be there."

Matt hung up and grinned at Vivian and Luis Hernandez. "The Great Man can hardly wait to see me. And I bet he'll be smug as hell because he holds all the high cards."

"You're acting like you're itching for the showdown," Luis Hernandez grumbled.

"I am. Guys like Sturdevant are vulnerable in certain areas. Aim for the right ones and you give them ulcers. That alone can be gratifying."

Vivian Auerbach nervously licked her lower lip. "Are you sure this isn't a mistake, Matt?"

"Absolutely, unequivocally certain, m'love." Matt laughed. "Anyway, remember that the original idea was yours. I've simply dreamed up a few frills. With any luck at all, I'll jolt the bastard off balance. With a little more, I'll leave him making what the Sakhanese call *gama-gama* in his handmade silk shorts."

"Rutledge will be here at half-past eleven," John Nicholson reported to Charles Sturdevant.

"Good. That'll be all for now, John." Sturdevant's expression was predatory as he watched Nicholson leave his office. He turned to Owen Raynor. "Rutledge is the prospector who got the Sakhanese concessions. He's coming to beg. Watch and see."

"You don't want me to be here when you talk to him?"

"Yes, I do."

"Is that wise, C. J.? If he finds himself discussing Sakhana with you in front of the Assistant Secretary of the Treasury, it might give him ammunition—"

"Ammunition for what? On the contrary. Rutledge will finally realize how much power he and that tinpot Maharaja are bucking. He'll crumple."

Not gay, just sexless, the perfect corporate eunuch, Matt Rutledge thought, sizing up John Nicholson.

"Please follow me, Mr. Rutledge," Nicholson said, and even his voice was depersonalized. He led Matt through a maze of reception rooms and corridors in the board chairman's seventy-second-floor office suite.

"In here, please, Mr. Rutledge."

Sturdevant's private office was designed to overawe and intimidate, a huge cathedral-like room celebrating the greater glory of Sturdevant National. There were thirty feet or more of parquet flooring to cross before reaching a desk so large it could have served half a dozen men. Rutledge saw the first chink in Sturdevant's personal armor.

"Mr. Matthew Rutledge." John Nicholson announced—and withdrew. Charles Sturdevant did not bother to stand. Neither did the man who sat in a chair facing him, whom Matt recognized from newspaper photographs as Owen Raynor, the Assistant Secretary of the U. S. Treasury Department. Fascinating, Rutledge mused.

The banker's greeting and his introduction of Owen Raynor were curt. There were no offers of handshakes. Sturdevant indicated a chair set a few feet to the right of the one occupied by Raynor. "Sit down, Rutledge, and let's get to whatever business you may have—or think you have—with me."

"Thanks." Matt eased himself into the chair, lit a Camel.

Raynor felt uncomfortable. The tall, wide-shouldered

prospector in the Bill Blass suit hardly gave the impression that he had come to beg anything from anyone.

"I'm here because of Sakhana," Matt said, smoke drifting slowly from his nostrils.

"Sakhana?" Sturdevant repeated. "Oh, yes. You won the mining concessions one of my companies—Miramines, Incorporated—was after there. I presume you're now interested in selling them?"

"You presume wrong. I'm holding on to the concessions regardless of your sandbagging and bushwhacking operations."

"I'd be careful about making accusations, Rutledge. Miramines is a world-famous company. And, I might add, although I control it, the company has an autonomous management. Its executives operate legally and legitimately—"

"Bullshit. That's not what I hear by way of M. Michel Auerbach—among others."

Sturdevant was stunned but controlled his expression. He and Sheikh Nasib planned to rid themselves of Michel as a partner in the gold-corner venture. Could it be that Michel guessed this plan and was revealing information to protect himself?

"Whatever Michel Auerbach might have told you—"

"He hasn't told me anything," Matt chuckled. "I never met the man."

"But you said—"

"You must have a guilty conscience, Sturdevant. You leap to conclusions. I've been making the rounds of the banking world recently. It's a small world. When you bankers talk, your colleagues often know what you're really thinking. And doing."

He got up, stubbed his cigarette out in an ashtray on Sturdevant's desk and returned to his chair.

"There's a lot of gold being bought recently," Matt continued. "Now, let's suppose you were speculating heavily on the gold market—who knows, maybe even trying for a speculative monopoly. That might explain why a company you control is eager to get the Sakhanese concessions." Matt grinned shrewdly. "Several million ounces of new gold coming onto the market in the next six or seven months could play hell with the price structure."

Owen Raynor swallowed. Rutledge obviously knew far more than Sturdevant imagined. The banker himself remained impassive.

"There is no gold coming out of Sakhana," he said.

"Not yet," Matt said and readied the partial truths and Big Lies with which he hoped to unnerve Sturdevant. "Soon, though." He spoke with easy assurance. "You see, I've scored runs on you, Sturdevant. I finally got the development capital I was after."

Impossible, Sturdevant thought, his face flushing.

Rutledge was greatly encouraged. His whole intent was to shake Sturdevant's confidence, leave him beset by doubts and stampede him into making rash, reckless moves that would help unpin his plans and operations regarding Sakhana.

"In short, the reason for my visit here is to thumb my nose," Matt said, and started to get up.

"Wait a minute, Rutledge," Sturdevant said.

Point for my side, Matt thought as he paused. I'm getting to him.

"Ah—that is, it's always possible that the executives of Miramines exceeded their authority," Sturdevant said in a conciliatory tone. "I can't keep day-to-day touch with all my companies . . ."

Keep talking, Matt urged silently. When you've run out of horsecrap clauses, you might even say something.

". . . but I know they've been aggressive in their attempts to win the Sakhanese concessions. Frankly, I'd like to see Miramines have them. The company could do a superior job developing the fields you discovered and make significant contributions toward improving the economy of Sakhana.

"Miramines would be prepared to make a most reasonable offer to you and the Sakhanese government."

"First things first," Matt said. "Before you make any offers, who's going to clamp down on the New Delhi fanatics your pratboys got to make claims on Sakhana?"

"What the hell are you talking about?" Owen Raynor blurted, only to be silenced by a glare from Sturdevant.

"Yes, I did hear something about India wanting Sakhanese territory," Sturdevant said. "Of course, while I'm only a private citizen and can't guarantee anything, I'll be pleased to have a word with certain people in Washington on the matter."

"People like Jeffrey Tillinger?"

"That's mighty high on the Potomac organization chart," Sturdevant replied. "On the other hand, I appreciate the need for proper diplomatic representations to New Delhi—"

"Uh-huh," Matt interrupted, and got to his feet. "It's as I said earlier. You bankers do talk too much sometimes." He looked at his watch. "I've been here exactly sixteen minutes. That's all it took you to confirm every suspicion I have and every rumor I've heard. All I've got left for you and Mr. Assistant Secretary Raynor is an old tunnel miner's exit line. You've tried to fuck everybody else—now go fuck yourselves!"

He turned and his slow, lazy amble to the door was a gesture of supreme contempt.

Charles Sturdevant's face was an enraged purple mask as he punched down an intercom key.

"Nicholson, C. J.," the box sounded off.

"Listen! Rutledge claims he got the loan he was after. Find out who gave it to him—and block it, I don't care how!"

He released the key and glowered at Owen Raynor.

"Rutledge knows too much," Raynor muttered. "Can't you—"

"Stop him?" Sturdevant broke in. "It's been tried—more than once and in more ways than one. So far, he's been lucky. But we'll keep trying until his luck gives out." His face was gradually returning to its normal hue. "In the meantime, we can also go after him from other angles."

"Namely?"

"You should be able to handle some of them, Owen. Get on the phone to Washington. Order a full I.R.S. investigation of Rutledge. Pull strings and have the C.I.A. and F.B.I. run complete checks on him. If anyone turns up anything that can be used against him, I want it used!"

Matt returned directly to his apartment. He had no illusions about the nature of the reactions and responses his session with Sturdevant and Raynor would trigger.

"They'll get every official bureau and agency in Washington after me," he told Vivian and Luis. "This being Friday, nothing much will actually start happening until Monday morning—but I have to be out of the country by then. Luis, start packing me up—for a long stay."

"You're not going directly to Sakhana, are you?" Vivian asked.

"No. Back to England—then on to the Continent. I'll have to buy equipment and other gear and arrange to have it air-freighted to Sakhana somehow." He reached for the telephone. "Good thing I have most of my money banked abroad—but I have to transfer whatever I have in the States over there right away."

"Why in such a great hurry?"

"Honey, by Monday morning, Owen Raynor's Treasury Department will find a way to tie up every dime that can be traced to me."

"Matt, I want to go with you," Vivian said. "I have to be with you in this."

"Viv—"

"It's no use. I'll only tag after you, stay on your heels."

"That goes for me, too, Matt," Luis Hernandez declared. "Tin leg or no tin leg, I'm still as good as most guys you can hire."

Matt saw the determination in their faces. He realized it was useless to argue, and he felt grateful—and, to his surprise, glad.

"Okay," he growled. "All three of us get packed and we all go. Now let me start saving my hard-earned dough from phony internal revenue grabs." He picked up the receiver and began to dial.

"Matt," Vivian said, touching his cheek. "I love you."

He stopped dialing. "I love you, too, Viv." The words came naturally, automatically. He blinked and wanted to say more, but Vivian had vanished into another room. He smiled, depressed the receiver hook, released it and began dialing again.

9

Matt spent a hectic Friday afternoon. He arranged to cable-transfer all but a few thousand dollars of his American funds to the Bauer Kreditbank in Zurich and obtained his securities certificates from his broker. He held a hurried consultation with his New York attorney and placed the eighteen-pound Sakhanese gold nugget in a safety-deposit box. He wanted to avoid further risks in taking the nugget through customs in Britain or elsewhere.

Luis Hernandez worked feverishly, with Vivian Auerbach pitching in to help. By Saturday afternoon, everything that was to be taken had been packed. The apartment was closed up, and Matt informed the building management he was going on an extended trip. That evening he, Vivian and Luis—and more than five hun-

dred pounds of excess baggage—were aboarded a BOAC
Boeing 747 bound for London.

Rutledge took his usual suite at the Dorchester Hotel, a
separate single room for Luis Hernandez and, to maintain
appearances, another for Vivian, who registered under
her own name. "Things are bad enough already between
you and your father without having him find out you're
living with me openly in London," Matt argued.

The situation proved even worse than Rutledge had
feared. Vivian went to see her father on Sunday evening.
She returned to the Dorchester in less than an hour. She
was deathly pale and had been crying.

"I shouldn't have gone," she told Matt miserably.
"Daddy's attitude is that I stopped being his daughter—
and an Auerbach—the night he called your apartment
and learned I was there."

Matt felt as though he had been kicked in the
stomach.

"Viv—suppose I tried to talk to him," he stammered, then blurted, "Maybe if we got married—"

"No." Vivian shook her head. "Let's be honest, Matt.
You and I are far from being sure that we want to marry
each other, and it wouldn't change a thing with Daddy.
You're a Gentile. The Auerbachs are Jewish. Auerbachs
don't marry Gentiles—or fall in love with them. He's
already disowned me—not that I care—and he's had all
my personal things packed and sent into storage."

Rutledge could think of nothing to say.

"So, you're stuck with me for a while," Vivian said,
discovering that she could smile after all. "Just tell me
you love me and take me to bed and make love to me."

He held her very tightly when he said, "I love you,
Viv," and when they were in bed his lovemaking was
more gentle and tender than it had ever been.

On Monday morning Matt visited Jacob Auerbach and
Company. He had a little more than $100,000 on deposit
in the bank and wished to have this amount also trans-

ferred to his Swiss account. He did not ask for Sir David Auerbach, but dealt with a junior officer of the bank. When the necessary paperwork had been completed, he left, feeling deep regret that his decade-long business association and friendship with Sir David were finished.

Matt and Vivian lunched in the Rose Room of the Dorchester for sentimental reasons. It was there they had met for lunch the first time.

"Will you take me straight upstairs to your suite after we're done?" Vivian asked.

"And have you insist you don't want to wait when I say we have plenty of time?" Matt smiled.

"Some things change. We do have plenty of time today, don't we?"

"The rest of the day—and all night," Matt said— but he was wrong. They were finishing their coffee when he was paged. There was a telephone call for him. He excused himself and took the call in the lobby.

"Inspector Kirkland here. Remember me?"

Matt remembered. Inspector Thomas Kirkland had been investigating the murder of Rafin Kalsi, the man with the Sakhanese passport who was killed aboard the plane Rutledge had taken from Calcutta to London.

"You didn't waste much time finding out I was in town."

"Had your name red-tagged so the immigration people would notify me whenever you entered the U. K." Kirkland's tone was cheerful. "Mind if I drop by in half an hour?"

"No, I'll be here, Inspector." Whatever was up, best to find it out quickly, Matt thought. He hung up and went back to Vivian. "Sorry, darling. No replay this afternoon. Man's coming to see me. I'll have to see him alone. Go to the room you're supposed to be using. I'll call you when he leaves."

Inspector Kirkland accepted the drink Matt offered him.

"Cheers!" Kirkland grinned. "I see you've remained intact."

"Did you expect anything else?"

"Couldn't be sure. Y'see, certain sources provided us with considerable fascinating information. For example, Rafin Kalsi wasn't a Sakhanese merchant. He was a major in the Maharaja's Palace Guard—sent by His Majesty to look after you. To prevent *you* from being killed."

"I'll be damned!"

"Rutledge, you and the Maharaja have some extremely nasty—and potent—enemies."

Matt lit a Camel and leaned back thoughtfully. "You're not ordinary police, are you, Kirkland?"

"Regulations require me to maintain that I am." Kirkland emptied his glass. "Even when under the influence of drink."

Rutledge poured two more whiskeys. Kirkland was no plain cop, but belonged to—or worked very closely with—some high-level secret British government agency.

"Three questions," Kirkland said. "Why are you in London, where do you go next and will you return to Sakhana?"

"You get quick answers. I'm shopping for mining equipment and good miners here and on the Continent— and, yes, I'll be returning to Sakhana."

"Thought as much." Kirkland swallowed whiskey. "So you're looking for miners, eh? Could you use one with a fair military record who's had experience in coal and copper mining, knows something about Asia—and also holds a pilot's license?"

For Christ's sake, Matt thought. Thomas Kirkland probably has an unemployed buddy—or brother-in-law— he wants to unload on me. "I might be interested," he said without enthusiasm. "I'd have to talk to the man, though."

Kirkland grinned. "Of course. Go ahead. Talk away."

Matt almost spilled his drink. "You mean—"

"I mean that certain individuals with considerable authority—especially over me—want to see Sakhana remain independent. They believe the country should be permitted to develop its gold resources under terms most favorable to it. They agree that you're to be preferred over your—ah—competitors. And, they've formed the notion that because of my oddly assorted qualifications, you and the Maharaja might find me handy to have around."

Rutledge's green eyes narrowed. "Why? So Britain can stick an 'advisory' foot inside Sakhana again?"

"Hardly. Those days are long past. My job would be to help keep you and the Maharaja alive—and him in power—and to do honest miner's work in assisting you to produce gold."

Intuition assured Matt that Kirkland was being truthful. But even if he weren't, it would be wiser to have him within easy reach.

"Okay, you're hired. Now what?"

"Oh, we're accustomed to arranging these things over here. My personnel folders simply disappear from the files. Whenever you're ready, I am—as an employee on your payroll, subject to your orders, obliged to go when and where you tell me."

Matt and Kirkland talked for another hour, much longer than Rutledge had anticipated. Just as Kirkland was leaving, the telephone rang. Matt assumed it was Vivian, wondering why he had been delayed. He grabbed the receiver and said, "Hold on a second," then laid the instrument on a tabletop. He saw Kirkland to the door, shook his hand, saying, "I'll be in touch with you before the end of the week." He closed the door and returned to the telephone, picked it up and said, "Hi, I'm sorry—"

"Is this Mr. Matthew Rutledge?" It wasn't Vivian. The voice was male, clipped to ultrafine Public School tolerances.

"Yes. Who's this?"

"My name, Mr. Rutledge, is Alan Leopold."

Oh, brother, this is all I needed, Matt thought.

"I'm in the lobby. I know it's most irregular and an imposition, but I'd appreciate a few minutes—"

"No imposition at all. Please come on up."

Matt depressed the hook, called Vivian's room.

"I'm still tied up, honey," he said. He did not reveal that Alan Leopold was on his way for what might well prove to be an abrasive confrontation. "Hang in for another half hour or so."

Alan Leopold was obviously one of those Englishmen who always did the right thing. He was dressed in an expensive—and mandatory—London-financial-section uniform. Conservative dark gray suit, and proper overcoat. He carried a bowler—and a brolly rolled to a thickness not much greater than that of a malacca cane. He shook hands with precisely the correct degree of pressure. He said he did not believe he would be staying long enough to bother taking off his overcoat and did not relinquish his bowler or brolly.

So this is my predecessor, Matt thought, eyeing Leopold. He was slender, with the lithely athletic body and healthy complexion that even those Britishers in sedentary occupations so often manage to maintain with little or no apparent effort. He was about five-eleven, tall but still three inches shorter than Matt. His age was perhaps twenty-eight or twenty-nine compared to Matt's thirty-four, and he had blondish hair and refined-handsome features.

"Sit down, please," Matt said. "Care for a drink?"

"No, thank you." Alan Leopold seated himself in an armchair, his manner making it clear he did not intend to remain long. He studied Matt for a moment. "I've already apologized for disturbing you. Now I should explain that I'm not here on my own account. It's because of Sir David."

"He asked you to talk to me?"

"Good Lord, no. He's far too proud for anything

like that. But I know how deeply he's been affected by Vivian's alienation from him, and I thought that if I—"

"Save it!" Matt rasped. "I've known David Auerbach more than ten years. I always thought he was intelligent, reasonable, understanding—a man with a heart and a mind. A real person. The *alienation*—as you put it—was his idea, not Vivian's. It turns out that he's intolerant, a prude and a bigot!"

"Mr. Rutledge. You do not—you cannot—appreciate that generations, even centuries, of religious tradition—"

"Balls! I personally have no religion. None. But I respect the religious feelings of others—until they reach a point where they become fanaticism, a form of obsession."

"The Auerbachs have been Jewish—"

"So what? Let's turn this whole business around and get a fresh perspective on it. If some pea-brained, prejudiced Gentile tells his child to stay away from Jews because they're Jewish, then the Gentile is labeled an anti-Semite, a bigot, God only knows what else. But when David Auerbach rejects his daughter because she falls in love with a Gentile, that's different. All of a sudden, it's hallowed religious tradition."

"You're oversimplifying—"

"Could be. In any case, it's not up to me to make any further decisions. I've made mine. I want Vivian to be with me. If any changes of mind are to be made, they'll have to be made by David Auerbach—or by Vivian. Talk to him—or to her."

"That's impossible. They and I are too—"

"Yeah, I know. Too proud."

Alan Leopold was on his feet and moving toward the door. He paused and turned to face Matt.

"There's only one thing more I have to say, Mr. Rutledge—a sort of footnote, really. It happens that I'm aware that a number of people dislike you intensely. They

223

are mainly individuals for whom I have very little respect. However, I find myself in wholehearted agreement where you are concerned. I promise you this. I shall do all I can to help them break you."

Alan Leopold made his exit. Matt hurried to the telephone and called Vivian's room.

"I'll be down to get you in a minute," he said. "In fact, I'm already on my way—and, hey, this time *I* don't want to wait!"

He said nothing to her then—or later—about Alan Leopold's visit.

10

On Wednesday, February 27, gold rose to $178 an ounce on the London Market.

Matt Rutledge considered it was time that he communicated with Maharaja Narayan Mahendra Karamchad. He composed a radiogram carefully.

> AM NOW IN PROCESS OF OBTAINING EQUIPMENT AND SKILLED
> MANPOWER WHICH WILL BE AIRLIFTED TO KANGTEK QUICKLY
> STOP WE WILL BEGIN DEVELOPMENT OF SER-GI RI SOON STOP
> AM PLANNING TO ARRIVE WITH MY ADVANCE PARTY IN NEXT
> WEEK OR TEN DAYS STOP BEFORE LONG WE SHALL SEE ALL
> THE STORM CLOUDS DISPERSE

Matt had the radiogram transmitted through ordinary commercial channels. He knew all radiograms to Sakhana were monitored by the Indian government. He strongly suspected that they were also monitored by the network of agents Charles Sturdevant and his Miramines had inside India. He felt that one way or another, his message would be made known to Sturdevant or his close associates.

He was right.

Charles Sturdevant had believed Matt's claim that

he had obtained the loan he sought. But, despite his orders—and all his aides' best efforts—Sturdevant was unable to obtain any clue as to who might have provided Rutledge with the money, and the billionaire began to wonder if Matt had been bluffing. A copy of the radiogram to Narayan reached Sturdevant. Its contents and confident tone appeared to confirm everything Matt had said. Sturdevant placed another of his frequent conference calls to Sheikh Nasib and Michel Auerbach. He read them the radio intercept.

"Rutledge wouldn't lie to the Maharaja," Sturdevant said. "Now, it will take him time to start production. We're bound to stop him before he makes much progress. All the same, I suggest we take some profits in case there's a price drop when the news breaks that goldfields are being opened up in Sakhana."

"Yes," Michel Auerbach agreed. "We can safely feed anywhere up to a third of what we hold into the market."

"The price will fall," Sheikh Nasib said, "but not below our present cost average. We can begin buying again once Rutledge has been neutralized or India has cracked the Sakhanese nut."

The syndicate in which the three men were partners started selling gold at a rate that was to depress the free market price by $20 an ounce within the following week.

Matt Rutledge appreciated that his maneuver was no more than a minor feint in his war of nerves against Charles Jordan Sturdevant and the billionaire's associates in the gold-corner scheme. He was also aware that the message he sent to Narayan was grossly misleading. The Maharaja would believe that Rutledge had gotten the entire $20 million he went after. He would have to make his explanations to Narayan personally and hope that he understood the reasons. In the meantime, although erroneous, the story that Rutledge had obtained $20 million would spread from one end of Sakhana to another. It would strengthen Narayan's hand and his hold on the throne and undermine whatever credence the dissident elements inside Sakhana might have gained.

It was a paradox that if Matt had really gotten the $20 million for a full-scale development program, he would have had a far easier task than he faced in planning a limited operation. With $20 million, he could have contracted with large construction companies to build work camps, roads and airstrips in Sakhana and have bought standard pattern gold mining equipment and machinery.

But he had only his own $2 million and the somewhat more than $750,000 Vivian insisted on transferring from her name into his Swiss bank account. With such comparatively limited capital, the process of recasting his plans and revising his goals became one of miniaturization.

Available funds would permit building only one or two new airstrips in Sakhana. These would have to be small, with short, unsurfaced runways that could not accommodate large transport planes. Since smaller aircraft were to be used, it followed that big, bulky items of machinery and equipment could not be air-ferried into Sakhana. The smallest, lightest mining gear and construction equipment had to be sought out. Even many of these items would have to be dismantled, air-shipped in sections and reassembled after arrival in Sakhana.

Matt reasoned that he could charter large aircraft to fly gear from England and Europe to Darjeeling. There, the shipments would have to be broken down into much smaller loads for loading into craft capable of landing on the airstrip in Kangtek. This required him to make additional precautionary allowances for extra expenditures.

"The Indian government is hard-assing Sakhana—thanks to Sturdevant and his crew," he told Hernandez. "That means they'll use every bureaucratic trick to hold up transshipments and clearances out of Darjeeling. And that, in turn, means I'll have to set aside at least a hundred thousand dollars for palm greasing."

"Why not fly our stuff in by way of Nepal?" Luis asked. "The field at Katmandu can take the big commercial planes."

"Wouldn't gain anything," Matt said, shaking his head. "It's too long a hop from Katmandu to Kangtek. The smaller planes we'd use for shuttling would have to carry overloads of fuel, leaving too little freight-carrying capacity. We'll just have to bribe our way in and out of Darjeeling."

"Suppose those politicians in New Delhi are so worked up that we can't bribe them?"

"Luis, there's one lesson I've learned in life. No politician ever reaches a state where he *can't* be bribed. All he does is raise the asking price."

Ordinary citizen Thomas Kirkland—his personnel files presumably having disappeared from whatever official offices in which they were kept—established instant rapport with Vivian Auerbach and Luis Hernandez. The burly, fortyish Kirkland had an easy, even-tempered manner, and beneath it one could sense solid integrity.

"You only have to look at his face and eyes," Vivian told Matt. "He looks a little Humphrey Bogart-ish. English Home Counties version, of course. He's the sort we used to send out to build Empire, yet there's no air of Old School Tie about him, thank God. But there is humor—and kindness—in his eyes."

Luis Hernandez stated his approving verdict, too. "Kirkland's the kind of guy I want on my side if I get into a jam—and I figure we're going to be in a lot of jams, Matt. You made a great choice—only where the hell did you find him?"

"I heard of him through a friend," Matt lied. Kirkland's background and the true nature of their relationship would have to remain a secret.

Tom—the nickname basis was formed quickly—Tom

Kirkland's qualifications were all he had claimed them to be and more. He did have much knowledge and experience of mining.

"Almost became a mining engineer like yourself," he told Matt. "But I got sidetracked."

"Into the service of Her Brittanic Majesty?"

"Something like that. I'll tell you the story—or rather parts of a reasonably accurate version—someday."

Matt's financial squeeze made improvisations and shortcuts imperative if they were to surmount their myriad problems. Having started his career as an independent, working on the thinnest of frayed shoestrings, Matthew Rutledge had mastered these arts. Hernandez had spent much of his life booming around the world as a miner and was no less adept, although somewhat more limited. To Matt's boundless relief—and delight—Tom Kirkland was not only their peer, but had the priceless added assets of a photographic memory and what seemed an almost limitless circle of acquaintances, as he demonstrated almost immediately.

Bulldozers were crucial items on Matt's shopping list. There were none in Sakhana. At least three would be needed to level airstrips and carve a minimal number of access roads. Commercial models were expensive and too heavy to airlift from Darjeeling to Sakhana by any plane capable of using the Kangtek strip. Matt mentioned the problem to Tom Kirkland, who thought for a moment and said, "Y'know, I may have the answer."

He remembered that during the 1956 Suez Crisis, Britain had ordered two hundred bulldozers for engineering units of airborne divisions. The dozers were tiny, light enough to be carried by two-engined propeller-driven transports and dropped by parachute. Subsequent cuts in the size of the British army and the adoption of new equipment had left one hundred fifty dozers in a Portsmouth depot. Ideally suited for Matt's purposes, they had long been for sale as government surplus.

"I'll ring up a chap I know in the Defense Ministry," Kirkland said.

It was arranged that Rutledge would buy six machines for the equivalent of $5,000, a fraction of what he would have to pay for a single standard commercial bulldozer. Naturally, the transaction required numerous government forms in innumerable copies.

To Matt's astonishment, Vivian Auerbach had an electric typewriter sent up to his suite and did the work with professional efficiency.

"I didn't even know you could type!" Matt exclaimed in wonder. "You're the last person I'd have expected—"

"Darling." She shot him an arch and provocative look from under her long lashes. "You've been far too obsessed with a single area of my talents even to ask if I had any others."

Matt, Vivian, Hernandez and Kirkland interacted with a rare degree of ease, forming a smoothly functioning and creative team, with one idea engendering another.

The night after Vivian had typed up the government forms, Luis Hernandez came to Matt's suite. He had spent much time poring over copies of the maps and aerial photos Rutledge had brought with him from Sakhana.

"You're going to set up a base camp, like you did before, and then hike overland to the Ser-gi Ri, right?" he asked Rutledge.

"That's the plan."

"You said there's no place to land a plane near those mountains."

"We've been over that before, Luis. No, there isn't."

"I'm not so sure." Hernandez spread a photostat of the map Rutledge had drawn of the final approaches to the Ser-gi Ri and the mountains themselves. "You went through this gorge"—Luis pointed—"and came out into a valley here. You crossed the valley, got to the riverbank at the mountain base and found the bench placer deposits. Isn't that how it was?"

"Sure. What are you getting at?"

"Why can't we fly right into that valley with a copter?"

"Because any chopper that could set down there, with the prevailing winds and air currents, would have to be in the Chinook class. It couldn't be rented. I'd have to buy it, and one of those babies costs millions."

"How about a rugged STOL plane like a Pilatus or Beaver?"

"Forget it. There isn't a level space bigger than a carpet in that valley, and there are nine million boulders in the way."

"A few guys, some A. N. Gelatine Dynamite seventy-five to bust up those boulders and a bulldozer are all it would take to clear a strip."

"You're hallucinating, Luis. You can't carry a dozer over the mountains on pack mules."

"And you're not thinking. Look. The men slog in overland with the explosives and start blasting boulders. Those dozers you're buying were built to be parachuted to airborne troops. We get some cargo chutes, we load a dozer into a Beaver, take it over the valley and drop it in. The guys already there can level off ground and inside a week, the next STOL lands like it was at Kennedy."

Matt stared at Hernandez. "I'll be a son of a bitch," he muttered. "Now why in the hell didn't I think of that?"

It was a stroke of genius, Rutledge reflected. One that would save untold time and labor, eliminating the need to bring every last item of supplies and equipment overland from a base camp. If Luis's suggestion worked— and there was no reason it shouldn't—almost everything could be flown into the valley at the foot of the Ser-gi Ri.

True, the STOL aircraft used for the purpose would have to carry numerous loads and each landing and takeoff was bound to be risky. Still, the entire operation would be greatly accelerated. Even more important, as gold was recovered from the fields, it could be flown direct to Kangtek. He had been estimating ten days for gold shipments from the fields via pack train to a base camp and then by air to the capital.

A direct airlift meant a reduction of shipment time to less than two hours. Of course, Rutledge reminded himself, all that still lay very much in the future. He was in England. A huge amount of preliminary work and purchasing remained to be done even before the first load of gear could be airfreighted to Darjeeling. There would be even more work after that before so much as an ounce of gold could be taken from the Ser-gi Ri.

Thomas Kirkland was enthusiastic the next morning when Matt told him of Hernandez's suggestion.

"It inspires me," he chortled. "There must be whole treasure troves for us in the various ministries' surplus catalogs!"

There were.

Kirkland called government offices, bureaus and agencies. Within two days, he had located a barely credible array of surplus materials—all excess and available for sale. He read off part of his list to Matt, Vivian and Luis.

"The bulldozers come with their loading pallets," he grinned. "And I found brand-new cargo chutes for them —the government will be overjoyed to sell any number at thirty pounds apiece. Ah, now here's a find. Hutments, six-man, portable, weatherproofed—unitized, air-transportable, complete with chemical amenities—"

"Mind translating that for me?" Luis broke in.

"Gladly. Hutments are crude cottagelike structures designed for use as temporary troop housing. These provide space for six men. They are packed in containers made to fit into any aircraft larger than a Piper Cub. Each has its own chemical toilet."

"They would take care of housing for the work force," Matt observed. "Can we buy twenty?"

"I've put in a request for twenty-four," Kirkland said. "They're only fifty pounds apiece."

He returned to his list. It was long and included handtools, beds and bedding, pneumatic drills, air compressors and electric generators. Many were suitable only for general construction, but several were readily adaptable for use in actual mining operations.

"Bargains, all of them," he concluded. "I suggest we buy what we think we'll need, have everything shipped to Gatwick Airport and stored there. I have a friend who owns a small charter airline based there. He has two DC-six's converted for carrying air freight. He'll give us a reasonable price on charters to Darjeeling whenever we're ready to start shipments."

"You handle it, Tom," Matt nodded. Kirkland was doing a magnificent job, saving him hundreds of thousands of dollars.

Free market gold slid to $160 an ounce on March 5.

In Washington, Secretary of State Jeffrey Tillinger received a midnight telephone call from the Indian ambassador advising him that Prime Minister Indira Gandhi's government would loose another diplomatic broadside against Sakhana late the following day.

"There will be a demand for a conference to study long-standing border disputes," the ambassador confided. "In addition, certain members of the Congress party will publicly denounce the Maharaja of Sakhana as a tyrant and despot."

Tillinger immediately relayed this information to Assistant Treasury Secretary Owen Raynor, calling him at his home. Tillinger could not know that he was calling at a very bad time for Raynor. The Assistant Treasury Secretary, his wife, Adele, and a buxom Department of Agriculture stenographer were busily engaged in a variety of imaginative sexual acts.

Owen Raynor was forced to detach himself from

232

the tangle on his bed to speak with Tillinger—and then regretfully take a longer recess while he telephoned Charles Jordan Sturdevant, passing on what he had heard. That done, Raynor returned to bed. He ruefully observed that Adele and the stenographer had apparently continued their strenuous activities without him. Indeed, he suspected that they had been oblivious to his absence.

Charles Sturdevant's conference call took longer than usual to complete. The Emir of Hajar was said to be meeting with his Council of Ministers. Michel Auerbach was not at home or at his office. An hour passed before he was located.

At last, the three men were linked together and Sturdevant related what he had been told by Owen Raynor.

"The New Delhi nutcracker is tightening," Sheikh Nasib commented. "The Sakhanese shell should break soon."

"Precisely," Sturdevant said. "In my opinion, we can resume our buying."

"Most definitely," Nasib declared.

Michel Auerbach was hesitant. "My Elysée Palace informants tell me Pompidou has taken a turn for the worse. You will recall that I warned of the possible ramifications if he dies."

Sturdevant remembered the incident clearly. Weeks before, when word of the French President's critical illness first leaked from the Elysée, Michel had become jumpy. He feared that the elections which would inevitably follow Pompidou's death might result in exposure of the gold-corner conspiracy and his part in it. He and his bank, the Société Auerbach, could not afford to have that happen, he had told Sturdevant.

"Michel, if you wish to withdraw from our venture, say so," Sturdevant said. Nasib and I will cut you out soon enough, no matter what you do, he added to himself.

"*Mais non,* Charles! I merely—"

"Then we are unanimous," Sheikh Nasib al Rahman interrupted impatiently. "We buy again."

A new surge of gold buying sent London Market prices up $4 dollars an ounce on March 7. And newspapers carried stories of India's new demands on Sakhana. No correspondent or editorial writer saw any connection between the two developments.

On March 8, more gold buying caused the price of gold to rise another $8—to $170 per ounce.

Matthew recognized the relationship between the news from New Delhi and the resurgence of gold buying as cause and effect. That evening, he talked with Vivian, Luis Hernandez and Tom Kirkland in his suite.

"I'm leaving London tomorrow for Sakhana," he announced.

"Not alone, Matt!" Vivian exclaimed. "If you're going, I'm coming with you!"

"I hoped you'd say that," Matt smiled at her. He did want her with him. But the decision had to be her own. Now that she had made and stated it, the question was settled. He turned toward the two men.

"The opposition is increasing the pressure on Narayan again," he said. "I have to be in Kangtek to bring him up to date and do whatever I can to keep the situation from deteriorating at that end."

Rutledge lit a cigarette. "Luis, Tom, you'll have to take care of the purchasing and hiring. You both know what material and what kind of people we need as well as I do. Keep me posted by radiograms to Kangtek— address them to the Maharaja. I'll keep in touch with you by radiogram. If anything urgent turns up, I'll go across the border to India and telephone you."

"Matt." Kirkland cleared his throat. "You seem to forget one of the principal reasons you hired me. I was to, well, stay close on your heels."

"A matter of priorities, Tom. It's more important

that you and Luis stay here and if necessary shop France and West Germany. The faster you get everything assembled and on its way, the better chance we will have of coming out of this business with whole skins"—he grinned broadly—"and fat bank accounts."

"Want to give us a deadline, Matt?" Luis asked before Kirkland could make any comment.

"If you can wrap everything up in three weeks, have the first air shipments en route by then, I'll be more than satisfied."

"How about ten days?" Tom Kirkland asked quietly.

"Ten days? Christ, that would need a miracle—a whole flock of miracles!"

"Then we'll just have to work them," Kirkland said. "And if you don't mind, I'll go to your bar and pour us all some very large whiskeys—so we can drink to it."

11

The diplomatic offensive launched from New Delhi on February 21 had caused consternation in Sakhana. Within the Sakhanese government, it was Maharaja Narayan Mahendra Karamchad who outwardly seemed to be the least disturbed. A tough, crafty statesman who had met countless diplomatic crises in his forty years on the throne, he knew it was imperative that he appear confident, even serene.

"India has tried to absorb Sakhana for centuries," he told Tsering Dorje. "This is but another attempt to create fear among our people. We must remain calm, avoiding both panic and any provocation."

"If the Indians attack, we are defenseless, Majesty," Dorje declared. "They have the most modern weapons, a huge army—"

"These are not always deciding factors, my friend. We need look no further than the American experience in Vietnam." Narayan's strong face was tranquil. "The Indian government is divided and rotten with corruption. India's economy is a shambles. India depends on foreign loans, credits and gifts to exist. It cannot afford to lose these—as it would if it moved against a tiny country like Sakhana."

Dorje said only, "I shall proceed as you command, Majesty."

"Then compose a long, flowery diplomatic note that makes vague promises to hold consultations in the unspecified future. We must gain time. Once the goldfields of the Ser-gi Ri are opened, every Western power will become our ally from fear that India might control the wealth. The clamor from New Delhi will fade into silence."

Tsering Dorje and Dep Bahadur Singh were unnerved by the Indian territorial claims. Both assumed they were another manifestation of Indian expansionism like the 1971 war with Pakistan over Bangladesh and the military occupation and takeover of Sikkim in 1973. Neither man dreamed that New Delhi's demands on Sakhana had been instigated by Charles Jordan Sturdevant through the agency of the American Secretary of State Jeffrey Tillinger.

Dorje and Singh realized that the threat of an Indian invasion of Sakhana endangered them as much as it did the Maharaja. They would lose their positions, power— and, not improbably, their lives—if India annexed their country. For this reason they reluctantly agreed it was necessary to suspend their plans for staging a coup d'etat and toppling Narayan Mahendra Karamchad from his throne.

Kancha and Baki, the two Palace Guardsmen who had accompanied Rutledge into the High Mountains, had been made lieutenants in reward for their bravery and loyalty. After Rutledge's departure from Sakhana they were assigned to personal attendance on the Maharaja.

It was Kancha who brought the radiogram to Narayan on February 28. The message was like an elixir to the Maharaja. He joyously read it to Kancha.

Then he said, "I shall miss you here in the palace."

Kancha misinterpreted the words.

"Your Majesty, I have offended—"

"Offended?" Narayan smiled. "On the contrary, you have performed your duties in superior fashion. I say that I shall miss you because when Rutledge *sahib* returns, you will again go into the Cen-po Ri with him."

"I humbly thank Your Majesty," Kancha said, meaning it. He held Rutledge in high esteem and was eager to participate in the project that would make Sakhana rich.

"Now hurry and summon the Prime Minister," Narayan said. "He must be informed of this good news."

"Fortune has smiled," Dorje told Singh after his audience with the Maharaja. "Make it known through the country that Rutledge will be back in Sakhana soon to mine the gold of the Ser-gi Ri. Have your agents paint glowing pictures of the wealth that all Sakhanese may expect to enjoy."

Singh's long face was dour. "There are many who will remember the stories spread about Narayan and Rutledge planning to keep the gold for themselves," he cautioned.

"Your men must say those were lies concocted by Indian spies and saboteurs." Dorje's close-set eyes hardened. "Of course, a few may remember too well and speak out too loudly. They are to be put to death publicly for treason."

"Tsering, it was last month that our Living God commanded there be no executions."

"That was before India made its demands on us. I shall explain to Narayan that those executed were agents in the pay of New Delhi. Like the people, he will believe what he is told."

* * *

Two days later, Ramesh Anwar appeared in Kangtek and demanded to see General Singh. Anwar had obtained a monitored copy of Matthew Rutledge's radiogram and received instructions from his clients.

"What do you intend doing after Rutledge arrives?" Anwar demanded.

"That remains to be seen," Singh responded. "You are Indian and live in Calcutta, Anwar. With India becoming more hostile, we Sakhanese cannot afford drastic action that may disturb our internal situation."

"What comes out of New Delhi is empty talk."

"For us to believe that would be a dangerous gamble. We have not forgotten Sikkim." General Singh brushed at the lapels of his military tunic. "You have constantly spoken of the immense power of the personages you represent. Yet they were no more able to eliminate Rutledge than we. His message shows they could not even prevent him from obtaining the huge sum he went to borrow in the West."

"I am not here to discuss anything but the promises and assurances you made in the past—and ask what you plan to do in the future."

"Listen to me, Anwar. *You* have assured me that you are employed by men who can—and do—control entire nations. Very well. Let them use their influence in New Delhi to silence those who are making threats against Sakhana. Then the Prime Minister and I will have free hands once more."

"General, you are a fool. Who do you think inspired New Delhi to make its claims against Sakhana? It was these men who have lost patience waiting for the Sakhanese concessions. They are building fires under you."

So, that is how it is, Singh reflected. This could make matters much worse—or much better—depending entirely on how Tsering Dorje and he made their moves.

"No, Anwar," he shook his head. "They—your men of great power—are the fools." The general's smile was sardonic. "If your word carries any weight, I recommend

238

you remind them that the Indians are even more avaricious than they. The Indian government gives away nothing of value. If India takes Sakhana, it will take the Ser-gi Ri too. For itself. There will be no concessions to any Western countries. That treacherous witch who governs India will turn to her Soviet friends for technical aid to develop the Ser-gi Ri."

Ramesh Anwar experienced a sinking sensation. General Singh was right. The Americans, never able to comprehend Asian psychology, had blundered again. They had used India to set a trap but, as Singh pointed out, when sprung, it would close on themselves. Anwar determined that he would send urgent warnings along the chain of communication.

"I repeat what I have said so often," General Singh murmured. "Leave us to ourselves and allow us to proceed at our own pace. Only then will your clients obtain the concessions now held by Rutledge."

The next word Narayan received from Matthew Rutledge came on the morning of March 9. It was a radiogram sent from London the night before.

AM FLYING TO CALCUTTA THEN DARJEELING TOMORROW STOP WILL RADIO MY EXPECTED TIME OF ARRIVAL FROM DARJEELING AFTER AIRPLANE RENTAL ARRANGED STOP AM BEING ACCOMPANIED BY MISS VIVIAN AUERBACH WHO IS BRITISH SUBJECT STOP PLEASE WAIVE ENTRY PERMIT FORMALITIES FOR HER AND YES YOUR MAJESTY SHE AND I WILL SHARE WHATEVER HOUSING ACCOMMODATIONS THAT MAY BE PROVIDED FOR US STOP IN FRIENDSHIP SIGNED RUTLEDGE

Narayan was delighted that Rutledge would be in Kangtek within a day or two and pleased that he was bringing a woman with him. A man like Matthew Rutledge needs a woman, Narayan reflected, and if he thinks enough of this one to bring her to Sakhana, so much the better. It was yet another indication that Rutledge was prepared for a long stay.

Lieutenant Baki was attending the Maharaja that

day, and he had brought the radiogram to the royal audience chamber.

"Lieutenant Baki."

"Your Majesty?"

"The large suite of apartments in the west wing of the palace—the one used for visiting princes. Give orders it is to be made ready today for Rutledge *sahib*."

"Yes, Majesty."

"And Lieutenant, select three of the best serving women in the palace. They will be assigned to wait on the lady who is coming with him."

The large amount of luggage that Matt and Vivian had brought with them was loaded aboard the Pilatus. Vivian got into the copilot's seat. For an instant, Rutledge felt a pang of grief. He remembered Sita, how she had sat in the same seat, flying with him over the Cen-po Ri, experting operating the bulky Fairchild K-22 camera....

"What's wrong, darling?" Vivian asked. "You seem— oh, I don't know, terribly sad."

"I'm only concentrating—thinking ahead," Matt said—and then smiled, his sense of sorrow disappearing. Sita was gone, dead, and nothing could bring her back to life. And he had not loved Sita. He did love Vivian. "Your belt fastened?"

"Yes."

He strapped himself into the pilot's seat, started the engine, and asked the control tower for takeoff clearance and taxiing instructions. Several minutes later, the plane was airborne and climbing to its cruising altitude. Matt switched on the transmitter again and called the Kangtek radio station.

Matt made three low sweeps over Kangtek to give Vivian the same view that he had enjoyed the first time he visited the Sakhanese capital. She was fascinated.

"That's the palace compound you've told me about?"

she asked. Matt said it was. "It's even bigger than I imagined," Vivian added. She laughed. "Maybe you shouldn't have brought me."

"Oh?"

"You said the Maharaja is a widower. I might decide to become the British Hope Cooke." Vivian Auerbach seldom giggled. She did now. "I've been cut adrift from the Auerbach family because you're a Gentile. Think of the reaction if I married an Oriental Living God!"

Matt thought it best to make no comment.

Matt noted that the reception committee at the Kangtek strip was the most elaborate yet. In addition to Tsering Dorje and General Singh, there were several other ministers, and the honor guard was larger and in full dress uniform. Nonetheless, despite the effusive greetings and the masses of flowers that aides presented to Vivian, Rutledge sensed disturbing undercurrents in the manner of the officials. The Indian threats are getting to them, he thought.

"His Majesty commanded that his own limousine be provided for you and Miss Auerbach," Dorje said. "It is over there." He paused, lowered his voice so that Vivian could not hear. "Naturally, the driver and his assistant are armed, and there will be cars with guards preceding and following."

Vivian stared at the scarlet and saffron-yellow Bentley for a moment before getting into the back seat.

"A striking combination—to say the least," she murmured to Matt.

"Royal colors," he said out of the corner of his mouth. He took her arm as if to help her into the car and lightly jabbed two fingers into her ribs, just below her breast. "You can wear them all the time after you're the Maharanee."

Vivian kept her face straight. "You are a bastard," she whispered, turning to smile at Dorje and Singh as she got into the Bentley.

12

When the convoy of vehicles drove into the palace compound grounds, Vivian's hazel eyes grew huge. "It's fabulous—a fairyland!" she exclaimed. They approached the palace itself. Vivian seized Matt's arm.

"Think of making love there!" Her tone was sultry —and serious. She was staring at the great marble pool in front of the palace. "On the grass beside the pool— some night when the moon is full!"

"Nymphomaniac." Matt chuckled, but squeezed her thigh. Then he caught a glimpse of the guest villa where he had stayed with Sita, and his mood changed. He wondered if her killer had been caught and punished. Probably not, he thought. Otherwise Dorje would not have made such a point about armed guards.

The limousine braked in front of the main entrance to the Maharaja's palace.

Narayan Mahendra Karamchad and his courtiers, gathered in the Council Chamber, were resplendent in ceremonial dress. Matt bowed. Tsering Dorje presented Vivian, who curtsied.

Rutledge guessed that Narayan was shrewdly using the occasion as a morale-building device. It would be an emphatic statement of his confidence that Matt's return signaled the beginning of a new and affluent era for Sakhana. This made Matt all the more apprehensive. How would Narayan react when he learned the truth about the failure to obtain the loan and the drastic scaling-down of development plans?

The Maharaja's formal remarks ended. Speaking informally, he announced that there would be an official banquet for Matthew Rutledge and Vivian Auerbach that night. All those gathered in the Council Chamber had already been commanded to attend. Now, they were dismissed. Miss Auerbach was to be escorted to the "Apartment of the Princes" in the west wing. Narayan wished to speak alone with Matt in the small audience chamber.

The room emptied. Matt had noticed that Narayan was flanked by Kancha and Baki, who now wore the ornate uniforms of commissioned officers in the Palace Guard. He shook the two men's hands warmly and congratulated them on their promotions. They responded proudly and, standing at attention, declared they earnestly desired to accompany Rutledge *sahib-kamal* into the High Mountains again.

Narayan and Matt seated themselves on couches in the small audience chamber. The Maharaja loosened the high standup collar of his royal ceremonial robes. Rutledge took a pack of Camels from his jacket pocket and lit one.

"Your lady is beautiful, and she has charmed me completely," Narayan said. "I congratulate you—but I see that I do not need to wish you happiness with her. It is obvious that you have it."

"Thank you, Your Majesty."

"It is I who should thank you, Matthew," Narayan said. "You succeeded. I knew in my heart that you would."

Rutledge drew on his cigarette nervously.

"No, Your Majesty." He eyed Narayan squarely. "I did not succeed. The conspiracy you sensed here in Sakhana reaches much further than either of us dreamed. The doors I expected to have open were shut in my face. I did not obtain the loan I sought."

A muscle in Narayan's saturnine face pulsed. It was the only visible indication of the impact that Matt's words were having on him.

"You gave no hint of this in your radiogram."

"I devised an alternative plan, Your Majesty. I have

243

my own money. Miss Auerbach has lent me almost eight hundred thousand dollars more—"

"Wait a moment. The lady's name has struck a bell. Is it not the same as that of the banker you know so well in London?"

"Yes. Vivian is his daughter. The money she lent me is her own."

Narayan's worldly eyes grew wise. "She did this against her father's wishes because of you?"

"Partly—even mainly. But her father is also a victim of the conspiracy. He cannot oppose the conspirators for reasons that are many and complex. Vivian is determined to fight them."

Matt took a deep breath.

"Perhaps if I start with the events that took place after I left Kangtek . . ."

"Please do."

Rutledge gave Narayan a complete account of his experiences. He began with the murder of Rafin Kalsi and the attempt made on his own life in London. He explained what he knew about the nature and extent of the Sturdevant-masterminded gold-corner plot and how it undoubtedly related to events and trends inside Sakhana. He told of the reception given him by bankers in London and New York and voiced his conviction that Sturdevant had manipulated India into making territorial claims against Sakhana. He finished by detailing the decisions he had made in London and what further steps would be taken.

"Our new plans are largely improvised," Matt admitted. "With financial resources only a seventh of what they should be, we will have to rely to a great extent on ingenuity, expedients and even makeshift arrangements. Nonetheless, if Your Majesty concurs, I'm going ahead. My people and I will bring gold out of the High Mountains—in significant quantities and in time to wreck the plans of those ranged against us."

Narayan smiled. He was over sixty years old, and he had learned much about life and about men. Matthew

Rutledge was a member of a rare breed. A man of honor and of his word, he was exhilarated by challenge.

"My confidence in you has not lessened, Matthew," he declared. "If anything, it has increased. Oddly enough, I feel that you will accomplish far more now than you would have if you had returned to Sakhana with twenty, fifty, even a hundred million dollars."

"I hope you're right."

"And so, my friend, do I. Bear in mind that as ruler of Sakhana I have only two choices in regard to the Ser-gi Ri. One is to open my kingdom to the great Western multinational corporations like the Miramines concern controlled by the billionaire Sturdevant. That, as I have told you before, would mean the end of Sakhanese independence and a culture shock of proportions my people could not withstand. It would also mean precious little revenue for Sakhana—and my finish as the ruler of my country."

He paused, making a gesture with his slender but sinewy-strong hands.

"Oh, I would doubtless be allowed to remain perched on my throne as a figurehead, but power would be wielded by those who know—or care—nothing about the deeper needs of the Sakhanese people. And when my son would succeed me, his power would be even further diluted."

He looked at Matt with an expression of trust and confidence.

"That is one choice—and I have rejected it. Your proposals offered me the alternative, the second choice. I accepted the proposals and made the choice. We shall proceed, together."

Matt was about to speak, but Narayan stopped him.

"I must make one request of you, Matthew. It is that you say nothing to anyone else in Sakhana about your failure to obtain the twenty-million-dollar loan."

"Your Majesty," Rutledge grinned. "I was about to make exactly the same suggestion. Our enemies should be left to believe we're practically drowning in money."

Narayan laughed heartily.

"We really must play a game of poker someday, Matthew. It would be a memorable experience—for both of us."

The banquet held that night was far more elaborate than the one given for Matt when he first came to Kangtek. Vivian, breathtaking in a white Givenchy gown, her long auburn hair backswept and coiled to emphasize her lovely neck and bare shoulders, sat on Narayan's right. Matt was seated on the Maharaja's left and, next to him, Narayan's favorite—and beautiful—almond-eyed concubine. This event was not for men only as the previous one had been. Palace dignitaries had brought their wives —or their Number One concubines if they were widowers. According to Sakhanese custom, the concubines of widowers enjoyed the same degree of social status and acceptance as wives.

The feast was sumptuous, with several dozen courses. It was followed by entertainment—Sakhanese music, performances by jugglers and acrobats and then a troupe of dancers, all lovely and sinuous young women. Matt realized it was the same troupe he had seen before. Sita had been a member of it. He avoided watching the dancers, but applauded politely when they ended their performance.

He tensed slightly, wondering if there would be a Kai-Shee exhibition as there had been before. There was none. Evidently, exhibitions of the combat art were given only at palace functions attended by all-male audiences. Instead, the festivities ended with a sort of chanted hymn of loyalty to the Maharaja, with everyone present but Narayan standing and the Sakhanese singing—if it could be called that, Matt reflected—in Hindi.

The apartment assigned to Matt and Vivian was immense. Going through it earlier in the day, they had counted twelve rooms and had given up. There must have been many more, for there were several doors they did not even open.

Two male and two female servants were waiting when Matt and Vivian returned from the banquet. It was after two o'clock in the morning. Matt dismissed them for the night.

"Tired?" he asked Vivian.

"I suppose I should be—but I'm not. I'm turned on. To full power." She gave him a look that sent a tidal wave of blood into his loins. "Shall we christen the rooms?"

"All twelve—in one night?" Matt laughed. "I'm afraid I'm not man enough—"

"We could make a start."

"The master bedroom?"

"Too much. It would be like making love in the Grand Ballroom at Buckingham Palace. Let's work our way up to it." Her eyes became bright, even more than they had been all evening. "I know!" Her hands worked some secret combination of dress fastenings. The Givenchy gown fell to the floor. "There's a small room over here"—she moved toward a door—"it has a couch and windows that look out over that gorgeous pool."

Matt reached her as she was opening the door. His hands drank in the feel of her flesh as he drew her to him and kissed her ravenously.

"Is there a full moon?" he asked.

"I feel like there is." She spoke against his lips, and her fingers were already pulling down the zipper of his trousers and reaching for his sex, which strained with the urgency of his own desire.

It was not quite eleven P.M. in London. Sir David Auerbach and Alan Leopold had been talking together in Sir David's study for almost three hours. Both men had begun to realize that their conversation had grown repetitious.

"It's quite useless, Alan," Sir David said. "Vivian has gone to Sakhana with Rutledge. All that either of us can do is something that's not really possible for me— try to forget her."

"It's not possible for me, either. I really wanted to marry Vivian."

"I know, Alan, and I'm sorry."

Leopold felt compelled to make an admission.

"I haven't told you before, sir, but I went to see Rutledge a few days ago, while he was still here in London."

"Did you?" Sir David was surprised. "Care to tell me what transpired between you?"

"I tried reasoning with him. I hoped to convince him that Vivian should be made to return home, that religious differences were an insurmountable barrier in their—their relationship. It was futile."

"Anything else?"

"Yes. In the end, I told Rutledge I'd do my utmost to help break him."

David Auerbach stared past Alan Leopold into empty space.

"A mistake," he murmured—addressing himself and not Leopold. The bitter irony was that Vivian would still be home and still engaged to Alan if he had not acceded to Michel Auerbach's request and done precisely that, helped in the attempt to break Matthew Rutledge.

In New York City, it was five hours earlier than in London. The Emir of Hajar had flown to New York on March 12 and, although intending to remain only a few days, had preempted an entire floor at the Carlyle Hotel for himself and his retinue. Sheikh Nasib al Rahman had come to the United States for several specific purposes, not the least among them being the one he was discussing privately the next day with Charles Jordan Sturdevant III.

"Gold has been drifting down on the London Market," Nasib was saying.

"I know," Charles Sturdevant nodded. "It closed at one sixty-three yesterday and stayed at the same level throughout today. The trend is unusual, considering the volume of our buying. Someone is selling heavily."

"Have you any idea who?"

"No, although I've tried to find out. Do you know?"

"Intuition tells me it must be Michel Auerbach."

"Nasib, no offense—but your intuition must be faulty. That would make no sense."

"Why not? The damned Jew has made it clear enough that he is becoming nervous. He is probably playing a double game. Buying with us on the one hand, feeding other holdings out to take profits on the other."

Sturdevant's angular features became harshly sharp.

"Perhaps the time is ripe for us to drop Michel," he muttered.

"I would say so." Nasib toyed with his *sibah,* fingering the beads of the Muslim rosary. News-magazine writers usually described the thirty-six-year-old Emir of Hajar as "falcon-faced." Now his expression was vulture-like. "You and I do our buying through intermediaries. We pass on instructions that they are to make no more transactions through Michel or his Société Auerbach."

"In a week or two, all visible—or traceable—ties we may have with him will be severed," Sturdevant nodded. "He'll be furious, of course—but not for long. When someone informs the Elysée Palace that he has been claiming to speculate in gold on behalf of the French government . . ."

"He and his bank will be ruined."

"Not quite."

"What if Hajari funds deposited with Société Auerbach are withdrawn?" Nasib inquired, still fondling his prayer beads.

"Suddenly, and with a public announcement of the withdrawal?"

"How else?"

"It would push Michel *and* his bank very close to the brink—possibly even over the edge."

"Into the outstretched hands of Sturdevant National, eh, C. J.?"

"Barring the unforeseen, yes."

"Then it is how we shall proceed," Nasib said. "Now, the question that recurs: what of our albatross Rutledge —and Sakhana?"

"Both are being pressured by my organization and an Indian government growing more belligerent daily."

Nasib slipped his rosary into a jacket pocket. The discussion of business had ended.

"Stay the evening," he urged. "I have a spectacular array of women due to arrive in an hour."

Sturdevant sadly shook his head. "Not in the States, Nasib. I can't risk any scandal."

13

Matt conferred with Sakhanese government officials the next morning. The special commissions and agencies established by the Maharaja before his departure had achieved positive results. A large work force had been registered for labor at the Kangtek airstrip. A considerably smaller number of Sakhanese had volunteered to enter the forbidden zone itself and work there. A supply of available hand tools had been obtained and stockpiled.

Rutledge outlined what needed to be done quickly, before supplies, equipment, miners and technicians began arriving. First, the Kangtek airstrip would have to be improved, potholes and fissures filled, and simple structures built at the strip to shelter materiel. Transient Housing accommodations had to be erected for the skilled men coming from Britain and Europe. Native laborers willing to brave the forbidden zone would have to be air-ferried to the site of his original base camp where they were to clear and level ground for a runway and for hutments.

Within three days, work was in full swing at the Kangtek airfield. Using fuel reserves left over from his aerial survey flights and still stored at the airstrip, Matt shuttled men and materiel to the base camp site, moving in a work crew of fifty men, who were then left in Lieutenant Kancha's charge.

Once these top-priority projects were underway, Matt and Vivian flew to Darjeeling. They spent two days there while Rutledge made preliminary preparations for his forthcoming airlift. He rented warehouse space at the Darjeeling airport, contracted with a freight-forwarding firm to handle unloading and reloading.

The company from which he rented the Pilatus also owned a DHC 6-200 De Havilland Otter. Matt dickered only briefly before agreeing to the asking price for a three-month rental of the Canadian-made Otter— a deep-bellied, twin-turboprop-engined craft that could carry more than two tons of cargo. It was capable of even shorter takeoffs and landings than the Porter Pilatus.

"Are you checked out in the Otter?" Matt was asked by the former R.A.F. officer in charge of the aircraft rental firm.

"No, but a man who works for me—Thomas Kirkland—is. He'll be arriving next week." I hope, Rutledge added to himself.

Matt had a question of his own. He asked about a new military tent-camp he had noticed not far from the Darjeeling airport. A battalion of infantry, he was told, had been moved up to Darjeeling from the large Indian military base at Bhagalpur.

"Probably brought 'em to be close to the Sakhanese border—ready to move," the man replied.

Matt and Vivian rode back to their hotel in a taxi. The cab was pulling up in front of the entrance when sudden realization hit Matt.

"Holy Christ!" he exclaimed. "I've got to get hold of Hernandez or Kirkland—like right now!"

"You sound as though there's been a disaster," Vivian said, completely baffled.

"There may be—unless I talk to those guys fast!"

The taxi stopped. Matt shoved a fistful of rupees at the driver and rushed Vivian into the lobby. He gave another handful of rupees to the desk clerk.

"I have to get a telephone call through to London—it's very important." He scribbled down the number of the Dorchester and the names of Luis Hernandez and Thomas Kirkland. "Either of them will do—please have your operator push the call."

Matt and Vivian had a third-floor suite. When they were inside, Vivian asked Matt what the emergency was all about.

"Honey, it's too complicated to explain—you'll know when you hear me talk to Luis or Tom." He stared expectantly at the telephone, even though he knew it would take an hour or more for the call to be completed. "There's a bottle of Chivas Regal in the top bureau drawer. Pour us some drinks, huh?"

Matt's generous tip to the desk clerk helped break the record for a Darjeeling-to-London connection. Matt was on the line with Hernandez less than forty-five minutes later.

"If you're calling to check up on us, we're doing great, Matt. We'll probably even meet that miracle deadline. Tom's in Frankfurt and found some machinery there. I expect him back here tonight. In fact—"

"Luis, for God's sake shut up and answer my questions!" Matt barked. "Where's all that British military surplus we bought?"

"Most of it's already at Gatwick—ready for loading whenever—"

"Look. Get your ass moving and hire men—I don't care how many or what it costs. Every piece of that stuff right down to the last shovel has to have a brand-new paint job. I don't care what color—red, purple or baby-blue—as long as it hides all British service markings and that olive drab or mottled camouflage paint that's standard on military equipment."

"Sure—only what's the big deal? Who gives a damn if the stuff comes in the usual army shit-color?"

"The Indian customs inspectors. They're liable to think we're running war materiel to the Sakhanese!"

When the conversation ended, Matt hung up and heaved a sigh of relief.

"Understand now?" he asked Vivian.

"Yes—lucky you thought of it." She frowned. "But why couldn't you have told me?"

Matt gave her a puzzled look. "Told you what?"

"About the equipment—it wasn't that complicated. Even I could understand it," Vivian replied tartly.

"Oh. Sorry, honey. Seemed silly to go over it more than once. But you're right. I've been making my own decisions and giving my own orders for so long that— well, I guess I'm just not used to working in tandem. I'll try—"

Vivian interrupted, immediately contrite. "I'm being silly, darling. It isn't that important." She reached out and touched his hand. "Ready for another drink?"

Matt received the radiogram he had been waiting for on the morning of March 17. The first DC-6 would leave Gatwick at around noon on March 19. There would be three more DC-6 flights from London spaced twenty-four hours apart. A fifth plane would leave Frankfurt on March 21. A dozen miners and skilled workers would be arriving on commercial flights. The radiogram listed their names, nationalities—mostly British—passport numbers, and specialties, so that Rutledge could arrange their entry into Sakhana. Kirkland would be aboard the first cargo flight, Hernandez on the last.

Rutledge conferred with the Maharaja.

"My men promised me a miracle—and they're delivering, Your Majesty," he said. "I'll have to go to Darjeeling and stay there until everything has arrived—and then been transshipped to Sakhana. I have to be certain of one thing though, that there won't be any red tape at this end."

"You will have carte blanche," Narayan assured him. "But should you not remain and supervise the arrival of the equipment and the men?"

"I'll probably send Luis Hernandez ahead as soon as he arrives," Matt said—then stopped. "If you'll excuse me for a few minutes, I may have an even better idea."

He hurried to his apartments in the palace. Vivian was just about to leave on a tour of the countryside that Narayan had arranged for her to take with his favorite concubine.

"The car and military escort are waiting," she said.

"I'll only take a minute—now. I've got a question. How'd you like a full-time job—as a combination cargo superintendent, forewoman, expediter, wet nurse—"

"Have you been drinking?" Vivian pretended to sniff for alcohol on his breath.

"Honey, I want you to run things for me here in Kangtek until we've finished—"

"Where will you be?"

"Darjeeling."

Vivian bit her lip. She so badly wanted to be with Matt. She hated the prospect of being separated from him for even a few hours—much less for several days. She was on the verge of saying as much, demanding that he take her to Darjeeling with him. Then her mind flashed back to an evening at the Dorchester when she had acted the spoiled little rich girl. She remembered how Matt left her in the sitting room, went downstairs to the lobby and returned with the stuffed toy panda-doll—his way of telling her that she was being willful, demanding—and childish.

My life has changed since then, Vivian Auerbach reflected. For the better, she reflected. And it's all because of Matt. The fact that he needed her, that she could really help him, that she could be part of his work and his life, was such an important breakthrough, not only for Vivian but for the both of them.

254

"Of course I'll do it," she said. She kissed him, feeling that the bond between them had taken on a new dimension, grown infinitely stronger. "Only I'll want overtime pay when you return."

"Cash?"

"In kind—your time and energy, my pet. There are rooms here we still haven't explored, much less christened."

Matt hurried back to the Maharaja to report what he and Vivian had decided. Narayan nodded his approval.

"And have no fears for Miss Auerbach's safety, Matthew," he said. "I will assign Lieutenant Baki and a squad of men to keep constant guard over her."

On March 18, 1974, seven of the nine Arab oil-producing countries that had been embargoing oil shipments agreed to end their boycott. But they refused to make any adjustment in the prices they would charge for crude oil. These had been trebled and quadrupled.

Now the worldwide energy crisis would end. Normal supplies of Middle Eastern crude would soon begin flowing. But the astronomical price of petroleum was certain to create economic havoc in the industrialized countries.

Secretary of State Jeffrey Tillinger found himself in a painful dilemma. On the one hand, he could—and did —publicly declare that American diplomacy had played a decisive role in convincing the Arab countries to end their embargo. On the other, representing a sorely embattled administration, it was necessary that he minimize the devastating effect skyrocketing petroleum prices would have on U. S. and world economies.

Jeffrey Tillinger used his favorite tactic. He did not mention the bad news at all. Instead, he diverted attention from it by dwelling on a totally unrelated international problem.

"Your government must now focus its attention further east in Asia," Tillinger declared. "It should study the implications of the territorial claims India has made recently against the Kingdom of Sakhana. The United States guarantees justice for small nations threatened by their larger and more powerful neighbors. I have instructed the State Department's Asian experts to examine this situation and evaluate the merits of India's position."

His statement brought instant response from two quarters. The first was from the Indian ambassador.

"Mr. Secretary, I was under the impression that my government had your tacit assurance of disinterest—"

"There is no fundamental change," Tillinger soothed him blandly. "After a month, at most two, I will issue a communiqué declaring that the merits have been weighed and evaluated. Your government will not be disappointed in it."

"Nonetheless, we shall be forced to retreat from our stand."

"I prefer to think of it as a short and minor strategic withdrawal in order to gather greater—even overwhelming—strength," Tillinger said.

Stronger protests came from Tillinger's patron Charles Sturdevant. The billionaire did not even bother to use Assistant Treasury Secretary Owen Raynor as his intermediary. He telephoned Tillinger directly.

"Your statement on India and Sakhana!" Sturdevant rasped. "Do you realize—"

"Sorry, C. J.," Tillinger apologized. "I didn't have time to clear it with you in advance." He felt secure that his explanation would satisfy Sturdevant. "Public attention had to be shifted away from the crude-price picture —and from the fact that oil companies like AMENOCO will now make record profits."

"God damn it!" Sturdevant said, but it was clear that he was having second thoughts. "You could have picked something else—let loose against the Russians—"

"When we've been selling détente? I took the only possible course, C. J. And it won't be any final curtain— only a short intermission." Tillinger's laugh sounded more like a snicker. "The Indians will be able to put just that much more wallop into their next act—it'll be final."

Matt Rutledge landed the Porter Pilatus in Darjeeling on the afternoon of March 19. He went to the operations office. Yes, the Darjeeling airport had been notified that a DC-6 had taken off from London some hours before, bound for Darjeeling via refueling stops in Beirut, Teheran and New Delhi. No, there was no information yet as to its Estimated Time of Arrival—but Mr. Rutledge would be informed at his hotel when that was received.

Matt checked to insure that all was in order with the freight-handling contractors and the company from which he was renting the Pilatus and the Otter. Then he went to the Indian Customs Office. He was prepared for an icy reception and difficulties that could be overcome only by distributing sheafs of the U. S. and British currency he carried in his attaché case.

"We shall be pleased to cooperate fully in expediting your transshipments to Sakhana," the chief customs officer said—to Matt's astonishment. "I will personally see to it that formalities are held to a minimum."

The Mysterious East, Rutledge thought as he took a taxi to his hotel. The highway led past the new Indian army encampment. Matt observed that the troops were hard at work, striking their tents and loading equipment into trucks.

Matt's hotel-suite phone rang at 4:40 A.M. A sleepy Darjeeling airport operations clerk said the flight he was waiting for was due to land in one hour.

"Thanks," Matt mumbled, climbing out of bed. "I'll be there."

Thomas Kirkland was the first person off the plane.
"Wait'll you see the cargo," Kirkland chortled,

wringing Matt's hand. "Luis and I followed your instructions—but used our own judgment. We had everything painted—the most revolting chartreuse green we could find."

Matt groaned, then laughed and pounded Kirkland's back.

14

Michel Auerbach was accustomed to dealing personally with the Finance Minister of whatever French government was in power. He did not take kindly to the announcement made by his secretary that a middle-rung civil servant from the Finance Ministry was demanding to see him without delay.

"He is a M. Etienne Jabot," the secretary said.

Michel grimaced his distaste. Etienne Jabot. Even the name was petite bourgeois. "Shunt him off to someone else."

"*Pardon*, M'sieu Auerbach. I have tried. He insists he must speak with you. He claims he is acting on the orders of the Finance Minister himself."

"Absurd. All right, show him in."

Etienne Jabot was no fussy, obsequious *sous*-official. Not yet forty, he had the steely eye of a Sureté inspector and entered Michel Auerbach's office insolently, a half-smoked cigarette pasted at the corner of his mouth.

Auerbach glared at him. "Yes, Jabot?"

"The Finance Minister sends his compliments, M'sieu Auerbach," Jabot said and seated himself without being invited to do so. He opened a briefcase, removed a document and all but flung it on Michel Auerbach's desk. The banker reached for it automatically, glanced at the heading—and grew deathly pale. It was a notorious Finance Ministry Form 63, "Advice of Withdrawal of

French Government Funds and Suspension of Bank from Participation in Official Transactions."

"*C'est impossible!*" Michel Auerbach spluttered. "This is a mistake. Some idiot has bungled—"

"*D'accord,*" Etienne Jabot agreed icily. "Some idiot has bungled—and badly. You, M'sieu Auerbach. The Finance Ministry has no objections to anyone speculating on the gold market. It is a French national pastime." He stood up, ready to leave. "However, as you will read in the document I have given you, the Ministry—and the government—cannot tolerate privately owned banks letting the world believe they are speculating on behalf of the French government. *Au revoir,* M'sieu Auerbach."

Michel Auerbach's hands trembled as he held the Form 63 and read the complex legal phrases. The Finance Ministry possessed evidence—even proof. As provided under the law, the Société Auerbach would no longer be the repository for the funds of any French government bureau or agency. Nor would it be permitted to act as an agent for any transaction involving official contracts, monies. . . .

It meant the loss of almost five billion francs in deposits! To say nothing of what private concerns and individuals would withdraw when the Ministry's action became known. Michel Auerbach's first impulse was to reach for his telephone and begin making frantic calls to highly placed political figures who owed him—or his bank—favors. But his secretary entered again.

"M. Lascelles is outside. He says it is urgent."

Lascelles was the Number Three man in the Société Auerbach organizational hierarchy.

"Very well," Michel said, an edge of fear in his voice.

Lascelles entered, a middle-aged, autocratic figure, his face as pale as Auerbach's and his hands trembling.

"Michel—we have received fully confirmed orders to close out all Hajari accounts and transfer them to other banks!"

The pieces fell into place with a crash that threatened to implode Michel Auerbach's throbbing skull.

"Go," he whispered to Lascelles. "I will talk with you later."

Auerbach had his secretary place a conference call to Charles Sturdevant in New York and Sheikh Nasib al Rahman in Hajar. Two endless, agonizing hours passed before it was completed.

"Whatever it is, Michel, make it fast," Sturdevant's voice said. "I have a full schedule today."

"Yes, I too am busy," Nasib said.

"You—you two have stabbed me in the back," Auerbach stammered. "You—"

"Aren't you getting things mixed up, Michel?" Sturdevant demanded. "You began the double-dealing."

"You are mad, Charles!"

"Am I? You've been taking profits, selling your private gold holdings when we were buying in a rising market."

"It is not true. I have never done anything of the kind." Auerbach was telling the truth, but neither Sturdevant nor Nasib cared.

"Too late, Michel," Sturdevant said. "You're out."

"*Mon dieu!* You even informed against me to the Finance Ministry!"

"You'll have a tough time trying to prove that."

"I wish to prove nothing, save that I lived up to our agreement. To the letter!"

"Did you?" Sheikh Nasib's tone was cold and threatening. "All we have heard from you are whimpers about your fears of risk—"

"They have been realized." Michel was slowly gaining a grip on himself. "Thanks to both of you."

Nasib was enjoying himself now. "You can always take refuge in Israel, Michel. I doubt if you'll be safe there for very long, though. Now that we Arabs have beaten the entire world, we'll strangle—"

Michel Auerbach hung up his telephone. To his amazement, his hands were steady. A phrase from his schoolboy days came to his mind. If you go to bed with dogs, don't be surprised if you wake up with fleas, he repeated to himself. For the first time in his life he was laughing bitterly at himself.

Michel grew ever more calm. He would fight with shrewdness and determination.

On March 20, gold rebounded to $173.50 an ounce. Charles Sturdevant and the Emir of Hajar had resumed purchasing on a massive scale. With Michel Auerbach out of the syndicate, they would corner the market—and evenly divide the profits.

Vivian Auerbach gladly began doing her work in Kangtek, because she felt she was helping Matt Rutledge. After the Otter piloted by Thomas Kirkland arrived with the first load of cargo, she found herself becoming deeply involved in checking freight manifests and setting up inventory records. She gained increasing satisfaction from the realization that she performed a vitally important job and did it well. I *am* a functioning, contributing member of the team, Vivian thought with pride when Kirkland brought the Otter in on its second flight from Darjeeling. She met him as he emerged from the plane. Sakhanese laborers were already swarming around the craft to unload its cargo.

"Here, Viv—more damned paperwork," Kirkland said, thrusting a mass of documents at her. He started toward the open cargo hatch where a labor gang was wrestling with a particularly large and cumbersome crate, stopped and turned back to her. "Almost forgot. Matt told me to give you his love. He also babbled something to the effect he wished he was spelunking through every room in the palace with you. I haven't the foggiest notion what he meant."

"I do," Vivian chuckled and went into the concrete hut she had appropriated for use as an office.

* * *

Kirkland could make two round trips daily between Darjeeling and Kangtek. Thus it was possible for Matt to clear the full load of each DC-6 arriving out of Darjeeling within twenty-four hours after the plane touched down.

The men Kirkland and Hernandez had hired started coming in on commercial flights. Rutledge interviewed each briefly and outlined the problems and difficulties that lay ahead. He was completely satisfied with the personnel chosen by Tom and Luis. Thoroughly experienced in their specialties, they were tough and dependable veterans of mining operations in practically every corner of the world, accustomed to hard work and hardship. They were eager to start for the High Mountains and participate in opening up a great new virgin goldfield. As they arrived in Darjeeling, Matt obtained rooms for them in his hotel. All twelve were present when Hernandez came in aboard the final DC-6 flight on March 25. The plane had been delayed first due to loading problems, then because of mechanical difficulties.

Rutledge gathered the dozen hired hands, Hernandez, and Kirkland in his suite that evening. A folding table was set up in the middle of the sitting room and Matt spread maps and aerial photographs on it and held what he had planned as a short preliminary briefing. It turned into something quite different.

First Matt, then Luis and Tom went over the intended procedures. The hutments and supplies needed at the base camp would be air-ferried there, with the men being housed in Kangtek until this task was completed. Then Matt, the men, some Sakhanese workers and a military escort would trek overland to the Ser-gi Ri. Once the valley at the base of the mountains had been reached, Kirkland would air-drop more prefabricated hutments, and these would be assembled. Additional supplies were to be parachuted into the valley along with two of the undersized bulldozers.

"And how long d'you think all that'll take?" a grizzled British miner named Frederick Coyne asked.

"Two weeks, if there aren't any hitches, Fred," Matt replied.

Coyne gnawed on a scarred briar pipe. He leaned down, peering at maps and photos. "Bloody waste of time!" he snorted. He nudged the lean, hardened man who stood next to him, Timothy—"Tim"—Donahue. "Hell, Tim and me could jump into that valley. Drop us a tent, some fodder, a dozen crates of dynamite and those dozers. We'll level a strip long before anybody gets over the mountains from that base camp."

A third man pushed forward to the table. His face was badly scarred, and he had the build of a blacksmith. He was Gerhard Schurz, a German, but he spoke almost perfect English—which he had learned in a POW camp. Schurz had been taken prisoner by the British while serving in the Wehrmacht's parachute corps.

"Three could do it better," he said.

Matt stared at Hernandez and Kirkland. He knew that for some reason many World War Two paratroopers had gravitated into mining after returning to civilian life. Even so, to have three in a group of only a dozen men was an unusually high proportion. Unfortunately, the men were no longer young. Tim Donahue had lied his way into the British army at sixteen and was now forty-nine, but Fred Coyne and Gerhard Schurz were in their fifties.

"You'd never make it; the air currents are violent," Matt said. "We can drop cargo but not men."

"We made practice jumps in the Austrian Alps with gale-force winds blowing," Gerhard Schurz said.

"Bring a plane in low, not over a thousand feet above the valley, and we'll be safe as babies," Fred Coyne declared, giving his pipe stem an extra-hard bite.

Matt studied them. Despite their ages, they were in superb physical condition.

"I thought the first lesson soldiers learned was never to volunteer," he said.

"Well, now." Coyne took the pipe from his mouth.

"Time saved is money earned. Me and Tim are looking to our pockets. We're not volunteering. It's hazard pay we're after."

"Double wages," Donahue grinned. "Should be worth it."

And then some—several times over—Matt thought. If the three men could bring it off, the camp near the Ser-gi Ri would be ready weeks ahead of schedule.

"How long has it been since any of you jumped?" he asked.

"A year," Coyne grunted.

"About the same for me," Donahue said.

"And you, Schurz?" Matt inquired.

"Last month. I've continued to parachute for a sport." He smiled. "But they call it sky-diving now."

Rutledge hesitated. "All right," he said finally. "I want you all to get a look at the terrain first, though. You may change your minds. Tom or I'll fly you over the valley in a couple of days, after we're in Kangtek."

The last of the cargo was delivered and the twelve employees were transported to the Sakhanese capital two days later. Kirkland promptly began airlifting materiel to the base camp in the Otter. Matt took the Pilatus and flew the three former paratroopers over the Ser-gi Ri and the valley adjoining them. The trio remained adamant. They would jump into the valley.

"Just make sure we get two chutes apiece," Fred Coyne told Matt when he landed the Pilatus at Kangtek. "A regular and an emergency. And we repack the chutes ourselves."

15

Matt rode as Tom Kirkland's copilot on the morning of March 30. They could not have wished for better weather conditions. The skies were cloudless over the Middle

Hills and even the lower reaches of the Cen-po Ri. The prevailing winds were comparatively mild—little more than middling-strong breezes compared to what Rutledge had previously encountered in the High Mountains.

Fred Coyne, Tim Donahue and Gerhard Schurz were in the cargo compartment of the Otter. They lay sprawled on the floor amidst the bundles and containers of supplies that were to be dropped before they made their jumps.

Matt left the flight deck and came aft to join them. The cluster of three mountains that were the Ser-gi Ri loomed less than ten miles ahead. Tom Kirkland banked the Otter so that the three men could get their initial bearings. He circled for several minutes, allowing them to observe the terrain through the Otter's double-paned ports.

"We've got the lay as good as we can from the air," Fred Coyne told Matt.

Rutledge called Kirkland on the intercom. "Let's do some sightseeing over the valley."

The Otter banked left, angling down. Kirkland leveled off at a thousand feet above the valley floor, throttling the engines back to near-stalling speed. He made several passes over the valley, enabling the men to study it.

"No hard feelings if anybody wants to change his mind," Matt said. "This is about the last chance to do it."

The men didn't bother to make any comment. They would jump.

"Then we'll open the hatch."

Matt depressed the cargo-hatch lever. It was a large door that snapped back onto tracks inside the fuselage and was then rolled clear on casterlike bearings. Frigid air blasted into the plane. A stout quarter-inch steel cable had been rigged the length of the cargo compartment. The webbed static lines attached to the ripcords of the cargo chutes were latched to the cable.

Kirkland started a new pass over the valley. Matt Rutledge and his three companions shoved and heaved containers and bundles through the hatch. As each dropped, the static lines snapped taut for an instant, then whipped free and slack. Large, varicolored parachutes blossomed in the Otter's wake. About half the cargo was dropped before Kirkland circled to make another pass, during which the remaining cargo was dropped.

Now it was the men's turn. Fred Coyne hooked up first, then Tim Donahue. Gerhard Schurz was last. Matt shook hands with each of them. "We'll be back this afternoon with the dozers—for Christ's sake, keep your heads up and yourselves clear when we dump those."

They waited until the Otter made another circuit. Coyne stepped to the open door, crouched with his hands clutching the frame. He watched the ground below, jumped. Donahue took his place, counted three, followed. Schurz went to the door. Another three count, and he leaped.

All the chutes opened, began floating down. Kirkland brought the plane around, easing the Otter to within three hundred feet of the valley floor. He on the flight deck and Matt in the cargo compartment could see the men, waving their arms, signaling that they had landed safely. Matt felt an immense load lift from his mind. Straining, he slid the cargo hatch forward, shoved it flush and worked the locking handle. He returned to the flight deck, dumped his large frame into the copilot's seat.

The Otter could only carry one of the bulldozers at a time. Sweating native work crews got the first machine aboard by using an improvised ramp and rollers under the airdrop pallet on which it was mounted. Eight of the Sakhanese laborers were taken along to help push the dozer out.

Rutledge and Kirkland laughed when they approached the valley. They saw a series of what looked like artillery-shell explosions. Coyne and his companions were already blasting boulders into small, manageable bits of rock.

"They worked fast," Kirkland said, pointing down. The tent the three men would use for the first few days had been pitched at the mouth of the gorge opening into the valley. Kirkland flew back and forth over the valley until a green flare was fired into the air from the mouth of the gorge. This was the signal that the men were clear of the drop zone.

Matt went aft again and opened the cargo hatch. There were three static lines for the chutes attached to the dozer. He latched them to the cable. Using crowbars and rollers, the Sakhanese laborers worked the dozer to the door—and at his order, gave the final push. The machine landed intact.

The second, flown to the valley an hour and a half later, did not. The cargo chutes were faulty. Two did not open. The third was torn to shreds in midair. Bulldozer and metal pallet were smashed to junk as they struck the ground.

There was sufficient daylight remaining for them to return to the base camp, load a third dozer and fly it to the valley. The chutes opened properly. The machine floated down and settled to the ground gently.

The three men on the ground had a radio that could be used for communicating with aircraft flying above the valley—but was incapable of transmitting or receiving across the mountains. Matt called down to them while Kirkland kept the Otter circling overhead.

"Everything in good shape down there?" he asked.

"All snug and tidy." It was Fred Coyne. "We even took a walk over to the bench placer on this side of the river. Never saw so much bloody gold." There was a pause. "Found some skeletons, too. Three men, two mules. Want us to do anything about them?"

"Leave them where they are," Matt said. "When the first Sakhanese troops land, they'll take care of them. We're going to head back now. Anything you want?"

"Sure—add a bottle of whiskey to tomorrow's supply drop."

"Wilco," Matt chuckled. "Over and out."

Rutledge could have easily commuted by air daily between the base camp and Kangtek. Although it would have taken days to travel one way by foot, flying time was little more than forty-five minutes. He resisted the temptation on the entirely valid ground that it would have an adverse effect on the morale of the men working for him. He spent the evening after the airdrop in the hutment he shared with Kirkland, Hernandez and Kancha. The three Americans drank coffee and played poker. Kancha watched them, silently and intently, for more than an hour.

At about ten P.M., Kancha spoke. "Rutledge *sahib-kamal*. Is it permitted for me to play also?"

"Why sure, Kancha," Matt nodded, giving Luis and Tom warning glances. They were playing for low stakes—by their standards. No pot had been over $60. But Lieutenant Kancha was paid the equivalent of only $27 a month by the Sakhanest government.

"We'll make it penny-ante—in rupees," Rutledge said.

Kancha won the first ten hands.

"Beginner's luck—with a vengeance," Kirkland commented.

"Is it permitted to make larger bets?" Kancha asked.

"Sure," Matt told him. "But we're old-time poker players. You're liable to lose everything you've won."

"I take chance."

Out of the next dozen hands, Kancha won nine. He dropped out of the other three, losing only his ante.

"If we weren't passing the deal—and if these weren't my cards, I'd swear you were using markers," Hernandez grumbled.

"Markers? What are those?" Kancha asked.

"Never mind—it's just a joke," Matt said.

The game did not end until nearly four in the morning. Kancha had periodically asked that the bets be raised. The Americans had gone along. And Lieutenant Kancha finished the evening more than $600 ahead.

"I'll be a son of a bitch if I can figure how you did it, Kancha," Hernandez said, unstrapping his artificial leg and getting into his bunk.

"I watch, Hernandez *sahib*. Poker almost same like *tang-fu*."

"Like what?"

"*Tang-fu*. Game we play with cards in Sakhana for maybe thousand years. Only cards different."

"I *am* one dumb son of a bitch," Luis moaned. "Suckered by a Sakhanese . . ."

Rutledge and Kirkland roared with laughter. Lieutenant Kancha grinned.

Matt had a legitimate reason for flying to Kangtek on April 2. Supplies of fresh meat, vegetables and fruits were running low. He went to buy more in the capital's markets.

"Stay overnight," Kirkland urged him. "Vivian will be thrilled if you do."

"I don't need much convincing," Matt said.

Rutledge had much to think about on the hop to Kangtek. The price of gold was continuing to soar. It had leaped to $180 and more an ounce on some markets—and during certain peak periods during trading sessions on the London Market.

Matt could not help but reflect that he had enjoyed a long series of narrow escapes—and extremely lucky breaks. These ranged from his meeting Thomas Kirkland to the unexpected about-face of the Indian government and even to having three experienced parachutists turn up on his small staff of miners and technicians. And they, he reminded himself, were doing a fantastic job. The airstrip in the valley near the Ser-gi Ri would be in shape to permit both the Pilatus and Otter to land with light loads within a day or two. After that, another week or ten days—and he and his men would begin producing gold.

Matt called Kangtek radio.

"This is Matthew Rutledge. I'll be landing in twenty-five minutes. I'd like to have a car meet me."

By God, I have had luck, Rutledge mused after receiving an acknowledgment and switching off his radio. A sudden twinge of anxiety, then fear manifested itself. You can't beat the law of averages, an inner voice warned, there's no such thing as an uninterrupted winning streak.

"But you can beat the law of averages," Matt was surprised to hear himself saying aloud. "Just remember Kancha and *tang-fu*."

The fear receded, only a feeling of uneasiness remaining as he made an easy, smooth landing, found a palace Bentley waiting for him and climbed into it for the drive to Kangtek.

Tsering Dorje and General Singh were having yet another of their private discussions.

They had been taken aback by India's abrupt about-face. There had been no further diplomatic notes—or even propaganda blasts—out of New Delhi. The Indian army units which only such a short time ago were reported concentrating near the Sakhanese frontier had been quietly withdrawn and returned to their bases.

The net result was a dislocation of the most recent strategy employed by Dorje and Singh. The external threat had apparently ceased to exist. Yet their agents operating throughout the country were carrying out their latest instructions, exhorting the population to stand firm and loyal behind their Maharaja.

"We've executed nearly a hundred of the most outspoken dissidents on the pretext they were Indian agents," Singh declared ruefully. "Many were men we could have counted upon to foment riots and lead mobs when we were ready to seize power."

"The winds have been shifting much too rapidly," the Prime Minister philosophized. "You and I have had no choice but to swing like weathervanes with them. Take comfort that we've done so successfully. We have survived this long, and our store of options is by no means empty."

"There are few remaining," General Singh muttered. "Rutledge is reported to be making excellent progress in the High Mountains. Before long, he will be taking gold from the Ser-gi Ri. Once the treasury is rich with gold, our Living God will be invulnerable."

Singh ran his right hand along the Sam Browne belt around his waist as though feeling for a holstered pistol or other weapon that was not there.

"And Rutledge is already invulnerable," he said. "He is surrounded by his band of Westerners, men from Narayan's Palace Guard and Sakhanese workers loyal to him and to the wages he pays them."

Dorje was forced to concede the point. Any further attempts to kill Matthew Rutledge or force him out of Sakhana would be futile.

"Rutledge's woman," Dorje murmured, half to himself. "She could prove to be the chink in his armor."

"You joke. The English slut is watched over night and day by Palace Guardsmen. Even if she were not, what possible use could we make of her?"

"As yet, I am not certain, Dep. But a thought—still as nebulous as an early morning mist—is forming somewhere deep inside my brain. I can feel it gathering substance. When its shape has taken form, I will tell you."

16

Matt's first wish was to see Vivian, but on arriving at the palace he was told that the Maharaja directed that Rutledge be taken directly to the small audience chamber. He found Vivian there with Narayan and his favorite concubine.

"I shall not detain you long, Matthew," Narayan said. "Simply tell me how the work goes"—he smiled at Vivian—"and the two of you may leave and be by yourselves."

"Everything's proceeding beautifully, Your Majesty," Matt reported. "We're so far ahead of schedule that I can hardly believe it myself." He was sitting beside Vivian and reached out to hold her hand. He squeezed it. "And I have a strong recommendation to make."

"Make it, by all means."

"The time has come for us to crow—and loudly— to the world. The Kangtek radio should broadcast announcements describing the proven wealth of the Ser-gi Ri and freely predict that large amounts of gold will be coming from the fields in the very near future."

The Maharaja's brow furrowed.

"Is that wise?"

"Imperative," Matt said. "The news—if presented confidently, even boastfully—will serve to spread much confusion among our various enemies. I don't doubt for a moment that it will stop the gold price trend and probably cause a noticeable drop. The men trying to corner the market will begin to have serious doubts."

"And react violently—against Sakhana," Narayan interposed. "They will make greater efforts than ever before to prevent the production of Sakhanese gold."

"I've accepted that as a calculated risk, Your Majesty. But whatever they may do, it will be too little and too late. Once it becomes generally known that Sakhana is on the verge of actually producing great quantities of new gold, Western financiers and politicians will do everything in their power to demonstrate friendship. They'll realize that Sturdevant and his associates have lost their battle. They'll look out after their own interests, compete with

272

each other to appear as though they are Sakhana's staunchest supporters and protectors."

"That is not how India will react, Matthew. New Delhi is certain to renew its demands—perhaps go further, send troops across our borders."

"I'd discount that possibility entirely. India can't afford to antagonize the Western governments—and banks —whose money is propping up the Indian economy." Matt fished a Camel from the pocket of his khaki bush jacket and stuck it between his lips. He flicked his lighter into flame and inhaled. "India would lose infinitely more than it would gain, even if it seized the Ser-gi Ri."

"Your logic is convincing."

"I had to convince myself first," Matt smiled. "An Indian takeover would leave me penniless. Which brings me to another reason why I believe an announcement should be made. My"—he glanced at Vivian and corrected himself—"our financial resources are dwindling rapidly. Oh, we're safe for another three weeks or so at the present rate of expenditure. After that, we won't be able to meet the bills."

Instead of appearing downcast, he grinned, his green eyes lighting up.

"The news broadcast will stir up interest—to say nothing of avarice—among Western financiers and bankers. They'll disregard their unwritten laws and start poaching on what Charles Sturdevant and his friends thought they had staked out as their private hunting preserves. You and I will begin receiving inquiries from the same banks that turned me down flat, asking if we wouldn't like to have additional capital."

"Matthew, the distance between an inquiry and a commitment of funds could be very great," Narayan warned. "Certainly, not even the most profit-hungry banker will establish credits on the basis of a news broadcast or two."

"They might, Your Majesty," Vivian Auerbach

spoke up. "Being a banker's daughter, I know how fast they often act when they believe a situation is especially promising."

"Oh, I'd never count on bankers putting out money just because they hear a newscast, Viv," Matt chuckled. "With Your Majesty's permission"—he cocked his right eyebrow at Narayan—"we'll arrange a spectacular show that'll let them inspect the shiny merchandise."

"A show? Merchandise?" Narayan said.

"Yes. Our airstrip near the placer fields is almost completed. We'll begin mining the placer deposits within days after we've flown in men and rudimentary equipment. Those deposits are so rich, we'll barely have to do more than strain the gravel through a kitchen colander!"

Matt paused, lit a fresh cigarette off the end of the one he had smoked.

"The object of the starting exercise is to recover a thousand pounds—possibly even a ton—of nuggets and large flakes from the placer deposits," Rutledge continued, a note of excitement evident in his tone. "We'll worry about the veins up in the mountains later. I'll fly that initial load—half ton or whole, depending on our luck—here to Kangtek. We'll have it piled in one place—in the Grand Ballroom of the palace. Then your own people—and Very Important Personages and possibly a few journalists you invite to Sakhana—can gape and salivate. Your Majesty, if we use that kind of showmanship, the Rockefellers, Mellons, Rothschilds and all the rest of the international bankers will be begging for the chance to lend money by the hundreds of millions. Credits will be established within twenty-four hours!"

The Maharaja shook his head good-naturedly. "What amazes me, Matthew, is that my instinct and reason both tell me that you are absolutely right." He pursed his lips. "The initial announcement should be broadcast in English," he said.

"I agree," Matt nodded.

274

"It must be carefully prepared, with much attention to the wording."

"Your Majesty." It was Vivian Auerbach. "I can write it. My knowledge of bankers' psychology is practically encyclopedic."

"You have my permission."

Narayan said they could talk again later and asked if there was anything further Rutledge desired.

"I need a supply of fresh food for my men, Your Majesty."

"My aides will see it is obtained and aboard your aircraft tomorrow." The Maharaja's wink was that of an exceedingly human—and earthy—Living God. "The two of you must spend a long night refreshing and replenishing each other."

French President Georges Pompidou died on April 2, 1974. Financial analysts unaware of the existence of a continuing gold-corner campaign theorized that this event was somehow responsible for the next day's leap in gold prices. On the Paris Market, gold rose by $13—to an absolute all-time high of $197 an ounce.

This seemed to bear out the prediction made on March 13 by Samuel Montagu and Company, one of the member firms of the London Gold Market:

"The price of gold could easily rise above $200 an ounce," the merchant banking firm stated in its annual *Bullion Review*. The publication had gone on to state its forecast was based on the fact that there would be no significant increase in gold production or for an increase in gold supplies reaching the market during 1974 or 1975.

"Indeed," the *Bullion Review* declared, "it is anticipated that the production available to the Western world will at best remain constant."

The Samuel Montagu and Company prophecy was widely quoted by the media reports on the April 3 price jump. It now seemed certain that gold prices would crash through the magic $200-an-ounce barrier and zoom up into the stratosphere within a day or two.

There was chaos in the gold rooms of banks in Paris, Frankfurt, Zurich, Beirut and elsewhere around the world. Teletypes clacked incessantly. Telephones stopped ringing only when they were snatched up by trading clerks who took down orders given in dozens of languages.

The orders were fed to the telex operators whose machines in most instances were on direct lines to member firms of the London Gold Market.

"BUYING ONE THOUSAND OUNCES ACKNOWLEDGE"
"OUR BUY ORDER NUMBER 2573 FOR THREE THOUSAND OUNCES TELEXED FIFTEEN MINUTES AGO STILL UNACKNOWLEDGED PLEASE EXPEDITE"
"BUYING TWO HUNDRED FINE KILOGRAMS . . ."

Thousands of speculators on every continent were frantically seeking to purchase gold before the price went over $200 an ounce.

The chaos was multiplied in the gold rooms of the six firms that formed the London Gold Market. It was into their gold trading centers that orders poured from banks, brokers and secondary markets all over the globe.

The afternoon fixing session of the London Gold Market was one of the longest on record to that date. Representatives of the six member firms remained in constant, direct telephone communication with their respective gold rooms. The flood of orders was such that each firm's trading position changed from one minute to the next.

It was impossible for the N. M. Rothschild and Sons representative—who, as always, chaired the session—to obtain agreement on a fix.

"One eighty-one," the Samuel Montagu representative said—then hastily pulled up the tiny Union Jack on his desk. "Sorry. I have to flag."

"I also flag," the Mocatta and Goldsmid representative said. All six flags were up, as they had been un-countable times that afternoon.

Each man listened to the information being relayed to him from his firm's gold room, using all his experience and mental reserves in the attempt to establish his relative trading position.

Then there was a flurry of profit taking. The London Market's afternoon fix was set at $179.50 an ounce, still the highest fix price ever. The member firms' representatives returned to their own gold rooms. A late surge of additional buy orders sent the price well above the fix. Before the firms had ended their trading for the day, some had made sizeable sales at more than $190 an ounce.

Kevin Sundbury, manager of gold trading operations for Jacob Auerbach and Company went to Sir David Auerbach's office at five P.M.

"The market has truly gone insane," Sundbury said. "Lord only knows what the price will be tomorrow—or where all of this will end."

"What does your intuition say, Kevin?" Sir David asked.

"I anticipate the morning fix will be above two hundred dollars and a further increase of twenty dollars or more in a week. Barring some unforeseen development, of course." He shrugged. "It is inevitable. There appears to be no limit to the number of people who want to buy —and it's as the *Bullion Review* said—there's only so much gold being produced and there aren't any new sources."

Kangtek radio went on the air with an English-language broadcast giving the first public information about the discovery of gold in the Ser-gi Ri and the progress of development operations.

". . . extensive placer deposits and rich ore. Nuggets ranging up to eighteen pounds in weight have already been brought out of the mountains. Sakhanese government officials declare that within the next month, gold worth millions of dollars will be produced, and that when the fields are in full production . . ."

The broadcasts were picked up in Europe and Great Britain before the members of the London Gold Market met to establish the morning fix on April 4. Some public skepticism about the announcement from a tiny Asian kingdom, and a great backlog of buy orders cushioned the broadcast's impact. Nonetheless, it had its effect. There were waves of orders to sell. Instead of being higher than the afternoon fix of the day before, the morning fix had to be lowered $2 an ounce.

It was the end of the upward trend that had begun the previous November.

Sir David Auerbach heard the news without change of expression. It would have no effect on Jacob Auerbach and Company—or any other London Market member firm—at the business level. The merchant banks made profits on gold trading as "bullion brokers" whether the market went up or down. At the personal level, Sir David could think only of his daughter. Vivian was in Sakhana. With Matthew Rutledge. If only . . .

"Sir David," his secretary interrupted the banker's thoughts. "Mr. Michel Auerbach is telephoning you from Paris."

David Auerbach hesitated. "Very well. Put him through." How long had it been since he had last spoken directly with his second cousin? Weeks—a month or more? He could not remember exactly. A light flashed on his telephone. He lifted it.

"David?"

"Yes, Michel."

"David, you have no doubt heard of what has happened?"

"Of course. The story has been making the rounds of banking circles." Sir David's tone was dry. "I'm surprised you didn't get in touch with me before."

"I had hoped to overcome the problems myself."

Unusual for Michel, Sir David reflected. It was his custom to ask for help—for "cooperation" whenever anything went wrong.

"I take it you cannot."

"No, David. I am in need of thirty million pounds to maintain the liquidity of the Société Auerbach. If I have it, the situation will clear in six months—and the money will be repaid."

There was a new strength and a note of determination in Michel's tone, Sir David realized.

"Invoking the Auerbach code again, Michel?" he asked.

"Yes. I have no alternative, David."

David Auerbach was silent for a moment. "All right, Michel. You can count on me. Good-bye." He replaced the phone in its cradle. Michel was an Auerbach—and the family and its traditions had to survive.

But Vivian was an Auerbach, too—and his daughter, his only child—Sir David thought. Once again, he felt a turmoil of feelings sweep over him—love for Vivian, anger over her actions, remorse over his own. Perhaps if he could see her, speak to her again—no, his pride refused to permit him to make the first move.

Then he thought of the news item from Sakhana. He could use that as an excuse. Matthew Rutledge had approached him first for a development loan—and he had refused it at Michel's request. An apparent change of mind about the loan would serve as a pretext—a transparent one, perhaps—but it would salvage his own pride. Yes, he could make a convincing show of going to Sakhana for the purpose of providing development capital —and even claim that he wanted to contract for Sakhana's gold production on behalf of Jacob Auerbach and Company.

Sir David telephoned a high official in the Foreign Office, a man with whom he had attended Oxford.

"Hello, George—I'm favor seeking this morning."

"A large favor, I hope, David. I owe you several."

"I'd like an entry permit into Sakhana."

"Aha! Hot on the gold trail already. It'll be a bit difficult, I'm afraid. They don't call Sakhana the Closed Kingdom without reason. It can be done, though—by pushing some of the right buttons. May take a little time—"

"How long would you say, George?"

"Two weeks, possibly a bit less if I have luck."

"No sooner than that?"

"They say nothing's really impossible. I'll give it my best try."

Maharaja Narayan Mahendra Karamchad had guessed correctly about how Charles Sturdevant would react to the news from Sakhana. Cold with rage, Sturdevant summoned one of his most trusted aides.

"Leave for Calcutta on the first available plane. Get in touch with Ramesh Anwar—"

"You mean speak with him personally and not through the usual middlemen, C. J.? Isn't that sticking your neck out—"

"God damn it! Listen—and do what you're told. You see Anwar. Inform him that *I* sent you. With an ultimatum. If he completes the job he was retained to do, he gets a bonus of two million dollars. In cash. If he fails, I'll spend whatever it costs to have him finished off. Now go and get packed and on your way!"

Sturdevant's mood was not improved by the telephone call he received half an hour later from Sheikh Nasib al Rahman in Hajar. Nasib coolly reminded Sturdevant that at last calculation, their combined gold holdings totaled some 90 million ounces—still 35 million ounces short of what was needed to gain an effective corner on the gold market. Because of extremely heavy buying in a rising market, their cost averaged $163 an ounce.

"If the market declines, we'll have to hold until it stabilizes at some lower level—otherwise our heavy selling would drop the bottom out of it," Nasib said. "I could lose several billion dollars on this scheme that was originally your idea." He paused. When he spoke again, his voice had a sharp edge. "If anything of the sort happens, you will lose a great deal more, I assure you."

Sturdevant did not need to have the threat spelled out for him. If the corner failed, the Emir of Hajar would take retaliatory action by nationalizing the Sturdevant-controlled American Ensign Oil Company. That would represent a loss running into the *tens* of billions.

"Take out your *sibah* and stop worrying, Nasib." Charles Sturdevant managed to sound as though he were maintaining his composure. "The price dip doesn't bother me at all. It's temporary. I'm going to step up my buying."

17

Matt made the first landing in the valley at the base of the Golden Mountains on the morning of Friday, April 5. The landing strip was narrow and anything but smooth. However, the Pilatus handled easily on it, the landing gear absorbing the bumps, and came to a stop after a short run.

Rutledge got out of the plane awkwardly, for he was holding three bottles of Dimple Haig in his arms—one each for Fred Coyne, Tim Donahue and Gerhard Schurz. The three men had done a magnificent piece of work, and he told them as much as he handed around the whiskey.

"Get as drunk as you want," he said. "I brought in four Sakhanese soldiers and some gear—which they'll unload. Tom Kirkland will be coming in with the Otter and more men and supplies before noon. You birds can lie around and watch for a change."

Fred Coyne gripped his pipe tightly between his teeth. His hands were at work opening his bottle. "You could've brought us some women, too," he grumbled.

Tim Donahue already had his bottle open and was

taking a heroic swallow of whiskey. Gerhard Schurz screwed his badly scarred face into an imitation sneer.

"Scotch whiskey again?" he grumbled. "I expected a bottle of Steinhager or a good Moselle on an occasion like this."

Rutledge laughed. He knew the type of men who worked on mining operations. Open bitching and belly-aching in front of their employer was a sign they were proud of their work and satisfied with the man who paid their wages.

"Disappear before I fire all three of you—or put you to work," Matt said.

"Not before you have a drink with us, by God!" Coyne growled.

Rutledge had to take a swallow from each of the bottles. Then the three men who had parachuted into the valley and built the landing strip wandered off.

Using both the Pilatus and Otter to shuttle men and materiel from the base camp, Matt and Tom Kirkland managed to bring up everything needed to start operations in two days. Their men—Westerners and Sakhanese—worked steadily and efficiently under Luis Hernandez's supervision. Hernandez seemed to have lost ten years.

"Jesus, Mary and all the damned saints!" he told Matt exultantly. "You can't believe what it's like for me to be out in the field again. I hardly even remember that I got a tin leg!"

Matt and Luis were sufficiently close for Rutledge to speak frankly.

"Maybe you don't—while you're on ground that's more or less level," he warned. "Don't try climbing any mountains—or even hills. I need you around here too God-damned much to have you laid up—or have to fly you out to some fucking hospital. I mean that, Luis."

"Okay, Matt."

Hutments were assembled. Two cook shacks were erected—one to feed the Westerners, the other for the use of the cook who prepared the highly spiced food preferred by the Sakhanese. The bulldozers were used to transport heavy machinery and equipment across the valley to the placer deposits by the riverbank.

Lieutenant Kancha and a three-man detachment of Palace Guardsmen detailed to Rutledge disposed of the skeletons of Captain Nyamgal, Sergeant Lapka and Private Ang, the men Kancha and Baki had killed months before. They followed the ritual Sakhanese custom prescribed. The skeletons were disjointed, each individual segment of bone being removed separately. Then the men under Kancha's command spent half a day carrying the bone considerable distances and dispersing them over a wide area.

In the meantime, work crews began setting up electric generators, air compressors, water pumps, box sluices and the other paraphernalia needed for comparatively simple placer mining. The remaining dozers were brought in by air. They would be used to scrape gravel into mounds near the sluices and troughs.

The gold-bearing earth would be strained, screened, washed with water. Riffles—baffles placed at right angles to the flow of water and sand in the sluiceboxes—would catch the gold, with the smallest grains being trapped by coarse corduroy cloth on the corduroy tables. The tailings would be washed back to the river and carried downstream.

Later, when adequate financing was obtained and full development made possible, there would be dragline and ladder dredges to mine deeper and work the riverbed itself. Great swivel-mounted nozzles would be brought in for full-scale hydraulic mining. With this process, jets of water under high pressure break down the gravel beds and wash the material through long lines of sluices. Later still, lode mining would commence in the mountains upstream.

If Matt had obtained the $20 million he had wanted as capital, the operations could have begun simultaneously. As it was, he had to be content with working the bench placer deposits and the near bank of the river.

Tsering Dorje and General Dep Bahadur Singh recognized that they no longer required outside help. Rutledge and his men were in the High Mountains, producing gold. When a large and impressive quantity had been recovered, it would be brought to Kangtek.

"He who has control of that gold once it reaches Kangtek will control Sakhana," Dorje declared. "If it goes into the hands of our Living God, no power can remove him from the throne. If, on the other hand, you and I take possession of it after it is brought to Kangtek, we can do whatever we wish with Narayan, and none will dare to question our actions."

"Rutledge will hand the gold over to Narayan."

"Unless matters are arranged otherwise."

"Can you also arrange to have the sun rise in the west and set in the east?" General Singh said sarcastically.

"Not even our Living God can do that." Dorje smiled—and the smile was cryptic. "Rutledge and the gold are not the sun. The thoughts I told you of are slowly taking their form. Be patient with me—as I am with myself—and we may yet win the prizes we have so long sought."

Singh returned to his office after this talk with Dorje and within the hour was notified that Ramesh Anwar had again come to Kangtek. He was waiting to see the general, an adjutant declared.

"Have him wait a little longer."

Singh hurried through the palace to confer again with the Prime Minister.

"Anwar is here," he said. "What should I tell him now?"

Tsering Dorje's fingers touched to form a steeple. "I have the answer, not only to your question but to the question of Ramesh Anwar himself. Listen to me."

Dorje spoke rapidly for ten minutes. Singh went back to his office, making two short detours on his way.

"Good day, General," Anwar said, entering Singh's office. "We have much to discuss. I have received an ultimatum."

"From your American men of limitless power?"

"There is scorn in your voice, General. Do not underestimate them—for your own sake."

"You hear things that are not in my voice, Anwar. I speak with the utmost respect. And I take it that you have come—as always—in regard to Rutledge and the concessions."

"What other purpose would I have?"

"I have news for you," Singh smiled. "Good news. We are holding Rutledge a prisoner."

"What?"

"You will enjoy seeing him—come, let us go to him together."

Anwar followed Singh eagerly. They went out into a corridor, where they were joined by three soldiers in Royal Constabulary uniform. One was a corporal and, Anwar quickly realized, a deaf-mute.

The party went down a long flight of stairs into the palace cellars. A soldier—the deaf-mute—produced a powerful flashlight and lit the way down other dark corridors. The group halted in front of an iron door.

"He is inside?" Anwar asked.

"Yes," Singh said. He rapped out some words in Tibetan. Ramesh Anwar felt sudden fear. He whirled around—too late. A rifle butt swung and crashed down on his skull. He fell to the stone floor.

The deaf-mute unlocked and opened the iron door. The other two soldiers dragged Anwar's limp body inside the cell.

"Leave us," Singh ordered. "Return to your posts."

It was the same dungeonlike chamber in which the Kai-Shee master Danu had been interrogated—and the deaf-mute corporal was the same, too. The gestures Singh

285

made to the corporal were different. The man mewled understanding, drew a revolver from its holster on his belt, bent down and held the muzzle to Ramesh Anwar's head. He pulled the trigger twice. The blasts were deafening in the closed room, and the second shot was totally unnecessary, for the first had blown away half of Ramesh Anwar's head.

Obeying another combination of gestures made by Singh, the corporal held the flashlight while the general knelt down and searched the dead man's clothing. He removed only the permanent entry permit he had issued Anwar months before and a letter Anwar carried that contained information linking him with representatives of Miramines. He left everything else intact—including Ramesh Anwar's Indian passport. Then he added something else. It was a card and he slipped it into Anwar's wallet. The card was a perfect forgery. It indicated that Ramesh Anwar was employed by the Indian army's military intelligence section.

General Singh had the corporal light his way back along the corridors. He went to his office and called his adjutant.

"The man who was here—and has been here before —Ramesh Anwar, has turned out to be an Indian spy and agent. He has been executed by my order. His body is in the interrogation cell in the cellars. Strip off his clothing, save whatever documents you find—and have the body buried secretly."

"Yes, General!" The adjutant saluted and hurried off.

General Singh wrote a short memorandum to cover himself. It stated that he had been informed of the spying and agent-provocateur activities of one Ramesh Anwar and, as provided by law, had had him summarily executed. He took the memorandum to Tsering Dorje.

"The Anwar saga is finished," Dorje mused aloud. "Believe me, the tale of Matthew Rutledge, Narayan and the gold of the Ser-gi Ri will also be finished before long. Not quite as simply, but as surely."

* * *

Rutledge's miners and laborers were obtaining spectacular results. Production strained the credulity even of the veteran workers who participated in the placer mining operation. Although the nuggets recovered did not approach the size of the gold "boulders" found in Australia in the 1850s, they were many and large. The gravel was richer in gold than any they had ever seen or heard of.

Nuggets weighing many ounces—and some weighing pounds—were being taken regularly from the sluice-boxes. Production exceeded even Rutledge's most sanguine expectations. By April 13 his men had recovered 2,105 pounds of gold from the gravel terrace. Even though free market gold prices had by then eased down to around $165 an ounce, the value of this hoard far exceeded all his expenditures to date.

Matt reflected that if worse came to worst and large sums in additional capital were not forthcoming, he could pay for further operations with actual gold production. To count on this occurring, however, was risky. It was impossible to estimate when the placer deposits might play out, and the truly heavy expenditures lay ahead. Funds would be needed for dredges to mine the riverbed, to start lode mining, to build a crushing mill and smelter, and for other costly, complex installations and operations.

"Keep an eye on things," he told Kirkland and Hernandez on the morning of April 14. "I'm making a quick trip to Kangtek."

Vivian was ecstatic at the news Matt brought.

"A ton—a whole ton!" she repeated over and over in wonder, hugging him tightly. She saw the results as far more than fabulous success for their joint efforts and the promise of personal wealth in the future.

By now, Vivian was incurably infected with gold fever—the timeless prospector's drive to find gold, wrest it from the earth, and revel in triumphing over the forces Nature deployed against those who searched for the metal. Even beyond that, Vivian had grown fiercely protective of Sakhana, its ruler and its people. She marveled at the inner strength and determination of the Sakhanese. They had retained independence and remained self-contained and self-sustaining for over a millennium.

Analyzing her responses and feelings, Vivian concluded hers was simply a classic case of a pampered and sheltered rich girl coming face to face with elemental realities. It's my value sense that's changed, she told herself, failing to recognize the vital factor deeply ingrained in her unconscious.

In an odd, refracted, and microcosmic sense, the history of the Sakhanese people paralleled the five-thousand-year heritage of her Jewish forebears. The Sakhanese had proudly and bravely clung to their group identity, their beliefs, and their traditions. Bizarre as it would have seemed to Vivian if she had recognized the similarities, they made her relate to the Sakhanese at some deep emotional level.

Matt took Vivian with him when he went to the Maharaja's small audience chamber. Rutledge's weathered face glowed with pride and enthusiasm as he described what had been accomplished at the forward mining camp and revealed how much gold had already been recovered. It could all be brought to Kangtek in one load aboard the De Havilland Otter, he said, and suggested that a timetable be established.

"Radio messages should be sent right away to British, French and other major European foreign offices over your name," Matt suggested. "Invite members of the London Gold Market, important European bankers and financiers, and leading financial writers to Kangtek—"

"I've already made a list of names," Vivian broke in.

Matt gave her a probing look. "Including Jacob Auerbach and Company?" he asked.

Vivian flushed and averted her eyes. "No."

"Add it, honey."

"If—if you think it's wise."

"I know it's necessary—for a lot of reasons." He addressed Narayan again. "We'll bring the gold in two more days, Your Majesty. The invitations should be for three days after that—for April eighteenth. It allows enough time to organize security, arrange for shuttling the guests in from Darjeeling, get villas and apartments ready for them and make other preparations."

"It seems very short notice," Narayan said. "Rich and powerful men do not like to be hurried."

Matt's expression became cynical. "The people you'll be inviting would leave on an hour's notice to see positive proof that a huge virgin goldfield has been opened up. Especially when they scent a possible share in the profits."

Narayan sighed, studied his hands. "Odd. I shall be the first in my long line to open the Closed Kingdom wide to foreigners."

"You'll be selective," Vivian Auerbach interjected with an amused smile. "Asking only an elite group of men whose money will enable you to keep Sakhana a Closed Kingdom—and make it a rich one."

"Let us hope that is how it will be," the Maharaja murmured. His eyes were focused somewhere in the distance, as though trying to look into the future.

The prickle of apprehension Matt had felt earlier returned as Narayan spoke. By the time he and Vivian left the audience chamber, it had turned into a heavy—and, he told himself in vain, wholly unreasonable—sense of foreboding.

18

"The gold will reach Kangtek tomorrow," Prime Minister Tsering Dorje informed General Dep Bahadur Singh. "Foreign bankers are being invited to view it. Those who accept will arrive on April eighteenth."

"I have heard," Singh muttered. "Narayan has given

me many orders. Half the Royal Constabulary is to be brought to Kangtek without delay. The men will guard gold, protect guests and maintain order." He scowled. "But they must also clean the streets of the city, improve the appearance of the palace compound and refurbish the guest villas before the foreigners come. Narayan is turning fifteen hundred of my troops into common laborers!"

"Do not complain. Our Living God is giving us the means to make the sun rise in the west and set in the east. With your soldiers in the capital, our way is clear."

"Clear for what? To bow and scrape before him and his foreign guests?"

"Your warrior's instincts make you purblind, my friend. Picture this schedule in your mind: The gold arrives. We seize it at the airstrip. An hour later at most, Narayan is hastened on to his next incarnation. As Prime Minister, I announce the succession of his son to the throne."

Dorje's plump features radiated serenity.

"I also announce that you and I will act as coregents for the young King until he reaches the age of twenty-one. Mind you, all these events transpire within hours. Four days later, the foreigners arrive." He paused and smiled. "They find the nation in mourning, the air reeking of burning sandalwood incense. But they will be received with due ceremony by the new Living God and his two faithful regents. Being hungry for gold, the foreigners will express their condolences and accept the authority of the new Maharaja. They will have but one thought— to open negotiations with us, the regents, who control the gold of the Ser-gi Ri."

Dep Bahadur Singh was much impressed. The plan was remarkable in its simplicity and logic. Yet he frowned.

"How is Narayan's passing to be explained?"

"Easily. The many tensions of the last few months brought on a fatal heart attack."

"The court physician?"

"He and I have talked. He will attest to the sudden cardiac arrest in return for a generous gift of gold."

"What of Rutledge and his Western technicians?"

"When Matthew Rutledge abruptly leaves Sakhana and returns to the West, his men will naturally believe he has taken some of the gold and deserted them. They will continue working. For us."

"Tsering, nothing can cause Rutledge to leave now."

"Ah, but there is something. The woman. The idea I said was gradually taking shape has formed itself." Dorje leaned forward in his chair. "Pay close attention while I tell you of it."

Phelan, Sir David Auerbach's butler, came into the library of the Auerbach townhouse on Belgrave Square shortly before noon on Sunday. His employer was reading the newspapers.

"A gentleman from the Foreign Office on the telephone, sir."

Sir David was surprised. He reached for the extension on the table beside him and recognized a familiar voice.

"Good morning, George. I always took it for granted that government stopped dead on weekends."

"Usually does, David. This is a most unusual exception. You asked me to request an entry permit into Sakhana—"

"You've managed it?"

"Not exactly. You can go, however."

"Without a permit?"

"By royal invitation, no less. It's the strangest coincidence, really. Got an official radio communiqué from Kangtek. The Maharaja's inviting London Gold Market member firms and some other banks to send representatives to Sakhana for a visit to begin on the eighteenth. Seems he wants to crow about his new goldfields. I thought I'd ring you first. The others will be notified through normal channels tomorrow morning."

"Sorry to trouble you, George, but do you have any more details?" Sir David asked.

"Very few. The communiqué is long and flowery, and it was read to me over the phone. Seems the guests need only their passports. They're asked to fly to Darjeeling. Planes will take them on to Kangtek from there. I take it you'll go?"

"I'll probably be the first to arrive. I'm most grateful to you, George—"

"What for, David? Save your thanks for His Nibs the Maharaja."

Matthew had advised Narayan to send no invitational communiqué to the U. S. State Department.

"Charles Sturdevant practically owns the administration, and his influence over the American banking community is enormous," Matt argued. "You'd only be asking for complications—or worse—by inviting American bankers."

Narayan followed the advice. Nonetheless, Washington learned of the invitations through radio intercepts, and these were brought to the attention of Secretary of State Tillinger on Monday morning. Tillinger recognized the significance of the messages. He telephoned Sturdevant and apprised him of the Maharaja's action.

"Is it possible the message to Washington was delayed somehow?" Sturdevant asked.

"No, C. J.," Tillinger told him. "This is a deliberate omission."

"Make an official protest on the grounds that Sakhana is discriminating against American enterprises—"

"Useless. It would only call worldwide attention to the snub. The Sakhanese would have a perfect answer ready, anyway. The statutes don't allow American individuals or firms to own or deal in gold except for manufacturing purposes. And there's no free market here— only the forty-two dollars and twenty-two cents an ounce official price."

Tillinger might have said more, but he discovered that he was holding a dead line. Charles Sturdevant had slammed down the receiver.

Sturdevant summoned the aide he had sent to Calcutta the previous week.

"Any word from Ramesh Anwar?" he demanded.

"Nothing, C. J. He was to leave for Sakhana the morning after I saw him in Calcutta and report to me as soon as he was back in India."

"Try his Calcutta number. If there's no answer, give the right people orders to have him tracked down."

Left alone, Sturdevant placed his own telephone call, to Sheikh Nasib al Rahman. Nasib could not be reached for almost an hour. When he came on the line, his voice sounded annoyed.

"You interrupted me in the midst of pleasure."

"Sorry, but this wouldn't wait." Sturdevant relayed what he had heard from Jeffrey Tillinger. "They got together some gold, possibly even bought part of it on the Indian market. They're staging a show in a desperate effort to raise more money."

"It's in your bankers' area of responsibility," said Nasib. "Now let me return to my sport."

He broke the connection.

Sturdevant stared at the telephone for a moment. He told himself there could not be any real threat to his gold-corner scheme. It was only necessary to keep on buying.

Early on Monday evening, Narayan Mahendra Karamchad strolled in his palace gardens. Twilight was gathering, but there was still ample light. He was accompanied by Vivian Auerbach and his Number One concubine. Lieutenant Baki and a private in the Palace Guard walked a short distance behind them. Actually, there was no real need for Baki and the soldier to be along,

Narayan reflected. Scores of Royal Constabulary troops were everywhere in the grounds, hard at work.

General Singh was performing in his usual, efficient manner, Narayan mused. He had obviously passed on the commands given him in a manner that motivated his men strongly. The palace compound grounds would be perfectly groomed and the buildings gleaming clean when the foreign bankers arrived.

Vivian paused. A tiny, white-faced monkey squatted at the base of a ginkgo tree beside the path, chattering at her. Vivian stooped down, held out her hand. The monkey stayed still, allowed her to scratch the top of his head with her fingertips for a moment. Then it turned and vanished among some bushes.

Vivian straightened up. She gazed again at the palace—as she did at every opportunity when walking through the grounds of the compound. There was a breathtaking beauty to the white marble structure. It was immense, yet delicately graceful. Much of the intricately carved stone ornamentation appeared as fragile as bone china, but it had endured and remained intact for more than three centuries. Everyone marvels at the Taj Mahal, Vivian thought. What would they say if they were told it had been copied—in considerably reduced size—from the palace of the Sakhanese Maharajas?

"The proverbial penny, Miss Auerbach," Narayan said, then grinned. "Don't tell me. You are thinking of Matthew's arrival tomorrow."

"I wasn't—not at that moment. But I am now. And I don't suppose I'll think of anything else until he gets here."

"Would you like to meet him at the airstrip when he and Mr. Kirkland land with the gold?" Narayan asked.

"Oh, yes!" Vivian's hazel eyes glowed.

What a uniquely lovely and genuine young woman, Narayan thought, and there were no bounds to her love for Rutledge. He wondered why they hadn't already married.

Vivian's expression changed. "Your Majesty, I've heard the airstrip is being sealed off by soldiers and that all traffic will be stopped tomorrow to protect the gold shipment. Wouldn't my going out there create problems and complicate things?"

"It is a Divine Right of Living Gods and Maharajas to command that there shall be no problems or complications," Narayan laughed. "Lieutenant Baki and a driver will take you out in my own limousine. No one will stop you." No one would dare.

19

Matt had definitely set ten A.M. Tuesday as the time he and Thomas Kirkland would land at Kangtek in the Otter. Vivian was up at six. Time passed slowly until the servingwomen assigned to her came to the west wing palace suite at seven-thirty and helped her bathe and dress. The weather was warm. She chose a crisp beige linen suit because she had worn it before and Matt had remarked how much he liked it.

Too excited to eat breakfast, Vivian drank two cups of tea. At nine o'clock, Lieutenant Baki came for her. He escorted her downstairs and outside to where the Maharaja's scarlet and saffron-yellow Bentley was waiting. A Palace Guardsman sat behind the wheel. Lieutenant Baki held the rear-compartment door for her. She got inside. Baki closed the door and took his place in the front seat beside the driver.

There was no traffic on the road from Kangtek to the airstrip, but detachments of Royal Constabulary troops were stationed at intervals along the route. Vivian noticed they were heavily armed and alert, but none made any move to impede the royal limousine. Instead, those who saw it pass snapped to attention and saluted smartly.

Then the military detachments seemed to thin out. After the car had gone some three miles beyond the city limits, there were no more soldiers to be seen. Vivian wondered about this idly and assumed that the security arrangements called for a series of cordons around the airfield. No doubt, there would be more troops farther ahead.

There were. As the limousine rounded a curve, the driver was forced to bring the car to a stop. A wooden barrier had been erected as a roadblock. It was manned by three members of the Royal Constabulary, one an officer.

"We go through in minute, *memsahib*," Lieutenant Baki said.

Like all the British-built Bentleys in Sakhana, the limousine had a right-hand drive. The officer strode forward and stood by the right front door. His men took up positions on the left side. The driver rolled down his window.

"I am Lt. Gopal Rangaswami," the Royal Constabulary officer said, leaning into the window. Vivian thought it rather strange that he was speaking English and addressing her, rather than the driver or Lieutenant Baki. "We have strict orders to allow no one past this place."

Vivian noticed that Lt. Gopal Rangaswami had a narrow, pockmarked face.

"His Majesty gave me special permission," she said. "As you can see, this is his personal limousine."

"I was told nothing."

Lieutenant Baki lost his patience. Although he and Rangaswami were equals in rank, the Palace Guard was the Maharaja's private and elite force and enjoyed higher status than the Royal Constabulary. What was more, halting the royal limousine was an affront to the Maharaja.

"*Tumhari bat sachchi nahin*—your words are not

true!" he rasped in Hindi. "Open the barrier or His Majesty will have you—"

Baki's words were cut short by the explosions of the revolver that Gopal Rangaswami had drawn without being seen and now thrust through the open window. He fired two shots into Baki, two more into the driver. Both men died instantly.

Vivian Auerbach might have screamed in horror or lunged for the door handle in an effort to escape from the car, but it had all happened too suddenly. Rangaswami, revolver still in hand, snapped orders to his men. They tore open the door to the passenger compartment and seized Vivian. Now she cried out and fought back. But the men held her. Gopal Rangaswami opened the other door. He holstered his revolver and produced a canteen. He unscrewed the cap, thrust the neck of the canteen between Vivian's lips and tipped it up.

"Drink—or I'll drown you in it!" he ordered. The liquid poured over Vivian's lips and chin. She recognized its taste. It was *rakshi*, the Sakhanese rice liquor. She spluttered, moving her head violently from one side to another. Rangaswami's free hand shot out. His fingers dug into her throat. "Drink—or I'll strangle you!"

Vivian had to swallow.

"More!" The fingers clutching her throat tightened.

She choked, but more of the liquid was in her mouth, and she swallowed again.

Rangaswami released her and took the canteen away. His men continued to hold her pinned against the seat. She felt her legs and arms grow heavy. She tried to speak. The only sound that came from her lips was a ragged, coughing groan. She felt her eyes closing, fought to keep them open, failed—and consciousness left her.

The two soldiers got out of the car. At Rangaswami's order, they pulled the bodies of Lieutenant Baki and the driver from the front seat, dragged them to a ditch beside the road and dumped them into it. They pulled back the roadblock barrier. Gopal Rangaswami was already behind the wheel of the limousine. He started the engine. One man got in beside him, the other seated himself on the back seat. Vivian's unconscious body had slumped from the seat and lay doubled over on the floorboards. The soldier left her where she was.

Rangaswami shifted into gear. The Bentley started forward, gathering speed. Half a mile farther along the road, Gopal Rangaswami slowed and turned off onto a crude and deeply rutted dirt track that appeared to lead toward a grove of pepper trees.

Kirkland was bringing the Otter in on a direct approach to the Kangtek airstrip's single runway.

"Damned if I don't feel like buzzing the bloody field and doing a victory roll," he said to Matt Rutledge, who was in the copilot's seat.

"Go right ahead, smartass. It can't do more than send a ton of gold and those three soldiers riding shotgun on it bouncing all over the cargo compartment. Of course, you might even tear the wings off this kite—which would make things just that much more interesting."

But Kirkland wasn't listening. He was concentrating on instruments and controls now. Matt peered ahead through the windshield. The conquering heroes are about to be hailed, he thought. The largest reception committee yet had apparently turned out to greet their arrival. There were more soldiers, more cars, more trucks than he had ever seen in one place in Sakhana lined up along the runway.

"We may have to make speeches, Tom," he said.

Moments later, the Otter was on the runway. Kirkland brought it to a stop after a remarkably short run, gunned the engines, turned the plane and taxied up to the concrete hut before which were ranged two full companies of Royal Constabulary troops.

"Dorje and Singh—as usual," Matt remarked. Kirkland swung the plane broadside and cut the engines. Unfastening his seat belt, he stretched. Matt went aft to

crack open the cargo hatch. The three Sakhanese soldiers
who had made the trip gave him toothy grins. They were
glad to be on the ground.

Matt opened the hatch, dropped to the ground. The
soldiers followed. Kirkland, who was already out of the
plane, ambled back toward Matt.

They heard someone bark a command in Hindi and
turned.

"Jesus Christ!" Kirkland exclaimed.

Matt stared, too, in disbelief. It was a repeat performance of what he had experienced when he had first
come to Kangtek in November. An entire platoon of
Royal Constabulary troops had their rifles raised to their
shoulders. The weapons were aimed at Kirkland, the
Palace Guardsmen who had been aboard the plane—and
at him.

There was another command. A dozen rifles cracked.
The three Guardsmen were slammed to the ground by
the bullets that riddled their bodies.

"Do not move—either of you!"

It was General Dep Bahadur Singh's voice. He strode
forward, flanked by a dozen soldiers who held their rifles
at the ready.

"What's our opening line?" Kirkland asked from
the corner of his mouth. " 'There must be some mistake'?"

" 'You're making a big mistake, a regiment of cavalry
is just over the rise' would be better."

The feeble attempts at wisecracking were a nervous
reaction. Fear clutched at both men's guts. Fear that was
made all the worse by their total inability to comprehend
what was happening—and why.

Singh halted five paces from them.

"Consider yourselves prisoners," he said. The
soldiers who had accompanied him formed into a rough
circle around the two men. "Follow orders, and you will
not be harmed."

299

Vivian, Matt thought. Whatever the hell was going on, his first concern had to be for her safety.

"We'll follow your orders, General," he said. "Just tell me one thing. Where is Miss Auerbach?"

"That is something you will be told soon enough."

Rutledge's blood froze. "Is she—"

"She is alive and unhurt. Whether she remains so or not is entirely up to you."

"General," Tom Kirkland spoke up, "I am quite prepared to be the most docile and well-behaved prisoner in history. My only problem is that I can't abide mysteries. They upset my entire metabolism . . ."

The British, Matt thought. Cool, unflappable, magnificent.

". . . make me unable to control myself."

"You rave like a madman. What is your point?"

"I'm asking for a hint—nothing more, simply a hint —as to what the bloody hell this is all about."

General Singh grimaced contemptuously.

"A coup d'etat," he said. "It is already well underway. You two will help bring it to a successful conclusion."

Tsering Dorje came forward and joined Singh.

"Why are we delaying?" Dorje asked—in English.

"The American begs for information about his woman. The Englishman asks for explanations."

The overweight Prime Minister was strutting—like a bush league Asian Napoleon, Matt thought.

"Very well," Dorje said, striking a pose he no doubt thought was menacing. "Rutledge, we have Miss Auerbach. She is being held as a hostage—"

"Hostage? For what?"

"To guarantee that you and Kirkland do as we tell you—and that all three of you leave Sakhana by nightfall. Our men who are holding Miss Auerbach will have no compunctions about killing her." Dorje glanced at Kirkland. "To satisfy your curiosity, General Singh and I are acting in the best interests of Sakhana. We are replacing Narayan with his son. Sakhana will develop her own resources"—he shifted his gaze back to Rutledge—"without sharing our wealth with foreign adventurers."

He turned on his heel, muttering to Singh in Hindi.

"Go with my men," Singh said.

Rutledge and Kirkland were marched to a Bentley sedan and ordered into the back seat. Two armed soldiers crowded in with them. There were two more in front.

A Leyland truck had already backed up to the open cargo hatch of the Otter. Men were clambering into the plane. Matt saw Dorje and Singh get into the car directly ahead, then saw it start. The Bentley he and Kirkland were in followed. The soldiers and other vehicles remained where they were.

Now, that's weird as hell, Rutledge thought. If Dorje and Singh had staged a coup d'etat, they should have carloads of officials and trucks filled with troops escorting them. He glanced sideways at Kirkland. His expression made it easy to figure out what was in his mind.

"Something's fishy," Matt said—and was instantly sorry that he had. The soldier squeezed in beside him rammed the muzzle of a Webley deep into his ribs.

"No talk!"

Weirder yet, Matt thought, as they passed military units stationed along the road to Kangtek—and the two cars pulled to a halt just before reaching the city's outskirts. He and Kirkland were ordered to get out. They did and were marched up to the automobile in which Dorje and Singh were riding. It was a seven-passenger sedan.

"You will accompany us the rest of the way," Singh said. Rutledge and Kirkland were told to sit on the jump seats. A soldier sitting next to the driver turned sideways and held a revolver pointed at them. The car drove on toward Kangtek. Matt did not want to take any chances by turning around, but he managed to look into the driver's rear-view mirror. The second car did not follow.

They were into Kangtek proper when Dorje spoke for the first time.

"When we reach the palace, you two will go with General Singh and me to the small audience chamber," he said. "The soldiers in the front seat will accompany us. They have orders to shoot you both if you do not cooperate completely. And of course Miss Auerbach will be killed too, Rutledge. Only her death will not be quick or easy for her."

"The Maharaja's still alive, isn't he?" Matt asked.

"Yes."

"But not for long. You're scheduled to take Kirkland and me into the small audience chamber—where your men shoot him down—is that it?"

"I congratulate you, Rutledge. That is how the drama is to be played out. Your bringing in the gold today and the audience with Narayan are perfect for us."

"Dorje—or do you insist on Your Excellency under the circumstances?—what assurances do we have that you won't gun us down and kill Miss Auerbach anyway?"

"You have several. First and foremost, we do not wish to create international incidents. The death of the Maharaja is an internal matter. The elimination of two British and one American subject is quite another matter —an eventuality General Singh and I wish to avoid. Not, however, at all costs. Only if we are able to reach our goals."

"I believe them, Matt," Kirkland said, still staring forward. "They want Narayan and the Ser-gi Ri. When they have both, then Vivian, you and I will be allowed to leave. It stands to reason. We'd be very serious liabilities to these gentlemen if we were to remain in Sakhana— whether dead or alive."

The limousine drove through the palace compound gates. The sentries stationed there saluted. As the car rolled along the graveled roads leading to the palace itself, Matt saw large numbers of Royal Constabulary troops raking leaves, clipping hedges, performing a multitude of cleanup tasks. He reflected grimly on the irony of the situation. Narayan had unwittingly enabled General Singh to bring a hostile invading army to the very doors of his palace.

And the car had reached the palace entrance.

"Do not forget for a moment that our men are ready to shoot you," Tsering Dorje warned again as the soldiers got out of the front seat and came to open the back doors.

"An excellent rule to remember at all times," Thomas Kirkland said. "Never forget for a moment when any man is ready to shoot."

Matt did not look at Kirkland, but his hopes soared.

Rutledge and Kirkland went first. The two soldiers walked on either side of them, a pace to their rear. Behind them came Dorje and Singh, both acting official in their manner. Singh sharply returned the salutes rendered him by Palace Guardsmen stationed at the entrance.

Palace protocol had to be followed. Dorje informed a court chamberlain that he and Singh were bringing Matthew Rutledge and Thomas Kirkland for an audience with the Maharaja at His Majesty's command. The chamberlain scurried off and returned within moments. The Maharaja awaited them in the small audience chamber.

He led the way.

"Y'know, Matt," Tom Kirkland said in a casual, drawling tone. "I've always had great respect for the common soldier. Look at these chaps with us. Disciplined, loyal. I'll take them over motley civilians any day."

"Everyone to his own taste," Matt said. He had gotten Kirkland's second message.

The court chamberlain opened the doors to the small audience chamber, announced the visitors and, when they had filed inside, bowed himself out and closed the doors.

Narayan rose from his chair and came toward Rutledge and Kirkland, his hands extended, his face wreathed in a welcoming smile.

Stay back—don't come any closer, Matt wanted to shout, and he tensed, more alert than he had ever been.

"Well, fuck me blind if it isn't that son of a bitch, the Living God!" Thomas Kirkland exclaimed.

Narayan stopped, stunned. Dorje and Singh whirled, staring at Kirkland, dismayed by the outburst. The two soldiers, although not understanding the words, realized that something unplanned was taking place. They looked at each other indecisively, then toward Dorje and Singh, pleading for some sign as to what they should do.

Beautiful, Tom, Matt cheered silently and snatched up the diversionary thread.

"Living God, my ass."

Tsering Dorje and Dep Bahadur Singh spun on their heels to gape at Matt now. The two soldiers followed suit. It was the split-second for which Kirkland had been waiting. His right hand plunged under the waistband of his trousers. A snub-nosed .38 caliber Smith and Wesson revolver flashed into view, already roaring. His first shot caught one soldier in the groin, his second plowed into the other's chest.

Matt's muscles uncoiled. He sprang at General Singh, his right hand chopping at the side of his head. The blow connected. Singh staggered, but did not fall. Rutledge followed up with a savage kick that drove into Singh's genitals. The general screamed, doubled over. Matt rabbit-punched him, and he fell.

Kirkland triggered his revolver two more times, putting bullets into the bellies of both soldiers. Tsering Dorje was trying to flee, running toward the door. He had almost reached it when Matt caught up with him. Dorje was fat, flabby, a man who did no physical work or exercise. One hard punch in the area of his right kidney was enough. He did not fall. He seemed to slump to the floor in a sitting position.

Narayan had recovered from his initial, disbelieving shock. He did not try to run, even though he believed that Rutledge and Kirkland had either gone mad or that they were seeking to make him a captive or even kill him. He stood his ground and shouted for his guards.

Kirkland sensed that Narayan had misunderstood and that if the guards burst into the room, the results could be disastrous for him and Rutledge. He flung his revolver to the floor.

"Hold up your hands, Matt!" he called to Rutledge, raising his own high above his head. "Don't move, for God's sake!"

Matt understood and lifted his arms.

"Your Majesty—when the guards come, have them seize Dorje and Singh!" he said. "Don't let either of them get away."

Half a dozen Palace Guards burst through the doors. They carried drawn guns. When they saw the Prime Minister and General Singh and the bodies of the two soldiers on the floor they stopped. They pointed their guns at Rutledge and Kirkland.

"Do not shoot them," Narayan said, his voice miraculously steady. He walked across the room, stood before Matt and gazed deeply into his eyes. No, Rutledge was not insane. Then what? Had the two Westerners hoped to steal gold they had brought from the Ser-gi Ri?

The Maharaja could not bring himself to believe that Tsering Dorje and Dep Bahadur Singh had done anything . . .

It was at that moment that Singh recovered partial consciousness. He stared up from the floor through eyes filmed with pain from the punishment he had received from Matt Rutledge. His mind was not functioning clearly, and he could only make out the figures of men in uniform. Men in uniform who had guns. He thought they were his own men.

"Shoot Narayan, you fools!" he croaked. "Kill him!"

The Maharaja paled.

"Put down your weapons," he ordered his guards in Hindi. His voice had suddenly old and tired. "You can stop holding your hands in the air," he said to Rutledge and Kirkland in English. He passed a hand in front of his face. "Begin, Matthew. Tell what you have to tell. I will listen."

20

Dorje and Singh knew they had only one chance of saving their lives. Even though they now stood before the Maharaja, with their hands manacled and Palace Guardsmen at their sides, the two men were defiant.

"We hold the woman," Dorje said. "Give us safe conduct to India, and she will live. Anything less than that, and she dies."

Nayaran looked at Matt.

"They'll never keep the bargain," Rutledge said. "They gave themselves away at the airstrip. Singh said that if their coup was not completely successful by nightfall, Vivian would be killed. Even if we flew them to India right away"—he looked at his watch—"it's one-thirty, they could never get word back to Sakhana in time."

The Maharaja could not admit openly that Matt's answer was an enormous relief to him. He would have been willing to let Dorje and Singh go free to save Vivian Auerbach, but he knew that if he did, the two men would only continue to conspire against him. And if they reached India, they would find hosts of strong allies there.

"They will be made to talk and tell us where Vivian is," Narayan said.

Dorje sneered. "Torture? We shall say nothing. When one knows he is to die in any event, he can withstand great pain."

"Especially when he thinks of the revenge he will have even after his death," Singh said. "Believe us. Whatever torture we may suffer, it will be painless compared to what we have ordered for the woman."

Matt moved as if to hurl himself on Singh. Kirkland grabbed him and held him back.

"Take them to the cellars," Narayan ordered the Guardsmen. Dorje and Singh were led away.

"I shall be present when they are—interrogated," the Maharaja said to Matt. "You and Mr. Kirkland may decide whether or not—"

"I want to be there," Matt said.

"And I," Kirkland nodded.

Tsering Dorje and Dep Bahadur Singh lay on high wooden tables, bound tightly to them. Their clothing had been removed. Dorje's body was fat, puffy. Singh's was lean and muscular.

"I will not ask you again," Narayan said. "Will you speak—or shall the men begin?"

Dorje clamped his jaws. Singh spat. Narayan nodded. A Guardsmen stepped forward. He held a razor-sharp knife. He went to General Singh first and made long, comparatively shallow incisions in the flesh of his arms, chest, stomach and thighs. Singh groaned and he strained against his bonds. The wounds, surprisingly enough, did not bleed much.

The Guardsman moved to the table on which Dorje lay. He cut somewhat more deeply, for there were thick layers of fat. Dorje screeched in pain once, then willed himself into silence.

"It is only the beginning," Narayan murmured.

Rutledge and Kirkland stood beside the Maharaja, their faces impassive.

Another Guardsman held a metal canister that had a spout like a teapot. He stood over Singh, tipped up the canister. Black, granular powder poured from the spout into the knife cuts. Satisfied that every incision had been filled with the powder, he repeated the process with Dorje.

"It is black gunpowder," Narayan said quietly. He raised a hand. A third member of his Palace Guard came forward with a long stick of burning punk. He touched the lighted end of the punk to one gunpowder-filled incision after another. Black gunpowder does not explode when loose and exposed to air. It only burns, very rapidly and at very high temperature. The streaks of powder flared as they ignited. Small clouds of white smoke puffed out of the open wounds. The room suddenly reeked with the stench of charring human flesh.

Neither Dorje nor Singh could prevent themselves from screaming.

"The pain is agonizing," the Maharaja said between their shrieks. "But the burning cauterizes the wounds." He scowled. "If they do not talk, much deeper cuts can be made, and still they will not bleed to death."

The screams subsided somewhat.

"Where is Miss Auerbach being held?" Narayan demanded.

Both men remained silent.

"Continue," Narayan said to the Guardsmen. He turned to Rutledge and Kirkland. "Let us leave for a while and think together. Perhaps we may hit on some clue."

By then, it was two forty-five in the afternoon.

They went to a room on the main floor of the palace, not far from the head of the stairs that led down to the cellars and the interrogation cells.

Narayan yet again repeated what was known about Vivian's departure that morning. She had started for the airstrip in his limousine, accompanied by Lieutenant Baki and a Palace Guardsman who served as the driver.

"I have sent men to search for the car and for any person who might have seen it," the Maharaja declared. "Some soldiers placed along the road as security guards for the gold shipment say they remember it passing in the morning. Then it seems to have vanished."

The three men sat silently for several minutes. They were interrupted by a palace aide who came to make a report.

"The truck bearing the gold has arrived, Your Majesty. Where do you wish it taken?"

Narayan blinked. Yes, of course, he realized. Once they seized power, Dorje and Singh intended to receive the foreign guests and let them see the gold. But who cared about that now?

"I suggest the Council Chamber, Your Majesty," Matt said, appreciating how Narayan felt, but also realizing that no matter what happened to Vivian, Narayan was still the ruler of his country. He would have to go through with what had been planned and arranged.

"Thank you, Matthew," Narayan murmured. "Yes, have the gold displayed in the Council Chamber," he told the aide.

The aide withdrew.

A Guardsman came up from the cellars. The interrogation was continuing. The torture had been intensified. The scrotums of both Dorje and Singh had been slit open and packed with black powder. When the powder had been lit, they had screamed and Dorje had bitten through his own tongue.

"But they have revealed nothing, Your Majesty. The sergeant recommends cutting out their eyes."

"Do whatever is necessary."

Matt tried not to let the words register or picture in his mind what was being done in the cellars. He paced the floor, thinking only of Vivian, hoping desperately that Dorje or Singh could be forced to disclose where she was being held in time to save her.

"She could be anywhere in Kangtek," he muttered, half to himself. "Anywhere within a hundred miles—or even more."

"Doubt that," Kirkland said. "Even though they might have used the Maharaja's car or another motor vehicle, they would have kept her fairly close to the city. They had to keep her close enough so that they could produce her quickly, if necessary."

That made sense, Matt thought—for whatever good it did.

"Your Majesty!" Another palace aide, and he was breathless. "A patrol has found the bodies of Lieutenant Baki and his driver!"

"Where?"

"On the road that goes toward the airfield. Not very far from where it takes a sharp curve to the left."

"Send a messenger to the airstrip. Have the troops there begin searching the entire area—"

"Your Majesty, there are no troops at the airfield. General Singh gave orders that all who were there should return immediately to Kangtek after the truck loaded with gold left for the city."

Matt stopped pacing. "Wait a minute. You mean the airstrip is deserted?"

"Yes, Rutledge *sahib-kamal*."

"I think—sure, it holds together!" Matt exclaimed. "That's where Vivian is—at the strip. In that hut she made into an office. It's the last place any of us would dream of looking—and the one place they could have handed her over to me fast if Kirkland and I helped them and then agreed to leave Sakhana."

"By God, I believe you're right," Kirkland said, leaping out of the chair in which he was sitting. "It even explains their 'before nightfall' deadline. We either took off before dark, or we couldn't take off at all."

Narayan turned to the aide. "Rush a hundred men—"

"No!" Matt protested. "We can't send soldiers. Your Majesty, any men Dorje and Singh detailed to guard Vivian would kill her the minute they saw troops approaching."

"Then what—"

"Your Majesty, I want a gun and a throwing knife—"

"You can't go alone, Matthew."

"He won't be alone," Kirkland said. "I'm going with him."

The *rakshi* Lieutenant Gopal Rangaswami had forced Vivian to drink was heavily laced with *charas*. She had swallowed enough to put her into a deep sleep for twelve hours or more. She did not know that Rangaswami had hidden the royal limousine in a grove of pepper trees until after one o'clock, when the last soldiers departed from the airstrip. Then Rangaswami and his two men had driven to the strip, carried her into the concrete hut and placed her on the floor.

Rangaswami left his two men to watch her and hid the limousine in the grove again. He walked back to the airstrip, entered the hut and settled down to await developments—or further orders. At around three in the afternoon, he began to grow edgy.

"You will take turns as sentries outside," he told his two men. "You first—you'll be relieved in an hour."

The man started for the door, paused. He looked toward the corner where Vivian Auerbach lay unconscious.

"Lieutenant, sir. If it becomes necessary to kill her, it would be a waste—"

"Certainly," Rangaswami said, understanding. "All three of us will use her first. For as long as we like." He snickered. "Perhaps that may even be the way in which we kill her."

The man left. The other soldier eyed Rangaswami quizzically.

"Why should we not start with her now, Lieutenant, sir? We need only pull her legs apart."

"Our orders are that she is not to be harmed—or touched in that manner—until nightfall or until the orders are countermanded."

"I shall pray that the sun goes down quickly today," the soldier said.

Major General Dep Bahadur Singh broke under torture minutes before Matt Rutledge and Tom Kirkland left the palace.

"Your Majesty, Singh has talked," a Guardsman rushed up from the cellars to report. "Miss Auerbach is at the flying field. There are three men guarding her."

"Is that all Singh said?" Narayan asked.

"No, Your Majesty. He begged us to end his suffering and kill him."

"Then he has told the truth. Grant his wish."

Narayan tried once more to convince Matt that he should take a detachment of soldiers with him. Rutledge refused. He had been provided with a Webley revolver and a throwing knife. Tom Kirkland had his Smith and Wesson, which he reloaded. At Matt's request, the Maharaja furnished them with an automobile.

"How do we go about this business?" Kirkland asked as Matt drove the car through the palace compound gates.

"There's only one way that I can see," Rutledge began. "Listen and tell me if you don't agree. . . ."

The second of Lt. Gopal Rangaswami's men had relieved the first on sentry duty outside the concrete hut. When he saw the car approaching, he rushed into the hut and told the officer.

"Stay inside," Rangaswami said, drawing his revolver. "And close the door." He went to the tiny, dust-glazed window that looked out in the direction from which the car was coming. "Hold yourselves ready," he told his men over his shoulder.

The automobile was one of the palace Bentleys, Rangaswami saw. He relaxed a little. It was probably bringing someone with a message from General Singh. The car turned in toward the airstrip. As it drew closer, Rangaswami's eyes widened, and he clicked off the safety catch on his revolver. Even at two hundred yards' distance, he recognized the driver. It was Matthew Rutledge, and he was alone. This defied understanding, the lieutenant thought.

The car drove directly to the hut, stopped in front of it. Rutledge got out, walked toward the door. Rangaswami's first impulse was to open fire, but he held back. There was a possibility that Rutledge had been told to come after his woman by General Singh. In that case, he would have a written message from Singh.

"You!" the lieutenant snapped at the nearest of his men. "Open the door, point your gun at him and tell him to stop."

The man did as he was told. Matt halted less than three feet from the door. The soldier holding the gun gestured. Matt nodded, raised his hands.

"Search him!" Rangaswami ordered from inside the hut.

The soldier obeyed, tapping Rutledge's pockets. He found the big Webley in Matt's hip pocket, yanked it out and tossed it off to one side.

"Get out there, too," Rangaswami said to his second soldier. "If he has no letter from General Singh, we will blow his brains out." He raised his voice. "Why are you here?"

"I was sent," Matt replied.

Another soldier emerged from the hut.

"Who sent you?"

"General Singh!" Matt shouted the words. It was the agreed signal. Tom Kirkland raised himself from the back seat of the Bentley where he lay, the Smith and Wesson ready in his fist. The gun roared twice—and the first soldier fell, already dead. At the same instant that Kirkland fired, Matt's right arm lashed down. The throwing knife concealed in his sleeve whizzed through the air, driving into the second soldier's chest.

Gopal Rangaswami realized he was trapped. Rutledge was not alone. If he exposed himself to aim at

Rutledge, the other foreigner would kill him. He had one hope. Instead of moving out of the hut, he retreated into it and went to the corner where Vivian Auerbach lay. He knelt beside her, thrusting the muzzle of his revolver against the side of her face.

"Come in—both of you—or I shoot the woman!" he called out. "You—who has the gun—throw it on the ground where I can see it."

Matt stepped over the bodies of the two soldiers and crossed the threshold. His eyes focused quickly in the dim light. He could see Vivian clearly—and see the officer holding the revolver against her face.

Tom Kirkland stepped in front of the doorway. He held the Smith and Wesson by its muzzle and let it fall to the ground.

"Inside!" Rangaswami barked at him.

Kirkland entered the hut.

The lieutenant laughed. Now he could shoot both men—and then the woman.

"I failed to hit you in the marketplace, Rutledge," he said, unable to resist the sadistic urged that moved him. "The bullet meant for you struck the dancing girl—your woman. Now you have another woman, and I will not miss either of you."

He swung his revolver away from Vivian's face, pointing it at Matt.

Rutledge and Kirkland sprang as one. Rangaswami's revolver exploded and spat flame. A sledgehammer struck Matt's left arm, but Kirkland was gripping and twisting Rangaswami's hand. Rutledge ignored the pain that tore at his arm and the blood that ran hot down over his hand. He raised his foot, stamping down against Rangaswami's pocked face. Rangaswami howled like a wounded animal.

Kirkland now had the lieutenant's revolver. He stood up, hurried out of the hut and bent down over the soldier Matt had killed with the throwing knife. He pulled the knife from the man's chest and returned to the hut.

314

"Here, Matt," he said, handing Rutledge the knife.

"Thanks. Can you get Vivian out of here by yourself?"

"I think so."

Kirkland leaned down and lifted Vivian bodily. He carried her to the car. Matt waited an extra moment; then he took a firm grip on the throwing knife with his good hand and cut Gopal Rangaswami's throat.

21

Sir David Auerbach had worried about what he would say to Matthew Rutledge when they met in Sakhana. The problem resolved itself when Sir David disembarked in Darjeeling and went into the passenger terminal. He found Rutledge there, waiting for him. Matt's left arm was in a sling.

"Hello, Matthew—what happened to you, have another accident?" The words came out naturally, automatically.

"Sort of," Rutledge said, smiling and holding out his right hand. "I'm glad you came, David—and yes, Viv is fine and she can't wait until she sees you."

Auerbach found himself taking Rutledge's hand and shaking it.

"So I'll have you flown right into Kangtek before any of the others arrive—"

"Then I am the first? I hoped I might be."

"You are, and I'm glad about that, too. You and Viv could use a little quiet time together."

David Auerbach wet his lips.

"Matthew. Please tell me. Is Vivian angry or—"

Matt smiled warmly as he put his arm around the older man's shoulder. "Vivian wants nothing more than to hold her father and kiss him. She might even have a good, old-fashioned cry. I know it's terribly un-British, but that's how it stands. Now for God's sake let me get you aboard the plane for Kangtek."

"What about you—when will you get there?"

"With the last batch of visiting firemen."

Vivian did have a good old-fashioned cry, and Sir David found himself shedding tears, too.

"We're not being very British, are we, Daddy?" Vivian said, wiping her eyes.

"That's strange. Matthew used almost the same words when he met me in Darjeeling."

"Not strange at all. Matt and I think very much alike about a great many things. We're very close. Infinitely closer than I ever believed I could be to any man." All her tears were gone now and she kissed his cheek. "Except to the grumpy, prudish man who happens to be my father, that is."

"Viv, I know now that I was wrong, but I thought I was right—"

"Come, I'll take you to the Maharaja. He wants very much to meet you."

A total of twenty-seven visitors arrived in response to the Sakhanese Maharaja's invitation. They were of several nationalities. Most were senior vice-presidents of large banks. Except for Jacob Auerbach and Company, each of the London Gold Market member firms sent the assistant director of its gold trading operations. And there were several financial writers including two Britons and a West German.

Narayan feted the men at an extravagant banquet. He introduced them to his Prime Minister and the chief of the Sakhanese armed forces, carefully refraining from mentioning that they had been appointed to their posts only the day before.

The climax came when the guests were ushered into the Council Chamber. Smartly uniformed Palace Guardsmen were ranged along the walls. A glittering heap of gold nuggets and flakes was displayed in the middle of the room.

"Slightly more than a short ton of gold," Matt told the group. "All taken from a one-square-mile section of a placer deposit that has a total area thirty-seven times as great. Then there is the riverbed, and higher up in the mountains, there are thick—believe me, gentlemen, extremely thick and rich—lodes." He walked to a large table on which there were a hundred or more chunks of rock.

"These are ore samples taken from the mountains," he said. "You are welcome to help yourselves to them as souvenirs. No doubt, you may wish to have them properly assayed"—he chuckled—"and when you do, you won't be able to believe the results."

The visitors tried not to gape openly.

Almost all the bankers indicated they would like to begin discussions about loans immediately. Matt reported this to the Maharaja.

"Has Sir David approached you yet?" Narayan asked.

"No," Matt said, shaking his head.

"Please wait until he does."

"What if he doesn't?"

"I believe he will, Matthew, and if his terms compare favorably with those offered by others, I would much rather that we deal with him."

Matt withheld comment. He did not believe that David Auerbach would offer to make a loan—not after having refused it in the first place.

Sir David surprised him the next evening, when he chatted with Vivian and Matt in their place apartments.

"The fact that we're sitting here as we are is all the evidence any of us needs that we consider bygones as bygones," Sir David began. "Now, I would like to convey a message to His Majesty. Jacob Auerbach and Company is prepared to advance all the development capital you will need—even going above the twenty million dollars you originally requested."

Matt was smoking a cigarette. He crushed it out in a ceramic bowl he used as an ashtray.

"A very blunt question, David. If you're changing your decision because you want to salve your conscience—"

"Ridiculous. Listen, Matthew. I was prepared to lend you the twenty million when you first approached me about it in February. I considered it an excellent investment then. I consider it far better now." He frowned. "I don't need to remind you why I turned you down."

"Dear Uncle Michel," Vivian muttered.

"Yes. I deferred to Michel's wishes—much to my regret." Sir David sighed. "Michel has since learned a bitter lesson, and so have I. However, let's return to the main theme of our conversation. I am offering you a minimum twenty-million-dollar loan because it's excellent business for me, and for no other reason."

Auerbach paused, took a cigar case from his pocket and extracted an Upmann panatela from it. He replaced the case and held the cigar unlit.

"There is one condition attached to the offer."

"Oh?"

"You must agree to push development of the fields but delay shipping gold until they are in large-volume production."

"You baffle me, David. The point of any such delay eludes me."

"It's a bonus—for all of us. I want Sakhana to produce enough gold to shake the market. Or rather, to shake out one or two undesirable speculators."

Rutledge finally understood.

"And wreck Charles Sturdevant's gold corner?"

"Exactly."

"David, as far as I'm concerned, you've just made yourself a deal!"

News of the great Sakhanese gold strike became public. Although all reports emphasized that a period of time must pass before new production would begin reaching the market, the news had its effect. Small-scale speculators grew nervous first and began unloading their ten- or twenty- or hundred-ounce holdings. The selling wave spread, grew. Gold prices drifted lower. By the end of May, the London Market quotation stood at $156.50 an ounce. In late June, it fell to $147, and all signs were that it would continue to drop.

The presidential administration was in deep trouble. Inflation, recession, Watergate and related scandals were ongoing and ever-deepening crises.

Tardily—ever so tardily—members of the administration recognized that President Nixon's "New Economic Policy" was a disaster. It was remembered that this "policy" had been the brainchild of Assistant Treasury Secretary Owen Raynor. A scapegoat was needed. Owen Raynor's resignation was demanded. He had no choice but to tender it. The ultimatum was "resign—or be thrown out."

There were many Executive Branch resignations in June, 1974. That of the Assistant Secretary of the Treasury was lost in the shuffle and largely ignored by the media. It was not ignored by the shrewd, hard-nosed Secretary of the Treasury. He ordered a quiet investigation into the affairs and activities of Owen Raynor.

On June 28, Jacob Auerbach and Company made public the fact that it was the firm that had provided the kingdom of Sakhana with development capital two months before. The announcement added that Sakhanese production was now three tons monthly—and that this quantity would be shipped regularly from Sakhana on the fifteenth of each month.

By July 2, the free market price of gold had fallen to $138 per ounce.

The U. S. Secretary of the Treasury realized it was useless to seek an appointment with the President. Sorely beset from all sides, accused openly of serious crimes, the Chief Executive was becoming more and more reclusive, and his decisions and orders carried less and less weight.

Instead, the Treasury Secretary conferred with House and Senate leaders, officers of the Federal Reserve and a meticulously chosen group of bankers. The Secretary revealed to them what had been uncovered by investigators checking into the activities of former Assistant Treasury Secretary Owen Raynor.

"He was being paid secretly by Charles J. Sturdevant, and Sturdevant has been trying to corner the gold market since last year," the Cabinet officer told them. "A gold corner will be a catastrophe to our economy —which is already in bad condition. It will also dislocate the whole world's monetary balance."

Then he made certain recommendations.

"I propose two moves. First that laws prohibiting ownership of gold by Americans be repealed—and second, that we sell a million or more ounces of U. S. gold reserves on the open market. We won't announce our intention to sell publicly until later in the year— but we let the information leak in the right places."

Charles Jordan Sturdevant III was forced to admit defeat. The vast quantities of new Sakhanese gold were real. The rumor that the United States Government intended to sell part of its gold reserves was not a rumor.

There was no longer any hope of obtaining sufficient gold to have a monopoly on the free market.

"Nasib, we'll have to throw in our hand, sell our gold holdings and salvage what we can of our investment," he told the Emir of Hajar.

"I started selling two months ago," Sheikh Nasib said, making no effort to hide his contempt for Sturdevant. "Much of the gold you've been buying has been mine, C. J."

"You can't be serious!"

320

"I haven't yet begun to tell you how serious I'm going to be. Remember that I warned you. The idea to corner gold was yours. I told you that if I lost on the scheme, you would lose much more than I!"

On July 5, 1974, gold skidded to $131.50 an ounce.

Five days later, U. S. newspapers carried front-page stories reporting that Sheikh Nasib al Rahman, Emir of Hajar, had nationalized the properties of the American Ensign Oil Company in Hajar.

As the *Wall Street Journal* said:

"AMENOCO is an American petroleum industry major controlled by the Sturdevant family interests. Its nationalization by the Hajari government means a loss of more than $25 billion to the Sturdevants, according to reliable sources . . ."

Sir David Auerbach returned to Sakhana on July 24. His daughter Vivian and Matthew Rutledge met him at the Kangtek airstrip. It would not long be a mere airstrip, Matt boasted.

"They've started construction on a new concrete-surfaced runway," he told Sir David.

"Another few months, and the road to Kangtek will have an asphalt pavement, Daddy," Vivian added.

The gardens of the Maharaja's palace compound were illuminated by more than a thousand lanterns on the following night. Five hundred guests sat outdoors at tables that sagged under the weight of silver platters heaped with succulent foods.

Sir David Auerbach occupied the place of honor on Narayan Mahendra Karamchad's right at the royal table. Vivian Auerbach and Matthew Rutledge were the only guests who were not seated at tables. They sat on cushions placed on the grass in front of the Maharaja's table. An embroidered cloth was spread before them.

321

On it were two plates and two cups. The plates contained millet gruel, the cups goat's milk.

Sir David Auerbach cleared his throat and addressed Narayan.

"Your Majesty, I'm sure there's some symbolism involved here, and I must apologize for my ignorance. But why are my daughter and Matthew sitting there on the grass?"

"Vivian is your daughter," Narayan replied. "You see that she is seated directly opposite you—but at a lower level. Matthew is an orphan. He sits opposite me because I am taking the place of his father."

"May I ask what it all signifies?"

"A symbolic acknowledgment of deference to their parents. They have only millet gruel and goat's milk to eat and drink. This, too, is symbolic. It is a reminder that while others may feast on the richest of foods, human happiness is possible even for those who have little."

"It's fairly obvious, now that you've explained it, Your Majesty. But I still have a question. You radioed me an invitation to a party in my honor—and I find my daughter and Matthew Rutledge deep in some sort of ritual."

Narayan's eyes twinkled and he smiled.

"Sir David, in Sakhana, the girl's father is always the guest of honor at events such as this."

Auerbach's expression showed puzzlement.

"Ah, my apologies!" Narayan exclaimed, his smile deepening. "Our radio operators are sometimes slovenly in their transmissions, omitting words or even entire sentences. Possibly that is what happened—the reason why you were not informed that this is a betrothal ceremony."

Sir David gaped. "A *what kind* of ceremony, Your Majesty?"

"Betrothal." Narayan raised his wineglass. "Of course, under Sakhanese law—and because I am a Living

322

God—it can be even more than that. I need only to chant a prayer and the betrothed pair are married."

Matt nudged Vivian.

"Honey, look at your father. I think he's having a coughing fit."

"That can only mean one thing. The Maharaja's told him."

"He's stopped coughing."

"I don't dare look up at him, Matt. What's he doing now?"

"Leaning over and whispering in Narayan's ear."

"I'd give anything to find out what he's saying."

"Me, too."

They learned a moment later. Narayan raised a hand. The guests immediately fell silent. The scarlet-uniformed servants scurrying back and forth stopped, stood still.

Narayan Mahendra Karamchad, the Maharaja and Living God of Sakhana, began to chant a prayer . . .

Footnote

As I stated in the opening pages of this book, there was a very real plot to corner the world's free market in gold during 1974. That conspiracy and its outcome form the factual basis on which this work of fiction has been constructed.

The gold-corner plot failed in fact, and the failure cost the men I have chosen to call Charles Jordan Sturdevant III and Sheikh Nasib al Rahman many billions of dollars. While "Sturdevant" was badly hurt by the failure, he was far from ruined. A "Sturdevant dynasty" has far too much wealth and power to be destroyed by even such an enormous loss.

Nor did the change in presidential administration have much adverse effect on "Charles Sturdevant." There are other "Owen Raynors" holding government positions in Washington. They are beholden to "Sturdevant" because of loans he has made them or salaries or retainer fees he secretly pays them.

As for the gold market itself, it has been freed of the pressures of monopolistic speculation. It is finding its own levels in accordance with the timeless laws of supply and demand. At this writing, London Gold Market quotations are in the $160-$170-an-ounce range. They have reached this level again because of the operation of free market forces such as deepening recession and a weakening of confidence in the strength of the American dollar and other currencies.

Countless people are still mesmerized by the mystique of gold. They believe it safe, certain that it will always retain value. Whether it will or not is a moot question. Gold has been virtually demonetized throughout the entire world. To all practical purposes, it is now merely another commodity metal.

One final note. Since the beginning of 1975, American citizens have been permitted to buy, sell, and own gold bullion. It had been predicted that Americans would buy enormous quantities of gold to hoard as a hedge against inflation. U. S. citizens disappointed the prophets. Their gold buying and hoarding to date have been negligible. To their credit, they at least have refused to be beguiled and bedazzled by the gold mystique. Or perhaps it is simply that the everyday American citizen has more faith in the strength and future of the United States and its economy than do parasites like "Charles Sturdevant," "Owen Raynor," "Sheikh Nasib al Rahman" and their ilk.

—*Jonathan Black*